K를 팝니다

All The Korea You May Not See

다 아는데 왜 재밌을까 싶은
대한민국 영어 설명서

박재영 지음

ㄴㄴ > < ㄷㄴ

#.
한국인 독자들만을 위한 서문

한국에 대한 전 세계 사람들의 관심이 지금처럼 높았던 때는 단군 이래 없었다. 사실 우리 스스로도 얼떨떨할 지경이다. K팝을 필두로, 영화, 드라마, 음식, 뷰티 등 여러 분야에서 'K'가 열풍을 일으키고 있다. K콘텐츠를 즐기는 사람은 수십억 명에 달하는 듯하고, 한국을 방문하는 외국인 관광객의 수는 연간 천만 명이 넘는다. 정부는 2027년까지 이 숫자를 3천만 명까지 늘린다는 목표를 세웠다(늘 그렇듯 목표는 있는데 구체적인 전략은 별로 없어 보인다).

'여행 준비'라는 독특한 취미를 즐기다가 『여행준비의 기술』(글항아리, 2020)이라는 책까지 쓴 사람으로서, 문득 궁금했다. 한국을 알고 싶어하는 외국인들은 어떤 책을 읽고 있을까? 아마존에서 검색해본 결과는 놀라웠다. 한국어 공부와 관련있는 책들을 빼면, 한국 혹은 한국 여행에 관한 정보를 담고 있는 '영어로 된' 책은 열 권이 채 되지 않았다. 심지어 그것들 중 한국인이 쓴 책은 단 한 권도 없었다!

가장 유명한 『론리 플래닛 한국편』을 사서 대충 읽어봤다. 우리가 흔히 보아온 전형적인 가이드북이었다. 정보는 많지만 '이야기'가 없는, 읽다보면 지루해져서 대충 넘기고 마는, 읽고 나도 뭐 하나 기억에 남지 않고 그곳에 가고 싶은 마음이 용솟음치지도 않는 그런 책.

그래서 내가 쓰기로 했다. 내가 과거에 만났던 외국인들에게 들려주었을 때 그들이 가장 재미있어했던 이야기들만 모은, 그들이 나에게 던졌던 의외의 질문들에 대한 답을 정리해놓은, 찐 한국인이 알려주는 놀랍고도 신기한 K스토리 책을. 읽고 나면 한국에 대한 관심이 증폭되고, 한국 방문의 욕구가 배가되고, 한국 여행이 훨씬 흥미진진해지는 책을. 한국이 얼마나 매력적인 나라인지, 한국의 역사와 언어와 문화와 음식 등이 얼마나 독특한지, 구글링만으로는 절대 파악할 수 없는 한국의 진면목은 무엇이 있는지 알려주는 책을.

문제는 나에게 영어로 책을 쓸 능력이 없다는 점이었다(지금까지 이런 책이 나오지 않은 것도 어쩌면 당연한 일이다. 한국인 중에서 영어로 책을 쓸 만큼 영어 실력이 출중한 사람은 별로 없을 테니 말이다). 그래서 일단 한글로 썼다. 한글 초고를 마친 시점은 2022년 말이었다.

이후 평소 신뢰하고 존경해온 한영 번역가를 만나 이 프로젝트의 의미를 설명했고, 샘플 원고도 보여드렸다. 그분은 큰 관심을 보이며 기꺼이 번역할 뜻을 밝혔지만, 기존 계약 때문에 7개월 후에나 작업을 시작할 수 있다는 문제가 있었다. 7개월을 기다릴 것인가, 아니면 다른 번역가를 찾아볼 것인가 고민하던 차에, 세상의 변화를 감지하는 촉이 뛰어난 후배 'K'가 한마디 툭 던졌다. 요즘 인공지능 프로그램 좋은 거 많이 나왔는데, 선배가 직접 영어로 바꿔보면 어때요?

그때는 지금까지 나온 번역기 중에서 최고로 손꼽히는 딥엘(DeepL)과 지금은 누구나 그 이름을 아는 챗GPT가 등장한 지 얼마 되지 않은 시점이었다. 두 프로그램은 정말 놀라울 정도로 정교하게 작동했고, 다행히 내 영문 독해력이 인공지능이 번역해준 영어 문장이 내가 원래 하고자 했던 말과 얼마나 부합하는지 파악할 정도는 되었기에(땡큐, 『성문 종합영어』), 긴 시간이 걸렸지만 원고지 9백 매 분량의 한글 원고를 8만6천 단어의 영문 원고로 바꾸는 데 성공했다.

대충 뜻이 통할 정도로 번역하는 작업이라면 몇 달이면 충분했을 것이다. 하지만 나는 이 원고를 영미권 출판사와 계약해서 수출하는 것이 최종 목표였고, 그러려면 영문 원고의 수준도 상당히 높아야만 했다. 한글 원고를 쓸 때부터 영어로 번역될 것을 염두에 두면서 작업했고, 딥엘이 바꿔준 영어 문장(당연히 오류가 많다. 군만두를 military dumpling으로 번역하는 식이다)을 다듬은 이후 챗GPT와 끊임없이 대화하면서(챗GPT도 military dumpling

이 진짜로 있는 줄 안다) 점점 더 '그럴듯한' 문장들로 바꾸어나가는데 1년 가까운 시간이 걸렸다(물론 직장 생활을 병행하느라 더 오래 걸리긴 했다). 한글 원고를 영어로 바꾸는 과정에서 적지 않은 시행착오도 겪었지만, 몇 마디 말로 설명하기 어려울 정도로 엄청난 노하우도 얻게 되었다. 이 노하우를 궁금해하실 분이 많을 것 같아서, '인공지능을 활용하여 영어로 책 쓰기'를 주제로 몇 차례 강연도 했고, 같은 주제로 아예 책도 한 권 쓰기로 계약했다.

원고를 정리하는 동시에, 수많은 영미권 출판사와 출판 에이전시에 출간 제안서와 샘플 원고를 보내기도 했다. 처음부터 '수출'이 최종 목표였으니까. 몇 군데에서 약간의 관심을 표하기는 했지만, 아직 계약이 성사되지는 않았다. 지금까지 백 번 넘게 거절당했지만, 조앤 롤링의 『해리포터』 원고가 2백 번 거절당했다는 사실에서 위안을 얻으며 계속 시도할 예정이다. (한국에서 먼저 출간되는 한영 대역판의 반응이 좋으면 계약 가능성이 높아질 것이니, 많은 성원 부탁드린다.)

외국인을 상대로 쓴 책을 왜 국내에서도 출판하는 것인지 궁금해하실 분이 있을지도 모르겠다. 일단 국내에 장기 체류하는 외국인이 2백만 명이 넘는다는 것이 한 가지 이유이지만, 더 중요한 이유가 있다. 이 책을 읽은 많은 한국인이 '외국인에게 K 설명하기'의 달인이 되기를 소망하기 때문이다. 한국인이라고 해서 한국에 대해 다 알고 있는 것은 아니다. 알고 있다고 생각하는 것조차 막상 설명하려고 하면 어디서부터 이야기를 시작해야 할지 고민스러울 때가 있다. 그리고 그것을 영어로 옮기는 것은 또다른 차원의 문제다.

꽤 영어 실력이 좋은 한국인들도 깻잎, 콩나물, 미역, 꼰대, 주량, 파도타기 등에 해당하는 영어 단어까지 알기는 어렵다. 한국의 간장과 일본의 간장이 어떻게 다른지, 간장과 된장과 고추장은 어떻게 만들어지는지, 왜 한국의 밤거리엔 빨간 십자가가 그렇게 많이 보이는지, 한국인에게 삼겹살과 치킨과 냉면과 김치와 소주가 어떤 의미인지, 한국 영화에 흔히 나오는 학원과 회식과 찜질방과 노래방은 어떤 곳인지, 왜 한국의 식당에는 테이블 아래에 수저통이 있고 호출 벨이 있으며 가위와 집게가 등장하는지 등을 '제대로' 설명하는 것은 영어 회화에 능통한 사람들에게도 쉽지 않은 일이다. 또한 우리는 우리 문화에 너무나 익숙해서, 무엇이 외국에도 흔히 있는 것이고 어떤 것들이 우리에게만 있는 독특함인지 구별하지 못하는 경우도 많다.

나는 이 책이 다음과 같은 역할을 하기를 기원한다. 첫째, 외국인들이 던지는 한국 관련 질문에 훨씬 더 풍부한 대답을 할 수 있는 한국인이 많아지는 데 도움이 되면 좋겠다(두 유 노우 싸이? 말고도 할 수 있는 말은 정말 많다). 둘째, 외국인들이 한국을 훨씬 더잘 이해하게 되고 훨씬 더 많은 이가 한국을 방문하게 되는 계기가 되면 좋겠다(한국을 방문하는 외국인들에게, 혹은 해외 출장을 가서 만나는 외국인들에게, 공항 면세점에서도 살 수 있는 평범한 기념품보다 이 책이 몇 배는 더 좋은 선물이 될 것이라 확신한다). 셋째, 한국의 저자들이 쓴 좋은 책들이 해외에 더 많이 수출되는 단초가 되면 좋겠다. 한국의 출판사들은 (아주 유명한 저자가 아닌 이상) 초판

1쇄를 천 부에서 3천 부 찍는 것이 보통이지만, 미국의 출판사들은 신인 작가의 책이라도 기본 3만 부를 찍는다(책을 써서도 돈을 벌 수 있다는 뜻이다). 나는 외국인 저자들이 절대 쓸 수 없는 아이템을 골랐지만, 언어의 장벽만 없다면 전 세계 작가들과 동등하게 경쟁할 수 있는 훌륭한 작가들이 한국에도 매우 많다고 생각한다. K콘텐츠가 다 성공하는데, K소설이나 K논픽션이 성공하지 못할 이유가 없다. 한국의 책이 더 많이 해외에 수출되지 못한 것은, '1인치'의 장벽만 넘으면 되는 영화나 드라마와 달리 책은 장벽의 높이가 '1미터'는 되었기 때문일 것이다. 인공지능의 도움을 받으면 이 장벽을 훨씬 낮출 수 있다. (한국의 출판사들에게도 적지 않은 자극이 되려면 이 책이 해외에 꼭 수출되어야 할 텐데.)

이 책을 쓰는 과정에서 물론 '인간지능'의 도움도 많이 받았다. 에세이스트 김혼비님은 한글 원고를 모두 검토하고 탁월한 피드백을 주었다(구체적인 의견들 외에 "다 아는 이야기인데 왜 재밌지?"라는 말과 "다 아는 이야기일 줄 알았는데 의외로 몰랐던 이야기가 많더라"라는 말이 특히 힘이 되었다). 존스홉킨스대학의 교수 클레어 허님은 미국인의 시선으로 영문 원고를 꼼꼼하게 검토한 후 어마어마한 분량의 피드백을 보내왔다(고치라는 곳이 너무 많아서 모두 반영하지는 못했지만, 덕분에 원고의 수준이 크게 향상되었다고 생각한다). 한국에서 국제학교를 졸업하고 곧 미국 브라운대학교에서 영문학을 전공할 예정인 이나혜님은 인공지능도 간과했던 세세한 부분에서 어색한 영어 표현들을 바로잡는 데 큰 도움을 주었다(앞으로 더 많은 것을 경험하고 꿈꾸는 모든 바를 이루기를 기원한다). 또한 오랜 기간 힘이 되어준 이은님에게도 깊은 감사를 드린다.

이 책에 실린 모든 원고는 (이 글만 빼고) 한국어와 영어, 두 가지 언어로 실려 있다. 당연히 책이 상당히 두껍고 제작비도 많이 든다. 독특한 아이디어에서 출발한 프로젝트라는 건 분명하지만, 많이 팔린다는 보장은 전혀 없다. 그럼에도 불구하고 원고를 보자마자 흔쾌히 출간을 결정해준 난다 김민정 대표에게 깊이 감사드린다. 이번에 처음 만났지만, 출판계에서 그가 왜 유명한지를 확실히 깨닫는 데는 한 번의 만남으로 충분했다.

0.

序

안녕. 당신이 이 책을 펼쳤다는 건, 한국을 방문할 계획을 갖고 있다는 뜻이겠지. 구체적인 여행 계획이 잡혔을 수도 있고, 언젠가 한 번쯤 가보고 싶다는 생각을 하고 있을 수도 있겠지. 출장이나 휴가와 같은 단기 방문이든, 유학이나 취업과 같은 장기 체류든, 한국을 방문한다는 멋진 생각을 갖게 된 것을 진심으로 환영해. 물론 당신이 K팝이나 한국의 드라마나 영화를 좋아하다가 한국에 대해 더 알고 싶어져서 이 책을 골랐을 수도 있을 거야. 어느 쪽이든, 이 책을 읽으면 한국에 대해서 더 많이 알게 될 것이고, 한국을 방문하고 싶은 마음이 더 커질 것이고, 당신이 한국에서 보내는 기간이 더 즐거워질 것이라고 확신해.

어떻게 그걸 확신하느냐고? 놀랍게도, 이 책은 외국인을 대상으로 출판된 한국 여행 관련 서적들 중에서 진짜 한국인이 쓴 최초의 책이거든. 이미 적지 않은 수의 한국 여행 가이드북이 영어를 비롯한 여러 언어로 출간되어 있지만, 그중에 진짜 한국인이 쓴 책은 하나도 없어. 전부 외국인 여행자들이 그리 길지 않은 기간 동안 한국을 돌아다닌 다음에 쓴 거지. 이 책은? 그야말로 '찐'이지.

나는 진짜 한국인이야. 한국에서 태어나서 50년 넘게 살았어. 한국어도 정말 끝내주게 유창하지. 한국에서 초등학교부터 대학원까지 다니면서 이것저것 공부도 많이 했고, 한국 음식도 엄청나게 많이 먹어봤고, 한국의 역사나 문화에 대해서도 제법 잘 알아. 이름난 곳도 많이 다녀봤지. 하지만 이런 조건에 부합하는 한국인은 수도 없이 많아. 그 많은 사람 중에서 하필 내가 이 책을 쓰게 된 것에는 몇 가지 이유가 있어.

첫째, 직업이 저널리스트라서 대중적인 글쓰기에 능한 편이야. 20년 넘게 보건의료 전문 미디어에서 일하는 동안(미처 말을 못했는데, 내가 사실은 의사야. 비록 환자를 진료하지는 않지만), 복잡하고 어려운 내용을 간단히고 쉽게 풀이 쓰는 일을 줄곧 해왔지. 보건의료와 관련된 기사, 칼럼, 책 들 이외에 종합병원을 배경으로 하는 장편소설도 쓴 적이 있는데, 그게 텔레비전 드라마로 만들어지기도 했으니, 제일 잘하는 게 글쓰기라고 할 수 있겠지.

둘째, 나는 여행과 여행 준비를 좋아하는 사람이야. 오죽하면 『여행준비의 기술』이라는 책도 썼겠어. 그 책은 영문판이 없어서 아쉽긴 한데, 엄청 웃기고 상당히 독특한 여행 에세이라는 소문이 자자해. 말하자면 나는 일종의 여행작가인 셈이지. 내 친구 몇 명은 나를 보고 '한국의 빌 브라이슨'이라고 불러주기도 해.

셋째, 맛있는 음식을 먹고 만드는 일에 관심이 많아. 유명한 음식점을 찾아다니기를 즐기고, 직접 만들 수 있는 요리도 꽤 많이 있어. 아주 오래전의 일이지만 미식과 요리에 관한 책도 펴낸 적이 있을 정도야. 사실 한국에서 누릴 수 있는 가장 큰 즐거움 중의 하나는 한국 음식을 먹어보는 일이야. 아직 해외에 덜 알려졌을 뿐, 한국은 정말 음식 문화가 발달한 나라거든. 그래서 이 책에서도 음식 이야기를 정말 많이 했어. 독자들에게 한국의 음식 문화를 생생하게 알려주려고 말이야.

넷째, 외국 여러 나라를 돌아다녀봤지. 스무 개 정도 되는 나라를 여행했고, 미국에서 2년 동안 살아본 경험도 있어. 그러다보니 다른 나라와 한국이 어떻게 다른지, 외국인들은 한국에 대해 어떤 것들을 궁금해하고 어떤 것들을 신기하게 생각하는지 많이 알게 됐어. 그 나라에 사는 사람들은 너무도 익숙해서 그냥 지나치는 것들을 외국인들은 흥미롭게 바라보는 경우가 많은 법이잖아. 이를 바탕으로 외국인들이 가장 신통하게 생각할 한국 관련 이야기들을 이 책에 풀어냈어. 정보도 주고 재미도 주는 게 내 목표지.

다섯째, 사실 이게 가장 중요한 건데, 이런 콘셉트의 책을 쓰겠다고 마음먹은 한국인이 그동안 아무도 없었기 때문이지. 아무도 하지 않은 일을 하고 세상에 없는 뭔가를 만들어내는 일은, 그게 대단히 큰 것이든 아니든, 흥분되고 보람 있잖아. 열심히 펜을 굴

리게 된 핵심 동기가 바로 이것이야. 나의 독특한 시각을 독자들과 나누고, 아직 덜 알려진 한국의 이모저모를 여러분에게 들려줄 수 있어서 나는 정말 행복해.

한국이 세상에서 가장 좋은 나라는 아마 아닐 거야. 한국이 세계에서 가장 환상적인 여행지라고 생각하는 사람도 별로 없을 거야. 하지만 한국은 정말 재미있는 나라이고, 그 어떤 나라보다 많은 추억을 만들어줄 수 있는 곳이야. 아무런 사전 정보 없이 방문해도 즐겁고, 『론리 플래닛 한국』편을 미리 읽고 오면 더 즐겁긴 한데, 이 책을 읽고 나서 한국을 방문하면 당신의 한국 여행은 몇 배나 더 짜릿한 경험이 될 거라고 확신해.

한국인이라면 모두가 다 아는 일상 표현 중에 '아는 만큼 보인다'라는 말이 있어. 당신이 한국에서 더 많은 것을 볼 수 있도록, 더 많은 즐거움을 누릴 수 있도록, 더 많은 추억을 쌓을 수 있도록, 내가 다양한 '이야기'들을 들려줄게. 맞아, 이 책은 '정보'가 아니라 '이야기'가 있는 책이야. 구체적인 정보를 엄청나게 많이 나열해놓은 가이드북이 아니라는 뜻이지. 그런 책은 이미 많아. 한국을 방문할 구체적인 계획이 아직 없다면 이 책민 봐도 충분하지만, 비행기 티켓을 알아보는 단계라면 평범한 가이드북도 함께 보는 게 좋을 거야.

아무튼, 당신이 이 매력적인 나라 한국을 한 번쯤 꼭 방문하기를, 한국에서 머무는 동안 그 어느 여행지에서보다 신나는 시간을 보내기를, 그리고 그 즐거웠던 기억을 오랫동안 간직하기를 바라. 신기함과 즐거움들이 당신을 기다리고 있는 이 나라에 당신이 얼른 도착하기를 기다리고 있을게. 조만간, 한국에서 보자고.

0.

A Journey Beyond Guides: Unveiling the Untold Korea

Hey there! If you're reading this, chances are you're planning a trip to South Korea, and that's absolutely awesome! Whether you already have a specific itinerary in mind or you're simply dreaming of visiting someday, let me assure you that you're in for a real treat. South Korea offers a wealth of opportunities for exploration, whether it's a short-term visit like a business trip or vacation, or a long-term stay for studying or working. Maybe you're a K-Pop or Korean drama enthusiast, eager to delve deeper into the country's vibrant culture. Regardless of your motivations, I'm confident that reading this book will enrich your knowledge about Korea, ignite your passion to visit, and enhance your overall experience.

Believe it or not, this is the first book written by a bona fide, full-blooded Korean native, exclusively for you fine foreign readers. Now, I don't mean to devalue those other guidebooks in English or other languages, but all of them were written by folks who barely scratched the surface of Korea on a quick visit. This book, though? It's the real deal, straight from the source.

As a Korean native, who's spent over five decades in Korea, I've acquired an exceptional understanding of the Korean language, culture, and history. From my school days all the way to graduate school, I've dove deep into a wide range of subjects, relished the diverse flavors of Korean cuisine, and explored numerous iconic landmarks across Korea. Yet, I'm fully aware that many Koreans have had similar experiences. So, what sets me apart as the author of this book, and what makes me the one behind this book? Allow me to share a few reasons that compelled me to undertake this endeavor.

One of the primary reasons is my background as a journalist. With over 20 years of experience in the healthcare media industry, my expertise lies in translating intricate medical concepts into easily understandable language for a broad audience. It's worth noting that I am also a doctor, although my current focus does not involve direct patient care. Throughout my career, I have published numerous articles, columns, and books on healthcare-related topics. Additionally, I have even authored a novel set in a hospital, which was later adapted into a popular TV drama. Writing is truly my forte, and I am confident in my ability to effectively convey the essence of Korea to readers.

Next, I'm a seasoned traveler with a true knack for planning and preparing for trips. My previous book, *The Art of Preparing for a Trip*, a humorous and unique collection of travel essays unfortunately not yet available in English, is a testament to my passion for traveling and planning. Some of my friends have even playfully referred to me as the "Bill Bryson of South Korea," so you could say that I'm a bit of a travel writer myself.

Furthermore, I have a profound passion for delectable cuisine and take great pleasure in exploring renowned restaurants and experimenting with various dishes in my own kitchen. While it may have been written some time ago, I also possess experience in writing about food and cooking. Undoubtedly, one of the most remarkable aspects of immersing oneself in Korea is the chance to savor its incredibly diverse and relatively undiscovered food culture. With that in mind, this book encompasses a multitude of captivating anecdotes and insights into the world of Korean cuisine.

Moreover, my globetrotting adventures have taken me to over 20 countries, and I even resided in the United States for a couple of years. Through these experiences, I've gained a unique perspective on how Korea stands apart from other nations and what aspects of Korean culture tend to captivate foreigners. I've discovered that outsiders often find fascination in things that locals may overlook or take for granted. Drawing from this understanding, I've crafted this book with a keen awareness of what foreign visitors find alluring about Korea. My goal is to provide readers with an informative and entertaining journey that showcases the intriguing aspects of Korean culture.

Last but certainly not least, the most crucial factor driving me to write this book is that no other Korean has ever embarked on a project quite like this. It's a thrilling and fulfilling endeavor to undertake something that has never been done before and to create a singular work that hasn't existed in the world until now, regardless of its perceived significance. This unwavering motivation has played a pivotal role in propelling me forward to pen this comprehensive book on Korea. I am genuinely excited to share my distinctive perspective with readers and offer a fresh take on the wonders of Korea that has yet to be explored.

Now, let me shoot straight with you. I won't claim that Korea is the absolute best country in the world - few would make such a bold assertion about South Korea as a top-tier travel destination. However, what I can assure you is that Korea is an incredibly enjoyable country, a place where you can create an abundance of unforgettable memories unlike anywhere else. It's a thrill to venture into Korea with little prior knowledge, and it's even more exciting to dive into the pages of *Lonely Planet Korea* before your trip. But mark my words, after reading this book, your journey to Korea will become infinitely more exhilarating.

There's a well-known phrase that every Korean is familiar with: "You can see as much as you know." And that's exactly what I'm here to do - help you see more, have a blast, and create countless memories in Korea by sharing an array of captivating stories. That's right, this book is all about stories, not just a repository of information. It's not your typical guidebook overflowing with details. There are already plenty of those on the market. If you haven't yet solidified your plans to visit Korea, this book will serve as an excellent starting point. However, if you're already in search of a plane ticket, it might be wise to also grab a conventional guidebook to supplement your journey.

Nevertheless, my genuine wish is for you to have the chance to experience this captivating country at least once. May you immerse yourself in the abundant wonders that you can hardly have in any other countries and create cherished memories that will last a lifetime. Until that day comes, I eagerly await your arrival in Korea, ready to share the enchantments and delights that await you. Safe travels, and see you soon!

Jaeyoung Park

#.
차례
Contents

1.

단 한끼만 먹는다면

사겨살
음부르

삼겹살. 발음하기도 어려운 이 단어는 당신이 꼭 기억해야 하는 한국어다. 당신이 한국에서 단 한끼만 먹을 수 있다면 먹어야 할 음식이 이것이기 때문이다. '세 개의 층으로 이루어진 고기'라는 뜻인데, 돼지고기 중에서 뱃살에 해당하는 부위다. 당신이 돼지고기를 먹지 않는 문화권에 속하거나 채식주의자라면, 매우 안타깝지만 실망하기는 이르다. 앞으로 수많은 한국 음식이 소개될 것이니 말이다.

조리법은 매우 단순하다. 사실 조리법이랄 것도 없다. 고기를 어떤 각도와 어떤 두께로 자를 것인지만 정하면 끝이다. 그다음엔 고기를 아무런 양념 없이 불판에 구워 먹으면 된다. 정말 그게 전부다. 하지만 이것이 이토록 특별한 음식이 되는 이유는 상당히 많다. 고기 자체의 품질도 물론 중요하지만, 고기와 함께 곁들여 먹는 식재료들, 그리고 그것들을 먹는 방법이 매우 다양하기 때문이다.

먼저 한국인들이 삼겹살을 얼마나 사랑하는지부터 살펴보자. 한국의 인구는 약 5천만 명인데, 한국에서 키우고 있는 돼지의 숫자는 약 천만 마리다. 5인 가족이 한 마리씩 돼지를 키우고 있는 셈이다. 이 정도면 충분해 보일지 모르지만, 돼지 한 마리를 잡아도 삼겹살이 15킬로그램밖에 안 나온다는 게 문제다. 그래서 한국은 열 몇 개 나라로부터 삼겹살을 수입한다. 전 세계 삼겹살은 전부 한국인이 먹는다는 농담도 있다. 그나마 다행인 것은 삼겹살을 즐겨 먹는 나라가 별로 없어서, 한국이 싼값에 외국의 삼겹살을 수입해올 수 있다는 사실이다.

모든 현상에는 이유가 있기 마련이다. 외국인들이 삼겹살을 그리 선호하지 않는 것에도 이유가 있고, 한국인들이 유난히 삼겹살을 좋아하는 것에도 이유는 있다. 물론 추정이지만. 삼겹살에는 지방이 많이 함유되어 있다. 그냥 먹으면 너무 느끼하다는 이야기다. 그래서 서양인들은 베이컨으로 만들어 먹는 부위다. 하지만 한국인들은 삼겹살을 먹을 때 고기만 먹지 않는다. 정말 다양한 부재료들과 함께 먹는다. 대표적인 한국 음식인 김치를 흔히 곁들이고, 된장을 기초로 해서 만드는 '쌈장'이라고 하는 소스를 찍어 버섯, 양파, 상추, 깻잎, 마늘, 콩나물, 파 등의 채소를 함께 먹기도 한다. 소금, 후추, 참기름 등도 삼겹살의 좋은 친구들이다.

이해한다. 벌써 너무 낯선 단어들이 여럿 등장하여 혼란스러울 것이다. 나중에 다 설명할 것이니, 일단은 넘어가자.

이 모든 것들을 다 한 번에 먹는 것은 아니다. 식당에 따라 위에서 나열한 부재료 중 몇 가지를 제공하는 것이 일반적이고, 테이블 위에 놓여 있는 여러 부재료 중에도 일부를 번갈아가며 삼겹살과 함께 먹는 것이 보통이다. 즉, 한국인들은 삼겹살이라고 부르는 한 가지 음식을 사실상 수십, 수백 가지 방법으로 변형을 주면서 먹는 것이다.

설명이 너무 길어지면 지루할 테니, 실제로 당신이 삼겹살 식당을 찾아가서 먹는 과정을 살펴보자. 한국인이 이토록 사랑하는 음식이니, 삼겹살을 파는 식당은 수도 없이 많다. 당신이 서울과 같은 대도시의 어느 지점에 서 있다면, 아무 방향으로든 몇 분만 걸어가면 반드시 삼겹살을 파는 식당이 있다. 영어로 'samgyeopsal'이라고 커다랗게 간판이 붙어 있……지는 않다. 한글로는 흔히 '삼겹살'이라는 단어가 식당 외부 어딘가에 붙어 있는 것이 보통이지만, 당신은 한글을 읽을 수 없고, 심지어 그 단어를 표시해놓지 않은 식당도 많다. 한국인들은 그냥 보면 안다.

하지만 다행스럽게도, 적지 않은 식당이 삼겹살 사진을 외부에 게시해놓는다. 지방과 살코기가 층을 이루고 있는 듯한 모양의 돼지고기 사진이 보이면, 제대로 찾은 것이다. 고기 굽는 고소한 냄새가 흘러나오고, 테이블마다 천장에서 연통 같은 것이 내려와 있는 모양이 보인다면 백 퍼센트다.

물론 허다한 삼겹살집 중에는 장사가 잘되는 곳도 있고 아닌 곳도 있다. 유난히 인기가 높아서 한 시간 이상 줄을 서서 기다려야 하는 집도 있다(그런 식당들은 이 책의 후반부에 따로 목록을 만들어놓았으니 참고하시라). 하지만 손님이 하나도 없는 텅 빈 가게만 아니라면, 그냥 아무데나 들어가도 된다. 당신이 삼겹살이라는 독특한 음식을 맛보며 즐거워하는 데는 전혀 문제가 없을 테니.

이제부터 당신은 놀랄 일이 많다. 우선 테이블 가운데에 가스레인지가 놓여 있을 거다. 캠핑 갔을 때나 사용하는 휴대용 버너가 놓여 있기도 하고, 아예 테이블에 화구가 매립되어 있는 경우도 많다. 만약 테이블 가운데에 정체를 알 수 없는 구멍이 뻥 뚫려 있다면, 당신은 식당 선택을 잘한 것이다. 잠시 후에 무시무시하게 시뻘건 숯불이 등장하는 신기한 장면을 구경하게 될 것이고, 상대적으로 좀더 고급 식당일 가능성이 높다.

신기하게 생긴 테이블 구경이 채 끝나기 전에 누군가가 주문을 받으러 올 텐데, 많은 경우 메뉴판을 주지도 않았으면서 뭘 먹을 건지 물어볼 것이다. 메뉴판은 흔히 벽에 붙어 있고, 한국인은 성격이 급하다. 당신은 당황하지 말고 '삼겹살'이라는 단어를 말하면서 인원수만큼 손가락을 펼치면 되겠다. 그리고 '소주'라는 한국 술을 주문하면 된다. 맥주를 주문해도 되지만, 한국에 왔으니 이왕이면 한국인이 가장 사랑하는 술을 맛보는 걸 추천한다.

운이 좋거나, 당신이 한국어를 못하는 걸 알아차린 종업원이 좀 센스가 있다면, 여기서 일단은 주문 완료다. 하지만 종업원이 '매뉴얼'을 고집하는 완고한 성격이면서 영어를 구사할 수 없는 사람이라면, 대화가 쉽게 끝나지 않을 수도 있다.

종업원이 물을 확률이 가장 큰 질문은 '무슨 소주?' 혹은 '무슨 맥주?'일 수 있겠다. 당연한 이야기지만 소주든 맥주든 여러 브랜드의 제품이 있다. 그래서 최소한 두세 가지, 많으면 대여섯 가지가 구비되어 있는 식당이 대부분이다. 못 알아들어도 큰 문제는 없다. 그저 어깨를 으쓱하면, 적당히 가져다줄 것이다.

어쩌면 '우리 식당에는 삼겹살은 없고 오겹살밖에 없다'라는 말을 했을 수도 있다. 삼겹살이 없다고? 여기서 '오'는 다섯을 뜻하는 말이다. 세 개가 아니라 다섯 개의 층으로 이루어진 고기라는 의미다. 껍질을 제거하지 않은 삼겹살을 오겹살이라고 한다. 오겹살은 삼겹살보다 조금 비싸고 조금 더 쫄깃하다. 그냥 오겹살을 주문하면 된다. 그리고 맛있게 먹으면 된다.

무사히 주문을 마치고 나면 잠시 후에 역시 매우 빠른 속도로 여러 가지 음식이 나온다. 크고 작은 그릇이 열 개 이상 등장할 것이고, 그중 태반은 정체를 알 수 없을 것이다. 정작 당신이 주문한 고기가 아직 나오기도 전에, 당신이 주문하지도 않은 많은 음식이 테이블에 놓이는 것이다. 하지만 놀랄 필요 없다. '반찬'이라고 하는 한국의 독특한 식문화이고, 아무리 많은 종류의 음식이 나와도 추가로 돈을 내야 하는 건 아니다. 심지어 그걸 다 먹으면 더 준다. 그걸 또 다 먹으면 또 더 준다.

포크와 나이프는 없다. 대신 숟가락과 젓가락이 있다. 젓가락을 한 번도 사용해보지 않은 사람도 없지는 않겠지만, 익숙하진 않아도 대부분 사용해본 경험이 있을 것이다. 하지만 젓가락을 사용하는 아시아의 여러 나라 중에서 한국의 젓가락이 가장 가늘다. 즉 사용하기 가장 어려운 편이라서, 처음엔 적응하기 쉽지 않을 수 있다.

가끔은, 온갖 반찬들이 테이블을 뒤덮은 다음에도, 숟가락과 젓가락이 안 보일 수 있다. 그럴 땐 테이블 아래를 확인해야 한다. 테이블 아래쪽에 길쭉한 상자가 붙어 있고, 그 안에 숟가락과 젓가락이 잔뜩 들어 있는 경우가 많다. 나중에 다시 말하겠지만, 효율성을 중시하는 한국의 식당에는 정말 특이한 문화가 많다.

똑같은 삼겹살이지만 식당에 따라 여러 종류가 있다. 우선 냉동시켰다가 살짝 녹인 다음 얇게 썰어서 굽는 집이 있고, 얼리지 않은 생고기를 조금 두껍게 썰어서 굽는 집이 있다. 고기의 두께도 집집마다 차이가 있다. 대부분의 식당은 전혀 익히지 않은 날것 그대로 고기를 내지만, 몇몇 식당은 살짝 익힌 다음 테이블에서 완전히 익혀 먹는 방식을 택한다. 불판의 종류도 다양하다. 두꺼운 철판을 불 위에 올리는 집도 있고, 그릴을 사용하는 집도 있다. 처음부터 끝까지 종업원이 구워주는 집도 있고, 손님이 직접 구워야 하는 집도 있다. 어떤 식당은 한입에 먹을 수 있을 정도로 작게 썬 고기를 내지만, 어떤 식당은 커다란 고깃덩어리를 통째로 불에 올려 구운 다음 가위로 자르는 방식을 쓴다. 그렇다. 칼이 아니라 가위를 쓴다. 이것도 한국의 독특한 식당 문화다.

테이블에서 직접 고기를 굽다보니 당연히 연기가 많이 난다. 그 연기를 빨아들이기 위해 천장에서부터 불판 바로 위까지 내려와 있는 후드가 있는 점도 다른 나라에서는 찾아보기 힘든 시스템이다. 어떤 식당은 연기가 테이블 아래로 빠져나가게 되어 있는 최첨단(?) 장치가 설치되어 있기도 하다.

고기와 함께 먹도록 제공되는 반찬들도 다양하다. 가장 일반적인 것은 김치이며, 파를 가늘게 채 썰어 비법 양념에 무친 한국식 샐러드도 많이 나온다. 여러 종류의 채소로 만든 장아찌라는 것도 흔히 나오는데, 이건 한국식 피클이다. 양파, 마늘, 버섯 등의 각종 채소가 역시 날것으로 제공되는데, 고기와 함께 구워 먹으면 된다. 그 과정 자체가 즐거운 경험일 것이다. 그리고 고기를 찍어 먹을 수 있는 여러 종류의 소스가 있는데, 소금, 참기름을 섞은 소금, 고추냉이, 쌈장 등이 기본이고, 다양한 해산물로 만든 젓갈까지 주는 경우도 있다.

자, 이제 먹을 차례다. 노릇노릇하게 잘 익은 고기를 다양한 방법으로 맛보자. 먼저 소금만 찍어서 먹어보고, 쌈장을 찍어서도 먹어보고, 고추냉이도 첨가해보고, 김치나 채소를 곁들여서도 먹어보자. 마지막으로, 상추나 깻잎을 손바닥에 펼친 다음 고기를 얹고 쌈장을 조금 넣어 먹어보기를 권한다. 입안에서 풍미가 폭발할 것이다. 이건 '쌈'이라고 하는 건데, 무언가를 싸서 먹는 일은 한식에서 매우 흔한 방식이다. 뭐, 한국식 타코라고 생각해도 좋겠다. 사실 쌈장이라는 단어는 쌈을 싸서 먹을 때 어울리는 소스라는 뜻이다. 여러 가지 방법으로 먹어본 다음, 가장 마음에 드는 방식을 더 자주 선택하면 된다.

아마도 당신이 생전 처음 먹어보는 오묘한 맛일 텐데, 맛있게 먹다보면 고기가 어느새 사라지고 있음을 발견할 것이다. 당신이 어지간한 소식가가 아니라면, 고기 추가 주문은 필수다. 한국의 고깃집에서 고기를 파는 단위는 '1인분'으로, 이건 '한 사람 분량'이라는 뜻이다. 그런데 식당에 따라 실제 양은 차이가 난다. 130그램(4.5온스)일 수도 있고 150그램(5.3온스)일 수도 있고 그보다 좀더 많을 수도 있다. 어느 경우든, 한 명이 1인분만 먹으면 뭔지 모르게 부족한 것이 일반적이다(미국에서 스테이크 한 접시는 대체로 8~10온스다). 한국인이 즐겨 하는 농담 중에 '맛있게 먹으면 0칼로리'라는 말이 있다. 그러니 더 주문하면 된다. 한 사람이 1.5인분 혹은 2인분을 먹는 건 지극히 정상적인 일이다.

추가 주문한 고기까지 다 없어졌다. 그럼 이제 계산을 하고 나가면 될까? 그렇지 않다. 대부분의 한국인은 이렇게 고기를 다 먹은 다음 '식사'를 시작한다. 실제로 종업원들이 다가와서 혹시 고기를 더 먹을 거냐고 물었을 때 이제 그만 먹겠다고 대답한다면, 종업원이 다시 물을 것이다. 그럼 식사는 뭐로 하시겠느냐고. 뭐라고? 지금까지 먹은 이 많은 음식은 식사가 아니었다는 말인가? 놀랍게도, 한국인들은 고기를 잔뜩 먹은 다음 김치찌개나 된장찌개 등 한국식 스튜와 밥을 함께 먹거나, 아니면 냉면이라고 하는 차가운 국수를 먹으며 한끼를 마무리하는 경우가 많다. 찌개와 냉면은 한식에서 대단히 중요한 메뉴이므로 나중에 자세히 설명할 터이니, 일단은 넘어가자.

이렇게 배불리 먹고 나면 돈은 얼마나 내야 할까? 두 명이 가서 삼겹살 3인분과 소주 한 병과 찌개 하나와 냉면 하나를 먹었다면, 식당에 따라 차이는 있지만 50달러 내외의 금액이 든다. 팁 문화가 없으니 이게 당신이 지불해야 할 총액이다. 한국의 높은 물가를 고려하면, 삼겹살은 비교적 저렴한 음식에 해당한다.

이 글의 첫머리에서 나는 당신이 한국에서 단 한끼만 먹을 수 있다면 삼겹살을 먹으라고 했다. 하지만 한국인들에게 '외국인이 한국에서 단 한끼만 먹을 수 있다고 하면 어떤 음식을 추천하겠느냐?'라고 묻는다면, '삼겹살'이라고 답하는 사람은 의외로 적을 것이다. 모르긴 해도 백 명에게 같은 질문을 하면 최소한 열 가지 이상의 음식 이름이 등장할 것이고, 삼겹살은 최상위권에 속하는 대답이 아닐지 모른다. 그런데 나는 왜 삼겹살을 추천했는가? 삼겹살집에 갈 경우 단순히 삼겹살만 먹을 수 있는 게 아니라 위에서 길게 설명한 것처럼 다양한 음식과 독특한 식당 문화를 모두 경험할 수 있기 때문이다.

앞에서 삼겹살에 가장 어울리는 술은 소주라고 했다. 다음 글에서는 소주가 어떤 술인지 본격적으로 알아보자.

1.

If you're only eating one meal, choose "samgyeopsal"

Samgyeopsal. Now that's a tongue twister you'll want to master if you're planning a trip to Korea. Trust me, if there's only one meal you can savor during your time in Korea, let it be samgyeopsal. Samgyeopsal literally translates to "three-layered meat," referring to the pork belly, and it's a must-try dish. But, don't worry if pork isn't your thing or if you're following a vegetarian diet. Korea has an abundance of other delicious dishes for you to explore.

It's ridiculously easy to make — so easy, in fact, that it hardly even qualifies as a recipe. All you need to do is choose how you want to cut the meat - how thick, at what angle - and then throw it on the grill, sans seasoning. That's it, folks. But despite its straightforward preparation, there's something undeniably special about this dish. Sure, the quality of the meat is crucial, but so too are the ingredients that accompany it, and the myriad ways you can enjoy it.

Let's talk about how much Koreans adore pork belly. With a population of roughly 50 million people and around 10 million pigs in the country, that means there's practically one pig per family of five. While this may sound like a substantial number, the issue is that each pig only provides 15 kilograms of pork belly, meaning that South Korea needs to import this cut of meat from roughly a dozen other nations. There's even a running joke that Koreans have managed to devour all the pork belly in the world. Thankfully, not many countries share the same pork belly obsession, allowing Korea to import it at a reasonable price.

There is a reason for everything, including why pork belly is a beloved dish in Korea and not as popular in other countries. Pork belly is rich in fat, which can make it too greasy for certain palates when consumed on its own. In the Western world, it is often cured and turned into bacon. However, in Korea, pork belly is elevated to new heights by pairing it with an array of complementary ingredients. It's commonly served alongside the spicy kick of kimchi, fresh vegetables like mushrooms, onions, lettuce, perilla leaf (known as "kkaennip"), garlic, bean sprouts ("kongnamul"), and scallions. And let's not forget the delectable "ssamjang" sauce, made with the flavorful "doenjang". Other seasonings like salt, pepper, and sesame oil add the perfect finishing touch.

It's understandable if you're feeling a tad bewildered. There's already a bunch of unfamiliar words swirling around. But fret not, my friend. We'll dive into all the nitty-gritty details later. For now, let's keep the momentum going and forge ahead.

No need to mix everything up at once. Depending on the restaurant, you may get a different selection of ingredients. Koreans enjoy pork belly by savoring each bite with different accompaniments like kimchi, lettuce, perilla leaf, and so on. In fact, Koreans have countless variations of the one dish they call pork belly, with each place offering its unique twist.

Now, let's skip the lengthy explanations and dive right into the experience of going to a samgyeopsal restaurant. As this dish holds a special place in Korean cuisine, numerous restaurants across the country serve it. In bustling cities like Seoul, you need only walk a few minutes in any direction to come across a pork belly restaurant. However, don't expect to see an English sign that says "samgyeopsal" outside these establishments. While the Korean term for pork belly (samgyeopsal) may be visible somewhere on the exterior of the restaurant, it may not be discernible to someone who can't read Korean (like you). Koreans just have a sixth sense when it comes to spotting samgyeopsal joints.

Luckily, a multitude of restaurants proudly showcase mouthwatering images of pork belly on their exteriors. So, if your eyes feast upon a tantalizing picture featuring layers of succulent fat and juicy meat, congratulations, you've stumbled upon a samgyeopsal haven. And if the irresistible aroma of sizzling meat dances its way to your nostrils, accompanied by the sight of smokestacks elegantly poised above each table, rest assured, my friend, you've hit the pork belly jackpot.

In the vast sea of samgyeopsal restaurants, there are those that flourish and those that struggle to make their mark. In fact, there are even establishments so wildly popular that you might find yourself patiently queuing for over an hour, eagerly anticipating your turn to dive into samgyeopsal's flavorsome gratification. (Fear not, for I shall provide a separate list of these highly coveted gems within the pages of this book.) However, rest assured that as long as you steer clear of desolate, empty establishments devoid of patrons, you can confidently step into any restaurant without a worry. Finding a place where you can indulge in the distinct and savory pleasure of pork belly should be a breeze.

As you enter a samgyeopsal restaurant, prepare yourself for a few delightful surprises. Right away, your attention will be drawn to a gas stove positioned at the center of your table. It could be a convenient portable burner like those used for camping, or a purpose-built fire pit seamlessly integrated into the tabletop. If you spot an intriguing hole in the middle of the table, you've chosen a great restaurant. Before you know it, a captivating spectacle will unfold as the charcoal fire roars to life, a clear sign of a more upscale and sophisticated establishment.

As you acquaint yourself with the idiosyncrasies of the table, a friendly server will approach you to take your order, and it's quite common for them not to provide you with a physical menu. Instead, you'll likely find menus adorning the walls, as Koreans are renowned for their efficiency and swift service. But worry not, my friend. Simply utter the magical word "samgyeopsal" and hold up the appropriate number of fingers to indicate the size of your group. Don't

hesitate to request a taste of "soju", a beloved Korean alcoholic beverage that comes highly recommended. Of course,
if you prefer, you can also opt for a refreshing beer. But
since you're in Korea, it's worth embracing the opportunity
to try their favorite libation and immerse yourself in the local culture.

If you find yourself lucky, or if the waiter is quick to catch
on, then you can proceed smoothly from there. However, in
the event that the waiter strictly adheres to the field manual
and doesn't have a strong command of English, the conversation may pose a bit more of a challenge.

The likely inquiry from the waiter will be, "What kind of
soju?" or "What kind of beer?" There are a variety of brands
of soju and beer available, with most restaurants offering at
least two or three, and sometimes even five or six options.
If you find yourself unsure about the question, don't fret too
much. Simply shrug your shoulders, and they will bring you
a suitable selection.

The waiter might inform you, "Apologies, we don't have
samgyeopsal, but we do have ogyeopsal." Don't be concerned if you were anticipating the former, as "ogyeopsal"
signifies that it has five layers of meat instead of three. If the
pork belly still retains the skin, it is referred to as ogyeo-

psal, which tends to be slightly more expensive and chewier compared to samgyeopsal. Simply order ogyeopsal and indulge in its gripping flavor.

Once you've successfully placed your order, the food arrives in a flash. The table will be adorned with a dozen or more plates of different sizes, some of which may hold unfamiliar dishes. Even before the meat you ordered arrives, a variety of dishes that you didn't specifically request will be placed on the table. But fear not, my friend, as this is a hallmark characteristic of Korean cuisine known as "banchan" or side dishes. And the best part? They come at no additional cost, and when you finish them, you'll be offered more. Finish those as well, and the servers will bring you even more to savor.

In Korean restaurants, you won't find forks and knives as the primary utensils. Instead, you'll be provided with spoons and chopsticks. While some travelers may not be accustomed to using chopsticks, many are familiar with them, even if they aren't entirely confident in their skills. It's worth noting that Korean chopsticks are known for being the thinnest among other Asian countries, which may require a bit of adjustment for those not used to them.

At times, even after all on-the-house banchans entirely

cover the table, you may not see your spoons and chopsticks on the table. In such cases, it's a good idea to check under the table. You'll often find a rectangular box attached to the underside of the table, which contains a set of spoons and chopsticks for your convenience. This is just one example of the peculiar features you'll encounter in Korean restaurants, reflecting their emphasis on efficiency. We'll delve deeper into these intriguing aspects later.

Despite the pork belly being the same, its preparation can vary across different restaurants. For example, some establishments freeze the pork belly, partially thaw it, slice it thinly, and then grill it, while others use raw meat sliced slightly thicker. The thickness of the meat can also differ from place to place. While most restaurants serve the meat raw and uncooked, some may choose to lightly cook it before allowing customers to finish grilling it at their table. The type of grill employed can also vary, with some restaurants using a thick griddle over the fire, while others opt for a classic grill. Furthermore, the level of involvement from the staff in the grilling process varies, as some restaurants handle the grilling from start to finish, while others leave it entirely to the customers. Lastly, some establishments serve small, bite-sized pieces of meat, while others grill larger chunks as a whole and then cut them with scissors instead of knives. The use of scissors is another characteristic element of Korean restaurant culture.

The presence of a grill at the table results in the generation of smoke during the cooking process. To address this, Korean restaurants incorporate an exceptional hood system that descends from the ceiling and hovers just above the grill. This feature is not commonly found in other countries and is unique to Korean dining establishments. In fact, certain Korean restaurants go as far as employing "state-of-the-art" devices that facilitate the escape of smoke underneath the table, further enhancing the dining experience.

The grilled meat is often accompanied by a diverse array of side dishes, enhancing the overall dining experience. While kimchi, a spicy fermented napa cabbage, remains the most common side dish, you will also commonly encounter Korean salads made with finely chopped green onions and vegetables, all mixed with a secret sauce that bursts with flavors. Another attractive addition is the Korean-style pickle called "jangajji", featuring a range of vegetables pickled in flavorful brine or other sauces.

In addition to the side dishes, the meal is complemented with a variety of raw ingredients such as onions, garlics, mushrooms, and other vegetables, which can be grilled right on the table alongside the meat. This interactive cooking process adds an element of fun to the dining experience. To enhance the flavors further, a wide selection of sauces is available to dip the meat in. Common choices include salt, salt mixed with sesame oil, wasabi, and ssamjang. For those seeking more adventurous flavors, "jeotgal", a salted and fermented seafood-based sauce made from an array of seafood, can also be found.

Alright, it's time to indulge in this mouthwatering, crispy meat! There are plenty of ways to savor the flavors and create your perfect bite. Start by enjoying the meat with just a sprinkle of good old salt to relish its natural taste. Then, explore the various sauces available to elevate the flavors further. Experiment with different combinations, dipping the meat into sauces like ssamjang, sesame oil mixed with salt, or even a touch of fiery wasabi for a kick. To add freshness and texture to each bite, accompany the meat with a side of kimchi or assorted vegetables.

For the ultimate culinary experience, try the favored Korean practice called "ssam". Take a lettuce or perilla leaf, lay it out in your hand, place a piece of meat on top, and add a dollop of ssamjang. Wrap it up tightly and enjoy the explosion of flavors and textures in a single bite. You can simply call it "Korean taco." Remember, ssamjang refers to the sauce (jang) that accompanies the ssam (wrap). Feel free to explore different combinations and discover your preferred way of enjoying this delicious dish.

The flavors of samgyeopsal may take a little getting used to, but once you start relishing its deliciousness, you'll find that the meat disappears quickly. Unless you have a small appetite, I highly recommend to order extra meat to truly indulge in the experience. In Korean restaurants, a unit of meat is typically marketed as a serving size for one person. However, the actual quantity can vary across establishments, ranging from 130 to 150 grams (from 4.5 to 5.3 ounces) or even more. Regardless of the advertised serving size, it's common to find that a single portion of meat is often not enough to satisfy your cravings. (In the United States, a standard serving of steak usually ranges from 8 to 10 ounces.) There's a well-known Korean joke that says, "If it tastes good, it has 0 calories." So, don't hesitate to order more meat to fully enjoy the flavors and make sure you're fully satiated. It's entirely normal for one person to consume 1.5 or even 2 servings of meat during their meal.

Once you've finished enjoying the extra meat, you might

think it's time to settle the bill and leave. However, in Korean culture, the dining experience doesn't always end there. If a waiter approaches you and asks if you want more meat, and you decline, they might ask again, "So what would you eat for a meal?"

You might be taken aback by this question, wondering if all the food you've been eating wasn't considered a meal. But in Korean culture, meat alone is not always considered a complete meal. Many Koreans continue their dining experience by ordering additional dishes such as a Korean stew called "kimchi-jjigae" or "doenjang-jjigae", which is enjoyed with rice, or they opt for cold noodles known as "naengmyeon". Jjigae and naengmyeon are indeed significant dishes in Korean cuisine, and we will explore them in more detail later. However, for now, let's move on.

If you're curious about the cost, let me give you an estimate. For a party of two who order three servings of pork belly, a bottle of soju, one jjigae, and one cold noodle dish, you can anticipate a bill of around $50, which may vary slightly depending on the specific restaurant. Unlike in certain countries, there is no tipping culture in Korea, meaning that this is the final price. Considering the generally high cost of living in South Korea, samgyeopsal is quite a bargain.

At the beginning of this article, I emphasized that if someone could only have one meal in Korea, it should be samgyeopsal. However, when you ask Koreans for their recommendation on the ultimate meal for a foreigner, surprisingly, samgyeopsal may not always be the top choice. It's challenging to pinpoint a single answer since, if you were to survey 100 people, you would likely receive at least 10 different responses. So, why did I initially recommend samgyeopsal? The reason goes beyond the food itself. It lies in the complete experience of visiting a Korean restaurant and immersing oneself in Korean food culture.

As previously mentioned, soju is widely regarded as the ideal pairing drink to complement the flavors of pork belly. In an upcoming article, I will explore the rich history and peculiar characteristics of soju.

2.
소주, 한국인의
솔 드링크

세상의 모든 사람이 소주를 아는 것은 아니다. 하지만 아마도 당신은 소주를 이미 알고 있을 가능성이 매우 높다. 비록 마셔본 적은 없을지 모르지만, 최소한 스크린에서라도 당신은 한국인의 솔 드링크, 소주를 접한 적이 있다. 이 책을 읽고 있다는 것은 한국에 대해 꽤 관심이 있다는 뜻일 테고, 그렇다면 한국의 영화나 드라마도 본 적이 있을 것이기 때문이다. 그것이 〈오징어 게임〉이든 〈기생충〉이든, 아니면 그보다 덜 유명한 작품이든.

한국의 (거의) 모든 영화나 드라마에는 소주가 등장한다. 내가 모든 작품을 처음부터 끝까지 체크해본 것은 아니지만, 시대 배경이 한국전쟁 이전이 아닌 이상, 한 번쯤은 반드시 등장한다. 소주를 빼놓고는 한국인의 일상을 제대로 표현할 수 없기 때문이다.

영화 〈기생충〉 초반에 최우식과 박서준이 만나는 장면. 두 배우가 아주 작은 유리잔에 따라서 마시는 그 술, 투명한 초록색 병에 담겨 있는 그 술, 그게 소주다. 드라마 〈오징어 게임〉에서 이정재와 오영수가 생라면을 안주 삼아 마시는 그 술, 그게 소주다 (원래 끓여서 먹는 라면을 익히지 않고 그냥 먹는 장면에 대한 설명은 나중에 '라면' 관련 글에서 하겠다). 공교롭게도 두 작품의 등장인물들은 모두 가게 외부에 놓여 있는 테이블에 앉아 소주를 마셨지만, 한국인들은 술을 마실 수 있는 거의 모든 곳에서 소주를 즐겨 마신다.

소주는 어떤 술인가. 글자 그대로는 '태운 술'이라는 뜻이다. 한국에서는 13세기부터 만들어지기 시작한 것으로 알려져 있고, 전통적으로는 쌀이나 다른 곡물을 발효시켜 만드는 증류주의 일종이다. 무색투명하고, 알코올 도수는 16도에서 50도 넘는 것까지 다양한 편이다.

그렇다. 소주는 증류주다. 술은 크게 맥주나 와인 등의 발효주와 위스키나 보드카 등의 증류주로 나뉘지 않나. 증류주가 알코올 도수가 훨씬 높고 가격도 훨씬 비싼 것이 일반적이고.

그런데 소주는 엄청나게 싸다. 360밀리리터 한 병을 기준으로 할 때, 음식점에서는 4달러 내외의 돈만 지불하면 된다. 슈퍼마켓이나 편의점에서는 1달러 조금 넘는 값이면 한 병을 살 수 있다. 전 세계에서 가장 싼 증류주 중의 하나가 아닐까(사실 외국인들이 소주에 대해서 가장 놀라워하는 것은 맛이나 향이 아니라 가격일지도 모른다). 어떻게 이런 일이 가능할까.

정확히 말하면 한국에는 두 종류의 소주가 있다. 외국의 여느 증류주처럼 비싼 소주와 매우 저렴한 값에 마실 수 있는 소주. 당신이 영화나 드라마에서 보았던 그 소주, 한국인이 유독 사랑하는 그 소주, 당신이 한국 여행중에 대부분의 음식점에서 마실 수 있는 그 소주는 후자다. 두 가지 소주는 모두 같은 이름으로 불리지만, 사실 만드는 방법이 다르다.

두 종류의 소주를 정확히 구별해서 말하자면, 한국에서 흔히 '프리미엄 소주'로 불리는 비싼 것들은 '증류식' 소주이고, 초록색 병으로 대표되는 대중적인 소주는 '희석식' 소주다. 희석식 소주는 연속 증류를 통해 만들어낸 높은 도수의 주정을 물로 희석한 다음 적당한 감미료를 첨가해서 만드는 것이다. 그래서 한국의 '보통' 소주는 증류주라 할 수도 있고 아니라고 할 수도 있다. 사실 다른 나라에도 희석식 소주와 비슷한 방식으로 만들어지는 값싼 증류주가 있지만, 한국의 소주처럼 큰 인기를 누리는 술은 별로 없다.

이 책은 과학책이 아니니 더 복잡한 이야기는 생략하자(사실 나도 잘 모른다). 다만, 증류식 소주와 희석식 소주의 관계가 버터와 마가린의 관계와 같다고 말하는 사람들도 있다는 점만 언급하자. (앞으로는 그냥 '소주'라고만 하면 희석식 소주를 말한다. 증류식 소주를 말해야 할 때는 '프리미엄 소주'라고 하겠다.)

소주는 언제부터 한국에서 인기를 끌게 되었을까. 원래 한국인들은 19세기까지만 해도 여러 종류의 술을 집에서 담가 먹었다. 그러다가 20세기 초부터 '세금'과 결부되면서 주류 산업은 특별해졌고, 허가 없이 술을 만들어 파는 행위는 금지되었다. 그때부터 소주 회사들이 생기기 시작했고, 오랫동안 가난한 나라였던 한국에서 가장 낮은 가격의 소주가 대중적인 인기를 끌었던 것은 어쩌면 당연한 일이었다. 심지어 한국전쟁 이후 식량 사정이 좋지 않았을 때는 쌀로 술을 빚는 것을 금지하는 법률이 만들어지기도 했으니, 한국인이 선택할 수 있는 거의 유일한 술이 소주였다고 해도 과언이 아니다.

20세기 후반 내내 소주의 알코올 도수는 25도가 표준이었다. 소주는 풍미를 즐기기 위한 술이라기보다는 취하기 위해 마시는 술이었다. 지금도 그렇지만 한국인들의 근로 시간은 꽤 길었고, 노동에 따른 스트레스도 높았다. 짧은 시간 동안 저렴한 비용으로 취하기에는 그 정도 도수가 딱 적당했던 것이다. 빨리 마시고 빨리 취하여 일상의 고단함을 잠시 잊고 얼른 집에 가서 휴식을 취해야 다음날 아침 일찍부터 다시 일할 수 있었던 것이다.

하지만 1998년에 한 회사가 23도의 소주를 출시했는데, 그게 큰 인기를 끌었다. 한국인들의 삶이 덜 팍팍해졌기 때문인지는 모르겠지만, 그 이후 여러 회사에서 경쟁적으로 조금씩 알코올 도수를 더 낮춘 소주를 출시하기 시작했고, 지금 한국인들이 마시는 소주는 대체로 16~18도 정도다.

한국인들은 소주를 얼마나 많이 마실까. 한국인의 소주 소비량은 한 병에 360밀리리터 기준으로 연간 40억 병 가까이 된다. 성인 인구가 대략 4천만 명 정도 되니까, 모든 성인이 평균 1년에 백 병 가까이 소주를 마시는 셈이다. 실제로 여러 통계를 보면 한국인들은 일주일에 두 번 정도 술자리를 갖고, 한 번에 소주 한 병 정도를 먹는 것으로 나타난다.

한국인들의 일반적인 인식과는 달리, 통계에 의하면 한국인이 특별히 술을 많이 마시는 민족은 아니다. 한국인의 알코올 소비량은 OECD 국가들 평균 수준이다. 하지만 특기할 만한 사실은, 한국인은 알코올 분해 능력이 다른 나라 사람들에 비해 매우 떨어진다는 점이다. 과학자들의 연구에 의하면, 한국인들의 약 30퍼센트는 유전적으로 알코올 분해효소가 매우 적다. 술을 거의 못 먹는 체질이라는 뜻이다(일본과 중국을 포함해 동아시아 3국이 이렇다고 한다). 이런 사람들은 술을 조금만 먹어도 얼굴이 빨개지고, 소량의 알코올도 건강에 매우 해롭다. 이런 점을 고려하면, 나머지 70퍼센트의 한국인은 술을 꽤 많이 먹는 편이라는 해석이 가능하다.

어쨌든, 당신은 일단 초록색 병에 들어 있는 저렴한 소주부터 맛보아야 한다. 그것이야말로 한국인의 솔 드링크니까. 어디서 마실까? 모든 곳에서 마실 수 있다. 대부분의 음식점에는 소주가 있다. 심지어 편의점에서 구입한 다음 공원이나 해변이나 길거리와 같은 공공장소에서도 마실 수 있다. 한국은 음주에 제법 관대한 국가라서, 특별히 음주가 금지된 구역만 아니면 어디서든 술을 마실 수 있다. 어떤 음식과 함께 마실까? (한국인들의 생각으로는) 소주는 모든 음식에 잘 어울린다(하지만 솔직히 말해 짜고 매운 음식이나 삼겹살과 같이 기름진 음식에 조금 더 잘 어울리는 편이다).

소주를 처음 맛보면 조금은 당황할 수도 있다. 아무런 향이나 맛이 느껴지지 않기 때문이다. 그저 에탄올에 물을 섞어 연하게 만든 것이라 느낄 수도 있다. 하지만 조금 더 마셔보면 약간의 단 맛이 느껴질 텐데, 이건 비법(?)의 감미료 맛이다. 세상 어디에서도 맛볼 수 없는 독특한 술이라며 좋아하는 외국인들도 있지만, 대다수의 외국인에게 소주는 '매우 싼 가격을 고려하면 (특히 한국 여행중에는) 그럭저럭 마실 만한 술'이라는 게 맞을 것이다. 솔직히 말해, 소주가 엄청나게 훌륭한 술이라고 주장할 생각은 없다. 하지만 이 저렴한 술이 한국인들에게 매우 특별한 것임은 분명하다.

우선 소주는 한국에서 '서민', 즉 보통 사람의 상징이다. 정치인이나 대기업 CEO나 '셀럽' 들은 소탈한 이미지를 보여주기 위해 일부러 소주 마시는 장면을 노출하기도 한다. 좋아하는 술이 무엇이냐는 질문을 받았을 때, 와인이나 맥주라고 대답하는 것보다는 소주라고 대답하는 것이 훨씬 안전하다. 특히 남자가 이 질문에 와인이나 위스키라고 답하면 자칫 '재수없는 놈'이라는 느낌을 줄 수 있기 때문에(물론 늘 그런 것은 아니지만), 상대방과 계속 친하게 지내고 싶은 마음이 있으면 실제로 좋아하는 술이 무엇이든 '소주'라고 대답하는 것이 현명한 답이다. 같은 맥락에서 '언제 소주 한잔하자'는 말은 '너랑 좀더 가까워지고 싶다'는 뜻이 된다.

한국에서는 술의 종류 자체가 미묘하게 다른 사회적 의미를 갖기도 한다. 친구에게 연락해서 '소주 한잔하자'고 말할 때와 '맥주 한잔하자'고 말할 때의 느낌도 다르다. 맥주 한잔하자는 말은 말 그대로 '친교의 시간을 갖자'거나 '(그리 심각하지 않은) 할 이야기가 있다'는 뜻이지만, 소주 한잔하자는 말은 '털어놓을 특별한 사연이 있다'거나 '힘든 일이 있어서 취하고 싶으니 같이 취해달라'는 속뜻이 있을 수 있다.

소주는 술을 얼마나 마실 수 있는지를 표현할 때 사용하는 '단위'가 되기도 한다. 사실 외국에서는 '당신은 술을 얼마나 많이 마실 수 있습니까?'라고 묻는 행위가 보편적이지 않다. 하지만 한국에서는 거의 인사말이다. 직장 동료나 친구에게, 혹은 처음 만난 사람에게, 심지어 회사에서 면접을 볼 때도 이 질문이 가능하다. 굳이 해석하자면 알코올 분해 능력이나 음주 역량 정도의 뜻을 가진 '주량'이라는 단어도 있다.

주량을 물어봤을 때 대답은 '소주 몇 병'으로 해야 한다. 주종에 대한 언급 없이 '몇 병'이라고만 할 때도 당연히 소주가 기준이다. 재미있는 것은 한국 사회에서 (특히 남자들의) 주량은 일종의 특기이자 경쟁력으로 취급되기 때문에, 실제 자신의 주량보다 부풀려 대답하는 경우도 흔하다는 사실이다. 심지어 일부 직종에서는 '술이 세다'는 사실이 직원 채용에서 약간의 가산점으로 작용하기도 한다.

소주는 그냥 마셔도 좋지만, 많은 한국인은 소주와 맥주를 1:3 정도의 비율로 섞어서 마신다. 소주와 맥주를 섞은 이 칵테일(?)의 이름은 '소맥'이다. 바에서 바텐더가 만들어주는 칵테일은 아니지만, 황금 비율로 소맥을 잘 만드는 사람이 있으면 친구들 사이에서 큰 칭찬을 받을 수 있다(물론 바텐더 역할을 한다고 해서 누가 팁을 주거나 하지는 않는다). 당신도 소주를 그냥 마셨을 때 그다지 흥미를 느끼지 못했다면, 이렇게 마셔보기를 권한다. 평범한 맥주에 저렴한 소주를 살짝 섞으면 의외로 알코올 도수가 좀 높은 '프리미엄 맥주'처럼 느껴질 수 있다.

외국인들에게는 다 똑같이 느껴질 수 있지만, 많은 한국인은 브랜드에 따라 소주의 맛이 다르다고 생각한다. 그래서 각자 선호하는 소주 브랜드가 있는 편이다. 실제로 블라인드 테스트를 하면 이게 어느 브랜드의 소주인지 정확히 구별할 수 있는 사람도 많다. 그러다보니 대부분의 음식점은 최소한 세 가지 정도의 소주를 구비하고 있다. 당신이 음식점에서 소주를 주문하면, 대부분의 종업원이 '무슨 소주?'라고 재차 질문하는 건 당연한 일이다. 하지만 당신은 한국어를 잘 모르니 이 말을 알아듣기가 어렵고, 대충 짐작한다 하더라도 특정 브랜드 이름까지 언급하기는 쉽지 않다. 이럴 때 알아두면 좋은 한국어 하나. 아무거나! 이건 뭐든지 좋다는 뜻이다.

하지만 좀더 재미있는 추억을 만들고 싶다면, 술을 주문할 때 다음 단어를 외쳐보라. '테슬라!' 음식점에서 웬 전기 차? 하지만 이건 많은 한국인이 즐겁게 하는 농담 중의 하나다. 당신이 테슬라를 주문하면 종업원은 더이상 묻지 않고(마음속으로 '외국인이 이런 말은 어떻게 알지?'라고 의아해하면서), '테라'라고 하는 한국 맥주와 '참이슬'이라고 하는 소주를 각 한 병씩 가져다줄 것이다(테라에서 테, 참이슬에서 슬. '라'는 왜 붙었느냐고 묻지 마시라. 웃자고 하는 말장난이다). 참이슬은 백 년 가까운 역사를 지닌 한국의 대표적인 소주 브랜드로, '전 세계에서 가장 많이 팔리는 증류주'라는 기록도 갖고 있다. 수출된 물량까지 포함하면 이 브랜드의 소주만 1년에 이십억 병 가까이 팔리기 때문이다.

당신이 테슬라를 주문하면 잔도 두 종류를 모두 가져다준다. 먼저 작은 잔에 소주를 따라 스트레이트로 맛보고, 큰 잔에 소주와 맥주를 적당히 부은 다음 소맥까지 맛보면 완벽하다. 참, 소주라고 해서 모두가 초록색 병에 담겨 있는 것은 아니다. 일부 브랜드의 소주는 투명한 병에 담겨서 판매되니, 당신에게 도착한 소주병이 초록색이 아니라고 해서 놀랄 필요는 없다.

당신이 한국에서 며칠 더 머문다면, 그리고 주머니 사정이 넉넉하다면, 프리미엄 소주도 한 번쯤 맛보면 좋겠다. 프리미엄 소주는 보통의 소주보다 다섯 배에서 열 배 정도 비싸다. 음식점에서도 그렇고 편의점에서도 그렇다. 알코올 도수가 40도 내외로 훨씬 높고, 말로 설명하긴 쉽지 않지만 '고급진' 맛이 난다. 이건 전통적인 방법으로 만들어지는 진짜 증류주이고, 한국식 위스키라고도 할 수 있다. 대표적인 프리미엄 소주 브랜드로는 '화요' '일품진로' '안동소주' 등이 있다.

2.

Soju, the Korean Soul Drink

Although not universally known, there's a good chance you're familiar with soju. Even if you haven't tried it, you've likely encountered it on the screen. If you are perusing this book, it stands to reason that you hold a notable interest in Korea, and as such, it is conceivable that you have been exposed to Korean films or dramas, whether it be the phenomenon of "Squid Game", the acclaimed "Parasite," or perhaps even a lesser-known production.

It's safe to say that almost every Korean movie or drama incorporates soju in some way. While I haven't personally examined each and every one of them, you can bet that soju will make an appearance at least once, unless the story is set before the Korean War. It's just impossible to truly capture the essence of Korean culture without touching on the ubiquitous drink that is soju.

Right from the start of Parasite, as Choi Woo-sik and Park Seo-joon's characters cross paths, they're knocking back shots of soju from those tiny glasses. Yup, that same clear green bottle that's widespread throughout Korea. And in Squid Game, we see Lee Jung-jae and Oh Young-soo indulging in the potent potable while munching on uncooked ramen. (I'll dive deeper into the raw ramen scene in an upcoming piece on the dish.) Interestingly enough, both scenes unfold outside a convenience store, but truth be told, Koreans will tip back soju just about anywhere they can.

Soju, which literally translates to "burned liquor", is a time-honored distilled spirit originating from Korea and has been cherished for centuries, dating back to the 13th century. Traditionally produced by fermenting rice or other grains, this libation boasts a transparent, colorless complexion. Though the alcohol strength can fluctuate, it is not unusual for soju to deliver a potent kick, ranging from 16% to well over 50%.

Correct! Soju falls into the category of distilled spirits.

Alcoholic beverages can be broadly classified into two main types: fermented beverages like beer and wine, and distilled beverages such as whiskey and vodka. Distilled spirits undergo a process of distillation, which separates and concentrates the alcohol content, resulting in higher alcohol levels compared to fermented beverages. Due to their production method and increased potency, distilled spirits often come with a higher price tag.

The affordability of soju is a source of wonder for many foreigners. It's astounding how inexpensive it can be. A customary 360 ml bottle can be acquired at a restaurant for approximately $4, while supermarkets and convenience stores often sell it for just a little over a dollar. In fact, when compared globally, soju stands out as one of the most budget-friendly spirits available. (Ironically, what often astonishes foreigners about soju is not its flavor or fragrance, but rather its price.) Now, what's the secret behind its remarkable affordability?

In Korea, there exist two distinct types of soju, each occupying a different price range. The first type encompasses premium or high-end soju, comparable to other costly spirits found worldwide. On the other hand, the second type, which is more prevalent and affordable, is the beloved soju that graces the screens of films and dramas and finds its place in the hearts of Koreans. It's the kind you'll commonly encounter at restaurants throughout Korea. Despite sharing the same name, these two variations of soju diverge in their production techniques and ingredients.

The more expensive, premium soju in Korea is meticulously distilled, offering a refined and signature flavor profile. On the other hand, the widely beloved and affordable variety, recognizable by its iconic green bottles, is known as diluted soju. Diluted soju is created by blending high-proof alcohol with water and incorporating a moderate sweetener, resulting in a remarkably smooth and pleasing taste. (So, soju may or may not be a distilled spirit.) It's worth noting that while the practice of diluting spirits is found in several countries, none have attained the same level of popularity as Korean soju.

Now, I don't want to get all scientific on you because, let's face it, even I'm not entirely sure about all the intricate details. But here's the deal: think of the relationship between distilled and diluted soju like the difference between butter and margarine. I'll refer to the diluted version as 'soju' from here on out, and if I need to mention the distilled kind, I'll call it 'premium soju'.

When did soju attain its widespread acclaim in Korea? Historically, Koreans brewed various types of alcohol at home until the 19th century. However, in the early 20th century, the alcohol industry underwent significant changes as it became heavily regulated and associated with taxation, making it illegal to produce and sell alcohol without a license. This shift gave rise to the emergence of soju companies, and the beverage quickly gained prominence, particularly the more affordable options that appealed to a nation facing economic challenges. During periods of scarcity, such as in the aftermath of the Korean War, laws were even enacted to prohibit the production of rice-based alcohol, further solidifying soju as one of the few available alcoholic beverages for Koreans.

For much of the latter half of the 20th century, soju in Korea commonly had an alcohol content of 25 percent. Its purpose was primarily to facilitate inebriation rather than being savored for its flavor. Even in the present day, Koreans endure grueling work hours, but in the past, their workloads were even more arduous, accompanied by elevated stress levels. Soju served as a quick and affordable means of getting intoxicated, offering a brief respite from the daily grind before returning to work the following morning. The aim was to consume it swiftly, become inebriated rapidly, temporarily escaping life's hardships, and then recuperate at home in preparation for the challenges of the next day's work.

In 1998, the world of soju experienced a breakthrough when one company introduced a 23 percent variant that quickly made a splash among drinkers. The exact reason for its success remains uncertain, whether it was due to a shift in Koreans' daily lives towards a less hectic pace or other factors. Following this, other companies joined the trend by launching their own versions with slightly lower alcohol content. As a result, the majority of Korean soju available today features an alcohol content ranging from approximately 16 to 18 percent.

The consumption of soju in South Korea is nothing short of staggering, with an estimated 4 billion bottles consumed annually. Each bottle generally holds 360 ml of this beloved spirit. Considering the adult population of approximately 40 million, it means that, on average, each adult consumes nearly 100 bottles of soju per year. It's intriguing to note that statistical data suggests Koreans indulge in soju approximately twice a week, typically savoring one bottle during each drinking session.

Contrary to the common perception of Korean people, statistics indicate that Koreans do not have a particularly high alcohol consumption rate compared to other OECD countries. However, it is important to note that Koreans have a lower tolerance for alcohol due to their genetics. Approximately 30% of Koreans are genetically predisposed to have limited levels of the enzymes required to break down alcohol, making it challenging for them to consume even small amounts without experiencing adverse effects such as facial flushing and headaches. This genetic condition is also prevalent in Japan and China. Considering these figures, it wouldn't be unfounded to suggest that the remaining 70% of Koreans exhibit considerable enthusiasm when it comes to their drinking habits.

To embark on your soju journey, I recommend starting with the iconic green-bottled soju, which proudly holds the title of South Korea's national drink. You can find it everywhere, from restaurants to convenience stores, and it's even allowed to be consumed in public places like parks, beaches, and streets. South Korea boasts a liberal drinking culture, allowing you to enjoy your soju in a multitude of settings, unless expressly prohibited. When it comes to food pairings, soju is known to harmonize well with almost anything, according to the Korean palate. However, to be honest, it tends to find its truest match with salty, spicy delicacies, and fatty dishes like pork belly.

When you take your first sip of soju, you might find it surprising and unfamiliar to your taste buds. It lacks a pronounced flavor or aroma, almost resembling a diluted blend of ethanol. However, as you continue to indulge, you may detect a subtle sweetness that stems from a mysterious sweetener. While some global wanderers appreciate the novelty of this singular libation, for many foreigners, soju is simply an average drink, especially during travel to Korea, that offers affordability. Let's be honest, soju may not be considered one of the most extraordinary beverages in the world. Nevertheless, it's undeniable that this inexpensive elixir carries immense cultural importance for Koreans.

To start with, soju is widely regarded as a drink for the "average Korean Joe". High-ranking officials, CEOs, and famous personalities are often photographed drinking soju intentionally to appear more down to earth. In Korean social dynamics, responding to the question of your preferred drink with wine or whiskey, especially for men, might lead to being perceived as pretentious. (Of course, not always.) To maintain a friendly atmosphere and avoid any potential misinterpretation, it's often considered wise to respond with soju regardless of your actual preference. Similarly, when someone suggests, "Let's drink soju sometime," it often carries an underlying message of wanting to deepen the connection and get to know each other better.

The choice of drink can also convey subtly different social meanings in Korea. For instance, inviting a friend to "have a beer" is often seen as a casual social activity, while asking to "have a soju" may indicate a desire to confide or release pent-up emotions. The latter expression can sometimes imply a more serious or even melancholic tone, as if to say "I need to forget about my troubles for a while, so let's drink together."

In Korea, soju serves as a unique unit of measurement when it comes to discussing one's alcohol consumption. It's interesting to note that asking "How much can you drink?" is not a common question in many other countries, but in Korea, it's almost a customary greeting. Whether you're interacting with coworkers, friends, new acquaintances, or even having a job interview, it's not uncommon for the topic of alcohol tolerance or drinking capacity, known as "jury-ang" in Korean, to come up.

When asked about their drinking capacity, people in

Korea often measure it in terms of bottles of soju. (If they mention just number of bottles, it automatically refers to soju.) It's worth noting that in Korean culture, drinking capacity is often regarded as a way to compete, especially among men. It is not uncommon for individuals to exaggerate their drinking ability as a means to showcase their resilience and social prowess. Notably, in certain professions, being known as a 'big drinker' can even provide an advantage during the hiring process.

Soju can certainly be enjoyed on its own, but it is also frequently mixed with beer to create a refreshing cocktail called "somaek". The common ratio is approximately 1 part soju to 3 parts beer. While somaek is not commonly found at bars, mastering the art of mixing it to the right proportions can earn you praise from your friends, even though you shouldn't expect tipping for your mixing skills. This combination is particularly appealing for those who find straight soju too strong or not so attractive. Mixing a small amount of affordable soju with a regular beer can create the illusion of a 'premium beer' with higher alcohol content.

To foreigners, the taste of soju might all taste the same, but to Koreans, it can vary depending on the brand. Actually, many Koreans have a preferred brand of soju and can discern the differences between brands even in a blind taste test. As a result, it is common for most restaurants in Korea to offer a selection of at least three different types of soju for customers to choose from. When ordering soju at a restaurant, servers may ask you to specify which brand you would like, which can be challenging if you're not familiar with Korean. Fortunately, there is a handy Korean phrase to know: "Amugona!" which means "Anything is OK."

If you're looking to add a touch of humor to your drink order, you can try shouting "Tesla!" This might seem peculiar since it's the name of an electric car, but it's actually a well-known joke among Koreans. When you order a 'Tesla' at a restaurant, you'll be served an amusing combination of beverages: a bottle of Terra, a Korean beer, and a bottle of "Chamisul" soju. (The name 'Tesla' comes from combining 'Te' from Terra and 'sul' from Chamisul. Why the 'a' is added? Don't ask. It's a playful wordplay.) The server will bring your order without further questions, though they may be curious how a foreigner is aware of this inside joke. Chamisul is a widely recognized brand that has been a favorite for nearly a century and holds the distinction of being the 'best-selling distilled spirit in the world'. It's worth noting that Chamisul alone sells nearly 2 billion bottles annually, including exports.

When you order a Tesla, you'll be presented with two different glasses. Begin by savoring the soju on its own from a small glass, appreciating its own flavor. Then, in the larger glass, combine the soju with beer to create a refreshing concoction known as somaek, which offers a glimpse into Korean drinking scene. It's important to note that not all soju brands come in green glass bottles; some are packaged in clear glass, so don't be surprised if you're served soju in a clear bottle.

If you have a few extra days in Korea and are willing to splurge, I recommend exploring the world of premium soju. While it may come at a higher price, both in restaurants and convenience stores, the experience is well worth it. These premium varieties, which can cost five to ten times more than regular soju, offer an alcohol content of around 40 percent, providing a considerably stronger kick. The taste of premium soju is difficult to capture in words, but it exudes a sense of luxury. Crafted using traditional methods, it embodies the essence of a true spirit and can be likened to a Korean interpretation of whiskey. Notable premium soju brands to consider include Hwayo, Ilpoom Jinro, and Andong Soju.

3.
서울은 정말로 복잡하다

북한을 제외한 한국의 면적은 약 10만 제곱킬로미터(38,600제곱마일)이다. 면적 기준으로는 전 세계에서 107위다. 캐나다, 미국, 중국 등의 100분의 1이 조금 넘는 수준이고, 가장 넓은 나라인 러시아와 비교하면 170분의 1에 불과하다(한국이 작은 게 아니라 러시아가 지나치게 큰 거다). 스페인의 5분의 1, 이탈리아의 3분의 1 정도이며, 한국과 비슷한 면적을 가진 나라로는 쿠바, 아이슬란드, 헝가리, 포르투갈 등이 있다.

그리 크지 않은 면적이지만 인구는 약 5천만 명이다. 1제곱킬로미터당 몇 명이 살고 있는지를 나타내는 인구밀도는 5백 명이 조금 넘는다. 인구 천만 명이 넘는 나라들 중에서는 방글라데시에 이어 2위이며, OECD 국가들 중에서는 1위다. 이 수치만 봐도 한국은 좁은 땅에 많은 사람이 모여서 복작복작 사는 나라임을 알 수 있다.

그런데 한국은 전체 면적의 무려 72퍼센트가 산이다. 이처럼 산지 비율이 높은 나라가 없는 것은 아니지만, 한국의 산은 대부분 경사가 급하고 지형이 험준한 편이라서 건물을 짓거나 개발을 하기 어려운 진짜 산악지대가 대부분이다. 국토의 대부분이 평지인 방글라데시보다 '실질적인' 인구밀도는 한국이 더 높다고 할 수 있다.

참고로 위에서 한국과 면적이 비슷하다고 언급한 나라들 중 쿠바, 헝가리, 포르투갈의 인구밀도는 모두 100~110명 수준으로 한국의 5분의 1 정도다. 아이슬란드는 한적하기로 유명한 국가이니 언급하는 게 무슨 의미가 있겠나 싶기는 하지만, 인구밀도가 3.6명이다(러시아나 캐나다보다 낮고, 호주보다 조금 높은 수치다). 아이슬란드 사람이나 호주 사람 한 명이 사용(?)하는 면적을 한국인 150명이 사용하고 있는 셈이다.

하지만 이게 끝이 아니다. 수도 서울의 혼잡함은 상상을 초월한다. 면적이 약 6백 제곱킬로미터(231제곱마일)인 서울에만 전체 인구의 20퍼센트인 천만 명이 살고 있어서, 서울만의 인구밀도를 계산하면 무려 1만 6천 명이 넘는다. 서울의 인구밀도가 싱가포르(7천6백 명)나 홍콩(6천5백 명)의 두 배가 넘는 것이다. 물론 방글라데시나 인도 등의 나라에 서울보다 인구밀도가 높은 도시가 여럿 있긴 하지만, 서울이 전 세계에서 가장 복잡한 도시 중의 하나인 것은 분명하다(심지어 서울조차 전체 면적의 4분의 1은 산이다).

서울 주변도 복잡하기는 마찬가지다. 서울을 둘러싸고 있는 경기도에는 1천3백만 명이, 서울에서 그리 멀지 않은 인천광역시(인천국제공항이 여기에 있다)에도 약 3백만 명이 살고 있다. 서울, 경기, 인천을 모두 합쳐서 흔히 '수도권'이라고 부르는데, 수도권에만 전체 인구의 절반 이상이 모여 살고 있는 셈이다.

아니, 싱가포르 같은 도시국가도 아니고, 10만 제곱킬로미터의 면적이면 아주 작은 것은 아닌데, 아무리 산지가 많다고 해도 좀 여기저기 흩어져 살면 되지, 왜 이렇게 특정 지역에만 모여 사는지 궁금할지도 모르겠다. 거기에는 역사적 맥락이 좀 있는데, 그 이야기는 나중에 다시 하기로 한다.

아무튼 서울이 이렇게 복잡하다보니 외국인들의 눈에는 낯설게 보이는 부분이 적지 않다. 가장 먼저 말하고 싶은 것은 한국인들은 비교적 좁은 '개인 공간'만 사용하며 생활하는 데 익숙하다는 것이다.

문화권에 따라 개인에 따라 편차는 크지만, 대체로 서구인들은 전혀 모르는 사람과는 3미터 정도는 떨어져야 편안함을 느낀다고 한다. 또한 대충 아는 사람과도 최소 1미터 이상의 간격을 두는 것이 보통이고, 친구나 가족들도 최소 50센티미터의 거리는 유지한 채 대화를 나누는 것이 일반적이다.

하지만 한국의 대도시에서는 이런 거리를 유지하는 것이 불가능하다. 물론 한국인들도 넓은 공간에 사람이 별로 없는 한적한 곳을 좋아하는 편이며, 휴가를 떠날 때는 최대한 덜 북적이는 곳을 열심히 찾기도 한다. 하지만 워낙 복잡한 도시에 살다보니 타인과의 거리가 꽤 가까워질 수밖에 없는 생활에 익숙해져서 별로 큰 불편이나 불안을 느끼지 않는 편이다.

개인 공간에 대해 한국인은 조금 다른 인식을 갖고 있다. 사람들이 줄을 서는 모습만 보아도 알 수 있다. 한국인들은 앞사람에게 바싹 붙어서 줄을 선다. 간격이 1미터가 안 되는 것은 보통이고, 경우에 따라서는 50센티미터 정도의 간격만 두고 긴 줄이 형성되기도 한다(그럼에도 불구하고 한국인들이 코로나 팬데믹 기간 중에 사회적 거리두기를 철저히 지킨 것은 정말 놀라운 일이다). 즉, 한국인들은 타인의 공간을 침범하는 것에 무신경한 것이 아니라, 각자 자신에게 할당된 공간이 아주 작다고 생각한다는 것이 옳다.

하지만 많은 경우에 한국인들은 그 작은 자신의 공간조차 온전히 확보하지 못한다. 거리에서, 시장에서, 지하철에서, 미술관에서, 한국인들은 흔히 다른 사람들과 약간의 접촉을 할 수밖에 없다. 실수로 아주 강하게 남에게 접촉한 경우가 아니라 지나가다 슬쩍 몸이 닿은 정도라면, 한국인들은 특별히 사과를 하거나 사과를 받아야 한다고 생각하지 않는다. 프랑스 사람처럼 몸이 실제로 닿지 않고 닿을 뻔만 해도 무조건 '파르동'이라고 말하면서 다닌다면, 지하철로 출퇴근하는 한국의 직장인들은 하루에 이 말을 수백 번은 해야 할지도 모른다. 그러다 제시간에 출근을 못 할 것이고.

비슷한 이유로, 한국인들은 엘리베이터와 같은 공간에서 타인에게 인사를 건네거나 눈을 마주치며 웃는 일도 별로 하지 않는다. 엘리베이터에 17명 정도 탔는데, 그들하고 어떻게 일일이 인사를 나눈단 말인가. 한국인들은 오히려 엘리베이터에서 누군가가 말을 걸면 혹시 '이상한 사람'이 아닐까 하고 약간은 긴장하는 편이다.

그러니, 한국을 여행하는 외국인들은 한국인이 타인의 공간을 아무렇지도 않게 침범하고 상대방을 슬쩍 건드려도 미안하다고 말하지 않는 무례한 사람들이라고 생각하지 말아주길 바란다. 한국인은 결코 특별한 사람들이 아니다. 우리도 복잡한 도시에 사는 것에 지쳐 있다. 우리도 (돈만 있으면) 인적이 드문 지중해의 해변이나 남태평양의 섬에서 휴가를 보내고 싶고, 사람들과의 거리가 충분히 보장되는 비즈니스 클래스에 탑승하고 싶고, 테이블 사이의 간격이 널찍널찍한 우아하고 조용한 레스토랑에서 밥 먹고 싶다.

혹시 서울이 얼마나 복잡한 도시인지 생생하게 체험하고 싶은 마음이 드는가? 그럼 출퇴근 시간에 지하철을 타보면 된다. 오전 8시경이라면 어디에서 타든 꽤나 많은 사람이 가득 들어찬 지하철을 볼 수 있을 것이고, 당신이 극한 체험을 좋아하는 취향이라면 지하철 9호선을 선택하기를 권한다. 9호선은 '일반'과 '급행' 두 종류가 있는데, 반드시 급행을 탈 것. 한 조사에 의하면 출근 시간 이 노선의 혼잡도는 무려 234퍼센트에 달한다. 잠시 계산을 해보면, 기차 한 칸의 정원이 158명인데 실제로는 360명이 탄다는 뜻이다. 오 마이 갓!

1호선과 2호선이 만나는 신도림역, 2호선과 신분당선이 만나는 강남역(〈강남 스타일〉의 그 강남 맞다), 2호선과 4호선이 만나는 사당역, 3·7·9호선이 만나는 고속터미널역, 2·4·5호선이 만나는 동대문역사문화공원역도 '혼잡 체험'을 하기에 적절한 지하철역이다. 당신이 사는 곳이 세계의 여러 메트로폴리탄 도시 중 하나라면 굳이 이런 체험을 해볼 필요가 없겠지만, 당신이 아이슬란드나 호주나 캐나다의 어느 시골 마을에서 온 여행자라면 구경삼아 한번 시도해보길. 출근 시간만큼은 아니지만 퇴근 시간의 혼잡도 만만치 않다.

그래도 좋은 소식이 몇 개 있다. 우선, 그렇게 혼잡함에도 불구하고 소매치기가 거의 없다. 물론 몇십 년 전에는 꽤 있었다. 과거의 신문 기사를 찾아보니 1980년대 후반에는 백화점 한 곳에서만 하루에 50건의 소매치기 범죄가 발생하기도 했다. 하지만 최근 한국에서는 소매치기 범죄가 1년에 약 5백 건 정도 발생할 뿐이다. 몇 안 되는 소매치기도 태반이 잡힌다. 한국의 소매치기 검거율은 60퍼센트 수준이다. 소매치기가 없어진 가장 큰 이유는 한국이 이미 (거의) 현금 없는 사회가 되었기 때문이다. 아직도 현금을 주로 사용하는 소수의 고령자를 제외하면, 한국인들은 거의 모든 소비를 신용카드나 스마트페이를 통해서 한다. 커피 한 잔이나 생수 한 병도 신용카드로 사고, 식당이든 미용실이든 현금을 꺼내는 일이 거의 없다. 훔칠 현금이 없으니 자연스럽게 소매치기가 영업(?)을 할 수가 없다.

핸드백이나 시계나 휴대폰 등의 물품을 훔쳐갈 수 있지 않느냐고? 그건 한국의 보안 체계를 모르고 하는 소리다. 한국에는 정말 많은 CCTV가 있고, 모든 성인은 얼굴 사진과 지문이 정부 데이터베이스에 등록되어 있다. 범죄가 아예 없는 것은 물론 아니지만, 현금이나 물건을 직접 훔치는 범죄는 정말 적다. 보이스피싱이나 스미싱과 같은 정보통신기술 기반의 범죄는 꽤 많이 발생하고 있지만, 적어도 외국인 관광객이 걱정해야 할 범죄는 별로 없다. 기껏해야 바가지요금 정도일 텐데, 이것도 요즘에는 많이 줄었다.

같은 이유로, 한국에서는 공공장소에서 물건을 아무렇게나 두고 다녀도 분실할 위험이 매우 낮다. 가령 당신이 혼자 스타벅스에서 커피를 마시다가 노트북이나 휴대폰이나 지갑을 테이블에 올려놓은 채 화장실에 다녀온다면? 아무 일도 일어나지 않는다. 실제로 한국의 많은 젊은이는 카페 같은 곳에서 공부도 하고 일도 하는데, 동행이 없더라도 도난이나 분실의 위험 없이 마음 편하게 자리를 비울 수 있다. 낯선 사람에게 내 물건 좀 지켜달라고 말할 이유도 없다. 화장실에 다녀와도 되고, 밖에 나가서 담배를 피우고 와도 된다. 식당에서 실수로 지갑이나 전화기를 자리에 두고 왔다면? 당황하지 말고 그곳을 다시 찾아가면 된다. 대부분의 경우 주인이 잘 보관하고 있을 것이고, 손님이 별로 없는 식당이라면 당신이 물건을 둔 바로 그곳에 여전히 놓여 있을 수도 있다.

경기가 벌어지는 날 야구장 인근의 지하철역에 가면 정말 진기한 장면을 볼 수 있다. 대부분의 지하철역 구내에는 물품보관함이 있는데, 보관함의 숫자는 기껏해야 백 개 내외일 수밖에 없다. 몇만 명의 관중이 한꺼번에 몰릴 때는 당연히 보관함이 모자란다. 복잡한 야구장에 들고 들어가기는 불편할 정도로 큰 짐이 있는 관객은 어떻게 하면 좋을까? 적어도 한국에서의 정답은 이렇다. 물품보관함 '근처'에 그냥 놓아두었다가 경기 후에 가지러 가면 된다. 진짜다. 열린 공간에 그냥 두는 것이니 보관료 따위는 없다. 빅게임이 열리는 날이면 이렇게 '방치'(?)되어 있는 가방의 숫자는 수백 개에 달한다.

한국에서 CCTV를 피하기는 정말 어렵다. 한국에는 공공기관이 설치해놓은 CCTV의 숫자만 130만 대가 넘는다. 중국보다는 훨씬 적다고 하지만, 해마다 빠른 속도로 늘어나는 중이다. 최근 10년 사이에만 백만 대가 늘어났을 정도다. 게다가 한국에는 민간이 설치한 CCTV도 상당히 많아서, 전국에 7백만 대 안팎의 CCTV가 존재하는 것으로 추산되고 있다. 2011년에 한 국가기관이 조사한 바에 의하면 수도권 시민들은 하루 평균 83회 CCTV에 찍히는 것으로 나타났다. 하지만 지금은 그때보다 몇 배 많은 CCTV가 설치되어 있으니, 당신에게 엄청난 재주가 있지 않은 이상, 최소한 수백 번은 찍히고 있는 셈이다. 매일같이 말이다.

더욱 놀라운 것은, 한국에 있는 모든 자동차의 약 90퍼센트에 블랙박스가 설치되어 있다는 사실이다. 한국에는 약 2,500만 대의 자동차가 있으니, 자동차 블랙박스만 2천만 대 이상 거리를 돌아다니고 있다는 의미다. 걸어다니든 차를 타고 다니든, 한국인들은 끊임없이 흔적을 남기고 있는 셈이다.

이렇게 이야기하니 한국이 '빅브라더' 사회인 것처럼 들릴지 모르겠다. 신용카드와 CCTV와 스마트폰과 인터넷 때문에 한국인들의 일거수일투족은 어딘가에 '기록'되고 있다. 그리고 그 모든 데이터는 일정 기간 '저장'도 된다. 하지만 한국에서는 '빅브라더'에 대한 사회적 우려는 그리 크지 않은 편이다. 사생활 침해나 개인정보보호에 관한 이슈는 가끔 불거지지만, 기술의 사용을 억제하자는 의견은 많지 않다. 오히려 민감하고 중요한 정보들을 더욱 철저하게 지키기 위해 보안 관련 기술을 더 높이자는 의견이 주류인 것으로 보인다. 한국이 정보통신기술 강국이라서 그런 건지도 모르겠다.

참, 역사적·문화적 맥락과 관련이 있는 한국인들의 행동 양식이 하나 더 있다. 문을 열고 지나갈 때 뒤에 오는 사람이 있는지 여부를 확인하고 뒷사람을 위해 문을 잡아주는 것은 서구에서는 매우 흔한 문화다. 하지만 한국에서는 이런 문화가 별로 없다. 두 가지 이유가 있지 않을까 짐작해본다. 하나는 앞서 말했듯이 워낙 인구밀도가 높고 사람들 사이의 거리가 좁기 때문이다. 사람들이 다닥다닥 붙어서 문을 통과하는 경우가 많기 때문에, 굳이 앞사람이 문을 잡아주지 않아도 자연스럽게, 그리고 빠른 속도로 많은 사람이 문을 통과할 수 있다. 다른 하나는 한국의 전통적인 건축 양식에서는 앞뒤로 움직이는 여닫이문보다 좌우로 움직이는 미닫이문이 더 흔히 사용됐기 때문이다. 앞사람이 신경쓰지 않아도 움직이는 문에 뒷사람이 부딪힐 일이 원래부터 없었던 것이다. 그러니 서구에서 온 여행자 여러분, 무심한 앞사람 때문에 움직이는 문에 얼굴을 다치는 일이 없도록 문을 통과할 때 조금은 조심하면 좋겠다.

비록 몸을 조금 부딪쳐도 미안하다고 말하지 않고 뒷사람을 배려해 문을 잡아주지도 않지만, 한국인들은 기본적으로 착하고 친절한 사람들이다. 외국인 관광객들에게는 특히 그렇다. Bon voyage!

3.

The Hustle and Bustle of Seoul

Excluding North Korea, South Korea has an area of approximately 100,000 square kilometers (38,600 square miles) and is ranked 107th in the world for land area. Although not a very small country itself, it pales in comparison to the size of Canada, the United States, and China, being only a little over one hundredth of their size. Russia, the world's largest country, is 170 times the size of South Korea. (Korea isn't too small, it's just that Russia is too big.) South Korea is roughly one-fifth the size of Spain and one-third the size of Italy. Some countries with similar areas include Cuba, Iceland, Hungary, and Portugal.

Despite its small land area, South Korea is home to around 50 million people, making it one of the most densely populated countries in the world. With a population density of just over 500 people per square kilometer, it ranks second only to Bangladesh among countries with over 10 million inhabitants and first among OECD countries. These figures indicate that South Korea has a considerable population living in a compact area.

Notably, a staggering 72% of South Korea's overall land area is mountainous. While other countries also have high proportions of mountainous regions, most of South Korea's mountains are incredibly steep and rugged, making it challenging to build and develop in those areas. As a result, South Korea's population is even more tightly packed than Bangladesh, which has mostly flat terrain.

For comparison's sake, countries like Cuba, Hungary, and Portugal, which are comparable in size to South Korea, have population densities of 100~110 people per square kilometer, which is around one-fifth of South Korea's density. While Iceland is known for its isolation, it's still worth noting that its population density is only 3.6 people per square kilometer, which is lower than both Russia and Canada but slightly higher than Australia. This means that 150 Koreans occupy the same space as one person in Iceland or Australia.

Moreover, the congestion in South Korea's capital city, Seoul, is simply overwhelming. With 10 million residents, which accounts for 20% of the country's population, squeezed into an area of just 600 square kilometers (231 square miles), the population density in Seoul alone exceeds 16,000 people per square kilometer. To put it another way, Seoul's population density is over double that of Singapore (7,600) or Hong Kong (6,500). While there are cities in countries like Bangladesh and India that are more densely populated than Seoul, it's evident that Seoul is one of the most densely populated and crowded cities in the world. Notably, Seoul even has a quarter of its land area covered by mountains.

The surrounding areas of Seoul are equally packed with people. Gyeonggi Province, which encircles Seoul, is home to around 13 million individuals, while Incheon Metropolitan City, which is not far from Seoul (and is where Incheon International Airport is located), has approximately 3 million inhabitants. Collectively, Seoul, Gyeonggi, and Incheon are often known as the "capital area," indicating that over half of South Korea's population resides in this region alone.

South Korea is not a city-state like Singapore, and even though it has a substantial number of mountains, 100,000 square kilometers is not a small area. Therefore, one might wonder why the population is concentrated in a specific area instead of being spread out across the country. While there is some historical context to this phenomenon, we will delve into it later.

Regardless, with such a densely populated city, there are many aspects of Seoul that may appear unfamiliar to outsiders. Firstly, it's worth noting that Koreans are accustomed to residing in relatively smaller personal spaces.

Cultural norms regarding personal space can vary significantly from one society to another and even between individuals. In Western culture, for example, people often feel comfortable standing at least three meters away from complete strangers. Even between casual acquaintances, it is customary to maintain a distance of at least a meter or more, while conversations with close friends and family usually take place at a distance of around half a meter.

Living in densely populated cities in Korea, it becomes challenging to maintain such distances. However, Koreans also appreciate open spaces and secluded areas with fewer people, and when they go on vacation, they often seek out less crowded destinations. Despite this, due to the experience of living in densely populated cities, they have grown accustomed to close proximity with others, so they don't feel excessively inconvenienced or anxious about it.

Koreans have a different concept of personal space. When standing in line, Koreans tend to stand near the person in front of them, sometimes less than a meter apart. Long lines can form with only 50 centimeters of space between individuals. (Considering this, it's amazing how well Koreans have been able to maintain social distancing during the coronavirus pandemic.) Koreans believe that each person has a very small allotted space, and it's not that they are insensitive to invading other people's spaces.

To continue, in many crowded situations in Korea, such as on the streets, in markets, on the subway, and in museums, physical contact between people is unavoidable. Koreans have adapted to these situations and are generally comfortable with passing touches, not feeling the need to apologize or expect an apology for them. Unlike in France where people may say 'pardon' when their bodies come close without actually touching, Koreans do not have such a practice. If Koreans were to follow this custom like the French do, subway commuters in Korea might find themselves saying 'pardon' hundreds of times a day, and being tardy for work.

Due to the reasons mentioned earlier, Koreans tend to avoid initiating greetings, making eye contact, or smiling at others in confined spaces like elevators. With a crowd of 17 people in an elevator, it would be nearly impossible to acknowledge each person individually. Koreans may also feel uneasy if a stranger attempts to start a conversation in an elevator, fearing that the person may be a weirdo.

As a foreigner traveling to Korea, don't jump to the conclusion that Koreans are a bunch of boorish space invaders who don't apologize when they bump into you. Koreans are just like you, worn out by the hustle and bustle of big cities and craving for some peace and quiet in a serene locale, perhaps a remote beach in the Mediterranean or a tranquil island in the South Pacific, if they can afford it. Koreans also relish the luxury of having ample personal space, be it on a flight or in a fancy restaurant where tables aren't crammed together like sardines in a can.

By any chance, if you're eager to get a genuine taste of the vibrant energy of Seoul, then why not brave the subway during the rush hour? At roughly 8 in the morning, regardless of which station you hop on at, the train is bound to be crammed to the rafters. And if you're the type of person who loves the thrill of living on the edge, I highly recommend you give Line 9 a try. This line has two options: the "all-stop" and the "express", and trust me, you want to opt for the express. According to a recent survey, this particular line is a whopping 234% over capacity during peak hours. Just let that sink in for a moment. That means a train designed to accommodate 158 passengers will instead be crammed with a staggering 360 passengers. Yikes! Can you imagine?

Sindorim Station, where Line 1 and Line 2 meet; Gangnam Station, where Line 2 and Bundang Line meet (yes, the same Gangnam from Gangnam Style); Sadang Station, where Line 2 and Line 4 meet; Express Terminal Station, where Line 3, 7, and 9 meet; and Dongdaemun History and Culture Park Station, where Line 2, 4, and 5 meet, are other great subway stations for the "congestion experience". If you live in one of the world's many metropolitan cities, you won't need to do this, but if you're a traveler from Iceland or a small town in Australia or Canada, it's worth a try. Don't think the chaos is limited to the morning commute either—evening rush hour is just as packed, if not more so.

Well, here's some good news: you won't have to constant-ly check your pockets for sneaky pickpockets in South Korea, despite the crowds. Back in the day, these culprits were rampant. I did some digging in the archives and discovered that back in the 80s, one department store in South Korea had to deal with a whopping 50 pickpockets a day. But these days, the game has changed. The number of pickpocketing crimes has gone down to a measly 500 a year in the country. (Besides, more than half of those sneaky thieves get caught. The arrest rate for pickpockets in South Korea is around 60%.) South Korea's low pickpocketing rates can be attributed to its near-complete transition to a cashless society. The majority of South Koreans use credit cards or SmartPay for their daily purchases, with only a handful of elderly folks still hanging onto cash. Even something as small as a cup of coffee or a water bottle can be purchased with a swipe of a card, and cash is seldom seen at eateries or hair salons. Since there's no physical money to pinch, pickpockets in South Korea have been forced to hang up their thieving hats.

You may be questioning if pickpockets in South Korea go beyond just stealing your cash and target your fancy handbag, watch, or smartphone. Well, let me tell you, the country has implemented robust security measures. With loads of CCTV cameras in almost every nook and cranny, and every adult's face and fingerprints on file with the government, the direct theft of cash or goods is pretty darn low. Sure, there are a few tech-based crimes like voice phishing and smishing, but as a foreign tourist, you don't have to stress about that. Worst-case scenario, you may encounter some overpriced goods, but that's not a common occurrence anymore.

Because of the low incidence of theft in public places, South Korea is a great place to relax and not worry about losing your personal belongings. For instance, if you need to step away from your laptop, phone, or wallet at a Starbucks, you can do so without concern or asking strangers to watch your belongings. You can leave your belongings unattended when you go to the bathroom or step out for a smoke. Many young people even study and work in cafes with their belongings unguarded. If you accidentally leave your phone or wallet at a restaurant, there's no need to panic. Just head back to the restaurant and the owner will likely have taken care of it, or it might still be where you left it if it's a quiet time of day.

If you happen to visit a subway station near a baseball stadium on game day in Korea, you'll witness a pretty bizarre sight. Although most subway stations have coin lockers, there are only about a hundred or so available, which isn't nearly enough to accommodate the tens of thousands of spectators that arrive at the same time. So what do fans do with luggage that's too big to bring into the packed ballpark? Well, the answer is simple: they can just leave it "near" the lockers and come back for it after the game. No joke. And get this—there's no storage fee since it's just out in the open. On busy game days, the number of bags left unattended can reach into the hundreds.

In South Korea, there's no escaping the watchful eye of CCTV cameras. With over 1.3 million cameras installed by public institutions, it's evident that extensive surveillance is in place. While this number may not be as high as in China, it's still growing at an alarming rate—in just the past decade, they've added a whopping 1 million cameras! Additionally, it is worth noting that South Korea boasts an estimated 7 million privately installed CCTVs within the country. In fact, a 2011 survey found that citizens in the Seoul metropolitan area were captured on CCTV an average of 83 times a day, and with the number of cameras increasing rapidly every year, that number is likely even higher now. So, unless you're exceptionally adept at avoiding surveillance, assume that you're being recorded hundreds of times each day.

It is also worth noting that an astonishing 90% of all cars

in South Korea have dash cameras installed. With around 25 million cars in the country, that translates to over 20 million dash cameras on the road. Consequently, Koreans are leaving a constant trail or trace, whether they are traveling on foot or in a vehicle.

South Korea may seem like a society where every move you make is being monitored, creating a footprint of your activities through credit cards, CCTVs, smartphones, and the internet, with data being stored for a period of time. Despite this, there is not much public concern about the idea of "Big Brother" in Korea. While issues of privacy and invasion of privacy do arise, the majority view seems to be that more security technology is needed to better protect sensitive and important information. Perhaps this is due to South Korea's status as a global leader in information and communication technology.

There is one more behavior in Korea that is influenced by its historical and cultural context. In contrast to the Western practice of holding doors for others, this behavior is not as common in Korea. This could be due to two possible reasons. Firstly, the high population density in Korea means that people often stand close together and pass through doors quickly without requiring someone to hold the door for them. Secondly, traditional Korean architecture often includes sliding doors that move left and right, although swing doors that move back and forth are also used. This means that the person behind won't be hit by a moving door, even if the person in front doesn't care. Therefore, travelers from the West should be aware and cautious when passing through a door in Korea to avoid being hit by a swing door.

Koreans are basically nice and friendly people, which holds particularly true for foreign tourists. While they might not always say sorry if they accidentally bump into you or hold the door out of consideration for the person behind, you can still expect a warm reception and hospitality during your stay in Korea. So, bon voyage and enjoy your time in this welcoming country!

4.
세계 최고의
서울 지하철

외국인들이 서울에서 가장 놀라는 것 중의 하나가 지하철이다. 사실 지하철은 세계 각국의 수많은 대도시에 있지만, 서울의 지하철은 정말 특별하다. 노선과 역이 정말로 많고, 승객도 정말 많고, 요금은 주머니 사정을 고려하지 않고 마음껏 탈 수 있을 정도로 저렴하다. 거기에 더해 놀라울 정도로 청결하고, 거의 모든 역에 스크린도어가 설치되어 있어 공기도 맑다. 심지어 공짜 와이파이가 터진다.

물론 서울이 전 세계에서 가장 먼저 지하철이 건설된 도시는 아니다. 오히려 그 출발은 한참 늦은 편이다. 세계 최초의 지하철이 영국 런던에 건설된 것은 1863년이다. 미국에서는 1898년 보스턴에 처음 지하철이 생겼고, 라틴아메리카 최초의 지하철은 1913년에 아르헨티나 부에노스아이레스에 생겼으며, 아시아 최초의 지하철은 일본 도쿄에 1927년에 건설됐다. 서울 지하철 1호선이 개통된 것은 1974년이니, 런던보다 무려 111년이나 늦은 셈이다. 아시아에서는 도쿄, 베이징, 평양에 이어 네번째였다. 그렇다. 서울 지하철은 베이징(1969년)이나 평양(1973년)보다 늦게 시작됐다. 아프리카 최초의 지하철은 1987년이 되어서야 이집트 카이로에 건설됐다.

철도는 훨씬 오래전인 1899년부터 한국에 존재했다. 그런데 지하철은 왜 이렇게 늦었을까. 우선 근대화가 늦은 편이었던 한국은 수도 서울조차 인구가 그렇게 많지는 않았다. 1942년에 처음 백만 명을 넘긴 이후 인구가 꾸준히 증가했지만, 1950년부터 3년간 치러진 한국전쟁으로 도시는 심각하게 파괴되었다. 전쟁이 끝날 무렵 서울의 인구는 여전히 백만 명 수준이었다.

하지만 이때부터 서울 인구가 폭발적으로 증가하기 시작한다. 불과 6년 후인 1959년에 2백만 명을 돌파했고, 그 이후엔 2~5년마다 백만 명씩 계속 늘어나서 1988년에 드디어 서울 인구는 천만 명을 돌파했다. 인구 백만의 도시가 인구 천만의 거대도시로 변하는 데 겨우 35년 걸렸다는 뜻이다(물론 행정구역의 변경으로 서울의 면적 자체가 커진 효과가 더해지긴 했다).

런던에 처음 지하철이 만들어지던 시점의 인구는 250만 명이었고, 당시 영국의 1인당 GDP는 3천 달러 정도였던 것으로 추정된다. 한국이 전 세계에서 가장 가난한 나라들 중의 하나였던 1950년대까지는 서울 인구가 2백만 명을 밑돌았고, 지하철과 같은 인프라를 구축할 수 있는 경제력도 없었다. 인구가 급증하던 1960년대에도, 교통 혼잡이 점차 심각해졌음에도 불구하고, 지하철 건설에 대해서는 막연한 구상만 있었을 뿐 실행에 옮길 만한 역량이 없었다. 한국의 1인당 GDP가 처음으로 2백 달러에 도달한 것은 1969년이었고, 그때까지도 한국은 매우 가난한 나라였다(한국의 1인당 GDP가 처음 백 달러를 돌파한 시점은 명확하지 않다. 정확한 통계가 없어서인데, 1960년대 초반으로 추정될 뿐이다).

지하철 건설 이전 서울의 대중교통은 버스와 전차가 주축이었다. 승용차를 소유한 개인은 극소수 부자들뿐이었고, 택시도 아주 특별한 경우에나 타는 수단이었다. 서울의 인구가 빠르게 늘어나면서 교통 혼잡은 점점 심해졌고, 결국 서울은 전차의 운행을 포기하고 지하철 건설에 나서기로 한다. 전차가 멈춘 1968년부터 지하철 1호선이 개통된 1974년 사이의 기간 동안 서울은 '교통지옥'으로 불렸다.

우여곡절 끝에 서울에서 지하철 공사가 시작된 것이 1970년이었고, 마침내 1호선이 개통된 것은 1974년 8월 15일이었다. 노선은 길지 않았다. 서울역에서 청량리역까지, 길이는 겨우 7.8킬로미터에 불과했고, 역의 개수도 열 개뿐이었다. 하지만 이 짧은 노선의 중요성은 매우 컸다. 서울역과 청량리역이 서울에서 전국으로 떠나는 기차들이 출발하는 가장 중요한 두 개의 역이었기 때문이다. 지하철 1호선 개통과 동시에 기존의 철로들 중 일부가 복선 전철화되었고, 이로 인해 지하철 1호선이 실제로 운행하는 거리는 훨씬 길었다.

지하철 1호선 개통은 오랫동안 서울 시민의 염원이었다. 그래서 개통 기념식은 대통령까지 참석한 가운데 성대하게 열릴 예정이었다. 아마도 개통 날짜가 8월 15일로 정해진 것도 계산된 일이었을 것이다. 그날은 한국의 가장 중요한 국경일인 광복절이다 (한국은 수천 년의 역사 중에 딱 한 번 외국의 식민지였고, 35년 동안의 식민 지배에서 벗어난 날이 1945년 8월 15일이다).

하지만 지하철 개통 기념식 직전에 열린 광복절 기념식에서 큰 사건이 터졌다. 대통령 암살 미수 사건이 일어나며 영부인이 사망하고 만 것이다. 범인은 공산주의자였던 한국계 일본인이었고, 북한과의 관련성은 명확히 밝혀지지 않았다.

아무튼, 서울은 그 이후 오랫동안 공사판이었다. 2·3·4호선 지하철 건설이 거의 동시에 추진되었기 때문이다. 1980년에 2호선이 개통됐고, 1985년에는 3호선과 4호선이 개통됐다. 하지만 1985년에는 이미 서울 인구가 천만 명에 육박했고, 네 개의 노선으로는 불충분했다. 그럼에도 불구하고 서울의 지하철 건설은 여기서 한동안 중단되었다. 지하철 추가 건설보다 훨씬 더 중요한 대형 이벤트가 있었기 때문이다. 그것은 바로 1988년 서울올림픽이었다.

1970년대에 접어들면서 한국은 엄청난 속도로 발전하기 시작했다. 1969년에 1인당 GDP가 처음 2백 달러를 돌파했는데, 1973년에 4백 달러, 1975년에 6백 달러, 1976년에 8백 달러, 1977년에는 드디어 천 달러를 넘겼다. 그로부터 6년 후인 1983년에는 2천 달러를 넘겼고, 다시 4년 후인 1987년에는

3천 달러를 넘겼다. 개발도상국에서는 처음으로 개최된 서울올림픽이 열린 1988년, 한국의 1인당 GDP는 4,755달러였다. 이것이 소위 '한강의 기적'이다.

한국전쟁이 끝났을 때, 한국은 폐허 그 자체였다. 그런 나라가 불과 35년 만에 올림픽을 개최할 정도로 발전한 것에 전 세계가 놀랐다(사실 한국인들 스스로가 가장 놀랐다. 이게 된다고?). 1970년대 말과 1980년대 초에 걸쳐 올림픽을 유치하기 위한 노력이 진행됐을 때, 정말로 올림픽 유치가 가능할 것이라고 생각하는 한국인은 많지 않았다. 좀 긍정적인 사람들조차 이렇게 생각했다. 이번에 성공할 리는 없겠지만 실패의 경험을 잘 활용하면 먼 훗날, 1996년이나 2000년쯤에는 정말로 우리가 올림픽을 개최하는 날도 오지 않을까?

오십대 이상의 한국인들 모두가 그 이름을 아는 독일의 도시가 있다. 바로 바덴바덴이다(물론 정확히 어디 있는지 아는 사람은 거의 없다. 그게 독일에 있다는 사실조차 모르는 사람이 태반이다). 바로 그곳에서 1988년 하계 올림픽 개최지가 발표됐기 때문이다. 1981년 9월 30일이었다. 그날 이후 오랫동안 '올림픽'은 한국 사회에서 가장 중요한 단어 중의 하나였다. 마치 올림픽의 성공 개최 여부에 국가의 명운이 달려 있는 것처럼, 한국은 올림픽 준비에 매진했다.

김포공항(당시엔 인천공항이 없었다. 인천공항은 2001년에 문을 열었다)에서 올림픽 주경기장까지, 한강을 따라 도시고속도로를 건설했고(당연히 이름도 '올림픽대로'였다), 외국 손님들이 보면 부끄

럽다는 이유로 판잣집을 철거하고 도시 빈민들을 내쫓았다. 경기장과 선수촌을 부지런히 건설했고, 그로 인해 또 수많은 철거민이 발생했다. 당시 서울올림픽은 올림픽 역사상 가장 많은 철거민을 발생시킨 올림픽이었다(이 기록은 2008년 베이징올림픽에서 깨졌다). 군인들이 길거리를 돌아다니면 남북이 심각하게 대치하고 있는 것처럼 보이니, 군복을 입은 사람이나 군용차량은 서울 시내로 들어오지 못하게 하기도 했다. '올림픽의 성공을 위해서'라는 명분으로 하지 못할 일은 없었다.

그렇게 지하철 건설은 한동안 중단됐다. 올림픽 준비에 많은 돈을 쓰느라 예산이 부족했기 때문이기도 하고, 지하철 건설을 위해 주요 도로를 헤집어놓으면 '미관상' 좋지 않기 때문이기도 했다(당시 우리는 정말로 올림픽에 '진심'이었다). 결국 지하철 공사는 올림픽 이후인 1990년에 재개되었고, 5호선은 1995년에야 개통했다. 4호선이 완공된 지 10년 만이었다. 1996년에는 8호선이, 2000년에는 6호선이, 2009년에는 9호선이, 2012년에는 7호선이 각각 개통됐다(서울 지하철의 노선 번호는 완공 순서가 아니라 계획이 수립된 순서다).

9개의 노선이 끝이 아니다. 숫자가 아닌 다른 이름이 붙은 노선이 몇 개 더 있고, 서울에서 그리 멀지 않은 수도권에서 운행하는 노선까지 더하면 더 많다. 여기에 현재 건설중이거나 계획중인 노선도 계속 늘어나고 있다. 2022년 기준으로, 서울을 포함한 수도권 지하철의 현황은 이렇다. 모두 23개의 노선이 있으며, 총 연장은 1,262킬로미터, 역의 개수는 640개다. 하지만 당신이 서울을 방문했을 때는 이 숫자들이 또 달라져 있을 가능성이 크다.

한때 서울 지하철은 '지옥철'로 불렸다. 너무도 복잡했기 때문이다. '지하'와 '지옥'은 한국어에서 한 글자 차이다. 지금도 서울 지하철이 특히 출퇴근 시간에는 매우 혼잡하다고 앞에서 말한 바 있다. 하지만 과거에는 그 혼잡도가 훨씬 심했다. 얼마나 사람이 많았던지, 그 당시에는 '푸시맨'이라는 별명으로 불리는 요원들이 주요 지하철역마다 배치되기도 했다. 푸시맨이 뭐냐고? 단 한 명도 더 타기 힘들 정도로 승객이 가득 들어찬 객차 안으로 사람들을 추가로 밀어넣는 일을 하는 사람들이다(세상에 쉬운 직업은 없다). 농담 아니다. 1980년대 중반부터 2000년대 중반까지 실제로 존재했다(이 직종이 존재했던 다른 나라로는 일본이 있다). 앞에서 말했다. 한국인들은 낯선 사람과 몸이 살짝 부딪쳐도 사과하지 않는다고. 사정이 이러니 그럴 수밖에.

하지만 지금의 서울 지하철은 정말로 훌륭하다. 비록 일부 노선은 특정 시간대에 매우 혼잡하지만, 대부분의 경우에는 쾌적하다. 지하철이 과거에 비해 덜 혼잡해진 이유는 크게 두 가지가 있다.

첫째, 서울의 인구가 지난 30여 년 동안 별로 변화 없이 천만 명 수준을 유지하는 동안 지하철은 크게 확충됐다. 단순히 노선만 많아진 것이 아니라 기존 노선들도 지속적으로 연장됐다. 예를 들어 4호선의 경우 1985년에는 28.9킬로미터 길이에 24개의 역이 있었지만, 이후 양쪽으로 꾸준히 연장되어 지금은 86.6킬로미터 길이에 52개의 역이 있다. 3호선도 개통 당시와 비교하면 길이와 역의 개수 모두 두 배로 늘었다. 다른 노선들도 마찬가지다(물론 연장 구간은 흔히 서울시 바깥에 위치한다).

둘째, 자동차가 크게 증가했다. 서울에 등록된 자동차는 1988년에는 78만 대에 불과했지만, 1995년에 2백만 대, 2014년에 3백만 대를 넘겼다. 승용차로 출퇴근하는 사람이 크게 늘어났으니, 자연스럽게 지하철 이용객이 줄어들었다. 하지만 좋은 일이 있으면 나쁜 일도 있기 마련. 지하철의 혼잡도가 줄어드는 대신 도로의 정체는 더욱 심각해졌다. 서울 시내의 도로 역시 길어지고 넓어졌지만, 자동차의 증가 속도를 따라가지는 못했다. 당신이 서울에 머무르는 동안 극심한 교통정체를 만난다면, 대규모 행사나 집회 혹은 대형 교통사고 등을 떠올릴지 모르지만, 그럴 가능성은 별로 없다. 그저 지극히 평범한 서울의 일상을 체험하고 있을 뿐.

서울 지하철의 또다른 장점 중 하나는 '편리함'이다. 거의 모든 한국인은 지하철 요금을 '교통카드'로 지불한다. 선불 충전 방식의 교통카드도 있지만, 대부분의 한국인은 이 기능이 포함된 신용카드를 사용한다. 후불제라는 뜻이다. 교통카드 혹은 교통카드 기능이 내장된 신용카드로 지하철은 물론 버스와 택시 요금도 낼수 있다. 냉난방 시스템도 정말 잘되어 있어서, 사계절 언제나 쾌적한 온도를 유지하고 있다. 심지어 여름철에는 사람들의 취향을 고려하여 냉방을 세게 하는 객차와 약하게 하는 객차를 나누어 운행하기도 한다. 노약자나 장애인을 위한 좌석이 별도로 마련되어 있을뿐더러, 임산부를 위한 핑크색 좌석도 따로 지정되어 있다(이런 좌석은 비어 있어도 아무도 앉지 않는다). 와이파이가 공짜라는 점은 이미 언급했다(재미있는 것은 지하철 와이파이를 이용하는 한국인은 별로 없다는 사실이다. 대부분 LTE 혹은 5G라고 하는 초고속 인터넷 서비스를 넉넉히 제공하는 휴대폰 요금제를 선택하고 있기 때문이다. 그렇게 빠른 인터넷에 길들여진 한국인들에게 지하철의 와이파이는 너무 느려 답답하다).

또한 서울 지하철의 최대 장점 중의 하나는 저렴한 가격이다. 거의 모든 구간을 1달러 정도의 가격으로 이용할 수 있다. 지하철로 한 시간을 이동해도 1달러다. 극소수 구간을 제외하면 환승에도 추가 요금이 붙지 않는다. 물론 아주 긴 구간을 이용하면 가격이 조금 올라가긴 한다. 지하철을 갈아타는 것 말고, 지하철과 시내버스를 함께 이용하면 어떨까? 추가 비용은 사실상 없다. 집에서 버스를 타고 가까운 지하철역까지 간 다음 지하철을 두 번 갈아타고 목적지에 도착한다고 해도 비용은 여전히 1달러다(하지만 버스를 탈 때와 내릴 때 모두 교통카드를 센서에 접촉시켜야 할인 혜택을 받을 수 있다. 불필요한 추가 요금을 내지 않으려면, 특히 버스에서 내릴 때, 이 사실을 잊지 말아야 한다).

65세가 넘은 사람은 아예 공짜다(물론 한국인만 그렇다). 아무리 멀리 가도, 아무리 자주 타도, 지하철은 무료다(하지만 시내버스는 유료다). 처음부터 그랬던 것은 아닌데, 1984년부터 그렇게 됐다. 노인을 공경하는 한국의 문화도 영향을 주긴 했지만, 매우 인기가 없었던 당시의 대통령이 사람들의 환심을 사기 위해 추진했던 측면도 있다.

요금이 매우 낮은데다가 65세 이상 무료 승차까지 있으니, 당연히 서울 지하철은 늘 적자다. 1년에 10억 달러 정도의 적자는 보통이다. 선거를 염두에 둔 정치인들이 공공요금을 쉽게 올리지 못하는 측면도 분명히 있지만, 대중교통 요금을 낮게 유지하는 것은 국가의 경제 규모에 비해 아직도 취약한 편인 복지 시스템을 조금이나마 보완하는 수단이기도 하다.

비슷한 이유로 택시 요금도 다른 나라에 비해 저렴한 편이다 (택시 요금도 사실상 정부가 정한다). 서울의 택시 요금은 미국, 유럽, 일본 등의 대도시와 비교하면 3분의 1에서 5분의 1 수준이다. 지하철의 적자를 세금으로 메울 수밖에 없는 것처럼, 민간이 운영하는 버스나 택시 회사에도 정부가 보조금을 지급하기 때문에 이처럼 낮은 가격을 유지할 수 있는 것이다.

그래서 한국에서는 지하철 요금 인상, 택시 요금 인상, 65세 이상 무료 승차 제도 폐지 등에 대한 논란이 끊이지 않는다. 지하철을 거의 이용하지 않는 사람도 많은데, 이들이 낸 세금으로 다른 지하철 승객의 요금 일부를 지원하는 것이 과연 공평한가에 대한 논쟁이다. 하지만 서민과 저소득층, 그리고 고령자 들이 부담 없이 대중교통을 이용할 수 있도록 요금을 낮게 유지하는 것을 찬성하는 사람이 더 많다. 결국 이 논쟁은 정부의 개입 정도, 개인의 책임과 사회복지의 균형 등과 관련된 더 큰 논란과 연결되어 있다.

하지만 이건 한국인들이 고민할 문제고, 한국을 방문하는 외국인들은 저렴한 교통비를 마음껏 누리면 된다. 하루종일 서울 시내 곳곳을 돌아다니는 여행자들이 지불해야 하는 교통비는 정말 싸다. 지하철만 이용한다면 하루에 10달러 넘기가 어렵고, 택시를 한두 번 추가로 이용한다고 해도 어지간히 멀리 가지 않는다면 30~40달러면 충분하다. 그러니 당신은 저렴한 대중교통을 맘껏 누리면 된다(절약한 교통비를 먹는 데 써라).

외국인 관광객만을 위한 특별한 티켓도 있긴 한데, 별로 추천하고 싶지는 않다. 1, 2, 3, 5, 7일 등의 기간이 정해져 있는 티켓인데, 하루에 열 번 이상 지하철이나 버스를 타야 할인 효과가 생기기 때문이다. 지하철 많이 타기 기록에 도전하는 게 아니라면, 이 티켓을 선택할 이유가 없다. 서울은 물론 볼 것이 많지만, 천천히 보아야 제대로 볼 수 있는 것도 많다. 한때는 '교통지옥'이었지만, 지금의 서울은, 적어도 외국인 여행자에게는, '교통 천국'이다.

4.

Seoul Subway: The Best in the World

The Seoul subway system never fails to amaze foreigners. While other big cities may boast subways of their own, Seoul's is truly something special. Not only does it have an impressive number of lines and stations, but the fares are also incredibly affordable. You can ride to your heart's content without breaking the bank! But that's not all—the system is known for its exceptional cleanliness and fresh air, thanks to the screen doors that line almost every station. And to top it all off, there's free Wi-Fi for commuters to stay connected.

It's a fact that Seoul was not the first city to build a subway system. London, England, holds that title with the first underground railway constructed way back in 1863. The United States joined the subway club in 1898 when Boston built its first subway system. Buenos Aires, Argentina, became the pioneer in Latin America, opening its subway system in 1913, while Tokyo, Japan, took the lead in Asia with its subway system established in 1927. Surprisingly, Seoul didn't join the subway train until 1974, a striking 111 years after London! Among Asian cities, Seoul was the fourth to develop a subway system, following Tokyo, Beijing (in 1969), and Pyongyang (in 1973). Interestingly, Pyongyang had a head start, opening its subway system in 1973, a year before Seoul. Meanwhile, the African continent had to wait until 1987, when Cairo built its first subway system.

Railroads have been a part of South Korea's transportation infrastructure since 1899, but the development of a subway system was a much later endeavor. There are several reasons why Seoul's subway system was built so late. Firstly, Korea was a latecomer to modernization, and its capital, Seoul, didn't experience marked population growth until the mid-20th century. While Seoul's population had been steadily increasing since it surpassed the 1 million mark in 1942, the Korean War, which began in 1950, substantially disrupted the city's growth. By the end of the war, Seoul's population still hovered around 1 million.

Since the Korean War ended, Seoul's population explosion began. Just six years after the war ended, in 1959, the population had already doubled to over 2 million. From then on, the city's population continued to swell at an incredible pace, growing by 1 million every two to five years. By 1988, Seoul's population had finally surpassed 10 million. This astonishing growth meant that it took only 35 years for Seoul to transform from a city of 1 million to a megacity of 10 million. (During that period, due to the changes in administrative zones, Seoul's area was also enlarged, contributing to its population explosion.)

When London constructed its first subway in 1863, the city had a population of approximately 2.5 million with GDP per capita of around $3,000. In contrast, during the 1950s, South Korea was still grappling with significant economic challenges as one of the poorest nations, and Seoul's population was less than two million. Consequently, the financial capacity to invest in infrastructure projects like the subway was limited. Even as the population surged and traffic congestion became problematic in the 1960s, concrete plans for a subway system remained vague, primarily due to a lack of available resources. It wasn't until 1969 that South Korea's GDP per capita reached $200, although the country still faced persistent poverty. (It's unclear when South Korea's GDP per capita crossed the $100 mark, as accurate statistics weren't available, but experts estimate it to be in the early 1960s.)

Before the subway was built, Seoul had a public transportation system that mainly relied on buses and streetcars. Cars were only owned by a small number of wealthy people and taxis were not commonly used. As the population increased, traffic congestion worsened and the city eventually made the decision to discontinue the streetcars and construct a subway. From the cessation of the streetcars in 1968 until the opening of the first subway line in 1974, Seoul was notorious for its heavy traffic, and was called "traffic hell".

The construction of the Seoul subway began in 1970, overcoming a multitude of challenges, and culminated in the successful inauguration of Line 1 on August 15, 1974. Despite its initial length of only 7.8 kilometers and 10 stations, Line 1 played a pivotal role in connecting two of the most important stations in Seoul: Seoul Station and Cheongnyangni Station. Notably, these two stations served as crucial transportation hubs for trains departing from Seoul to other regions of the country. Additionally, during the construction of Subway Line 1, some of the existing railway tracks were double-tracked, effectively extending the length and scope of the subway line.

The opening of Subway Line 1 generated significant anticipation among the residents of Seoul, leading to the planning of a grand opening ceremony that would be graced by the president. Interestingly, the chosen opening date of August 15th held special importance as it coincided with South Korea's most notable national holiday, National Liberation Day. South Korea had endured 35 years of colonial rule until August 15, 1945, marking the only period of colonization in its extensive history spanning thousands of years.

However, during the National Liberation Day ceremony preceding the subway opening, a momentous incident unfolded. A tragic assassination attempt on the president occurred, resulting in the unfortunate death of the first lady. The assailant was identified as a Korean-Japanese communist, although the extent of his connections to North Korea remained undisclosed.

Seoul has been under construction ever since, with the building of subway lines 2, 3, and 4 taking place almost simultaneously. Line 2 opened in 1980, followed by Lines 3 and 4 in 1985. However, by 1985, the population of Seoul had already neared 10 million, and four subway lines were insufficient. Despite this, the construction of the subway system was put on hold for a while due to a much bigger and more important event on the horizon: the 1988 Seoul Olympics.

During the 1970s and 1980s, South Korea experienced a rapid pace of development. The GDP per capita surpassed $200 in 1969, $400 in 1973, $600 in 1975, $800 in 1976, and finally $1,000 in 1977. By 1983, just six years later, it had exceeded $2,000, and by 1987 it had crossed $3,000. In 1988, when the Seoul Olympics were held in a developing country for the first time, South Korea's GDP per capita reached $4,755. This economic transformation is often referred to as the "Miracle on the Han River."

After the devastation of the Korean War, South Korea was left in ruins. However, it was a truly remarkable achievement that within a span of just 35 years, the nation had undergone such rapid development that it was able to host the Olympics. This was not only surprising to the rest of the world, but also to Koreans themselves, who wondered whether such a feat was even possible. During the late

1970s and early 1980s, when the effort to bid to host the Olympics was being made, few Koreans believed it could be accomplished. Even the more optimistic among them thought that if they failed this time, they could use the experience to their advantage and perhaps host the Olympics in 1996 or 2000.

There's a German city that every Korean over the age of 50 knows. It's called Baden-Baden. Now, don't go thinking everyone knows where the heck it is - truth is, most folks haven't got a clue where it is! But, why does it matter, you ask? Well, let me tell you - it's where the host city for the 1988 Summer Olympics was announced on September 30, 1981. Since the announcement, for years, "Olympics" was the buzzword on everyone's lips, and it seemed like the fate of the entire country was riding on the success of those Games. South Korea went all-in, pulling out all the stops to make sure it was a roaring success.

They built the "Olympic Highway," a brand new urban expressway stretching from Gimpo Airport (back when Incheon Airport wasn't even a thing yet) all the way to the Olympic main stadium. They even cleared out run-down shacks that might've made foreign visitors turn up their noses, and evicted the city's poorest residents. Unfortunately, the construction of the stadiums and athletes' villages led to a huge wave of forced evictions - in fact, the Seoul Games had the highest number of evictions in Olympic history, a record that was only broken years later by the Beijing Games in 2008. To avoid any hint of military tension between North and South Korea, they kept all military personnel and vehicles out of the city, creating an atmosphere of absolute safety and security. When it came to ensuring the success of the Olympics, nothing was off the table.

Believe it or not, subway construction in Seoul actually came to a screeching halt for a bit. One reason was that the budget was already stretched thin after pouring so much cash into preparing for the Olympics. But, there was also a concern that ripping up major roads to build the subway would be "aesthetically unpleasant" (we've all got our priorities, right?). So, work on the subway system didn't resume until 1990, well after the Olympics had come and gone. Line 5 wasn't even up and running until 1995 - a full decade after Line 4 was completed! After that, it was a slow but steady process: Line 8 opened in 1996, Line 6 in 2000, Line 9 in 2009, and Line 7 in 2012. Oh, and fun fact - the Seoul Subway lines are numbered according to the order they were planned, not the order they were finished!

But wait, there's more! The nine numbered lines are just the beginning. There are a few more lines with fancy names instead of numbers, and even more that run throughout the greater metropolitan area just beyond Seoul's borders. And, there are still more lines currently under construction or in the planning stages. As of 2022, the entire metropolitan rail system (including Seoul) spans an impressive 23 lines, stretching over 1,262 kilometers and featuring a staggering 640 stations. But, let's be real - these numbers are always in flux. Who knows what kind of new lines and stations they'll have by the time you get there?

Back in the day, the Seoul subway system was infamously dubbed the "Hell Railway". Why? Well, "underground (ji-ha)" and "hell (ji-ok)" are only one letter apart in Korean. And while it's still pretty crowded during peak hours, it was much worse in the past. So much so that subway stations had "pushmen" assigned at every major platform. Yes, you read that right. These pushmen's sole job was to physically shove more passengers into an already-packed train. (Talk about a tough gig. Believe it or not, this was a real thing from the mid-80s all the way up to the mid-2000s. (Japan was the only other country with this kind of job, by the way.) I said it before. Koreans don't apologize if they bump into a stranger. It's just the way things are.

Fortunately, the situation has improved dramatically in recent years, and the current Seoul subway is actually quite efficient. While some lines may still get pretty crowded during rush hour, for the most part, it's a relatively smooth ride. How did things get better? There are two primary reasons why the subway is less crowded now than it used to be.

The first reason is that while Seoul's population has remained steady at around 10 million for the past three decades, the subway network has expanded substantially. It's not just that there are more lines, but that existing lines have been continuously extended. For example, Line 4 had 24 stations and was 28.9 kilometers long when it first opened in 1985, but it has since been steadily extended on both ends, and now includes 52 stations and covers 86.6 kilometers. Similarly, Line 3 has doubled in length and number of stations compared to when it first opened. This trend is also true for other lines, although many of the extensions are located outside of Seoul.

Secondly, the number of cars in Seoul has extensively increased over the years. In 1988, there were only 780,000 cars registered, but that number grew to over 2 million by 1995 and over 3 million by 2014. That's a lot of people choosing to commute by car instead of the subway. And while that might seem like good news for anyone riding the rails, it's not all sunshine and rainbows. Because with all those extra cars on the road, the traffic situation in Seoul has gone from bad to worse. The city's tried to fix the problem by lengthening and widening its roads, but it's just not keeping up with the demand. So, if you're stuck in gridlock during your visit to Seoul, don't worry. You're not witnessing a big event or rally, nor a major car accident, but rather just experiencing an ordinary day in Seoul.

One of the remarkable advantages of the Seoul subway is its convenience. Almost all Koreans utilize a "transportation card" to pay for their subway fares, which is either a prepaid or postpaid system linked to their credit cards. The transport card is not only used for the subway, but also for buses and taxis. The subway also boasts a top-notch air conditioning and heating system that ensures comfortable temperatures all year round. In fact, during the hot summer months, there are even carriages equipped with both stronger and weaker air conditioning to cater to everyone's preferences.

The Seoul subway also offers special seating arrangements for those who need them. Elderly and disabled individuals have designated seats, as do pregnant women, marked with pink-colored seats. It's a cultural norm to avoid sitting in these seats even when they're empty. As previously mentioned, the subway provides free Wi-Fi for passengers. It's worth noting that despite this amenity, few Koreans opt to use subway Wi-Fi as many have cell phone plans with generous amounts of high-speed internet service, such as LTE or 5G. For those accustomed to lightning-fast internet, subway Wi-Fi can be a frustratingly slow alternative.

The Seoul subway system is a steal with its affordable fares. You can travel almost anywhere within the city for just one dollar. Even if you ride for an hour straight, it's still just a dollar. There are no additional fees for transfers, with the rare exception of a few lines. For longer journeys, the price may go up a little. If you want to save money and add some adventure to your trip, why not combine your subway ride with a city bus? You can transfer between buses and subways without any additional cost. So even if you have to take a bus to the subway station and transfer twice to reach your destination, it's still only a dollar. (When riding a bus, it's crucial to tap your transportation card on the sensor both when boarding and disembarking. This is especially important if you plan to transfer to the subway, as failure to do so may result in extra charges. So, don't forget to tap your card, when you get off the bus at your stop!)

If you are 65 years or older (and a Korean citizen), you can ride the Seoul subway for free regardless of how far or how often you use it, although city buses still require payment. This policy has been in place since 1984, and it reflects the respect that Korean culture places on the elderly. However, it was also implemented in part by a president who was struggling with low approval ratings and sought to win public support.

Due to its low fares and free rides for citizens over 65, the Seoul subway often operates at a loss, with deficits of up to a billion dollars per year being common. Although politicians seeking reelection are reluctant to increase fares, keeping public transportation prices low is a way to make up for a welfare system that is still relatively weak compared to the size of the country's economy.

Seoul's taxi fares are relatively low compared to other countries due to similar reasons as the subway fares. The government effectively sets the taxi fares, and they are one-third to one-fifth the cost of large cities in the United States, Europe, and Japan. The government subsidizes privately run bus and taxi companies to keep the prices low, just like the subway's deficit is covered by taxes.

The issue of raising subway fares, increasing taxi fares, and eliminating free rides for people over 65 is a constant debate in South Korea. Some people who rarely use the subway argue that it is unfair for their taxes to pay for the fares of other subway riders. However, others believe that affordable public transportation is essential to ensure that low-income people and the elderly have access to transportation. The debate over transportation fares reflects a larger political and social debate about the role of government in society and the balance between individual responsibility and social welfare.

Attention, fellow travelers! While the public transportation fare debates in South Korea continue, you have the perfect opportunity to enjoy the incredible affordability of getting around Seoul. Exploring the city for an entire day won't break the bank. Unless you're a jet-setting high roller, it's unlikely you'll spend more than $10 on subway fares alone. Even if you opt for a taxi ride or two, your total transportation expenses will likely be around $30 to $40. So why not make the most of these fantastic deals and take advantage of the low-cost transportation options while you have the chance? (Spend the transportation savings on food.)

Foreign tourists in Seoul can also take advantage of special tickets, but beware that they may not be the best value. These tickets are available in different durations, ranging from 1 to 7 days, but to truly benefit from the discount, you would need to ride the subway or bus at least 10 times a day. Unless you plan to break a world record for riding the subway, it's probably not worth it. Take your time, immerse yourself in the city, and savor the experience. Seoul has transformed from a "traffic hell" to a "traffic paradise," especially for foreign travelers.

5.

야구장에서 치맥을*

2019년 10월 26일, 나는 평생의 소원 중 하나를 이루었다. 프로야구팀 두산베어스가 한국시리즈에서 우승하는 순간에 야구장에 있었다! 한국에서 프로야구가 출범한 1982년부터 품어온 소원을 38년 만에 이룬 것이다. 정말 엄청난 경기였다. 경기 초반에 3:8까지 뒤졌지만, 후반에 9:8로 역전했고, 9회 말에 다시 9:9가 되어 연장전까지 간 끝에 11:9가 되는 극적인 승부였기에 더욱 기뻤다. 우승이 확정되는 순간, 눈물이 핑 돌았다.

스포츠 팬이라면 다들 알겠지만, 챔피언이 된다는 건 쉬운 일이 아니다. 엄청난 실력과 회복력, 그리고 어느 정도의 행운까지 따라야 한다. 그 순간을 직관하는 것도 마찬가지다. 그런 경기의 티켓을 구하는 것은 우승 못지않게 어려운 일이다. (이 글을 쓰다 말고 그 경기 하이라이트를 다시 봤다. 당시의 황홀한 느낌이 새롭게 밀려온다.)

　나는 스포츠 관람을 좋아한다. 야구를 가장 좋아하지만, 축구를 비롯한 다른 종목들도 재미있게 본다. TV로 보는 것도 즐겁지만, 스포츠는 역시 직관이다. 솔직히 직관은 불편한 점이 많다. 해설도 없고, 리플레이 화면도 없고, 클로즈업도 없고, 더워나 추위를 견뎌야 하고, 가끔은 비도 맞아야 하니까. 하지만 경기장에 가면 TV로는 결코 체험할 수 없는 여러 가지 즐거움이 있다. 여행 중이라고 다를 까닭이 없다. 그래서 나는 여행 계획을 세울 때도 흔히 스포츠 이벤트 일정을 확인하곤 한다.

　내가 외국에서 운동경기를 처음 관람한 것은 첫 해외여행이었던 프랑스 파리에서였다. 어렵게 티켓을 구해 파리 생제르맹 FC(2023년부터 한국의 이강인 선수가 뛰고 있는 팀이다)의 홈구장인 '파르크 데 프랭스(Parc des Princes)'를 찾았다. 어차피 내가 응원하는 팀은 없으니, 경기보다는 경기장, 선수들보다는 관중을 더 자세히 보았다. PSG 팬들은 박자에 맞춰 단체로 발을 구르는 응원을 즐겨 했는데, 그럴 때는 정말 바닥이 쿵쿵 울리면서 심장 박동이 저절로 빨라졌다. 1897년에 처음 지었다는 이 경기장이 무너지지 않을까 걱정이 될 정도였다.

　그땐 처음이라 잘 몰랐다. 나중에 이탈리아, 영국, 네덜란드, 미국, 일본, 호주, 태국 등 여러 나라에서 다양한 스포츠 경기를 관람하면서, 나라마다 스포츠 경기장의 분위기가 상당히 다르다는 걸 알게 됐다. 좀 거창하게 말하면, 경기장에 모인 사람들의 에너

지와 응원 문화는 그 나라의 국민성을 그대로 반영한다고도 할 수 있겠다.

이탈리아에서 AS로마 홈경기를 보러 갔을 때였다. 프란체스코 토티(Francesco Totti)가 주장이던 시절이다. 경기가 시작하기도 전부터 분위기가 거의 난장판이었다. 곳곳에서 다양한 폭죽을 터뜨려 연기가 가득했고, 경기장 전체에 몽둥이를 든 경찰관과 호스를 든 소방관이 줄을 맞춰 서 있었다.

휘슬이 울린 뒤에는 더했다. 마치 폭동이라도 일어난 듯, 귀를 먹먹하게 만드는 소음이 스탠드를 채웠다. 열정적인 팬들이 내지르는 응원의 목소리와 야유의 목소리가 사방에 울려퍼졌다. 저쪽에서는 누군가가 싸우고, 이쪽에서는 누군가가 담을 넘고, 여기서는 무언가가 날아다니고 저기서는 누군가가 뛰어다녔다. 컵 대회 결승전이나 특별히 중요한 경기도 아니고 그냥 평범한 경기였는데도 그랬다.

로마가 두 골을 앞서가다가 동점이 되더니 후반 중반쯤 역전 골까지 먹었다. 그 순간, 경기장이 폭발했다. 아니, 관중이 폭발했다. 그런데 황당한 건, 아직 경기가 10분 이상 남았는데, 꽤 많은 관중이 자리에서 일어나 퇴장하기 시작했다는 거다. 한 골만 넣으면 동점인데, 왜 나가지? 끝날 때까지는 끝난 게 아니지 않아? 경기는 종반으로 치달으며 점점 치열해지고 있었는데, 경기장을 떠나는 사람은 점점 더 늘어났다. 도대체 왜 나가는 건지 궁금했다. 밖에 뭐가 있나? 나가는 선수들 얼굴 보며 욕해주려고 좋은 자리 잡으러 가는 건가? 나도 나가봐야 하나? 경기가 끝난 이후 경기장에서 벌어지는 풍경도 보고 싶은데, 바깥 풍경도 궁금했다. 갈등하다가 결국 종료 5분을 남기고 일어섰다.

경기장 주변이 엉망이었다. 수많은 인파, 수많은 오토바이, 그리고 이미 자동차로 가득찬 도로. 이들이 경기도 끝나기 전에 서둘러 나온 이유는 의외로 단순했다. 늦게 나오면 길 막히니까. 그렇다. 이탈리아 사람들은 축구를 죽도록 좋아하고, 기다리는 건 죽도록 싫어하는 거다.

그 경기장은 로마시 외곽에 있었는데, 시내로 들어오는 도로가 좁아서 정체가 극심했다. 유적들 때문에 개발을 잘 못해서 거긴 지하철도 없었다(로마는 정말 멋진 도시이지만, 지하철에 관해서만큼은 서울이 한 수 위다). 결국 나도 버스를 타기까지 20분 이상 걸렸고, 버스가 경기장 주변에서 완전히 벗어나기까지 또 20분 이상 걸렸다. 먼저 나간 사람들은 이 정체를 피하기 위해 동점 혹은 역전의 순간을 볼 수 있는 가능성을 포기한 것이었다.

네덜란드 암스테르담에 출장을 갔을 때 아약스 홈구장을 찾은 것도 기억에 남는다. 가장 인상적이었던 건 경기도 아니고 경기장도 아니고 관중도 아니고, 매점이었다. 정확히 말하면 매점의 대금 결제 방식. 아약스 경기장 내부의 모든 매점에서는 현금 결제가 불가능하고 신용카드 결제도 불가능했다. 그럼 뭐로? 처음엔 당황했다. 다들 맥주며 핫도그를 문제없이 사고 있는데, 나만 우왕좌왕했다. 알고 보니 '아약스 카드'로만 음식을 살 수 있었다. 충전식 선불카드였다. 내가 구입할 음식 가격을 잘 계산한 다음 한쪽 구석에 있는 충전 전용 창구로 가서 30유로를 충전했다(네 명이 먹었다. 나 혼자 먹은 거 아님). 여길 다시 올 가능성은 거의 없으니, 많이 충전할 필요는 없었다. 29유로를 쓰고 1유로가 남았지만, 그건 기념품 값이라 생각하면 아깝지 않았다. 아약스 로고가 새겨진 그 카드는 20년 가까이 지난 지금도 내가 잘 간직하고 있다(그곳은 그때 이미 현금 없는 사회였다).

상업이 발달한 나라다운 훌륭한 방법이라 생각했다. 결제가 간편하니 줄도 길어지지 않았고, 현금 주고받는 수고도 없고, 미리 받아놓은 돈이 모이면 이자도 발생할 테고, 나 같은 뜨내기손님이 충전해놓고 쓰지 않은 낙전도 모으면 꽤 될 터였다. 그러고 보니 네덜란드 관중은 응원도 실용적으로 했던 것 같다. 아무때나 소리지르며 기운 빼지 않고, 차분하게 경기를 보다가 꼭 필요할 때만 강하게 내지르는 응원.

미국에서 야구장에 가면 경기 자체보다 음식에 더 집중하는 관객들을 발견할 수 있다. 이들은 야구를 보러 온 건지 뭘 먹으러 온 건지 알 수 없을 정도로 끊임없이 먹는다. 멀쩡한 자기 자리를 비워놓고 매점에 있는 테이블에 앉아서 이것저것 먹으며 야구는 TV로 보는 사람도 많다. 그럴 거면 왜 왔는지.

영국에서 축구장에 가면 한없이 진지한 팬들을 볼 수 있다. 이들은 경기장에 온 건지 도서관에 온 건지 알 수 없을 정도로 심각하게 집중한다. 다른 나라와 달리, 하프타임 때 말고는 화장실에 가는 사람도 거의 없다. 경기가 한창 진행되는 동안 누가 나가려 하면 아주 짜증스러운 얼굴로 길을 비켜준다. 이 엄중한 시기에 화장실 가는 너는 생각이 있는 거냐 없는 거냐, 뭐 이런 표정이다. 어찌나 열중하는지, 경기를 보며 뭘 먹는 사람도 별로 없다.

일본에서 야구장에 가면 외야석을 가득 메운 관중의 일사불란한 응원에 놀란다. 내야는 그리 특별할 것이 없지만, 외야는 분위기가 사뭇 다르다. 거의 모두가 유니폼을 입고, 응원단장의 손짓 하나에 신속 정확하게 구호를 외치고 동작을 실행하는데, 이건 뭐 전문 응원단이 따로 없다.

이렇듯 각국의 경기장 풍경은 다양하다. 하지만 한국의 야구장은 세계의 그 어느 경기장과도 다른 독특함이 있다. 당신이 4월부터 10월 사이에 한국을 방문한다면, 당신이 머무는 기간 중에 당신이 있는 그 도시에서 프로야구 경기가 열린다면, 꼭 한번 방문해볼 만하다.

야구는 한국에서 가장 인기 있는 스포츠다(내가 비록 야구팬이긴 하지만, 이건 거짓말이 아니다). 직접 플레이하는 사람은 축구가 더 많을지 모르지만, 구경하는 스포츠로서의 인기는 야구가 일등이다. 프로야구 출범 이전에는 고교야구의 인기가 매우 높았고, 1982년 이후에는 프로야구의 인기가 높다. 리그의 이름은 흔히 KBO로 불리는데, 이는 한국야구위원회(Korea Baseball Organization)를 뜻한다. 지금은 각 지역에 연고지를 둔 열 개 팀이 경쟁을 펼치고 있다. 경기 수준도 높다. 올림픽에서 금메달을 딴 적도 있고, 미국 메이저리그에서 뛰고 있거나 뛴 적이 있는 한국 선수도 28명이나 된다.

한국의 야구장은 무엇이 그렇게 특별한가. 가장 먼저 손꼽을 수 있는 것은 독특한 응원 문화이다. 일단 한국의 야구장에는 응원단장과 치어리더들이 있다. 그들은 앰프를 크게 틀어놓은 채 관중의 호응을 유도한다. 경기가 한창 진행중일 때는 볼륨을 조금 줄여야 하는 규정이 있기는 하지만, 야구장은 전반적으로 경기 내내 매우 시끄러운 편이다. 특히 홈 팀이 공격을 할 때, 좋은 찬스를 잡았을 때는 더욱 그렇다.

모든 팀은 각기 다른 자신들만의 응원가가 있다. 한두 곡이 아니라 최소한 열 개 안팎의 노래를 사용한다. 한국 가요도 있고 유명한 팝송도 있고 널리 알려진 오페라 아리아도 있다(물론 저작권료를 지불한다). 간혹 원곡의 가사를 그대로 부르는 경우도 있지만, 대부분은 가사를 바꾸어 부른다. 노래가 아니라 응원 구호도 여러 가지를 쓴다. 박수를 치거나 비닐 막대기 등을 두드려 소리를 내는 경우도 많은데, 각 팀마다 선호하는 박자가 정해져 있다. 응원단장은 여러 옵션을 다양하게 조합하며 관중을 이끈다. 경기 초반과 후반의 분위기가 다르고, 이기고 있을 때와 지고 있을 때가 다르다.

이게 '팀'을 응원하는 방식이고, 각 선수들을 응원하는 노래나 구호는 따로 있다. 모든 선수들이 등장할 때, 경기장에는 그 선수만을 위한 멜로디가 울려퍼진다(물론 홈 팀 선수가 등장할 때만 그렇다). 이것 역시 유명한 기존 음원들이 사용되는 경우가 많다(그래서 당신이 어느 나라 출신이든, 경기장에 몇 시간 동안 머물면 반드시 귀에 익은 멜로디를 여러 번 듣게 된다). 등장할 때 사용되는 곡 외에, 각 선수들을 위한 맞춤 응원 구호 역시 경쾌한 리듬과 함께 마련되어 있다. 열성팬들은 이 모든 멜로디와 가사를 전부 다 알고 있고, 당연히 큰 목소리와 큰 동작으로 응원에 동참한다(이런 팬이 많아서 응원단이 잘 보이는 좌석은 가장 먼저 매진되기 쉽다. 경기가 제일 잘 보이는 구역이 아니라 입장료가 아주 비싸지도 않지만, 이곳이 가장 인기가 높다).

경기 상황에 따른 응원곡도 여러 개 준비되어 있다. 우리 팀이 확실한 승기를 잡았을 때 부르는 노래가 따로 있고, 8회 말 시작 직전에 부르는 노래가 따로 있다. 상대 선수가 삼진을 당했을 때 흘러나오는 멜로디가 따로 있고, 우리 선수가 볼넷을 얻어 걸어 나갈 때 흘러나오는 멜로디가 따로 있다. 남성 관중과 여성 관중이 부르는 파트가 나뉘어져 있는 응원곡도 있다.

공격과 수비가 교체되는 1분 남짓한 시간에는 응원단이 미니 공연을 펼치기도 한다. 이때는 주로 유명 아이돌 그룹의 노래가 흘러나온다. 모든 관중이 일제히 스마트폰으로 불을 밝히는 응원을 하기도 하고(과거에는 휴대용 라이터를 켰다), 한창 기분이 좋을 때면 '파도타기 응원(Mexican wave)'이 펼쳐지기도 한다. 많은 관중이 차례대로 자리에서 벌떡 일어나 손을 위로 드는 방식으로 물결을 만드는 응원 말이다. 이 응원 방식은 1986년 멕시코 월드컵에서 유래한 것으로 알려져 있지만, 한국인들이 멕시코 사람들보다 훨씬 자주 써먹는다.

구단에 따라 몇 가지 응원 문화가 추가되기도 한다. 일제히 찢어진 신문지를 흔들기도 하고, 비닐봉지에 바람을 불어넣어 풍선처럼 만든 다음 머리에 쓰는 이상한(?) 행위를 함께 하기도 한다. 사실 이 두 가지는 모두 한국에서 두번째로 큰 도시인 부산을 연고로 하는 롯데자이언츠의 응원 문화다. 특히 비닐봉지 응원은 2005년에 시작되어 한동안 큰 인기를 끌었지만, 일회용품 사용을 줄이는 차원에서 2021년에 없어졌다. 과거에는 매년 비닐봉지 150만 장이 이 응원에 사용됐다(이 비닐봉지는 사실 쓰레기봉투다. 경기중엔 응원 도구, 경기 후엔 쓰레기봉투). 롯데자이언츠는 (비록 성적은 그리 좋지 않지만) 팬들의 응원 열기가 특히 뜨거운 곳으로 유명하다. 투수가 견제구를 던지면 사투리로 야유를 보내는 것도 유명하고, 파울볼이 떨어지면 주변에 있는 아이에게 선물하라는 말을 역시 사투리로 입을 모아 외치는 것도 유명하다. 혹시라도 부산에 갈 기회가 있고, 그날 야구 경기가 열린다면, 한 번쯤 보러 가는 것도 좋겠다. 한국어도 모르는데 사투리까지 따라 하기는 쉽지 않겠지만 말이다.

최근 유행하는 응원 도구로는 스케치북이 있다. 스케치북에 여러 가지 응원 문구를 직접 써서 준비해두었다가 경기 상황에 딱 맞는 것을 펼치는 것이다. 아무런 소리도 나지 않고, 동작도 크지 않고, 여러 사람이 같이 할 수 있는 것도 아니다. 그런데 이게 왜 인기일까? 비밀은 TV 중계에 있다. 한국의 프로야구는 매년 정규 시즌만 720경기가 열리는데, 이 모든 경기가 TV와 인터넷으로 생중계된다. 플레이오프와 한국시리즈 등의 포스트시즌 경기도 당연히 생중계된다. 그리고 카메라맨들은 언제나 재미있는 화면을 원한다. 기발하고 재미있는 문장이 쓰인 스케치북을 펼친 채 간절한 표정으로 서 있으면, 당신의 모습이 TV에 나올 확률이 꽤 높아지는 것이다. 한국의 야구장은 경기장인 동시에 유머 경

연장이기도 하다.

당신도 TV에 나올 수 있다. 일단 유니폼을 하나 구입하여 걸친 다음, 당신과 같은 유니폼을 입고 스케치북 응원을 펼치고 있는 누군가에게 보디랭귀지로 '나도 해보고 싶다'는 뜻을 전하기만 하면 된다. 그가 적당한 내용이 적힌 면을 펼쳐서 당신에게 빌려줄 확률이 90퍼센트 이상이다. 물론 당신이 TV에 나올 가능성은 그것보다 훨씬 낮다. 확률을 높이고 싶으면 더 많은 응원 도구를 갖추거나, 표정과 몸짓을 최대한 과장하거나, 얼굴에 뭔가를 칠하고 빨간색 가발을 쓰거나, 엄청나게 웃기는 춤을 추거나 하면 된다. 진짜 카메라에 잡힌다면, 나중에 확인해볼 수도 있다. 모든 경기는 언제든 인터넷에서 '다시 보기'가 가능하다. 한번 해볼텨?

두번째로 특별한 것은 야구장에서 엄청나게 다양한 음식들을 먹을 수 있다는 점이다. 외국에서 흔히 볼 수 있는 핫도그나 햄버거 등은 당연히 있고, 당신은 잘 모르지만 한국인에게는 너무나 익숙한 길거리 음식들도 많다. 서울의 잠실야구장에서는 삼겹살 도시락도 판매하고, 항구도시 부산의 야구장에서는 생선회도 판매한다. 심지어 일부 야구장(인천 SSG 랜더스필드와 창원 NC파크)에서는 삼겹살이나 다른 고기를 구워 먹을 수도 있다. 바비큐 존으로 명명되어 있는 특별한 좌석에 테이블과 불판이 구비되어 있기 때문이다. 캠핑 분위기 내면서 야구 경기를 볼 수 있는 것이다(취사도구와 고기는 직접 준비해야 한다). 한국의 야구팬들이 미국의 야구팬들보다 많이 먹는 것 같지는 않지만, 훨씬 다양한 종류의 음식을 먹는 것은 사실인 듯하다.

하지만 뭐니뭐니해도 야구장 음식의 꽃은 '치맥'이다. 한국식 닭튀김에 맥주를 곁들이는 것이다. 닭을 튀겨 먹는 것은 매우 일반적인 조리법이고, 맥주야 전 세계에서 가장 대중적인 술이지만, 두 가지를 같이 먹는 것을 즐기는 나라는 의외로 별로 없다. 사실 치맥은 한국인이 정말로 사랑하는 것이어서, 당신이 야구장에 가지 않더라도 반드시 먹어봐야 하는 필수 아이템이기도 하다. 치맥 이야기는 다음 글에서 계속 이어갈 것이다.

끝으로, 당신이 야구장에 갔을 때 응원해야 하는 팀을 알려준다. 응원하는 팀이 있어야 관람이 더 재미있는 법이니까. 바로 KBO의 최고 명문 구단 '두산베어스'다(뭐, 동의하지 않는 한국인이 더 많겠으나, 이 책이 두산베어스 열혈 팬에 의해 쓰였음을 참고하시라). 두산베어스는 한국에서 최초로 창단된 프로야구팀이며, 원년 우승팀이기도 하다. 창단 이후 42년 동안 스물다섯 번이나 포스트시즌에 진출했고, 그중 여섯 번을 우승했다. 특히 2015년부터 2021년까지 7년 연속 한국시리즈에 진출한 기록도 갖고 있다. 몸을 사리지 않는 허슬 플레이로 유명하여 '허슬 두'라는 별명을 갖고 있으며, 끝까지 포기하지 않는 '가장 끈기 있는 팀'으로 유명하고, 기적적인 역전승을 많이 거두어 '미라클 두산'이라는 별명도 갖고 있다. 유니폼도 제일 예쁘고, 응원곡들도 가장 멋지고…… 아무튼 제일 멋진 팀이다. 서울의 잠실야구장을 홈으로 사용한다. 지하철 2호선과 9호선 '종합운동장역'에서 내리면 된다.

• 이 글의 전반부는 나의 책 『여행준비의 기술』에 실린 원고의 일부를 재구성했다.

5.

Enjoy Your Chimaek at the Ballpark

On October 26, 2019, I had the incredible opportunity to fulfill one of my lifelong dreams. I was fortunate enough to be present at the ballpark, where I cheered passionately as the Doosan Bears secured victory in the Korean Series. This was a moment I had been eagerly anticipating for 38 years, ever since professional baseball debuted in Korea back in 1982. Let me tell you, my friends, it was an exhilarating and nerve-wracking game from start to finish.

The score swung back and forth throughout the game, with the early inning showing a score of 3-8, then turning into a thrilling comeback at 9-8, and ultimately resulting in a tie at 9-9 by the bottom of the ninth inning. However, in the gripping extra innings, the Bears managed to take the lead and emerged as the champions with a final score of 11-9. I must confess, tears of joy streamed down my face at that victorious moment.

Every devoted sports fan understands that winning a championship like the Korean Series is no easy feat. It requires immense determination, resilience, and a bit of luck. Not only is winning challenging, but acquiring tickets for such highly anticipated events can also be equally arduous due to the intense competition. (As I revisited the captivating highlights of the game while composing this post, the euphoria I felt at that moment resurfaced once again.)

I'm a huge fan of sports, with baseball being my absolute favorite. But I also enjoy watching soccer and a variety of other sports. While watching games on TV can be entertaining, there's nothing quite like the exhilaration that comes from being there in person. Admittedly, watching sports at the stadium can come with its share of discomforts - no commentary, no replays, no close-ups, and you're even exposed to the elements like heat, cold, and rain. However, there's a unique sense of atmosphere and energy that you can only experience firsthand at a stadium. I find that this inclination towards experiencing games myself extends to my travels, and I frequently seek out stadiums in foreign countries as part of my itinerary.

During my inaugural trip abroad to Paris, France, I had the opportunity to attend a sporting spectacle at the iconic Parc des Princes, the hallowed grounds of Paris Saint-Germain FC. (This is the team that South Korean player Lee Kang-in has been playing for since 2023.) Without a specific allegiance to any team, my focus naturally gravitated towards the stadium itself and the spirited crowd rather than the players or the game unfolding on the pitch. The PSG supporters left an indelible impression on me, their synchronized foot-stomping creating an exhilarating rhythm that sent shivers down my spine. As I absorbed the electric atmosphere, a fleeting concern crossed my mind that the venerable structure, which traces its roots back to 1897, might struggle to withstand the unbridled fervor of the passionate fans.

Then, being a novice on my initial journey, I possessed limited knowledge. However, as my travels unfolded, I was fortunate to partake in sporting spectacles across a multitude of nations. From Italy and England to the Netherlands, the United States, Japan, Australia, and Thailand, each stadium experience showcased a distinctive ambiance that served as a true reflection of the country itself. It became apparent to me that, in my opinion, the collective energy of the crowd and the stadium culture encapsulated the very essence and character of the nation at large.

During my visit to Italy, I had the opportunity to attend an AS Roma home game, with the legendary Francesco Totti leading the team as captain. From the moment I arrived at the stadium, the atmosphere was boisterous, with firecrackers exploding, smoke in the air, adding to the charged ambience. The stadium was heavily guarded, with a strong police presence and firefighters equipped with hoses, creating an unusual sight.

Once the game kicked off, the intensity reached another level entirely. The deafening roar of the crowd reverberated through the stands, making it feel as though a riot could break out at any moment. The passionate fans shouted and jeered with fervor, their voices echoing in every direction. It was a sight to behold, amidst occasional objects being flung across the stands and some spectators even attempting to climb the fences. Here, someone was fighting, there, someone was running. What struck me the most was that this was not a cup final or a particularly significant match - it was just an average game.

AS Roma initially held a two-goal lead, but eventually conceded an equalizer and then fell behind midway through the second half. The stadium erupted, or rather, the crowd did. But surprisingly, many people began to leave with still more than 10 minutes left on the clock. I couldn't understand why they were leaving, especially when the game was far from over. As Yogi Berra once said, it ain't over till it's over. What the heck are they even doing? As time went on, more and more people continued to leave, which made me wonder what they were rushing to see outside. Were they hoping to get better seats to yell at the players? Should I also leave and see what was happening? It was a tough decision, but in the end, I stood up with five minutes left to see what was going to happen next.

The area surrounding the stadium was an absolute disaster. Massive throngs of people, hordes of motorcycles, and streets already packed with cars. The reason they bailed before the final whistle was surprisingly straightforward. If they hung around too long, they'd be snarled in traffic for hours. That's right. Italians are wild about soccer, but I thought they hate waiting almost as much as they love soccer.

The stadium's location on the outskirts of Rome posed

challenges for transportation, with narrow and congested roads making it difficult to access. Rome's subway system is limited due to the presence of historical ruins, which complicates construction. (Rome is a really cool city, but when it comes to subways, it doesn't quite measure up to Seoul.) I found myself waiting for over 20 minutes for a bus and then enduring another 20 minutes navigating through the crowded streets near the stadium. Those who bailed early traded the chance of witnessing an equalizer or an upset for avoiding a traffic nightmare.

During my business trip to Amsterdam, Netherlands, I visited Ajax's home stadium. To my surprise, the most remarkable aspect wasn't the game, the stadium, or the crowd, but the concession stands. I was initially puzzled when I realized I couldn't make a purchase with cash or credit cards, while everyone around me was happily enjoying their hot dogs and beers. I wondered how they managed to buy their food. It turns out that Ajax only accepts payments through a reloadable prepaid card featuring their logo. I went to the top-up station and loaded 30 euros onto the card, carefully calculating the cost of the food I wanted to buy. (There were four of us; I didn't eat alone.) Since I wouldn't be returning anytime soon, I didn't need to add too much. In the end, I spent €29 and had €1 left over, but it was worth it for the souvenir of that pretty Ajax card. (It's worth mentioning that this happened over ten years ago when the Netherlands was already embracing a cashless society.)

I have to say, the idea of having a prepaid card system for easy payments was a stroke of genius for a highly commercialized country like the Netherlands. No more long lines or fumbling for cash, plus they can earn interest on any leftover funds. And let's not forget about the potential big bucks from all those unused small amounts, like the change I left on my Ajax card. On a side note, the Dutch fans are also pretty chill with their support. None of that screaming and cheering at random, they keep it cool and only get hyped when it really counts.

When visiting a ballpark in the US, it's not uncommon to observe fans who seem more focused on their food than the baseball game itself. These dedicated eaters can be seen constantly snacking, to the point where it becomes unclear if they're attending for love of the sport or the culinary delights. In fact, some fans go as far as leaving their seats entirely, opting to sit at a table in the concession stand. From there, they can enjoy their snacks while simultaneously watching the game on nearby TVs. It may puzzle onlookers why these individuals choose to be at the ballpark if they're not going to watch the game from their assigned seats.

On the other hand, when attending a soccer game in the UK, one can't help but notice the gravity with which fans approach the sport. The atmosphere inside the stadium can be so focused and hushed that it resembles a library rather than a sporting event. Unlike in other countries, it is rare to see fans leaving their seats to use the restroom, except during halftime. If you dare to leave your seat during a crucial moment of the game, you may encounter disapproving looks from fellow fans. It's as if they view such actions as inconsiderate, interrupting the flow of the game. The level of engagement and concentration displayed by the fans is such that they rarely take a moment to indulge in food or snacks.

When you have the opportunity to attend a baseball game in Japan, one aspect that stands out is the extraordinary experience of the unified cheering in the outfield. While the atmosphere in the infield may be lively, it's the outfield that takes center stage. Almost all the spectators in that area don matching uniforms, creating a vibrant sea of colors. What makes it truly astounding is the synchronized coordination that takes place. With a simple cue from the cheerleader, the crowd engages in intricate moves and chants, displaying an impressive level of speed and precision that rivals even seasoned professional cheering squads.

As you can see, stadiums across the globe offer a range of pleasant experiences. But there's nothing quite like the baseball stadiums in South Korea. If you find yourself in the country between April and October, you absolutely must seize the chance to attend a game at one of their many stadiums scattered throughout the nation.

South Koreans' passion for baseball runs deep, making it the nation's most beloved sport. (I may be a baseball fan, but this is an unbiased opinion.) While soccer may have a higher participation rate, baseball holds the crown as the nation's favorite sport to watch. In the past, high school baseball captivated the nation's attention, but since the establishment of professional baseball in 1982, the sport has soared in popularity. The Korea Baseball Organization (KBO) oversees the league, which features 10 teams competing for the championship title, each representing a different region of the country. The level of baseball in South Korea is truly exceptional, highlighted by the remarkable achievements of its players. Their success is evident in the abundant accolades they have garnered, including Olympic gold medals.

Furthermore, an impressive total of 26 talented individuals from South Korea have made their mark in the prestigious US Major League Baseball.

What makes Korean ballparks so special? Korean baseball fields are famous for their vibrant and unique atmosphere, primarily driven by the enthusiastic cheering culture. At the center of this culture are the spirited cheerleaders and their powerful amplifiers, which are cranked up to the maximum to ignite the crowd's energy. While there are regulations to lower the volume during crucial moments of the game, the stadiums are consistently filled with a constant buzz of excitement throughout the entire match. This fervor reaches its peak when the home team steps up to bat, presenting a golden opportunity to score.

Each team in Korean baseball features an extensive repertoire of chants and songs, comprising a diverse array of Korean hits, popular tunes, and even opera arias (with proper royalties duly paid). The lyrics are often tweaked to fit the occasion. But it doesn't stop at singing alone; fans exhibit their ingenuity through synchronized clapping and plastic stick-banging, each team adhering to its preferred rhythm. Leading the charge are the cheerleaders, who expertly orchestrate a blend of these diverse options, deftly adjusting the crowd's mood as the game progresses—whether it be at the beginning or end, with the team in the lead or trailing behind, and various other occasions.

In addition to cheering for the team, each player has their own dedicated entrance song or chant, which fills the stadium when they step onto the field, but only when the home team is playing. These songs are often based on famous existing melodies, ensuring that fans from different countries can recognize familiar tunes during their visit to the stadium. Along with the entrance song, each player also has a personalized chant with an upbeat rhythm. Die-hard fans are well-versed in all these melodies and lyrics, and they actively participate in the cheering with loud voices and enthusiastic movements. This dynamic atmosphere makes seats with a good view of the cheering section highly sought after, despite not providing the best view of the game or being the most expensive.

Korean baseball fans have ingeniously crafted a repertoire of chants and songs tailored to different game situations, contributing to the vibrant atmosphere of the sport. They have specific chants for when their team secures an impressive lead and another for before the bottom of the eighth inning, creating a heightened sense of anticipation.

Additionally, they have celebratory songs that play when an opponent strikes out, as well as when their own player receives a walk. It's worth noting that there are separate chants designed for male and female spectators, often sung in alternating turns.

During the brief break between offense and defense, the cheerleaders in Korean baseball stadiums deliver an electrifying mini-performance that never fails to impress. They often showcase a hit song by a popular boy or girl group, setting the perfect mood for the crowd. And when the vibe is just right, fans eagerly take out their smartphones (or previously, lighters) and wave them in the air, creating a concert-like atmosphere with the lights twinkling throughout the stadium. As if that wasn't enough, the crowd even engages in a tradition known as the "Mexican wave," where everyone stands up and raises their hands in the air, producing a wave-like effect that ripples through the stadium. Although it is said to have originated from the 1986 World Cup in Mexico, Koreans use it way more than the Mexicans do.

Depending on the team, there are some other funky traditions that get thrown into the mix. Take, for instance, the bizarre practice of waving ripped-up newspapers in perfect unison, or inflating plastic bags until they're fit to burst and then wearing them like crazy hats. This is all part of the Lotte Giants' cheering culture, hailing from Busan - South Korea's second-biggest city. The plastic bag thing, in particular, took off like a rocket in 2005 and was a huge hit for a good long while. Unfortunately, it got the boot in 2021 as part of a push to cut down on single-use plastic. Get this: in the past, a whopping 1.5 million plastic bags were used for this cheer every year. (Yep, we're talking about garbage bags, folks. Cheering tools during the game, trash bags afterwards.) The Lotte Giants may not be top of the league, but their fans are known to be some of the most dedicated out there. They're famous for busting out their own specific dialect to boo the pitcher's pick-off throw, and when a foul ball is hit, they all scream in unison to give it to a nearby kid. If you're ever in Busan and there's a ball game happening, I say go check it out. Just be warned - if you don't speak Korean, you might struggle to keep up with the lingo.

Another well-loved tool for cheering in South Korean baseball games is a sketchbook. Fans keep a collection of different cheers and use the ones that fit the game situation. It's not noisy, doesn't involve any big gestures, and isn't a group activity, but it's still wildly favored. Why? Because of

TV coverage, my friend. Professional baseball in South Korea has a whopping 720 regular season games each year, all broadcast live on TV and the internet. Of course, playoffs and the Korean Series are also broadcast live. By holding an open sketchbook, writing witty and humorous phrases, and displaying an eager expression, fans increase their chances of being captured by the cameramen who are constantly searching for captivating footage. At South Korean baseball stadiums, cracking jokes and showing off your wit are just as important as the sport itself.

You too can have a chance to appear on TV during a South Korean baseball game. All it takes is buying a jersey, putting it on, and using your body language to signal to someone wearing the same jersey who is engaged in sketchbook cheering that you'd like to give it a try. There's a high likelihood, over 90%, that they will gladly lend you their sketchbook, opening it to the right page. However, the probability of actually being featured on TV is lower. If you're determined to increase your chances, you can acquire more cheerleading gear, amplify your facial expressions and gestures, paint your face, don a red wig, or even unleash some eccentric dance moves. If you do happen to be captured on camera, you can always catch the replay online at any time.

So why not give it a shot?

Another standout feature of Korean baseball stadiums is the impressive array of food options available to fans. In addition to the classic hot dogs and hamburgers, you'll discover a diverse selection of street food that might be unfamiliar to visitors but holds a special place in the hearts of locals. At Seoul's Jamsil Baseball Stadium, you can savor delectable pork belly lunch boxes, while in the coastal city of Busan, you can treat yourself to mouthwatering raw fish dishes. Some ballparks, such as Incheon SSG Landers Field and Changwon NC Park, even feature barbecue zones equipped with tables and grills, enabling fans to grill their own meats. Just remember to bring your own utensils and food—it's like camping at a baseball game! (While Korean baseball fans don't seem to eat as much as their American counterparts, they do eat a much wider variety of foods.)

Now, listen up folks, because I'm about to introduce you to the true MVP of ballpark food: chimaek. This enticing combination brings together Korean fried chicken and a cold beer (maekju), forming a culinary dream team. Fried chicken is no stranger to our taste buds, and beer is the most common alcoholic beverage in the world, yet surprisingly, there are few countries that enjoy eating both together. In fact, "chimack" is so beloved by Koreans that it's a must-try even if you don't go to the ballpark. Stay tuned for the next article, where we'll dive into the fascinating history behind this epic pairing.

Lastly, if you're wondering which team to root for at the ballpark, look no further than the Doosan Bears, the crème de la crème of the KBO (some may disagree - but this book is written by a devoted Doosan Bears fan). These guys were the original gangsters of professional baseball in South Korea and have been dominating the game for an impressive 42 years. They have an astonishing record of making it to the postseason 25 times and have clinched six championships, including the inaugural year of the KBO. And let's not forget their incredible seven-year streak of reaching the Korean Series from 2015 to 2021.

The team's relentless hustle on the field has earned them the nickname "Hustle Doo," and their unwavering determination has crowned them as "the most unwearied team." And let's not forget their proud moniker, "Miracle Doosan," which is a testament to their numerous incredible come-from-behind victories. With their stylish uniforms and captivating cheers, they truly are the complete package. You can catch them in action at Jamsil Baseball Stadium in

Seoul, conveniently located near the Sports Complex subway station on lines 2 and 9.

6.

코리안 프라이드치킨과 치맥

나는 앞에서 당신이 한국에서 단 한끼만 먹을 수 있다면 삼겹살을 먹어야 한다고 자신 있게 말했다. 그럼 두 끼를 먹을 수 있다면 무엇을 더 맛볼까? 이건 정말 어려운 문제인데, 오랜 고민 끝에 나는 당신에게 '치맥'을 추천한다. (당신을 매혹시킬 한국 음식은 그 외에도 정말 많으니, 제발 두 끼만 먹고 떠나지 말고 좀더 오래 머무르길 바란다. 최소한 열 끼니쯤은 먹고 가시길.) 맥주와 함께 먹으면 딱 좋은 한국의 치킨은 과연 무엇일까.

닭은 전 세계 어느 나라에서나 사랑받는 식재료다. 당연히 한국인들도 아주 오래전부터 닭을 즐겨 먹었다. 하지만 주로 삶아 먹었다. 나중에 당신에게 추천할 대표적인 한식 메뉴 중에도 삶은 닭요리가 있다. 한국인이 닭을 '다른 방식으로' 먹기 시작한 것은 1960년대다. 어느 식당에서 판매하기 시작한 '로티세리 치킨(rotisserie chicken)'이 큰 인기를 끌었던 것이다.

로티세리는 한국에서 그리 흔한 기구가 아니고, 당시만 해도 음식을 만들 때 전기를 이용하는 일은 극히 드물었기 때문에, 이 음식의 이름은 독특하게도 '전기구이통닭'이 되었다. 지금도 운영 중인 그 식당의 이름도 재미있다. 영양센터. 가난으로 인해 영양분 섭취가 부족하던 시절, 닭은 한국인에게 귀중한 단백질원이었던 것이다.

1970년대부터는 기름에 튀긴 닭요리가 널리 퍼지기 시작했는데, 닭을 토막 내지 않고 통째로 기름에 튀기는 방식이었다(지금도 이렇게 조리된 닭을 파는 식당들이 간혹 있다). 닭을 적당히 자른 다음 튀김옷을 입혀서 튀기는 미국식 프라이드치킨은 1977년에야 한국에 등장한 것으로 기록되어 있다. 미국 브랜드 KFC는 1984년에 한국에 들어왔다. 이후 프라이드치킨의 인기는 꾸준히 높아졌다. 프라이드치킨을 만들어 파는 수많은 식당은 튀김옷의 배합을 조금씩 다르게 하면서 경쟁했고, 그중 일부는 프랜차이즈 점포를 다수 개설하며 브랜드 가치를 높여갔다.

그러던 중 한국의 프라이드치킨 문화가 급격하게 확산되는 중요한 계기가 생긴다. 하나는 1997년에 한국이 겪었던 외환위기이고, 다른 하나는 2002년에 열린 한일 월드컵이다.

1970년대부터 20여 년 동안 놀라운 경제성장을 이룬 한국은 1997년부터 몇 년간 아시아 각국에서 발생했던 외환 유동성 위기의 직격탄을 맞았다. 한국 정부는 결국 국제통화기금(IMF)으로부터 구제금융을 받아야 했고, 약 4년간 한국인들은 큰 고통을 겪었다. 그전에는 국민 대부분이 이름조차 들어보지 못했던 IMF라는 용어는 지금도 한국인들에게 일종의 트라우마로 남아 있다(사실 IMF는 위기 극복을 도와준 고마운 존재이지만, 'IMF 외환위기', 'IMF 사태' 등의 용어가 널리 쓰였기 때문이다. IMF 미안).

1997년의 경제위기는 모든 한국인의 삶에 크나큰 영향을 끼쳤다. 고통도 컸지만 교훈도 컸다. 특히 온 국민이 펼친 '금 모으기 운동'은 위기에 처했을 때 더욱 빛을 발하는 한국인의 의지를 보여준 사례로 지금도 기억된다. 무려 351만 명이 집에 보관하고 있던 금을 내놓아서 약 227톤의 금이 모였고, 이를 수출하여 부족한 외화를 보충할 수 있었다(한국에는 아이가 첫돌을 맞으면 주변 사람들이 작은 금반지를 선물하는 문화가 있어서, 대부분의 가정이 조금이나마 금을 보관하고 있는 것이 일반적이었다). 당시의 금 수출액은 IMF로부터 빌린 돈의 10분의 1 정도였으니 이것이 위기 극복에 결정적인 역할을 했다고는 할 수 없겠지만, 온 국민이 힘을 모아 국가적 위기를 극복하자는 단합의 분위기를 조성하는 데는 큰 역할을 했던 것이 사실이다.

하지만 강도 높은 구조조정과 그로 인한 실업자의 급증은 피할 수 없었다. 다수의 대기업을 포함하여 수많은 기업이 도산했고, 다른 기업들은 도산을 피하기 위해 수많은 직원을 해고해야만 했다. 약간의 퇴직금과 위로금만을 손에 쥔 채 하루아침에 실업자가 된 사람이 부지기수였다.

특별한 기술도 없고 큰 자본도 가지지 못한 많은 사람은 어쩔 수 없이 자영업자가 되었고, 그들 가운데 적지 않은 수가 '프랜차이즈 치킨집'을 차렸다. 본사에서 공급하는 재료들을 받아서 본사가 제공하는 매뉴얼대로 닭을 튀기기만 하면 되니까, 상대적으로 진입 장벽이 낮았다. 마침 1990년대에 프라이드치킨 사업으로 성공을 거둔 몇몇 기업이 공격적으로 점포 수를 늘리기 시작하던 무렵이었다. 미국 프라이드치킨의 유래에 흑인 노예들의 아픔이 묻어 있다면, 한국 프라이드치킨의 유행에는 갑자기 직장을 잃어 어쩔 수 없이 자영업자가 된 사람들의 눈물이 숨어 있는 셈이다.

이즈음부터 한국인들이 '치킨'이라는 단어를 영어로 말할 때의 의미는 동물의 이름이 아니라 '튀긴 닭요리'가 되었다(편의상 앞으로는 '한국식 프라이드치킨'을 통칭할 때에 'chikin'으로 표기한다).

이렇게 치킨의 인기가 점차 높아지던 2002년, 한국에서 월드컵이 열렸다. 국내 리그만 놓고 보면 야구가 가장 인기 있는 종목이지만, 한국에서는 축구의 인기도 매우 높다. 특히 국가대표팀의 경기에 대한 관심은 엄청나다. 월드컵에 대한 한국인의 열정은 여느 유럽인들 못지않다. 비록 일본과의 공동 개최이기는 했지만, 월드컵이 한국에서 개최된다는 것은 수많은 한국인에게 꿈같은 일이었다. 게다가 그 대회에서 한국은 승리를 거듭하며 4강에까지 진출했다. 16강 진출이라는 목표를 두 단계나 뛰어넘은 것이다.

월드컵 기간 내내 한국은 축제였다. 특히 한국 팀의 경기가 열리는 날에는 전국의 크고 작은 광장에 붉은 유니폼을 입은 사람들이 적게는 수백 명, 많게는 백만 명 넘게 모였다. 길거리 응원에 동참하지 않은 사람들은 술집이나 영화관(그때는 영화 대신 축구를 상영했다)에 모였다. 기차역이든 병원이든 학교든 회사든 집이든, 전국의 모든 TV에는 축구 중계가 나왔다. 그리고 그 많은 사람이, 이유는 모르겠지만 약속이나 한 듯이, 치맥을 즐겼다. 어찌나 많은 사람이 치킨을 원했던지, 주문하면 두세 시간 후에 배달이 오는 경우가 흔했다(그렇다. 나중에 다시 이야기하겠지만, 한국은 전 세계에서 '배달' 문화가 가장 발달한 나라다).

이후 치킨은 진화를 거듭했다. 수많은 치킨집이 열정적으로 새로운 레시피 개발에 나섰다. 1990년대까지만 해도 치킨은 크게 '프라이드'와 '양념' 두 종류였고, 이색적인 치킨으로 간장 양념을 사용한 것이 있을 뿐이었지만, 지금은 그 종류를 헤아리기 어려울 정도로 다양한 치킨이 있다. 단언컨대, 한국의 치킨은 이탈리아의 피자보다 다양하고 미국의 햄버거보다 다양하고 독일의 소시지보다 다양하다. 여러 개의 가맹점이 있는 프랜차이즈 치킨 회사만 4백 개가 넘고, 독립적으로 운영되는 치킨집도 부지기수다. 치킨 전문점이 아닌 평범한 펍들에서도 대부분 치킨을 판매한다. 각 브랜드가 최소한 열 가지 이상의 메뉴를 선보이고 있으니, 치킨이라고 통칭되는 음식의 종류는 족히 수천 가지가 넘는 셈이다.

가장 유명한 몇몇 브랜드는 한국에만 천 개가 훨씬 넘는 점포를 운영중이고, 해외에 낸 매장까지 포함하면 2천 개가 넘는 브랜드도 있다. 그럼 한국에 치킨집은 몇 개나 될까? 놀라지 마시

라. 8만 개가 넘는 것으로 추산되고 있다. 전 세계의 맥도날드 매장(약 3만 8천 개)과 스타벅스 매장(약 3만 4천 개)을 합친 것보다 더 많은 치킨집이 한국에 있는 것이다. 그야말로 한국은 치킨 공화국이라 해도 과언이 아니다.

아마도 당신은 이렇게 생각할 것이다. 그래봐야 어차피 튀김옷을 입혀서 튀긴 닭이니 다 거기서 거기 아니냐고. 결코 그렇지 않다. 많은 한국인은 한 조각만 먹어도 이것이 어느 브랜드의 치킨인지 비교적 정확하게 구별할 수 있다(심지어 냄새만 맡고서 구별하기도 한다). 당연히 대부분의 한국인은 각자 자신이 가장 좋아하는 치킨을 아주 구체적으로 말할 수 있다. 특히 치킨을 좋아하는 소수의 사람은 단 한입만 먹고서도 어느 브랜드의 무슨 메뉴인지까지 정확히 맞힐 수 있다. 심지어 그런 능력을 매우 자랑스러워한다!

몇 년 전, 배달 앱을 운영하는 어느 회사가 재미있는 이벤트를 기획했다. '치믈리에 자격시험'을 통과하면 '치믈리에 인증서'를 발급해주는 행사였다. 치믈리에는 당연히 치킨과 소믈리에를 조합한 신조어다. 필기시험과 실기시험이 있는데, 실기시험은 블라인드 테스트 방식으로 다양한 브랜드의 치킨을 구분해내는 능력을 측정하는 것이었다. 장소의 제한 때문에 5백 명만 응시할 수 있었는데, 이 시험을 보고 싶다고 사전에 신청한 사람이 너무 많아서 추첨을 해야만 했다.

얼마나 많은 사람이 신청했을까? 응시자는 무려 57만 명. 온라인 시험을 통과한 사람만 2만 7천 명이어서 추첨을 통해 5백 명이 오프라인 시험에 초대됐고, 그중 47명이 영광스러운(?) '치믈리에' 호칭을 획득했다(이 시험은 두 차례 실시됐고, 한국에는 총 166명의 치믈리에가 있다. 이렇게 인기가 있었는데 더이상 이벤트가 열리지 않는 것은 시험 현장에서 '동물권' 활동가들이 시위를 벌이는 일이 있었기 때문이다).

또한 한국의 치킨 유행은 여러 가지 사회적 이슈와도 연결되어 있다. 첫째, 지나치게 높은 자영업자 비율을 상징적으로 보여주는 것이 엄청나게 많은 치킨집 숫자다. 꾸준히 내려가고 있기는 하지만, 한국의 자영업자 비율은 여전히 25퍼센트 수준이다. OECD 평균 15.8퍼센트보다 훨씬 높고, 회원국 중에서 한국보다 이 비율이 높은 나라는 콜롬비아, 그리스, 브라질, 튀르키예, 멕시코, 칠레뿐이다. 좋은 일자리가 경제 규모에 비해 많지 않고, 노동시장의 유연성이 적어서 한번 직장을 잃으면 재취업이 쉽지 않은 것은 한국 경제의 주요한 약점 중의 하나다. 국민들의 소득 수준이 불안정적일 수밖에 없고, 과도한 경쟁으로 적자를 보거나 망하는 자영업자가 많아진다(영화 〈기생충〉의 송강호도 치킨집을 열었다가 망한 경험이 있다). 또한, 창업이나 운영과 관련된 비용을 모두 스스로 조달하다보니 가계부채가 늘어나는 등의 문제가 있다. 때문에 정부에서 자영업자 비율을 낮추기 위해 많은 노력을 하고 있지만, 해결이 쉽지 않다.

둘째, 자영업자 중 상당수를 차지하는 프랜차이즈 가맹점과 본사와의 갈등이다. 본사가 가맹점으로부터 재료값 외에도 다양한 수수료와 마케팅 비용의 일부까지 받아가기 때문에, 본사는 돈을 벌어도 가맹점은 큰 수익을 올리지 못하는 구조가 있는 것이다. 이런 문제는 치킨업계 외에 24시간 편의점을 비롯한 모든 프랜차이즈 업종에서 공통적으로 발생하고 있다.

셋째, 배달업체와 음식점들 사이의 갈등도 있다. 한국은 배달 문화가 정말로 발달한 나라이다. 치킨이나 피자는 당연하고, 세상의 거의 모든 상품이 배달 가능하다. 당신이 무엇을 떠올리든, 그것도 배달이 된다고 생각하면 된다. 이런 문화는 코로나19 이후 더 확산됐다(통계청 자료에 의하면 2021년에 한국인은 1인당 70.3개의 택배 상자를 받았다. 경제활동 인구만 기준으로 하면 1인당 128.2개다. 음식 배달 건수는 정확한 통계가 없지만, 같은 자료에서 한국의 배달 음식 매출 규모는 연간 2백억 달러까지 늘었다. 한끼에 10달러라고 하면 20억 끼니가 되고, 5천만 명의 한국인이 '평균적으로' 연간 40끼니는 배달을 통해 해결했다는 뜻이 된다). 음식점들이 각자 인력을 고용하여 배달 서비스를 제공하던 과거에는 아무런 문제가 없었다. 하지만 스마트폰의 탄생 이후에는 거의 모든 배달 주문이 앱을 통해 이뤄지고 있고, 음식 배달 시장을 소수의 플랫폼 기업이 과점하는 상황이 벌어졌다. 자연히 영세한 음식점들과 자본력이 탄탄한 플랫폼 기업들 사이에 수수료를 놓고 갈등이 빚어지는 것이다.

넷째, 치킨 시장이 워낙 커지고 몇몇 대기업의 시장 점유율이 높아지니, 가격담합 등의 불공정거래에 관한 논란도 불거지기 시작했다. 실제로 대형 프랜차이즈 체인에서 판매하는 치킨 가격은 꾸준히 올라서, 지금은 20달러를 넘는 메뉴도 많이 생겼다. 한국은 물가가 제법 비싼 나라이고 꽤 많은 시장이 과점 상태에 놓여 있는 만큼, 다른 상품들에 대해서도 폭리 논란이 자주 있는 편이다. 하지만 한국인들은 치킨값에 특히 민감한 편이다. 워낙 치킨을 사랑하다보니, 이것도 일종의 공공재(?)로 생각하는 경향까지 나타나는 것인지도 모른다.

이런 복잡한 이슈들의 해결은 한국인들에게 맡기고, 여행자인 당신은 맛있게 치킨을 맛보면 된다. 당연히 맥주와 함께. 그런데 고민이 될 것이다. 그 많은 치킨집 중에서 어디를 갈 것이며, 그 많은 메뉴 중에서 도대체 무엇을 먹을 것인가. 치킨 브랜드 중 빅3로 꼽히는 교촌, BBQ, BHC 중의 한 곳을 방문하면 안전하겠다. 세 회사의 매장만 해도 전국에 5천 개 가까이 있으니, 웬만하면 당신의 눈에 띌 것이다(다행히 세 회사 모두 간판에 영어 표기가 있으며, 치킨 사진도 대부분 붙어 있다). 친절하게 대표 메뉴도 알려드린다. 교촌에서는 '반반오리지널'을, BBQ에서는 '황금올리브치킨반반'을, BHC에서는 '뿌링클콤보'를 주문하시라(반반은 'half & half'라는 뜻으로, 두 종류를 맛볼 수 있다). 일단 2인 1메뉴를 시키고, 양이 부족하면 추가 메뉴를 주문하거나 (반드시 그 근처에 위치하고 있을) 다른 치킨집으로 이동하면 되겠다.

참, 일부 치킨집은 테이블이 아예 없고 포장이나 배달만 가능하다. 하필 그런 가게를 발견했다면 당황하지 말고 조금만 더 찾아보시길. 아니면 (한국인들이 흔히 그렇게 하듯이) 포장 주문을 한 다음 주변 공원이나 당신의 숙소에 가서 먹어도 된다. 마지막 팁. 맛보아야 할 한식은 많은데 시간이 부족하다면, 치킨은 점심이나 저녁 식사가 아니라 '야식'으로 선택하면 된다(실제로 치킨은 한국인들에게 가장 인기 있는 야식 메뉴 중 하나다).

오랜 역사와 전통을 가진 진짜 한국 음식은 아니지만, 어느덧 한국을 대표하는 음식이 된 치킨. 한 번만 맛본다면, 아마도 당신은 치킨 때문에라도 한국을 재방문하게 될 가능성이 높다.

6.

Korea Fried Chicken and Chimaek

I confidently stated earlier that if you had only one meal in Korea, it should be samgyeopsal. Now, if you have the opportunity for two meals, my recommendation would be Chimaek. It was a tough decision, but after careful consideration, I believe the combination of crispy fried chicken and beer is a must-try experience in Korea. (Of course, there are many more Korean foods that will captivate your taste buds, so I encourage you not to limit yourself to just two meals and leave. I hope you'll stay a bit longer and indulge in at least ten meals or so.) Korean-style chicken is a delicious dish that perfectly complements a cold beer, but what exactly is it?

Chicken is a universally beloved food, and Koreans are no exception. In fact, they have been enjoying chicken for centuries, but historically, it was prepared through boiling. Actually, some of the classic Korean dishes that I'll suggest later also involve boiled chicken. However, it wasn't until the 1960s that Koreans began to consume chicken in a new way. A restaurant introduced rotisserie chicken to the public, and it quickly became a hit.

Rotisserie cooking wasn't a common practice in Korea, and using electricity to cook food was indeed a rarity back then. As a result, the dish was given a peculiar name - "electric grilled whole chicken." The restaurant that introduced this innovative cooking method, and continues to operate today, has a quirky name - Nutrition Center. During an era of poverty and limited food options, chicken served as a valuable source of protein for Koreans, making it a prized dish.

During the 1970s, a new trend emerged in Korea where the whole chicken was fried, and it quickly gained popularity. Some restaurants still offer this style of fried chicken today, preserving the original method. However, it wasn't until 1977 that the American-style of fried chicken, where the chicken is cut into pieces, battered, and then fried, made its debut in Korea. In 1984, the American brand KFC (Kentucky Fried Chicken) entered the Korean market, further fueling the widespread appeal of fried chicken. Since then, the fried chicken industry in Korea has experienced steady growth. Many fried chicken restaurants have competed with each other by adopting slightly different frying methods and flavors, and some have expanded their business by opening multiple franchise stores, thereby increasing their brand value.

However, two important events played a crucial role in the massive popularity of fried chicken culture in Korea: the 1997 foreign exchange crisis and the 2002 Korea-Japan World Cup.

After two decades of remarkable economic growth starting in the 1970s, South Korea faced a significant setback with the 1997 foreign exchange liquidity crisis, which also affected several other Asian countries. The South Korean government sought assistance from the International Monetary Fund (IMF) to navigate through the crisis, which had a profound impact on the Korean people for approximately four years. Even to this day, the term "IMF," though unfamiliar to most Koreans at the time, carries a sense of trauma for many. While acknowledging the IMF's vital support during the crisis, the frequent use of phrases such as "IMF crisis" and "IMF debacle" has contributed to the negative association with the IMF. (Apologies to the IMF for any unintended implications.)

The 1997 financial crisis had a profound impact on the lives of Koreans, leaving a lasting impression and valuable lessons. The "Gold-collecting campaign" is still revered as a testament to the nation's resilience in the face of adversity. Around 3.51 million individuals contributed their stored gold, resulting in approximately 227 tons of gold being exported to address the foreign currency shortage. (In Korea, it is customary to gift a small gold ring on a child's first birthday, leading to many households having stored gold.) While the amount of gold collected and exported during the campaign accounted for only about one-tenth of the IMF loan, it played a crucial role in fostering a sense of national unity and collective determination to overcome the crisis. Although the gold export alone did not provide a definitive solution, the symbolic act of sacrificing precious possessions in the midst of economic hardship remains a powerful and cherished memory for many Koreans.

However, the impact of the financial crisis was far-reaching, leading to the bankruptcy of many companies, including large corporations, and forcing others to undertake extensive layoffs to avoid collapse. Widespread restructuring efforts were implemented, resulting in a sharp increase in unemployment. Overnight, countless individuals found themselves without jobs, receiving minimal severance and compensation.

As a result of the widespread unemployment caused by the 1997 crisis, many people in Korea, lacking specialized skills or capital, were forced to become self-employed. One accessible option was opening a franchise chicken restaurant, which had a relatively low barrier to entry. With the ingredients supplied by headquarters and the manual provided, anyone could learn how to fry chicken. In the 1990s, successful fried chicken companies began rapidly expanding their number of locations. This rise of Korean fried chicken is tied to the difficult circumstances that forced many Koreans to start their own businesses, in contrast to the origin of American fried chicken, which is rooted in the pain of black slaves.

Subsequently, "chicken" became synonymous with "fried chicken" to Koreans, rather than referring to the animal itself or other chicken-based dishes. To avoid confusion, I will use the term "chikin" to specifically describe Korean fried chicken from this point onwards. (Warning: It's not a typo.)

In 2002, South Korea had the honor of hosting the World Cup, coinciding with the growing prevalence of chikin. While baseball remains the most popular sport in the country, soccer also enjoys a robust following, especially when it comes to supporting the national team. South Koreans are just as passionate about the World Cup as any European nation. Despite being co-hosted with Japan, having the World Cup in their own country was a dream come true for many Koreans. The Korean team's remarkable performance captured the hearts of the nation as they won game after game and exceeded expectations by reaching the quarterfinals, surpassing their original goal of making it to the round of 16 by two stages.

During the World Cup, South Korea was swept up in a wave of excitement and celebration. On match days for the Korean team, large crowds of people adorned in red jerseys flocked to public squares throughout the country, with some gatherings attracting over a million enthusiastic fans. For those unable to join the lively street festivities, bars and movie theaters transformed into soccer viewing venues, replacing movies with live game broadcasts. Soccer matches could be seen on televisions everywhere, from train stations and hospitals to schools, workplaces, and homes.

Nobody knows the reason, but many of these spirited fans embraced 'chimaek' as if it were a precatory ritual, and the combination of chikin and beer became inseparable from the experience of watching soccer matches. The demand for chikin during the World Cup was so high that it was not uncommon for delivery services to have a waiting time of 2-3 hours to fulfill orders. (We will delve deeper into the extraordinary culture of efficient delivery services in Korea later.)

After the surge in popularity of chikin in the early 2000s, Korean fried chicken restaurants embarked on a journey of innovation, introducing a wide array of new recipes. In the past, there were only two main types of fried chicken: naked and marinated, with soy sauce marinated chicken being the exception. However, the landscape has drastically changed, and today, there is an overwhelming variety of chikin options, making it challenging to keep track. Korean chikin has become more diverse than Italian pizza, American hamburgers, or German sausages. Remarkably, there are now over 400 franchised chikin companies with multiple franchisees, alongside plentiful independently owned chikin restaurants. It is not uncommon to find even non-specialty pubs featuring chikin on their menu. Each chikin brand has at least ten different menu items, resulting in thousands of different types of chikin.

With some of the most famous brands boasting well over 1,000 stores in Korea alone, and over 2,000 when considering their international branches, it's natural to wonder about the total number of chikin restaurants in Korea. Prepare to be amazed. It is estimated that there are over 80,000 chikin restaurants in South Korea, surpassing the combined count of McDonald's (38,000) and Starbucks (34,000) worldwide. This staggering figure solidifies South Korea's status as a true "chikin republic."

One might assume that fried chicken is a simple and generic dish, lacking pronounced characteristics. However, this couldn't be further from the truth in South Korea. Many Koreans possess a remarkable ability to identify the specific brand of chikin they're eating with astonishing accuracy after just a single bite, and some can even discern it solely by its aroma. It is not uncommon for Koreans to have a particular favorite type of chikin, and there are enthusiasts who can proudly divulge the precise brand and menu item of a specific chikin after merely one taste. This ability is something that some Koreans take great pride in.

A few years ago, a delivery app company organized a

whimsical event where individuals had the opportunity to take the "chimmelier exam" and earn a prestigious "chimmelier certificate." The term chimmelier cleverly combines the words chicken and sommelier. The exam consisted of both a written and practical section, with the latter challenging participants to identify and differentiate between various chikin brands in a blind taste test. Due to space limitations, only 500 lucky individuals were able to participate in the test, and the overwhelming demand led to a lottery system to select the fortunate participants.

How many people do you think would have applied? Over 570,000 enthusiastic individuals eagerly applied for the event. Among the applicants, a total of 27,000 people successfully passed the online test, setting the stage for the next phase. Through a fair lottery system, only 500 fortunate candidates were invited to partake in the offline test. Finally, a distinguished group of 47 individuals emerged victorious, earning the esteemed title of "chimmelier." Such was the event's widespread appeal that it was organized twice to accommodate the overwhelming demand, and there are a total of 166 chimmeliers through two events. However, it is important to note that due to protests by animal rights advocates at the test site, the event is no longer being held.

The Korean obsession with chikin not only showcases a culinary preference but also highlights some underlying social issues. Firstly, the proliferation of chikin restaurants reflects the disproportionately high rate of self-employment in South Korea. Despite a gradual decline, the country's self-employment rate remains around 25%, markedly surpassing the OECD average of 15.8%. Only Brazil, Chile, Colombia, Greece, Mexico, and Turkey have higher self-employment rates than South Korea.

One notable drawback of the South Korean economy lies in its insufficient availability of quality jobs relative to the size of the economy. Additionally, the labor market's inflexibility poses challenges in finding new employment once a job is lost. As a consequence, people's income levels tend to be unstable, and there is fierce competition among self-employed individuals, leading to financial losses or business closures for many of them. A vivid example of this can be seen in the character Song Kang-ho portrayed in the movie "Parasite," where he once opened a chikin restaurant that ultimately failed.

Moreover, the financial burden of launching and sustaining an independent business often contributes to mounting household debt. While the government is actively working to reduce the percentage of self-employed individuals, addressing this issue is complex and presents considerable challenges.

The second most pressing issue within the Korean chikin industry pertains to the conflicts between franchisees and the headquarters of franchised businesses. Given the diverse fees and marketing costs that the franchisor collects from the franchisee, in addition to the expenses for ingredients, the franchisee often struggles to make substantial profits, while the franchisor, on the other hand, benefits financially. This challenge is not exclusive to the chikin sector; it is a prevalent concern across various franchise industries, including 24-hour convenience stores.

Thirdly, a conflict arises between restaurants and delivery companies due to the highly developed delivery culture in Korea. Not only chikin and pizza, but also almost any type of food and goods can be delivered. This trend has seen a significant increase since the pandemic. With Statistics Korea reporting that in 2021, the average South Korean received 70.3 home delivery boxes per capita. Considering the economically active population alone, this figure amounts to 128.2 deliveries per capita. While specific data on the proportion of food delivery within these numbers is not available, the same statistics indicate that food delivery sales amount to $20 billion. Assuming an average meal cost of $10, we can estimate that approximately 2 billion meals are delivered in South Korea annually. With a population of 50 million people, this suggests that each person consumes an average of 40 meals per year through delivery services.

In the past, conflicts between restaurants and delivery companies were less common because restaurants handled deliveries through their own staff. However, with the rise of smartphone apps, food delivery orders have become heavily dependent on delivery platforms. This shift in the market has led to conflicts between smaller restaurants and the few dominant platforms, primarily centered around commission rates.

Fourthly, as the chikin market in South Korea has expanded and the market share of a few major companies has grown, concerns regarding unfair trade practices, such as price fixing, have emerged. Notably, the price of chikin sold by large franchise chains has been steadily increasing, with many menu items now exceeding $20. South Korea, being a relatively expensive country with some markets dominated by a few players, has seen instances of price gouging in diverse industries. However, when it comes to the price of chikin, Koreans are particularly sensitive. Perhaps, they may think chikin as a sort of "public good" due to their deep affection for this culinary delight.

As a traveler, it's indeed best to let Koreans handle the complexities of these issues while you enjoy the delicious chikin and a refreshing beer. Now, the question arises of where to go and what to order from the overwhelming number of chikin restaurants and menus. If you're looking for the most favored chikin brands, you can easily spot Kyochon, BBQ, and BHC, as they have nearly 5,000 branches across the country. Most of their signage is in English, with pictures showcasing their specialty dishes. Allow me to guide you on what to order. For Kyochon, I recommend trying the "ban-ban" original; for BBQ, the olive chicken "ban-ban"; and for BHC, the bburinkle combo. (Ban-ban means half-and-half, allowing you to taste two flavors in one order.) A single menu item from these brands is usually sufficient for two people. If you're still hungry, you can order additional dishes or explore other chikin restaurants which will surely be nearby.

It's worth noting that some chikin restaurants in Korea operate primarily as takeout or delivery establishments and may not have tables for dine-in customers. If you come across such a place, don't worry and simply look for another option that suits your preference. Alternatively, you can order your chikin to-go, which is a common practice among Koreans, and enjoy it at a nearby park or back at your accommodation. Here's a final tip: if you have limited time to explore Korean cuisine, consider having chikin as a late-night snack rather than for lunch or dinner. In fact, chikin is widely enjoyed as a choice for late-night dining among Koreans.

While chikin may not have originated in Korea and lacks a long-standing deep-rooted history, it has undeniably become a beloved national food. Once you've experienced the amazing flavors and deliciousness of Korean chikin, you might find yourself yearning to return to Korea just to indulge in its taste once more.

7.
김치와 된장, 그리고 〈올드보이〉

요즘 한국의 젊은이들이 즐기는 놀이 중에 '밸런스 게임'이라는 게 있다. 이름만 들으면 체육관에서 하는 게임처럼 들리지만, 두 가지 상황을 제시한 후 둘 중의 하나를 고르게 하는 간단한 놀이다. 예를 들면 이런 식이다. 5백만 달러 받고 스무 살 더 먹기 vs. 그냥 이대로 살기. 평생 양치질 못 하기 vs. 평생 머리 못 감기.

질문은 극단적이고 기발한 것이 많다. 여기에 옮기고 싶지 않을 정도로 '더러운' 질문도 많고, 성인에게만 물어야 하는 야한 질문도 많다. 정말 쓸데없는 장난 같지만, 의외로 많은 사람이 이런 질문을 받으면 '도대체 이런 거지같은 질문에 왜 대답을 해야 하지?'라고 생각하면서도 자기도 모르게 고민에 빠진다. TV 쇼에 출연한 대통령 후보에게 이런 질문이 던져지기도 했다. 다시 태어난다면 지금 아내와 다시 결혼하기 vs. 대통령 되기(이 질문을 받은 후보는 차마 대놓고 후자를 고르기가 민망했는지 '아마도 아내가 나랑 다시 결혼해주지 않을 것 같다'는 영리한 답변을 했지만, 당선되지는 못했다. 전자를 골랐으면 득표율이 올라갔을까?). 당신에게는 이런 질문을 던질 수 있겠다. 한국에서 단 한 끼만 먹을 수 있다면? 삼겹살에 소주 vs. 치킨에 맥주.

평생 김치찌개 못 먹기 vs. 평생 된장찌개 못 먹기. 이 질문을 던지면 대다수 한국인들은 충격과 공포를 느끼며 괴로움에 몸부림칠 것이다. 한국인이 김치찌개를 평생 먹지 않고 살 수는 없다. 된장찌개도 마찬가지다. 이 두 가지 음식이야말로 진정한 한국인의 솔 푸드다.

'찌개'라는 단어는 스튜라고 옮길 수 있겠다(하지만 건더기만 먹지 않고 국물까지 먹는다). 그럼 김치란 무엇이며 된장이란 무엇인가. 아마도 당신이 한 번쯤 맛보았거나 그 이름을 들어보았을 가능성이 조금 더 높은 김치부터 살펴보자.

넓은 의미의 김치는 채소를 소금에 절여 발효시킨 모든 음식을 통칭하는 말이다. 주재료로 쓰인 채소가 무엇이냐에 따라, 소금 외에 어떤 양념을 추가하느냐에 따라, 발효의 정도에 따라, 심지어 어떤 모양으로 만드느냐에 따라 수없이 많은 종류가 있다. 한국인에게 김치의 종류를 읊어보라고 하면 누구나 어렵지 않게 최소한 열 가지 정도는 말할 수 있으며, 그리 흔하지 않은 특이한 김치까지 모두 포함하면 수십 가지 이상의 종류가 있다(심지어 같은 김치를 두고 여러 개의 이름을 붙이는 경우도 적지 않다).

좁은 의미의 김치는 소금에 절인 배추에 고춧가루와 마늘과 젓갈 등으로 만든 양념을 버무린 다음 일정 기간 발효시켜 먹는 것이다(당신이 구글에서 김치를 검색하면 등장하는 시뻘건 그 음식이 가장 표준적인 김치로, 다른 김치들과 구별해야 할 때는 '배추김치'라고 부른다). 김치는 그 자체로 한끼 식사가 되거나 주요한 요리가 되지는 않는다. 밥이나 다른 주요리에 곁들여 먹는 '반찬' 중에서 가장 중요한 것이며, 수많은 주요리의 핵심 재료로 쓰이는 것이다. 당신이 일부러 피해 다니지 않는 이상, 한국을 방문하면 절대로 마주치지 않을 수 없는 것이 김치다(사실 한국에 며칠 동안 머물면서 김치를 완전히 피한다는 것은 불가능하다. 그건 톰 크루즈도 해낼 수 없는 미션 임파서블이다).

김치의 역사는 최소한 천 년 이상 되었을 것으로 여겨진다. 하지만 김치의 역사에서 가장 중요한 계기는 고추의 전파였다. 고추가 한반도에 전해진 것은 16세기 말 혹은 17세기 초로 추정된다. 그 이전의 김치는 빨갛지 않았다는 뜻이다.

당신에게 김치의 넓은 세계에 대해 자세히 설명할 필요는 없겠다. 당신이 한국에 아예 정착해서 거주하지 않는 이상, 수많은 김치를 모두 맛보는 일은 불가능하기 때문이다. 그러니 몇 가지 사실만 추가로 설명하겠다.

첫째, 김치의 주재료로 배추 다음으로 많이 쓰는 것은 무다. 큰 무를 깍둑썰기 하여 담근 김치를 깍두기라고 하는데, 이건 당신이 한국에서 만날 확률이 제법 높은 김치 중의 하나다. 나중에 다시 설명할 삼계탕, 곰탕, 설렁탕 등을 파는 식당에서는 거의 예외

없이 나온다.

둘째, 고춧가루를 넣지 않은, 즉 빨갛지 않은 김치도 있다. 붉은 양념이 없다는 점만 제외하면 보통의 김치와 비슷하게 생긴 것의 이름은 백김치다. 이것 역시 배추를 주재료로 만든다. 사실 이게 더 오랜 역사를 가진 형태다.

셋째, 맑은 액체에 배추나 무 등의 재료들이 둥둥 떠 있는 형태의 김치도 있는데, 이건 물김치라고 부른다. 국물의 색은 완전히 투명한 경우도 있고 살짝 붉은 빛깔이 도는 경우도 있다. 채소만 건져 먹는 것이 아니라 국물도 숟가락으로 떠먹으면 된다.

넷째, 김치는 담근 직후에 바로 먹기도 하지만, 대부분은 일정한 숙성 기간을 필요로 한다. 그 기간 동안 발효가 일어나서 특유의 풍미를 갖게 되는 것이다. 어떤 온도에서 숙성시키느냐에 따라 다르지만 대체로 1~2주의 시간이 필요하다. 그런데 숙성이 끝난 김치를 먹을 수 있는 기간은 훨씬 길다. 적당한 온도에서 잘 보관한다면 몇 주는 기본이고 몇 달에 걸쳐 조금씩 먹는 것도 가능하다(물론 맛이 조금씩 달라진다). 심지어 온도를 아주 잘 조절하면 6개월 이상, 길게는 2~3년까지 숙성시켜 먹을 수도 있다. 신맛이 강해져서 외국인들에게는 조금 어려울 수 있겠지만, 대부분의 한국인들은 이렇게 오래된 김치도 엄청나게 좋아한다(흔히 '묵은지'라 부른다. 가격도 더 비싸다. 하지만 김치에 '빈티지' 같은 표현을 쓰지는 않는다).

다섯째, 꽤 많은 한국 가정에는 김치의 보관을 주목적으로 하는 김치냉장고가 따로 있다. 냉장고가 두 개인 것이다. 혹시라도 한국인의 집을 방문할 기회가 있으면, (대체로 좁은 집에) 커다란 냉장고가 두 개나 존재하는 걸 보아도 놀라지 말길 바란다. 김치냉장고의 크기는 일반 냉장고와 비슷한 편이며, 가격은 오히려 조금 더 비싼 것이 보통이다. 김치의 숙성에 최적화된 온도는 영하 1도로 알려져 있어서, 김치냉장고의 온도는 일반 냉장고보다 약간 낮다. 물론 김치냉장고에는 반드시 김치만 보관해야 한다는 법률 같은 건 없으니, 많은 한국인이 고기, 맥주, 채소, 과일 등도 여기에 보관한다. (김치냉장고가 널리 보급된 것은 1990년대 중반부터다.)

앞에서 설명했듯이, 김치는 가장 중요한 반찬 중의 하나인 동시에 여러 음식의 재료이기도 하다. 잘게 썬 김치에 밀가루와 물을 잘 섞어서 팬에 구우면 김치전이 되고(돼지고기, 조개, 오징어 등을 섞어도 된다), 잘게 썬 김치를 밥과 함께 볶으면 김치볶음밥이 되며, 충분히 숙성된 김치와 돼지고기 혹은 고등어 등을 함께 냄비에 넣고 긴 시간 익히면 김치찜이 되는 식이다. (삼겹살과 함께 구워 먹어도 된다는 사실은 알고 있겠지?)

하지만 김치로 만들 수 있는 음식 중에 가장 중요한 것은 김치찌개다. 조리법의 핵심은 육수에 김치를 넣고 끓이는 것이다. 육수의 재료로 가장 대표적인 것은 마른멸치와 돼지고기이며, 김치 외에 추가할 수 있는 재료로는 파, 양파, 두부 등이 있다(하지만 고정된 레시피에 연연할 필요 없이 다른 재료, 예를 들면 '스팸'을 넣어도 된다). 김치의 맛이 워낙 다양하고 추가할 수 있는 부재료도 여러 가지라서, 김치찌개의 맛은 엄청나게 다양하다. 모든 식당의 김치찌개 맛이 다 다르다고 해도 과언이 아니다.

　김치찌개와 쌍벽을 이루는 한국인의 또다른 솔 푸드는 된장찌개이다. 된장찌개는 육수에 다양한 채소와 된장을 넣고 끓인 음식인데, 핵심 재료는 된장이다. 된장은 무엇이며, 어떻게 만드는 것일까(사실 대다수 한국인들도 된장 만드는 방법을 잘 모른다. 과거에는 집집마다 된장을 직접 만들었지만, 지금은 마트에서 사 먹는 것이 일반적이기 때문이다).

　된장을 만드는 방법을 설명하기 위해서는 어쩔 수 없이 된장, 간장, 고추장 세 가지를 한꺼번에 설명해야 한다. 만드는 방법이 다 연결되어 있기 때문이다. 이 세 가지는 한국 음식에서 가장 중요한 장으로, 한식의 삼위일체 같은 존재라고 할 수 있다. '장'이라는 단어는 양념 혹은 조미료를 통칭하는 말이다.

　마법과도 같은 '장 만들기' 과정을 알아보자(한국인도 잘 모르는 사람이 많다). 시작은 콩이다. 콩을 불린 다음 삶는다. 으깨서 직육면체 형태로 빚는다. 이렇게 만든 덩어리를 '메주'라고 부르는데, 이걸 새끼줄에 매달아 몇 주 동안 말린다. 따뜻한 곳으로 옮겨서 1~2주에 걸쳐 발효를 촉진한다. 충분히 발효가 된 메주와 진한 소금물을 항아리에 함께 넣고 2~3개월 정도 기다린다. 그다음에 축축해진 메주를 꺼내어 잘 버무린 것이 된장이다. 남은 액체를 체에 걸러 찌꺼기를 제거하고 끓인 다음 식힌 것이 간장이다. (이렇게만 말하니 간단해 보이지만, 이 모든 과정은 상당히 까다롭다. 발효 과정은 온도와 습도 등에 매우 민감하기 때문에 자칫하면 아예 못 먹게 되거나 맛이 없어진다.) 그럼 고추장은?

고추장은 잘 말린 메주의 일부를 소금물에 넣는 대신 가루로 만드는 데서 출발한다. 메줏가루, 고춧가루, 소금, 물, 그리고 쌀이나 보리와 같은 곡식의 가루를 적당한 비율로 섞어서 숙성시키는 것이 고추장이다. (얼마나 매운 고추를 사용하느냐에 따라 같은 고추장이라도 덜 매운 것이 있고 아주 매운 것이 있다. 물론 덜 매운 고추장도 당신에게는 매울 것이다.) 즉 된장, 간장, 고추장을 만들 때에 반드시 필요한 핵심 재료가 콩을 발효시킨 메주다.

과거의 한국인들은 이렇게 만들어진 된장, 간장, 고추장을 모두 장독이라고 부르는 항아리에 보관했다. 한번 만들면 1년 내내, 혹은 몇 년을 두고 먹는 것이기 때문에 한국의 전통 주택 뒷마당에는 이러한 항아리 여러 개가 놓여 있는 것이 보통이었다. 물론 지금은 플라스틱 용기에 담아서 냉장고에 보관하지만.

미국 샌프란시스코에는 '베누(benu)'라는 레스토랑이 있다. 미슐랭 3스타 레스토랑이자 세계 최고 레스토랑 목록에서 자주 최상위에 오르는 유명한 곳이다. 이 레스토랑의 입구에 서서 고개를 들면 공중에 매달려 있는 여러 개의 '메주'가 보이고, 시선을 옆으로 돌리면 '장독'들이 줄지어 서 있다. 한국계 미국인 셰프 코리 리가 한식에서 영감을 얻은 음식들을 내놓는 이 식당의 정체성을 표현하는 데 있어서 최고의 장식품이 아닌가 싶다. 나는 딱 한 번 베누에서 식사를 해봤는데, 모든 면에서 대단히 훌륭한 최고의 레스토랑이라는 데 동의한다. 하지만 다시 방문하지는 못할 듯하다. 정말 비싸기 때문이다. (이 책이 성공하면 한번 더 갈까?)

먼길을 돌아왔다. 이렇게 어렵게 만들어지는 된장을 베이스로

해서 끓인 스튜가 바로 된장찌개다. 된장찌개에 들어가는 채소는 감자, 호박, 양파, 당근, 고추 등이 가장 일반적이며, 육수의 재료로는 마른멸치와 소고기가 대표적이다. 된장찌개는 맵지 않은 것이 보통이지만, 고추장이나 고춧가루를 조금 추가하여 약간 맵게 만드는 경우도 있다. 두부도 흔히 첨가되는 재료이며, 다양한 해산물도 얼마든지 추가될 수 있다. 된장을 많이, 물을 조금만 넣어 끓이는 경우도 있고 반대로 된장을 조금, 물을 많이 넣어서 국물이 많은 경우도 있다. 당신이 어떤 된장찌개를 맛보게 될지 모르지만 무엇을 먹든 상당히 인상적인 경험이 될 것이다.

된장찌개 및 김치찌개와 가장 잘 어울리는 짝은 밥이다. 한국인의 주식은 밥이다. 밥은 쌀로만 짓기도 하지만 보리, 현미, 콩, 팥 등 다양한 곡식을 조금 섞어서 짓기도 한다. 한국인이라고 해서 모든 끼니에 밥을 먹지는 않는다. 면도 많이 먹고 빵을 곁들이는 서양식 식사도 흔하다. 하지만 밥과 몇 가지 반찬, 그리고 찌개와 같이 국물이 있는 요리를 함께 먹는 것이 한국인의 가장 평범한 식탁 위의 모습이다. 물론 삼겹살을 먹을 때처럼 밥이 없는 상태에서 찌개를 먹는 경우도 없지 않지만, 찌개의 참맛을 즐기려면 밥과 함께 먹는 것이 가장 좋다. 된장찌개에 유난히 수분이 없는 경우라면, 밥에 슥슥 비벼 먹는 것도 훌륭한 선택이다.

김치는 기본적인 반찬인 동시에 여러 요리의 핵심 재료라고 이미 설명했다. 하지만 된장은 그 자체로 좋은 반찬이나 어떤 음식의 핵심 재료가 되지는 않는다. 대신 수많은 요리를 만드는 데 반드시 들어가야 하는 양념이다. 그리고 된장은 '쌈장'이라고 하는 또다른 놀라운 양념의 기초가 된다. 삼겹살이나 생선회를 먹을 때 곁들이면 놀라운 풍미를 만들어내는 그 독특한 소스는 된장에 마늘, 고추장, 참기름 등을 섞은 것이다.

고추장도 비슷하다. 채소에 찍어 먹거나 비빔밥에 곁들일 때처럼 고추장 자체가 눈에 보이는 경우도 적지 않지만, 여러 양념들과 각기 다른 비율로 섞이면서 다양한 음식을 만드는 기본 재료로 활용되는 경우가 훨씬 많다. 고추장은 수많은 한국 음식에 감칠맛을 더해주는데, 최근에는 점점 더 많은 외국인이 고추장의 매력을 발견하고 있다.

간장에 대해서는 할 이야기가 더 많다. 사실 간장은 된장이나 고추장에 비하면 당신에게 훨씬 익숙할 것이다. 여러 나라에 있는 일본 식당에서 경험해봤을 것이기 때문이다. 하지만 일본 간장은 앞에서 길게 설명한 것과는 다른 방식으로 만들어진다. 한국 간장과 일본 간장이, 한국 된장과 일본 된장이 어떻게 다른지는 나중에 다시 설명할 것이다(한국인은 두 종류의 간장과 된장을 다 즐겨 먹는다).

당신은 아마도 박찬욱 감독의 영화 〈올드보이〉를 보았을 것이다(아직 안 보았다면 꼭 보시라. 최고의 한국 영화 중 하나임에 틀림없다). 〈올드보이〉의 주인공 최민식은 이유를 모른 채 골방에 갇혀 15년 동안 군만두만 먹는다. 하지만 군만두가 아니라 김치찌개나 된장찌개였다면 어땠을까? 한국인 관객들은 아주 조금은 덜 끔찍하게 느꼈을 것이고, 영화적 긴장감이 약간은 감소했을 것이다. 한국인이라고 해서 언제나 김치찌개 혹은 된장찌개만 먹으면서 사는 것을 좋아할 사람은 없겠지만, 15년간 모든 끼니를 한 가지 메뉴만 먹을 수 있다면 무엇을 택하겠느냐고 묻는다면 십중팔구는 김치찌개 아니면 된장찌개를 택할 수밖에 없을 것이다 (오랜 고민 끝에 결국은 김치찌개를 고르는 사람이 훨씬 많을 것으로 생각한다). 김치찌개와 된장찌개야말로 진정한 한국인의 솔 푸드다. 당신이라면, 15년간 한 가지 음식만 먹을 수 있다면 무엇을 고르겠는가? 아마도 그 음식이 당신네 나라 국민의 솔 푸드이리라.

7.

Kimchi, Doenjang, and ⟨Oldboy⟩

Among the trendy games enjoyed by young Koreans to-day is the "balance game." While the name might evoke thoughts of a physical workout, it is actually a fun and straightforward what-if game involving choices. In this game, players are presented with two options and must choose one. For example, they might be asked if they would rather receive $5 million right now but age 20 more years instantly, or staying as you are. Another question could be whether they would prefer to never brush their teeth for the rest of their life or never wash their hair.

The questions in the balance game can indeed be outrageous and extreme, to the point that some are too explicit to mention here. Others may contain risqué content that is better suited for adult participants. While the game may appear to be a lighthearted joke, it often leads people to genuinely ponder their choices and question, "why on earth do I have to choose between these absurd scenarios?"

In fact, the game was even posed to a presidential candidate on a TV show. During the show, he was asked if he would rather marry his current wife again or become president if he were born again. While the candidate may have intended to choose the latter option, he cleverly responded with "I don't think my wife would ever marry me again." Despite his clever response to a tricky question, the presidential candidate did not win the election. It remains unclear whether he would have gained more votes if he had chosen the former option. Now, let's turn the question to you: If you could only have one meal in Korea, which would you choose: Soju with pork belly or beer with chikin?

Asking most Koreans whether they'd rather give up kimchi jjigae or doenjang jjigae for the rest of their lives is equivalent to asking them to choose only one to live with among their children. Both dishes are so integral to Korean cuisine and culture that the mere thought of giving up one or the other is enough to elicit looks of shock, awe, and sheer horror. Kimchi jjigae and doenjang jjigae are more than just food - they're a part of Korean soul and identity.

The term "jjigae" translates to "stew" in English, but it encompasses more than just the meat in the dish—it also includes the flavorful broth. Now, let's delve into the details of kimchi and doenjang. We'll start with kimchi, a well-known and widely recognized fermented side dish. Perhaps you have had the pleasure of trying it before or at least heard about its popularity.

In the broadest sense, kimchi refers to a diverse range of fermented vegetable dishes prepared by salting and fermenting vegetables. The types and varieties of kimchi are extensive and often influenced by the main vegetable ingredient, additional ingredients used, level of fermentation, and even the shape of the dish. If you were to ask any Korean, they would likely be able to name a dozen different types of kimchi, and the total number of varieties can surpass several dozen when including lesser-known and unique types. Moreover, it's not uncommon for the same kind of kimchi to have multiple names.

In a more specific sense, kimchi specifically refers to a distinct Korean dish that prominently features Napa cabbage as the main ingredient. It is seasoned with a blend of chili peppers, garlic, and salted fish, and undergoes a fermentation process before being consumed. It is worth noting that when you search for "kimchi" on Google, the most common result is "baechu (Napa cabbage) kimchi," which serves as the baseline type of kimchi.

Kimchi is not typically consumed as a standalone dish or as the main course. Instead, it serves as a crucial side dish that accompanies rice or other main dishes, and it is an essential ingredient in many Korean dishes. In reality, attempting to avoid kimchi during a visit to Korea, even for just a few days, is an almost impossible task. It's akin to embarking on a mission impossible, one that not even Tom Cruise could successfully accomplish.

Kimchi indeed has a rich and captivating history that spans over a millennium. However, one of the most pivotal moments in its history was the introduction of chili peppers, which is considered a momentous event. It is believed that chili peppers were introduced to the Korean peninsula in the late 16th or early 17th century. Prior to their arrival, kimchi did not possess its characteristic vibrant red color.

Certainly, I understand that delving into the vast world of kimchi can be overwhelming. The sheer variety and depth of the kimchi universe make it nearly impossible for anyone other than permanent residents of Korea to experience all its different types. Instead, I'm more than happy to share a couple more intriguing tidbits about kimchi with you.

Firstly, besides Napa cabbage, radish is another commonly used ingredient in kimchi. Kimchi made with diced large radishes is known as "kkakdugi" or cubed radish kimchi. It is one of the most commonly encountered types of kimchi in Korea and is often served at restaurants that specialize in dishes like samgyetang, gomtang, and seolleongtang, which we'll discuss in more detail later.

Secondly, there are certain types of kimchi that do not contain red pepper flakes and are known as "baek-kimchi" or white kimchi. White kimchi is made with Napa cabbage as the main ingredient and has a similar appearance to regular kimchi but without the red seasoning. In fact, it's the type of kimchi that has a longer history.

Thirdly, there is a type of kimchi called "mul-kimchi" or water kimchi. It is made with a clear liquid in which ingredients like Napa cabbage and radish float. The broth of mul-kimchi can be transparent or slightly reddish in color, and it's important to not only consume the vegetables but also spoon the broth while eating it.

Fourthly, while some kimchi is consumed immediately after marination, most varieties require a period of aging. During this time, fermentation takes place, contributing to its signature flavor. The duration of the aging process depends on the storage temperature, usually ranging from one to two weeks. However, kimchi can be enjoyed for an extended period even after the fermentation is complete. When stored at the correct temperature, it can be consumed in small portions over several weeks or months, with the flavor evolving over time. In fact, some Koreans appreciate kimchi that has been aged for six months or longer, and there are even instances of carefully temperature-controlled aging for two to three years. While the increasingly sour taste may present a challenge to some foreigners, aged kimchi holds great value among Koreans. And no, they don't use the term "vintage" to describe it, although it may cost more.

Fifthly, it's quite common for Korean households to have a dedicated refrigerator specifically for storing kimchi. If you ever have the opportunity to explore a Korean home, don't be surprised to find two large refrigerators occupying valuable space in their usually compact living quarters. These kimchi fridges are approximately the same size as regular refrigerators but come with a higher price tag. To maintain the optimal condition of kimchi, the temperature in a kimchi fridge is set a few degrees lower than that of a standard fridge, typically around minus one degree Celsius (just below freezing). While kimchi takes center stage, it's not the sole occupant of these fridges. Koreans also utilize them to store various other items, ranging from meats and vegetables to beverages like beer. (The widespread use of kimchi fridges only became prevalent in the mid-1990s.)

As previously mentioned, kimchi is not just a simple side dish; it's also a vital ingredient in a variety of mouth-watering dishes. Take, for instance, kimchi jeon, a delectable kimchi pancake. To prepare this tasty treat, you mix shredded kimchi with flour and water, then fry it in a pan along with pork, clams, squid, or any other ingredients that tantalize your taste buds. Another enticing option is kimchi bokkumbap, which is kimchi fried rice. This dish involves stir-frying shredded kimchi with rice in a wok, creating a harmonious blend of flavors. For a hearty and flavorful meal, you can indulge in kimchi jjim, a braised kimchi dish. In this preparation, aged kimchi is simmered with pork or mackerel in a pot for an extended period, allowing the flavors to meld together. And let's not forget the heavenly combination of grilling kimchi alongside pork belly!

But, when it comes to the enchanting world of kimchi cuisine, few dishes can rival the savory and soul-warming goodness of kimchi jjigae. This stew holds such a special place in the hearts of Koreans that it's often considered the country's national dish. The key to a truly exceptional kimchi jjigae lies in the broth, which must possess a deep and rich flavor that can only be achieved by simmering kimchi with the perfect combination of ingredients. Commonly, this includes dried anchovies and pork, complemented by scallions, onions, and tofu to add an extra layer of deliciousness. But, there's no need to be boxed in by convention. You can experiment with different types of kimchi and other add-ins (like SPAM) to make your own unique flavor. This is precisely why every kimchi jjigae you encounter in restaurants across Korea offers a different taste.

Another captivating Korean comfort food to indulge in is doenjang jjigae. This delicious stew features a medley of vegetables, doenjang (soybean paste), and a flavorful broth, with doenjang taking center stage. If you find yourself curious about what exactly doenjang is and how it's made, you're not alone. Interestingly, while Koreans are familiar with doenjang, many are unaware of the intricate process involved in making it from scratch. In the past, it was a common practice for many Korean households to prepare doenjang at home. However, in modern times, the convenience of purchasing it from the supermarket has become the norm for most people.

To truly understand the art of making doenjang, we must explore the interconnected nature of three vital elements: doenjang (soybean paste), ganjang (soy sauce), and gochujang (red chili paste). These three components form an inseparable trio known as the "holy trinity" of Korean cooking. In Korean cuisine, "Jang" is a catch-all term for seasonings and condiments.

Alright folks, get ready to learn about the magical process of making Korean jangs! (Even Koreans are unfamiliar with it.) It all starts with some beans. To make doenjang, you begin by soaking and boiling the beans, then mashing and shaping them into cubes called "meju". After hanging the meju on twine to dry for a few weeks, they are moved to a warm place to ferment for an additional one to two weeks. Once the meju has sufficiently fermented, it is combined with a strong brine in a jar and left to sit for two to three months. Finally, the moist meju is delicately transferred into jars, resulting in the creation of doenjang.

To make soy sauce, the remaining liquid from the doen-jang-making process is strained through a sieve to remove any scum, then boiled and allowed to cool down. Despite the seemingly straightforward recipe, don't be fooled by its simplicity. Achieving the right balance of flavors and textures requires precision and experience, especially since the process is highly susceptible to environmental factors like humidity and temperature. Even a slight deviation can result in a rotten or tasteless outcome. Now, where does gochujang fit into the picture?

To make gochujang, a portion of the dried meju is ground into a powder and combined with chili powder, salt, water, and grain flour such as rice or barley in precise ratios. The resulting gochujang can vary in spiciness, from mild to very hot, depending on the potency of the chili peppers used. (Naturally, even a less spicy gochujang might still taste spicy to you.) In summary, at the heart of doenjang, ganjang, and gochujang lies the same fundamental ingredient - meju, a fermented soybean paste.

In the past, it was common to find several clay pots called 'jangdok' in the yard of traditional Korean households. These pots were used to store the homemade jangs, including doenjang, ganjang, and gochujang. The jangs would be carefully prepared and fermented, allowing them to last for a year or even longer. However, with the advent of modern convenience, many people now opt to store their jangs in plastic containers in the refrigerator.

In San Francisco, there's a prestigious establishment called Benu, which boasts an impressive three Michelin stars and consistently ranks among the world's best restaurants. As you approach the entrance, you can catch a glimpse of "meju" hanging in the air, while stacks of "jangdok" catch your eye on the side. These visual cues reflect the Korean-American Chef Corey Lee's strong culinary identity and his exceptional interpretation of Korean cuisine. I had the privilege of dining at Benu once, and it was truly an exceptional experience that ticked all the boxes. However, it's worth noting that the prices at Benu are quite high, which might be a deterrent for some. While the restaurant is undeniably fantastic, affordability could be a consideration for potential diners. (If this book turns out to be a success, I wouldn't mind indulging in another memorable meal at Benu.)

We've come a long way. Although the process of making doenjang can be challenging and intricate, crafting doenjang jjigae is a breeze if you have a good doenjang in your hand. This versatile dish embraces a range of vegetables like potatoes, zucchini, onions, carrots, and peppers, allowing for endless customization. The broth, typically prepared with dried anchovies or beef, yields a delightful umami flavor. While doenjang jjigae is classically not spicy, some prefer to add gochujang or red pepper flakes for a hint of heat. Tofu is a common addition, and seafood can further enhance the dish. The consistency of the broth can vary from thick and hearty to light and brothy, depending on the recipe. One thing is for sure, no two bowls of doenjang jjigae are the same, but they are always delicious and satisfying.

Rice, the beloved staple food of Koreans, is the perfect companion for doenjang jjigae or kimchi jjigae. While rice is commonly prepared as plain rice, it can also be a satisfying blend of various grains like barley, brown rice, soybeans, and red beans. Koreans do not consume rice at every meal, as Western-style meals with bread or various types of noodles are also popular. However, a typical Korean home-cooked meal includes rice, a variety of side dishes, and a steaming hot brothy dish like jjigae. While it is not uncommon to enjoy jjigae without rice, especially when indulging in pork belly, for the ultimate flavor experience, pairing your jjigae with a generous serving of rice is highly recommended. And if your doenjang jjigae happens to have a minimal amount of broth, fret not - simply mix it with rice and savor it like bibimbap.

While kimchi is a staple side dish and an essential ingredient in many Korean dishes, doenjang is not ordinarily used as a standalone ingredient. Instead, it is primarily utilized as a fundamental condiment that adds depth and complexity to a wide range of dishes. Additionally, doenjang serves as the base for other widely consumed condiments such as ssamjang, a savory sauce made by blending doenjang with garlic, gochujang, sesame oil, and other ingredients. Ssamjang is often paired with dishes like pork belly or raw fish, complementing their flavors and providing an enjoyable taste experience.

Gochujang, much like doenjang, is frequently utilized as a foundational ingredient for an array of dishes. While it can certainly be enjoyed on its own, such as a dip for vegetables or as a condiment alongside bibimbap, it is more commonly combined with other spices in varying ratios to create appetizing sauces or marinades for meats and vegetables. Gochujang's versatility shines through as it imparts a distinctive umami flavor to a multitude of Korean dishes, and its appeal is expanding globally as more individuals discover its inviting taste.

Attention, everyone! Let's delve into the fascinating world of soy sauce. You're probably familiar with soy sauce, as it's a common ingredient found in many cuisines, particularly in Japanese cuisine. However, it's important to note that Japanese soy sauce is produced using a different method from the one we discussed earlier. But fret not; we'll explore the intricate details of the differences between Korean soy sauce and Japanese soy sauce, as well as Korean doenjang and Japanese doenjang (miso) in the upcoming discussions. It's worth mentioning that Koreans have a deep appreciation for both types of soy sauce and doenjang.

You've surely come across the celebrated film "Oldboy," directed by Park Chan-wook. (If you haven't, you're missing out on one of the greatest masterpieces of Korean cinema.) In the movie, the protagonist, played by Choi Min-sik, endures 15 years of confinement with only fried dumplings to sustain him, all without knowing why he's there.. However, let's imagine for a moment if it had been kimchi jjigae or doenjang jjigae instead. Korean viewers might have been slightly less horrified, and the suspense of the film may have been slightly diminished. While no Korean would willingly choose to subsist solely on kimchi jjigae or doenjang jjigae for a lifetime, if they were to select one dish to consume for every meal for 15 years, it is highly probable that nine out of ten Koreans would opt for kimchi jjigae or doenjang jjigae. (I would be willing to wager that a greater number would ultimately choose kimchi jjigae after very careful deliberation.) These hearty bowls of stew represent the essence of Korean comfort food. Now, if you had to choose one dish to eat for 15 years, what would it be? More often than not, it would be your culture's soul food.

8.

알고 보면 놀라운 한국의 역사

앞에서 야구 이야기를 할 때, 두산베어스라는 팀이 '끈기 있는 팀'으로 유명하다고 했다. 이건 실제로 그 팀의 플레이가 그런 특성을 갖고 있기 때문이기도 하지만, 팀의 상징 동물인 '곰'이 주는 이미지 때문이기도 하다. 곰은 적어도 한국에서는 '인내'의 상징이다.

곰은 인류 문명에서 꽤 중요한 위치를 차지하고 있어서, 여러 문화권에 걸쳐 신화, 미술, 문학, 민속 등 다양한 분야에서 인기 있는 주제였다. 독일의 베를린이나 스위스의 베른처럼 도시의 이름 자체가 위풍당당한 곰에서 비롯된 경우도 있다. 인간의 상상력은 곰을 밤하늘의 별자리로 영원히 남겨놓기도 했다. 또한 곰돌이 푸나 테디 베어와 같은 친숙한 캐릭터로도 많이 활용되어왔다.

하지만 곰이 인내의 상징으로 활용되는 문화권은 한국 말고는 없는 듯하다. 곰을 뜻하는 단어와 '견디다'를 뜻하는 단어의 스펠링이 똑같은 영미 문화권에서조차 곰의 이미지는 난폭하거나 헌신적이거나 귀엽거나 하지 '인내심이 강한' 느낌은 아니지 않나.

모든 한국인이 알고 있는 한국의 건국 신화는 이런 내용이다(여러 가지 버전이 있지만, 가장 널리 알려진 것만 소개한다). 먼 옛날, 천제 환인의 아들 환웅이 3천 명의 무리를 이끌고 하늘에서 내려와 백두산 어귀에 도시를 세웠다. 이때 곰과 호랑이가 찾아와 사람이 되고 싶다고 청했고, 환웅은 곰과 호랑이에게 쑥과 마늘을 주면서 백 일 동안 햇빛을 보지 말고 쑥과 마늘만 먹으며 동굴 속에서 생활하면 사람으로 만들어주겠다고 약속한다. 호랑이는 중도에 포기하였으나, 곰은 백 일을 잘 견뎌 '웅녀'라는 여인이 된다. 나중에 환웅과 웅녀가 결혼하여 낳은 아들인 '단군'이 고조선이라는 나라를 세웠는데, 기원전 2333년 10월 3일의 일이다(지금도 10월 3일은 한국의 국경일이다. 토요일이나 일요일에 걸리면 다음 월요일을 대신 쉴 정도로 나름 중요한 날이다. 물론 단군 할아버지가 정말로 이날 나라를 세웠다는 증거는 없다).

그러니까 건국신화에 따르면, 한국인은 모두 곰의 자손인 셈이다. 곰은 인내심이 많은 동물이고, 곰의 자손인 한국인들도 인내심이 많다. 쑥과 마늘만 먹으며 동굴 속에서 백 일 동안 살 수도 있고, 군만두만 먹으며 15년을 버틸 수도 있는 민족이다. (그런데 왜 한국인의 성격은 이토록 급한 것일까? 평소에는 급하지만 위기 상황이 왔을 때는 잘 견디는 오묘한 캐릭터인가?)

신화는 신화일 뿐, 실제로 기원전 2333년에 제대로 모습을 갖춘 '국가'가 생겼다고 볼 근거는 별로 없다. 고조선이 실제로 존재했던 나라이고, 꽤 오랫동안 유지되어오다가 기원전 108년 무렵에 멸망했다는 것은 비교적 확실한 사실로 알려져 있다. 하지만 정확히 언제부터 국가의 형태를 갖추었는지, 수도가 어디였는지 등은 명확히 확인되지 않았다. 아무튼, 한국인들은 한국이 5천 년 정도의 역사를 가진 나라라고 학교에서 배운다.

고조선 다음은 삼국시대다. 고구려, 백제, 신라의 세 나라가 수백 년 동안 한반도와 지금의 중국 북동부 일대까지를 나누어 차지했던 시기가 있다. 여러 차례의 전투 끝에 신라가 최종 승자가 되고, 그 이후는 통일신라시대로 불린다. '신라'라는 나라는 명목상으론 천 년 동안(실제로는 6백~7백 년일 것으로 추정되지만) 지속되었고, 화려한 불교 문화를 꽃피웠다. 이후 잠시 동안 다시 세 개의 나라가 존재하던 시기를 거쳐 '고려'와 '조선'으로 왕조가 이어진다. 고려는 918년부터 1392년까지 500년 가까이 존속한 왕조이며, 조선은 1392년부터 1910년까지 500년 넘게 존속한 왕조이다. (좀 지루하게 느껴질 수 있겠지만, 재미없는 설명은 곧 끝난다. 잠시만 기다려주시라.)

1910년부터 1945년까지 35년간 한국은 일본의 식민지였고, 1945년의 해방 직후 남북으로 분단되어 혼란의 시기를 겪다가 1948년에 남쪽과 북쪽에 각각 정부가 수립되었고, 1950년부터 3년간은 한국전쟁을 치렀다. 1953년의 휴전 무렵에는 남북이 모두 세계에서 가장 가난한 나라에 속했고, 이후 70년이 지난 지금 남쪽은 당신이 제법 잘 알고 있는 그 한국이 되었고, 북쪽은 역시 당신이 (전혀 다른 느낌으로) 잘 알고 있는 그 북한이 되었다.

복잡해 보이지만, 단순히 말하면 지난 2천 년 동안 '삼국-통일신라-고려-조선-대한민국', 이렇게 연결된다고 보면 된다. 당신이 한국인 귀화 시험을 준비할 게 아니라면, 더 자세한 내용까지 알 필요는 없을 것이다. 그러니 한국 여행을 조금 더 재미있게 만드는 데 도움이 될 만한 역사적 맥락들만 조금 살펴보자.

첫째, 명칭부터 알아보자. 지금 당신이 알고 있는 '코리아'라는 명칭은 '고려'왕조의 이름에서 비롯됐다. 그 무렵에 한국의 존재가 외국에 알려졌기 때문이다. 20세기 초반까지 5백 년 넘게 지속된 왕조의 이름은 '조선'인데, 이는 사실 기원전에 존재했던 나라의 이름을 그대로 다시 가져온 것이다. 그래서 구별을 위해 과거의 조선은 '오래된 조선'이라는 뜻의 '고조선'이라 부르게 되었다.

남한과 북한 두 나라는 모두 영어 명칭에 '코리아'가 포함된다 (남한은 Republic of Korea, 북한은 Democratic People's Republic of Korea). 하지만 공식적인 한국어 국호는 완전히 다르다. 남한의 명칭에는 '대한'이라는 단어가, 북한의 명칭에는 '조선'이라는 단어가 들어간다.

조선왕조는 1910년에 끝났는데, 그 직전인 1897년에 나라의 이름을 한 번 바꾸었다(당시의 왕이 '제국'을 선포하며 스스로를 황제로 칭하기 시작했다). 그 이름에 쓰였던 단어가 '대한'이었다. 몇십 년이 지나 남한은 새로 바뀐 이름을 선택했고 북한은 5백 년 전부터 쓰인 왕조의 이름을 선택한 셈인데, 그래서인지 북한은 아직도 '(김씨)왕조'의 성격을 띠고 있다. 당신이 아마도 그 이름을 들어보았을 북한의 지도자 김정은은 북한의 창시자라고 할 수 있는 김일성의 손자이자 직전 지도자 김정일의 아들이다.

한반도에 존재했던 몇몇 나라 이름은 지금도 흔히 쓰이는 고유명사다. 신라는 호텔과 대학 이름으로, 고려는 대학과 철강회사와 제약회사 이름으로, 조선은 신문, 호텔, 대학 등의 이름으로, 대한은 항공사, 보험회사, 물류회사, 밀가루회사 등의 이름으로 폭넓게 쓰인다. 작은 기업이나 음식점 등의 이름에 이들이 사용되는 경우는 더욱 많아서, 신라, 고려, 조선, 대한 등은 매우 흔한 상호이다(고려대학교는 영어 표기에 'Goryeo'가 아니라 'Korea'를 사용하긴 한다).

둘째, 한국은 상당히 오랜 역사에도 불구하고 중세 유럽과 같은 형태의 봉건제 국가였던 적이 한 번도 없다. 언제나 강력한 왕권을 바탕으로 한 중앙집권제 국가를 유지해온 것이다. 왕권이 특히 강했던 시기와 유난히 약했던 시기가 있기는 하지만, 왕의 권한이 약했던 시절에도 그 권력을 나누어 가진 것은 각 지역의 맹주가 아니라 중앙정부의 고위관료들이었다. 물론 일부 지방 관리들이 권한을 남용하는 경우가 없지 않았지만, 그래봐야 왕의 대리인이자 부패한 공무원일 뿐이었다(이들을 견제할 수 있는 여러 장치도 마련되어 있었다). 역사학자가 아닌 나로서는 이러한 사실의 의미를 제대로 해석할 능력이 없지만, 호시탐탐 권력의 확대를 도모하는 각 지역의 맹주들이 아예 존재하지 않았으니, 한국사에는 내전이라고 할 만한 사건이 벌어진 적이 없다. 그저 규모가 크지 않은 반란이 몇 차례 있었을 뿐이다. 모든 시대에 걸쳐 문화예술이 매우 높은 수준으로 발달한 것도 중앙정부와 소수 지배계급의 권력이 막강했던 사실과 관련이 있다고 볼 수 있다. 서울에 유난히 많은 사람이 모여 살고, 모든 면에서 서울과 지방의 격차가 큰 것도 이런 역사와 무관하지 않다. 심지어 '말은 나면 제주도로 보내고 사람은 나면 서울로 보내라'라는 속담이 있을 정도다.

하지만 외국의 침략에 의한 전쟁은 몇 차례 경험했다. 13세기에는 몽골제국과의 전쟁이 수십 년 동안 이어졌고, 16세기에는 일본과의 전쟁이 7년간 벌어졌다. 몽골과의 전쟁에서는 패배하여 한동안 몽골의 눈치를 많이 보아야 했고, 일본과의 전쟁에서는 적군을 성공적으로 물리쳤으나 동시에 엄청난 피해를 보았다. 일본과의 전쟁을 승리로 이끈 영웅인 이순신 장군은 한국에서 가장 존경받는 인물 중의 하나다. 반대로 한국이 외국을 침략한 역사는 없다. 다른 나라로 진출할 만큼 국력이 강하지 않았기 때문일 수 있겠지만, 교과서에는 '한국인들이 평화를 사랑하는 온순한 민족이기 때문'으로 기술되어 있다.

셋째, 한국은 특이하게도 근대화 과정을 제대로 겪지 않았다. 극적인 시민혁명으로 왕정을 공화정으로 바꾼 경험도 없고, 18~19세기에는 쇄국정책을 펴면서 외국과의 교류가 극히 제한적이었기 때문에 근대적인 기술이나 제도의 도입도 늦었다. 그러다가 국력이 약해져서 20세기 초에는 일본의 식민지가 되었다.

이후 근대화가 진행되긴 했지만 그것은 일본의 지배를 용이하게 하기 위한 수단이었기 때문에, 비정상적인 측면이 많았다.

식민지에서 벗어난 이후의 70년 역사는 그야말로 격랑이었다. 천 년 이상 유지되던 하나의 나라가 둘로 쪼개졌고, 3년간 치열하게 전쟁을 벌였고, 이후에는 시민들이 독재자들과 싸우며 민주주의를 발전시키는 동시에 세계 최고의 교육열과 근면함으로 경제발전을 이루었다. 단순히 부유한 나라가 된 것을 넘어 K팝으로 대표되는 '힙한' 나라의 반열에까지 올랐다. 다른 나라가 백 년이나 2백 년에 걸쳐 경험했던 수많은 일을 한국은 50년 동안 압축적으로 겪었다고도 할 수 있다.

한국의 경제성장이 얼마나 놀라운 것인지를 보여주는 단적인 사례가 있다. 한국전쟁이 끝난 직후 당시 연합군 총사령관이었던 맥아더 장군은 "한국의 재건에는 최소 백 년이 필요할 것"이라고 말했다. 얼마나 상황이 심각했던지, 미국을 비롯한 여러 나라가 한국에 원조 자금을 지원했다. 한국이 수십 년에 걸쳐 받은 해외 원조는 6백억 달러에 달하는 것으로 추산된다. 한때는 해외 원조가 국가 예산의 4분의 1에 이르기도 했다. 하지만 한국은 1990년대 이후 다른 나라를 돕는 나라로 변신했다. 원조를 받던 나라가 원조를 주는 나라로 바뀐 사례는 한국이 유일하다. 한국은 2021년에만 28.6억 달러를 외국에 지원하여, OECD 산하 개발원조위원회(DAC) 29개 회원국 중에서 열다섯번째로 많은 금액을 지원했다(하지만 GNI 대비 원조 비율은 0.16퍼센트로, DAC 회원국 평균의 절반 수준에 불과하다. 한국 정부와 많은 한국인은 앞으로 이 비율을 더 높여야 한다고 생각하고 있다).

넷째, 한국은 중국과 특수한 역사적 관계가 있다. 중국은 지금도 거대한 나라지만 과거 동아시아에서는 그 영향력이 더욱 컸다. 한국은 한자를 비롯하여 중국의 선진 문화를 많이 받아들였고, '중국이 세상의 중심'이라는 중국인들의 중화사상에 동조하는 지식인도 많았다. 한국은 중국의 식민지가 된 적은 없지만, 오랫동안 중국의 눈치를 보며 살았다. 힘세고 부유한 형에게 주눅든 동생과 비슷했다고 할 수도 있겠다. 16세기에 일본이 한국을 침략했을 때는 중국이 군대를 파견하기도 했는데, 당시 전사한 중국 군인의 수가 3만 명에 달했다고 한다. 17세기부터 2백여 년 동안 수백 차례의 특별 사신을 중국에 파견하며 공물을 바치기도 했고, 자주 찾아오는 중국 사신들을 최대한 융숭히 대접해야만 했다. 19세기 말 일본이 중국과의 전쟁에서 승리하고 20세기 초에 한국을 병합하면서, 중국과 한국은 동병상련의 처지가 됐다.

20세기 중반 이후는 더욱 복잡하다. 북한의 기습 공격으로 시작된 한국전쟁은 짧은 시일 내에 북한의 완승으로 끝날 뻔했지만, 미국을 비롯한 UN군의 참전으로 전세가 완전히 역전되어 남한의 승리 직전까지 갔다. 하지만 그때 중국이 참전했고, 전쟁은 오랫동안 교착상태에 빠져 있다가 결국 전쟁 이전과 비슷하게 분단된 채 끝났다. 이후 중국이 별로 발전하지 않는 동안 한국은 놀랍도록 빠르게 발전했고, 한동안 한국인들은 중국과 중국인을 은근히 무시하는 태도를 보이기도 했다. 하지만 수출로 먹고사는 나라인 한국에게 중국은 경제적 측면에서 결코 무시할 수 없는 나라였고, 중국의 파워가 점점 강해지고 북한이 핵실험을 계속하는 등 복잡한 국제정세 속에서 한국은 여러모로 중국의 눈치를 보지 않을 수 없게 되었다.

중국에 물건은 많이 팔고 싶고 중국인 관광객이 한국에 와서 돈을 많이 쓰는 것도 원하지만, 한편으론 중국인들이 한국의 부동산을 자꾸 사들이고 한국인의 일자리를 빼앗는 것을 싫어하는 이율배반적인 정서가 한국인들의 마음속에 자리잡은 것이다. 하지만 한중 관계의 악화, 더 정확히 말하면 한국인들의 중국인에 대한 감정이 악화된 결정적인 계기는 역사 왜곡이었다. 21세기에 접어든 이후 중국은 신라, 백제와 함께 삼국시대를 이루었던 고구려를 중국의 일부였다고 주장하기 시작했고, 한국인의 상징과도 같은 김치를 중국 음식이라고 주장하기도 했고, 한국의 고유 의상인 한복을 중국 의상이라 주장하기도 했다. 이러한 주장들은 모두 한국인의 반중 정서를 크게 자극했다(이건 스페인이 스스로를 피자의 발상지라고 주장한다거나 독일이 스스로를 샴페인의 원조라고 주장하는 것과 비슷하다고 할 수 있다).

게다가 인기 있는 한국의 TV 프로그램을 저작권료 지불 없이 베낀다거나 유명한 한국 제품들의 짝퉁을 무단으로 생산하는 일도 빈번하게 일어났다. 한국 드라마의 방영이나 한국 가수의 중국 공연을 중국 정부가 금지하기도 했다. 최근에는 코로나19 팬데믹도 반중 정서에 영향을 끼쳤다. 실제로 미국의 퓨 리서치 센터의 조사에 의하면, 한국인 중에서 중국에 대해 부정적 인식을 갖고 있는 사람의 비율은 2022년에 80퍼센트에 달했다. 그 비율이 2002년에는 31퍼센트에 불과했던 것을 생각하면 놀라운 변화다(반중 여론은 팬데믹 이후 다른 여러 나라에서도 높아졌지만, 한국의 경우는 특히 독보적이다).

다섯째, 한국과 일본의 역사적 관계를 살펴보자. 두 나라는 고대부터 오랫동안 다양한 방식으로 관계를 맺어왔다. 유라시아 대륙의 동북쪽 끝에 한반도가 있고, 그 바깥에 일본이 있으며, 일본의 동쪽에는 태평양이 놓여 있는 지정학적 특성을 생각하면 당연한 일이라 할 수 있다. 다양한 문화와 적지 않은 사람이 한국에서 일본으로 건너갔다. 심지어 현재 일본의 왕이 백제 왕실의 후손이라는 기록도 있으며, 2001년에는 당시의 일본 왕이 이러한 사실을 직접 밝히기도 했다.

중세의 한일 관계는 특별히 우호적이지도 적대적이지도 않았던 것으로 보이지만, 한국인들에게 일본은 일종의 골칫거리였다. 13세기부터 수백 년 동안 일본인 해적들이 자주 한국의 해안에서 약탈 행위를 했기 때문이다. 하지만 한일 관계가 결정적으로 틀어진 것은 16세기 말이다. 일본이 한국을 침략하여 7년간 전쟁이 벌어졌고, 한국인들이 이루 말할 수 없는 고초를 겪었기 때문이다. 그로부터 약 3세기가 흐른 후, 일본은 한국을 병합한다. 한국이 외국과의 교류를 최소화하면서 정체되어 있는 동안 해외의 선진 문물을 적극적으로 받아들인 일본의 국력이 매우 강해졌기 때문이다.

35년간의 일제강점기는 한국인에게 매우 가혹했다. 무고한 사람들이 고문을 당하고 감옥에 갇히고 목숨을 잃었다. 곡식과 지하자원을 비롯한 물자를 빼앗겼다. 이름을 일본식으로 바꿀 것을 강요받았고, 한국어 교육도 금지됐다. 수많은 사람이 일본으로 끌려가 강제노동에 시달렸고, 2차세계대전중에는 수많은 여성이 위안부라는 이름으로 끌려갔다.

일제강점기가 끝나고 80년 가까운 세월이 흐르는 동안 많은 변화가 있었다. 지금은 두 나라가 모두 선진국이 되었고, 거의 모든 분야에서 엄청나게 많은 교류와 협력이 이뤄지고 있다. 양국 국민들은 상대방 국가의 음식이나 문화에 관심이 많고, 서로에게 매우 인기 있는 관광지이기도 하다. 물론 임진왜란과 35년 식민 지배의 아픔을 가진 한국인들은 지금도 일본을 '반드시 극복해야 할 대상'으로 생각하는 편이다. 두 나라의 축구 경기는 그야말로 전쟁이다. 선수들이나 국민들이나, 다른 나라에 지는 것은 괜찮아도 일본에는 결코 져서는 안 된다는 생각을 갖고 있기 때문이다. 또한 한국인들은 특히 다음 두 가지 이슈 때문에 일본에 대해 부정적인 인식을 지우지 못한다. 하나는 위안부 문제이고, 다른 하나는 독도 문제이다.

일본은 2차세계대전중에 아시아 전역에서 여성들을 납치하여 여러 전장의 군 위안소에서 성노예로 일하게 했다. UN은 이러한 여성의 숫자가 약 21만 명에 달한다고 추산하고 있는데(일본 정부는 5만 명 정도라고 주장한다), 그중 약 70퍼센트가 한국인이었다. 그들 중 소수는 아직 생존해 있으며, 일본의 만행을 생생히 기억하고 증언한다. 그럼에도 불구하고 일본 정부는 아직도 사실을 부인하거나 왜곡하고 있으며, 적절한 보상이나 사과를 하지 않았다. 유태인 학살 등 과거의 잘못을 적극적으로 반성하고 지금도 전범들을 법정에 세우고 있는 독일과 비교하며, 많은 한국인은 일본의 태도에 아쉬움을 느끼고 있다.

독도는 한국의 동쪽 끝에 있는 매우 작은 섬이지만, 한국인들에게는 대단히 중요한 곳이다. 단순한 섬이 아니라 주권의 상징이라고 해도 과언이 아니다. 면적은 0.2제곱킬로미터도 안 된다. 수많은 역사적 기록이나 고지도에 한국의 영토로 표기되어 있고, 지금도 한국의 영토이며, 약 50명의 한국인이 거주하고 있다. 그런데 언제부터인가 일본이 영유권을 주장하기 시작했고, 21세기 들어서는 교과서에 이를 명기하는 등 더욱 빈번하게 논란을 일으키고 있다.

한국인들의 독도 사랑은 아주 특별하다. 많은 한국인들이 독도의 정확한 위치(동경 132도 북위 37도)는 물론, 평균기온, 강수량, 면적, 우물의 개수, 인근에서 잘 잡히는 어종 등을 쉽게 말할 수 있다. 심지어 어느 역사책 몇 페이지 몇째 줄에 독도가 한국 땅이라고 쓰여 있는지도 기억한다. 결코 농담이 아니다. 어떻게 이런 일이 가능할까. 그건 1980년대에 발표되어 지금까지 널리 불리는 대중가요가 있기 때문이다. 〈독도는 우리땅〉이라는 제목의 그 노래 가사에 위에 말한 독도 관련 정보들이 모두 들어 있다. 놀랍게도, 이 노래의 첫 부분 멜로디는 당신도 알고 있는 것이다. 영화 〈기생충〉에 나오는 그 유명한 '제시카 송'의 원곡이 바로 이 노래이기 때문이다. "제시카 외동딸 일리노이 시카고 과 선배는 김진모 그는 네 사촌(Jessica, Only child, Illinois, Chicago,

Classmate Kim Jin-mo. He's your cousin)." 실제로 많은 한국인은 뭔가 긴 내용을 암기해야 할 때 이 단순하고 중독성 있는 멜로디를 활용하곤 한다(당신도 한번 해보라. 암기가 잘된다).

당신이 한국을 방문한다면, '독도'라는 이름은 기억하는 것이 좋다. 식당에서 '독도는 한국 땅'이라고 외치면 공짜 음식을 제공받게 될지도 모르며, 뭔가 곤란한 상황에 처했을 때 이 문장을 먼저 말한 다음 도움을 청하면 한국인들이 훨씬 적극적으로 도와줄 것이기 때문이다.

8.

Uncovering the Hidden Gems of Korean History

Earlier, I mentioned that the Doosan Bears embody the spirit of "never give up, never surrender." This is not only due to their tenacity and determination on the field but also because their mascot is a bear, which symbolizes unwavering persistence in Korean culture.

Bears indeed hold a significant place in wide-ranging aspects of human culture. They have a rich history in mythology, art, literature, and folklore, with their presence spanning across a diversity of cultures throughout the world. In some cases, cities have been named after bears, such as Berlin in Germany and Bern in Switzerland, reflecting the enduring symbolism associated with these majestic creatures. Bears have even been immortalized in the night sky, with constellations named after them, further emphasizing their prominence in human imagination. Moreover, bears have found their way into the hearts of people through beloved characters like Winnie the Pooh and teddy bears, becoming symbols of warmth, comfort, and strength.

Despite the popularity of bears in diverse cultures, Korea appears to be unique in its use of bears as a symbol of perseverance. Even in Anglo-American cultures where the word "bear" has the meaning of "endure", bears are often associated with traits such as fierceness, dedication, or cuteness, rather than patience.

Every Korean is familiar with the foundational myth of their country, which has several variations, but the most representative one goes as follows: In ancient times, Hwanung, the son of Hwanin, the Lord of Heaven, descended from the heavens along with 3,000 followers and established a city at the foot of Mount Paektu. A bear and a tiger approached him, expressing their desire to become human. Hwanung agreed to grant their wish under the condition that they stayed in a cave for 100 days, consuming only garlic and mugwort while avoiding sunlight. The tiger gave up halfway through, but the bear persevered and transformed into a woman named Ungnyeo. Eventually, Ungnyeo and Hwanung's son, Dangun, went on to establish Gojoseon (Old Joseon) on October 3, 2333 B.C., a date still celebrated as a national holiday in Korea, despite the lack of historical evidence supporting Dangun's founding of the nation on that particular day.

According to Korea's founding myth, there is a belief that all Koreans are descended from bears, symbolizing the virtue of patience. Bears are known for their endurance and ability to survive in a cave for 100 days with a limited diet of mugwort and garlic. Additionally, there is a humorous reference to Koreans being able to survive solely on fried dumplings for 15 years, highlighting their perceived patience. However, despite the mythological association with patience, modern-day Koreans are often perceived as being constantly in a rush. This raises the question of why this phenomenon exists. Is it because Koreans are an unprecedented people who are usually in a hurry but also exhibit exceptional patience during times of crisis?

Now, I don't want to burst anyone's bubble, but let's face it: myths are just myths. And it's highly unlikely that a nation with a fully-formed government actually existed way back in 2333 BC. We can be pretty sure that Gojoseon did exist at some point, and that it hung around for a while before finally falling apart around 108 BC. But when exactly it became a state, or where its capital was located, are still up for debate. Nevertheless, South Koreans are taught in school that their nation has been around for an impressive 5,000 years.

After the fall of Gojoseon, the Three Kingdoms era emerged, with Goguryeo, Baekje, and Silla vying for control of the Korean Peninsula and parts of Northeastern China for centuries. Among them, Silla eventually rose as the dominant power and established the Unified Silla period. While the state of Silla claimed a thousand-year duration, historians estimate its actual reign to be around 6-7 centuries. Nonetheless, it left a profound impact as a vibrant center of Buddhist culture. Following the Unified Silla, a brief period of three separate states ensued before the rise of the Goryeo and Joseon dynasties. Goryeo thrived for nearly 500 years, from 918 to 1392, while Joseon endured for over 500 years, from 1392 to 1910. Although this historical account may seem a bit tedious, fear not, for we are about to conclude the less eventful part. So kindly "bear" with us for just a little longer.

From 1910 to 1945, Korea was under Japanese colonial rule. After gaining independence in 1945, the country was split into North and South Korea, leading to a period of unrest. The two Koreas formed separate governments in 1948 and engaged in the Korean War from 1950 to 1953. At the end of the war, both Koreas were left impoverished, but over the past 70 years, while South Korea has evolved into the prosperous and modern nation you're familiar with, its northern counterpart has taken a vastly different path, becoming the country you also know well, but with a very different trajectory.

To sum it up, the last 2,000 years of Korean history can be traced through the Three Kingdoms (Goguryeo, Baekje, and Silla), Unified Silla, Goryeo, Joseon, and the Republic of Korea. Unless you're studying for the Korean citizenship exam, there's no need to get into the nitty-gritty details. But understanding some historical context can make your visit to Korea much more captivating.

Well, let's get started with the name. "Korea" as we know it today got its name from the Goryeo dynasty. It was at this point in history that the world started to take notice of Korea. The next dynasty to come around was Joseon(or Chosun), which, fun fact, was the same name of a BC-era country. To differentiate it, old one is called "Gojoseon," which translates to "Old Joseon." Joseon dynasty lasted over 500 years until the early 1900s.

Although commonly referred to as South Korea and North Korea, the official names of the two countries are quite different from what we know. The Republic of Korea is the official name for South Korea and the Democratic People's Republic of Korea is the official name for North Korea. Interestingly, both countries still include "Korea" in their English names. However, the official "Korean" names are completely different from each other, and do not have "Korea" or "Goryeo" either. South Korea's name includes the word "Daehan," while North Korea's name includes the word "Joseon."

Before the end of the Joseon Dynasty in 1910, the country underwent a name change in 1897, when the king declared an "empire" and began referring to himself as emperor. The word used for the new name was "Daehan". A few decades later, after the country's division, South Korea chose a new name, while North Korea chose to retain a dynastic name that dated back 500 years. Some might even say it's fitting for North Korea, which resembles a "Kim" Dynasty. (North Korean leader Kim Jong Un, whose name you've probably heard, is the grandson of Kim Il Sung, the founder of North Korea, and the son of the previous leader, Kim Jong Il.)

It's noteworthy to note that some of the names of the ancient kingdoms that existed on the Korean Peninsula still have a lasting impact today. Silla (or shilla) is a name commonly used for hotel and university, while Goryeo (or Goryo) is used for university, steel company, and pharmaceutical company. Joseon (or Chosun) is a favored name for newspaper, hotel, and university, and Daehan is widely used by airline, insurance company, logistics company, theater, and flour company. It is much more common to find the names of these historical Korean kingdoms in the names of small businesses and restaurants rather than larger corporations. Silla, Goryeo, Joseon, and Daehan are celebrated choices for business names in Korea. It's notable that one university writes its name in English as "Korea University," but in Korean as "Goryeo University."

Secondly, it is worth noting that despite its long history, South Korea has never been a feudal state like medieval Europe. Rather, it has always been a centralized state with a strong monarchy. While there have been periods when the royal power was particularly strong or weak, even during the weaker periods, power was shared by high-ranking officials in the central government, not local warlords seeking to expand their own power. Though some local officials may have abused their power, they were merely agents of the king and corrupt officials, and there were plenty of checks and balances in place. This absence of local warlords seeking power has contributed to the lack of civil war in Korean history, with only a few small-scale rebellions. Moreover, the high level of cultural and artistic development during all periods can also be attributed to the strong central government and minority ruling class. These historical facts may help explain the large population in Seoul and the pronounced gap between Seoul and the rest of the country. Like a well-known proverb in Korea states, "If it's a horse, send it to Jeju island; if it's a man, send it to Seoul."

Throughout its history, Korea has experienced several devastating wars due to foreign invasions. In the 13th century, the war with the Mongol Empire lasted for decades, and while Korea was not conquered, it was forced to pay tribute to the Mongols for a period of time. In the 16th century, the war with Japan lasted for seven years and caused great destruction to Korea. Despite winning against Japan, Korea suffered tremendous losses. The Korean hero General Yi Sun-shin, who led the victory against Japan, is still one of the most revered figures in Korea. On the other hand, Korea has not engaged in any acts of invading other countries. While some suggest this may be due to the country's lack of power to expand its territory, textbooks often attribute it to the Korean people's peaceful and gentle nature.

Thirdly, Korea didn't exactly get with the times when it comes to modernization. They never had a dramatic citizen revolution to overthrow their monarchy and turn into a republic, and they were pretty much cut off from the rest of the world during the 18th and 19th centuries thanks to a "closed-door policy". As a result, the adoption of modern technologies and institutions was slower compared to other nations. In the early 20th century, just as Korea was beginning to catch up, Japan colonized the country. Although there were attempts at modernization during this period, they were primarily driven by Japan's control over Korea and were not always beneficial for the Korean people.

In the aftermath of decolonization, the subsequent seven decades in Korea were akin to a thrilling rollercoaster ride. A nation with a history spanning over a millennium was torn apart and engulfed in a grueling three-year war. However, the resilient people fought back against dictatorship and established a flourishing democracy, while simultaneously propelling their economy forward through a fervor for world-class education and unwavering dedication. Their achievements surpassed mere prosperity, as they also became a "cutting-edge" country, partly due to the global phenomenon of K-pop. South Korea managed to condense numerous milestones, generally requiring other nations 100 or 200 years, into a phenomenal span of just 50 years.

Here's an example that highlights the incredible economic growth of South Korea: After the devastation of the Korean War, General MacArthur, then commander-in-chief of the Allied forces, famously predicted that it would take at least 100 years to rebuild Korea. The situation was so dire that several countries, including the United States, provided aid to South Korea, amounting to an estimated $60 billion over the decades. At one point, foreign aid accounted for a quarter of the country's budget.

However, since the 1990s, South Korea has experienced a remarkable reversal of fortune, transforming into a generous provider of aid to other nations. It is the only country in the world to have transitioned from being an aid recipient to becoming an aid donor. In 2021, South Korea provided a staggering $2.86 billion in foreign aid, ranking 15th among the 29 members of the OECD's Development Assistance

Committee (DAC). Despite this achievement, South Korea's aid-to-GNI ratio of 0.16% is less than half the average for DAC members. Consequently, the South Korean government and many of its citizens are advocating for increased aid contributions in the future.

Fourthly, the relationship between South Korea and China holds an intriguing place historically. China, a major global player today, had an even greater influence in Asia in the past. South Korea was deeply influenced by Chinese culture, adopting elements such as Chinese characters, and many intellectuals embraced the idea that "China is the center of the world." While Korea was never a Chinese colony, it lived under Chinese influence for an extended period, akin to a poor younger brother under the authority of a powerful older brother.

During the 16th century Japanese invasion of Korea, China sent troops to aid Korea, and tragically, up to 30,000 Chinese soldiers lost their lives. For the following 200 years, Korea regularly dispatched special envoys to China as a form of tribute, while Chinese envoys were warmly received and treated with utmost hospitality. However, when Japan emerged victorious in its war against China in the late 19th century and subsequently annexed Korea in the early 20th century, both China and Korea shared a sense of empathy and solidarity, as the saying goes, "misery loves company."

The mid-20th century and beyond brought even greater complexity to the relationship between South Korea and China. The Korean War, initiated by a surprise attack from North Korea, initially saw the North making striking advances and nearly achieving a swift victory. However, the intervention of UN forces, including the United States, shifted the balance and brought the South to the verge of success. Subsequently, China entered the war, leading to a prolonged stalemate that resulted in the country being divided as it was before the conflict.

In the years that followed, while South Korea experienced rapid development, China's progress was comparatively slower, leading to a certain degree of dismissiveness among some Koreans towards China and its people. However, as a country heavily reliant on exports, South Korea has become increasingly dependent on China's thriving economy, which has become a force that cannot be ignored. Given China's growing influence and the recurring nuclear tests conducted by North Korea, South Korea often finds itself having to gauge China's stance and disposition.

South Korea finds itself in a difficult position as it seeks to maintain good economic relations with China while also grappling with conflicting emotions regarding Chinese investment to Korean real estates and job opportunities in Korea. However, the most significant factor in the worsening of Sino-South Korean relations has been China's distortion of history. China's claims that Goguryeo, one of the three ancient Korean kingdoms, was part of China, as well as its assertion that kimchi and "hanbok" (traditional Korean costume) have Chinese origins, have been met with strong opposition and have fueled anti-Chinese sentiment in Korea. (These claims are as far-fetched as Spain claiming to be the originator of pizza or Germany asserting to be the birthplace of champagne.)

Furthermore, China's disregard for intellectual property rights has caused additional strain on Sino-South Korean relations. Unauthorized production of knockoffs of famous Korean products and unlicensed distribution of Korean TV shows have been common occurrences. In addition, the Chinese government has banned Korean dramas from airing in China and Korean singers from performing in China. Moreover, the COVID-19 pandemic has contributed to the rise of anti-China sentiment in South Korea. According to a 2022 survey by the Pew Research Center in the U.S., South

Koreans' unfavorable perception of China reached a staggering 80%, a stark contrast from just 31% in 2002. While anti-China sentiment has risen in many other countries since the pandemic, South Korea stands out as a notable exception.

Fifthly, let's delve into the relationship between Korea and Japan. These two countries have had a long history of interaction, which is not surprising given their close proximity. Korea is located at the northeastern end of the Eurasian continent, while Japan is situated just across the water, with the Pacific Ocean to the east. Throughout ancient times, multifarious cultures and people have migrated from Korea to Japan, resulting in cultural influences. In fact, historical records even suggest that the current king of Japan is a descendant of the royal family of Baekje, one of the three ancient Korean kingdoms. This fact was confirmed by the king of Japan himself in 2001.

During the medieval period, Korea and Japan had a complicated relationship that was neither fully friendly nor hostile. However, Japan proved to be a thorn in Korea's side for many centuries, as Japanese pirates frequently raided Korean coasts starting in the 13th century. It wasn't until the 16th century that Korea-Japan relations took a definitive turn for the worse when Japan launched an invasion of Korea and engaged in a brutal seven-year war that caused immense suffering for the Korean people. Fast forward to the late 19th and early 20th centuries, Japan eventually annexed Korea, showcasing its modernization while Korea struggled to keep pace.

During the 35-year colonization period from 1910 to 1945, the Korean people experienced immense suffering and hardships. Countless innocent civilians were subjected to torture, imprisonment, and executions by the Japanese colonial authorities. Furthermore, the Japanese exploited Korea's valuable natural resources, confiscating grains and underground resources for their own benefit. Additionally, Koreans were forced to relinquish their Korean names and adopt Japanese names, and the teaching of the Korean language was prohibited. Many Koreans were forcibly taken to Japan as laborers, and during World War II, a myriad of women were coerced into becoming "comfort women" for the Japanese military.

In the almost 80 years since the end of colonization, significant changes have occurred in the relationship between Korea and Japan. Both countries have emerged as major players in the global economy, fostering extensive exchange and collaboration across myriad fields. There is a strong mutual fascination with each other's cuisine and culture, and both countries have become beloved destinations for tourists from the other. However, the deep wounds inflicted during the 16th century's Imjin War and the 35 years of colonization continue to affect their relationship, and many Koreans still perceive Japan as a rival that needs to be surpassed. A soccer match between these two nations often carries intense emotions, as Korean players and fans consider it unacceptable to lose to Japan. Moreover, there are two sensitive issues that contribute to Koreans' negative view of Japan: the problem of comfort women and the territorial dispute over Dokdo, a small group of islets.

During World War II, Japan committed grave atrocities across Asia, including the abduction and enslavement of women as sex slaves in military brothels. The United Nations estimates that approximately 210,000 women were affected, with around 70% of them being Korean (although Japan claims it was only around 50,000). These women, often referred to as "comfort women," endured unimaginable suffering, and their harrowing experiences continue to haunt them to this day. Sadly, the Japanese government has not fully acknowledged its responsibility for these crimes. It has also not provided adequate compensation or sincere apologies to the victims. This lack of accountability has deeply disappointed many Koreans, who draw comparisons to Germany's genuine efforts to confront its dark past, such as acknowledging the Holocaust and bringing war criminals to justice.

Dokdo may be small, but it holds immense importance for Koreans. This tiny island, located off the eastern tip of the country and measuring less than 0.2 square kilometers, has been recognized as Korean territory for centuries. Numerous historical records and ancient maps confirm its Korean heritage, and it is currently inhabited by around 50 Koreans. Despite this, Japan has been making its own territorial claims, and in recent years, the dispute has only intensified, with Dokdo even being included in Japanese school textbooks as Japanese territory. For Koreans, Dokdo represents more than just a piece of land—it is a symbol of sovereignty.

Koreans indeed hold a deep attachment to Dokdo. Many South Koreans are familiar with the precise coordinates of Dokdo (132 degrees East longitude, 37 degrees North latitude) and possess knowledge about its climate, size, number of wells, and the marine life in its surrounding waters. Some can even cite the exact title, page, and line of the specific book where the ownership of Dokdo by Korea is mentioned. Surprisingly, this is not a joke or exaggeration. It is attributed to a well-known song titled "Dokdo is Our Land," which was released in the 1980s and remains popular today. The song's lyrics contain the aforementioned information, and interestingly, the melody of its first part shares similarities with the famous "Jessica Jingle" from the movie Parasite. (Can you remember? Jessica, Only child, Illinois, Chicago, and Classmate Kim Jin-mo, He's your cousin.) Believe it or not, this catchy melody has become a mnemonic tool for many Koreans to memorize various facts. It's an effective and fun way to retain information. Why not give it a try yourself?

If you ever find yourself in South Korea, remember one word: "Dokdo." Why, you may ask? Well, uttering "Dokdo is Korean Territory" at a restaurant might surprise you with some free food. And if you happen to be in a difficult situation and need assistance, starting with this magic word might improve your chances of getting some help from the locals.

9.

이런 것들은
한국이 세계에서
1등

어떤 민족의 습속을 결정하는 데 있어서는 분명히 유전적인 요인도 중요하다. 하지만 최근 몇 세대에 걸치는 기간 동안 사회 구성원 전체가 공통적으로 겪은 체험도 매우 중요한 역할을 할 것이다. 한국인들이 최근 백여 년 동안 겪은 엄청나게 많은 일도 한국인들의 특성에 큰 영향을 주었음이 분명하다.

한국인들은 19세기 말까지 수백 년 동안 충효를 중시하는 유교적 전통 속에서 살았다. 그리 부유한 나라는 아니었지만, 고유의 언어와 문화를 가진 안정적인 국가였다. 신분제 사회라서 양반이 아닌 대다수 평민의 삶은 고단했겠지만, 주어진 운명에 비교적 순응하는 편이었다. 농경사회를 기본으로 했기에 사람들 사이에는 공동체 문화가 잘 형성되어 있었고, 국왕으로 대표되는 정치 시스템은 국민의 안녕과 행복을 위해 노력하는 존재로 (어느 정도는) 받아들여졌다.

그러던 중 19세기 말부터 격동의 시기가 시작됐고, 20세기 초에는 나라가 망했다. 아무런 잘못이 없었던 국민들은 무능한 지도자들로 인해 식민지 백성이 되어 고초를 겪었다. 끈질긴 저항 끝에 나라를 되찾았지만 우여곡절 끝에 분단과 전쟁이 이어졌다. 정부가 국민을 지켜줄 것이라는 믿음이 깨진 것이다. 망국과 혼란과 전쟁과 빈곤을 겪으면서, 국민들은 생각했다. 나를 지켜줄 수 있는 존재는 어디에도 없다. 아무도 믿을 수 없다(타인이든 타국이든 마찬가지다). 나의 살길은 내가 알아서 찾아야 한다. 또 생각했다. 명분보다는 실리가 중요하다. 현대 사회에서는 지식이 중요하고, 그래서 교육이 중요하다. 힘을 기르지 않으면 당한다. 이런 생각은 개인적 차원에서도 널리 퍼졌고, 국가적 차원에서도 마찬가지였다.

이러한 문화 속에서 자연스럽게 생겨난 두 가지 키워드는 '각자도생'과 '국뽕'이다. 각자도생은 '제각기 스스로 살길을 찾는다'는 뜻이다. 공동체 의식의 붕괴를 뜻하는 서글픈 말인 동시에 나 아닌 모든 사람을 경쟁자로 생각해야 하는 피곤한 말이다. 국뽕은 국가와 필로폰을 뜻하는 한국어 단어를 조합한 말로, 극단적이고 무비판적인 애국심을 부정적으로 지칭하는 말이다. 애국심을 매우 강조하는 사회가 오래 지속되는 과정에서 생겨난 단어라 할 수 있다.

다행스럽게도 각자도생의 문화는 점차 옅어지고 있다. 나라가 점차 부유해지면서 과거에 취약했던 복지 시스템이 상당히 많이 정비되었고, 국민들도 여유가 생기면서 사회적 약자를 배려하는 문화가 (조금씩이나마) 형성되고 있는 것이다. 다른 사람들과의 경쟁에서 이기는 것보다 자신의 행복이 더 중요하다는 당연한 생각이 퍼졌고, 오로지 양적 성장에만 집착하던 과거와 달리 분배나 형평과 같은 가치에도 눈을 돌리기 시작했다. (옅어지고 있다고는 했지만, 각자도생의 분위기는 한국 사회에 여전히 꽤 만연해 있다.)

국뽕은 최근 10여 년 사이에 널리 쓰이는 단어다. 어느 나라 국민이나 애국심이 있겠지만, 한국인의 애국심은 남다르다. 고유의 언어와 문화를 유지하면서, 국경의 변화도 거의 없으면서, 인종적으로도 별로 섞이지 않은 채 천 년 이상 유지된 나라는 많지 않다. 전쟁과 같은 국가적 위기를 맞을 때마다 한국인들은 자발적으로 군대를 조직하여 외세와 맞서 싸웠다. 한국인들은 평소에는 한국 정부의 무능이나 한국의 좋지 않은 관습에 대해 흔히 자조적으로 폄하하지만, 외국인들이 똑같은 비판을 하면 발끈하는 경향이 있다(나는 우리나라를 욕할 수 있지만 외국인이 우리나라 욕하는 건 못 참는다!).

또한 한국인들은 외국인들이 우리를 어떻게 생각하는지에 대해서 매우 큰 관심이 있다. 소위 '글로벌 스탠더드'를 매우 중요하게 생각하고, 'OECD 평균'과 같은 수치들에 과도하게 집착한다. 이런 건 아마도 19세기 말까지 수백 년 동안 외국과의 교류 없이 '우물 안 개구리'로 살다가 큰 낭패를 본 경험 때문이기도 할 것이고, 최근 몇십 년 동안 놀라운 발전을 거듭하면서는 '도대체 우리가 얼마나 발전한 것인지?' 객관적으로 알아보고 싶기 때문이기도 할 것이다. 마치 공부를 아주 열심히 한 학생이 다음 시험 날짜를 기다리는 것처럼 말이다.

이런 경향이 강하게 드러난 사례가 외국인에게 '두 유 노우 ○○○?'라는 질문을 (맥락 없이) 던지는 것이다. ○○○에 흔히 들어가는 단어로는 싸이 혹은 강남스타일, 김연아, 김치 등이 있다(요즘은 〈기생충〉이나 〈오징어 게임〉 등도 추가됐다. BTS는 잘 묻지 않는다. 당연히 모두가 알 것이라고 생각하기 때문이다). 외국인이 안다고 대답하면 기뻐하고, 너무 좋아한다며 호들갑스럽게 반응하면 격하게 기뻐하는 식이다. 평범한 사람들이 거리에서 만난 외국인에게 이런 질문을 하기도 하지만, 한국을 방문한 외국의 셀럽을 인터뷰하는 리포터가 TV 카메라 앞에서 이런 질문을 하기도 한다(대체로 무례한 행동으로 여겨지지만, 종종 발생한다).

사실 이 책도 국뽕 논란을 일으킬 가능성이 있다. 내가 한국에 대해 긍정적으로 기술한 부분을 두고 국뽕을 경계하는 사람들이 비판할 수도 있고, 부정적으로 기술한 부분에 대해서는 국뽕에 취해 있는 사람들이 비판할 수도 있기 때문이다(물론 나는 최대한 객관적으로 서술하기 위해 노력했다).

아무튼 한국인들은 여러 항목에서 국가별 순위에 집착한다. 좋은 쪽으로 높은 순위에 올라 있는 항목에 대해서는 더 높이기 위해 노력하고, 나쁜 쪽으로 높은 순위에 올라 있는 항목은 개선하기 위해 노력한다. 한국이 얼마나 독특한 나라인지 이해하는 데 도움이 되는 몇 가지 순위를 살펴보자.

첫째, 한국의 문맹률은 전 세계에서 가장 낮은 편이고, 대학 진학률은 전 세계에서 가장 높은 편이다. 한국은 고유의 언어와 고유의 문자를 갖고 있는데, 나중에 자세히 살펴볼 '한글'이라는 문자는 배우고 사용하기가 매우 쉽다. 한글을 읽지 못하는 한국인은 거의 없다고 해도 과언이 아니다. 소위 기본 문맹률은 제로에 가깝다는 뜻이다. 또한 한국의 대학 진학률은 거의 70퍼센트에 달한다(OECD 평균은 40퍼센트 정도다). 앞에서 설명했지만 한국인들은 가난에서 벗어나기 위해 자녀 교육에 목숨을 걸었다. 점차 감소하고 있기는 하지만, 대학을 졸업한 사람과 그렇지 못한 사람 사이의 임금 격차도 큰 편이었다.

하지만 이게 무조건 좋은 것은 아니다. 단순히 문자를 읽고 쓸 수 있는 기본 문해율은 매우 높지만, 사회생활에 실제로 필요한 능력을 의미하는 실질 문해율은 전혀 높지 않은 것으로 나타나고 있기 때문이다. OECD가 실시하는 국제성인문해조사(IALS, International Adult Literacy Surveys)에서는 산문 문해(prose literacy), 문서 문해(document literacy), 수량 문해(quantitative literacy)를 측정하는데, 한국은 세 부문 모두 OECD 국가 중 중하위권에 머물렀다. 대학 진학률이 높기 때문이기는 하겠으나, 대학 졸업자끼리 비교했을 때는 성적이 더 나빴다. 논리적 사고력보다는 지식의 습득과 암기를 더 중요하게 평가하는 한국의 교육 및 평가 시스템 탓이기도 할 것이고, 독서 인구가 적기 때문이기도 할 것이다(한국인들은 책을 많이 읽지 않는 편이다. 내가 오죽하면 외국인을 대상으로 하는 책을 썼겠나. 과거에 나름대로 좋은 책을 몇

권 썼는데, 좋은 평판에도 불구하고 한국에서는 그리 많이 팔리지 않았기 때문이다). 또한 대학 졸업자 비율이 너무 높다보니 취업 시장에서 수요와 공급의 불균형이 발생하는 문제도 있다. 화이트칼라 직종에서는 구직자에 비해 일자리가 턱없이 부족하고, 블루칼라 직종에서는 정반대의 현상이 나타나는 것이다.

둘째, 한국이 기적과 같은 경제성장을 하는 데 밑거름이 된 몇 가지 산업 분야에서 세계 최고 수준을 자랑한다. 우선 IT 강국답게 인터넷 속도와 스마트폰 보급률 등에서도 세계 최고 수준이다. 조사 기관이나 시점에 따라 차이는 있지만, 한국의 인터넷 속도는 세계 평균보다 3~4배는 빠른 것으로 정평이 나 있다. 스마트폰 보급률은 95퍼센트 수준이며, 5G 기술의 상용화 측면에서 세계에서 가장 앞서 있다. 온라인 게임 산업은 물론, 프로 게이머들이 격돌하는 e-스포츠 분야에서도 세계 최고 수준이다. 메모리 반도체 분야도 세계 1위로, 삼성전자와 SK 하이닉스 두 회사의 점유율을 더하면 약 70퍼센트에 이른다. 조선업도 매우 발달하여, 세계 시장 점유율에서 1, 2위를 다투고 있다. 전 세계에서 만들어지는 선박 중 40퍼센트 이상이 한국에서 만들어진다. 철강산업도 발달했다. 세계 시장 점유율 1위는 아니지만, 세계에서 가장 큰 제철소와 두번째로 큰 제철소가 모두 한국에 있다. 당신도 잘 알고 있는 콘텐츠 산업은 최근에 한국이 두각을 나타내는 분야다. 영화, 드라마, 대중음악 등 여러 분야에서 한국의 약진은 두드러진다.

셋째, 한국은 탄소중립과 관련해서 아주 재미있는 나라다. 우선 쓰레기 분리수거 분야는 독일과 세계 최고를 다투고 있다. 한국은 오래전부터 재활용이 불가능한 쓰레기를 버릴 때는 반드시 정부가 지정한 (제법 비싼) 쓰레기봉투를 사용해야 하는 정책을 펴왔기 때문이다. 하지만 그 외 지표는 어둡다. 재활용이 가능한 쓰레기를 버리는 데는 돈이 들지 않기 때문인지, 한국인의 플라스틱 배출량은 매우 많다. 한국의 1인당 연간 플라스틱 배출량은 88킬로그램으로, 미국(130킬로그램), 영국(99킬로그램)에 이어 세 번째로 많다(배달 문화가 특히 발달한 것도 관련이 있을 것이다). 한국인은 전기도 많이 쓴다. 1인당 전기 사용량은 OECD 34개 회원국 중 캐나다와 미국에 이어 3위다. 이는 가정용 전기요금이 너무 싼 것이 주요한 원인일 것이다(OECD 34개 회원국 중에서 31위다). 당연히 탄소 배출량도 많다. 총량 기준으로도 세계 10위권에 해당하고, 1인당 배출량으로는 전 세계 평균치의 두 배가 넘는다(나름대로 여러 가지 노력을 하고 있긴 한데, 수출 위주의 산업 구조 등 여러 이유로 인해 탄소중립으로 가는 길이 험난한 편이다).

넷째, 한국인은 전 세계에서 가장 오래 일한다. OECD에 따르면 2020년 기준 한국의 연간 근로시간은 평균 1,908시간이다(이것도 과거에 비하면 많이 줄어든 것이긴 하다). 멕시코(2,124시간)와 코스타리카(1,913시간)에 이어서 세번째이고, OECD 평균인 1,687시간보다 221시간이나 길다. 출근하는 거의 모든 날에 한 시간씩 일을 더 하는 셈이다. 파트타임 근로자의 비율이나 자영업자의 비중 등 여러 변수가 있기는 하지만, 한국인이 미국이나 유럽 선진국들 사람들보다 오래 일하는 것은 분명해 보인다. 이에 더해 출퇴근에 걸리는 시간도 한국이 가장 길다. 통근 시간의 OECD 평균은 28분인데, 한국 근로자의 평균 통근 시간은 58분으로 조사됐다. 근로시간도 길고 통근 시간도 기니, 휴식이나 여가 활동에 쓸 시간은 그만큼 부족할 수밖에 없다.

그런데 안타까운 것은, 한국의 노동생산성이 OECD 회원국 중에서 매우 낮다는 사실이다. 근무시간이 너무 길다보니 일을 덜 열심히 하기 때문일까? 그런 측면도 없지는 않을 것이다. 실제로 대부분의 한국 근로자는 점심시간 한 시간은 확실히 쉰다. 한 시간을 조금 넘겨 회사에 복귀하는 것도 흔히 용인된다. 퇴근 시간을 넘겨 일하는 경우가 흔하기 때문이다(낮잠을 자거나 하지는 않는다). 하지만 더 중요한 이유가 있다. 노동생산성이라는 것은 근로자가 생산한 물품의 양을 측정하는 것이 아니라 근로자가 생산하는 부가가치를 돈으로 환산하는 것이므로, 결국 근로자의 임금 수준과 밀접한 관련이 있다. 같은 일을 하더라도 그가 받는 임금이 두 배라면 생산성이 두 배 높은 것으로 측정되는 방식이다. 당연히 평균 임금이 높은 나라가 생산성도 높다. 한국은 자영업자 비율이 높고, 서비스업 종사자 비율이 높은 나라다. 그들의 평균 임금 수준이 낮기 때문에 생산성이 낮은 것으로 집계되는 측면도 분명히 존재한다.

다섯째, 한국은 성평등 지수가 낮은 편이다. 세계경제포럼이 발표하는 성격차지수(Gender Gap Index, GGI)에서 한국은 조사 대상 146개국 중 99위였다. 유엔개발계획(UNDP)이 발표하는 성개발지수(Gender Development Index, GDI)로 보아도 한국은 조사 대상 62개국 중에서 57위였다. 영국 매체 『이코노미스트』
가 발표하는 유리천장지수(Glass-ceiling Index)에서는 아예 꼴찌
다. UNDP가 발표하는 성불평등지수(Gender Inequality Index,
GII)에서는 189개국 중 11위로 매우 높지만, 이 지수는 의료나
교육 인프라에 크게 좌우되는 지표이므로 한국에 성차별이 없다
는 뜻으로 해석하기는 어렵다. 한국이 여성으로 살기에 매우 좋은
나라는 아니라고 보는 게 맞다. 한편 가부장적인 문화, 성범죄나
스토킹 관련 법규의 내용, 남자에게만 적용되는 병역 의무 등 여
러 이유로 특히 젊은 세대에서는 젠더 갈등이 제법 심한 편이다.

빈부격차가 큰 것도 사회문제 중의 하나다. 중위소득의 50퍼
센트 이하의 소득을 올리는 가구의 비율을 의미하는 상대적빈곤
율은 15퍼센트 수준으로, OECD 국가 중에서 미국 다음으로 높
다. 노인들의 경우 빈곤율이 더욱 높아서, 사회경제적으로 큰 문
제가 되고 있다.

여섯째, 한국은 세계 최저의 출산율과 세계 최고의 고령화 속
도가 나타나는 나라다. 특히 저출산 문제는 정말로 심각한 수준
이다. 한국의 출산율은 전 세계에서 가장 낮다. 2022년 한국의
합계출산율(total fertility rate, TFR)은 0.78에 불과하다(만성적인
저출산으로 고민하는 일본도 2022년 기준 1.26은 된다). 한국도 한때
는 인구 급증을 막기 위해 산아제한 정책을 펴던 나라였다. 한국
전쟁 직후인 1950년대에는 베이비붐 현상으로 출산율이 6.0을
넘기도 했기 때문이다. 1960년대 초반부터 1980년대 초반까지
매우 강력한 출산 억제 정책이 실시됐고, 그 결과 1983년에는

출산율이 인구 대체 수준인 2.1 밑으로 감소했다. 이후로도 감소세는 지속됐다. 1997년의 외환위기와 2009년의 세계금융위기, 여성의 사회 진출 증가 등 여러 요인이 작용한 것으로 보이지만, 가장 큰 문제는 한국이 '아이 키우기 힘든 나라'이기 때문이다. 한국 정부가 출산 장려 정책을 펴기 시작한 2003년 이후에도 출산율은 꾸준히 내려가서, 2018년에는 0.98을 기록했다. 전 세계에서 출산율이 1.0 미만을 기록한 것은 당시 한국이 최초다. 이후 4년 동안 더욱 떨어져 급기야 0.78까지 내려갔으니, 이제는 '국가 소멸'을 걱정해야 하는 수준이 되었다.

평균수명이 늘어나는 것에 낮은 출산율이 더해지니, 한국의 고령화 속도는 정말 무서울 지경이다. 2022년 현재 한국의 65세 이상 고령인구의 비율은 17.5퍼센트이다. 이보다 높은 나라도 많으니, 그 자체로 특별히 심각한 것은 아닐지도 모른다. 하지만 증가 추세가 문제다. 현재의 추세가 지속되면 한국은 2025년에 고령인구 비율 20퍼센트를 넘겨 초고령사회가 되고, 2045년에는 고령인구 비율이 37퍼센트에 도달, 세계에서 가장 늙은 나라가 될 전망이다.

일곱째, 앞에서 국뽕이라는 단어를 설명했지만, 이와 정반대에 놓여 있는 단어가 '헬조선'이다. 조선왕조의 이름에 지옥을 붙인 이 단어는, 현재의 대한민국이 '너무너무 살기 힘든 곳'이라는 자조적인 의미를 담고 있다. 긴 근로시간, 지나치게 경쟁적인 문화, 심한 빈부격차, 터무니없이 높은 부동산 가격, 양질의 일자리 부족 등 수많은 요인 탓이다. 같은 맥락에서 한국은 세계에서 가장 자살률이 높은 나라이기도 하다. 10만 명당 자살자 수가 연간 24.6명으로, OECD 평균 11.3명의 두 배가 넘는다.

사실 '헬조선'은 이미 안정적인 기반을 구축한 기성세대보다는 아직 가진 것이 별로 없는 젊은이들이 더 많이 쓰는 말이다. 경제 상황 등을 종합적으로 고려할 때, 현재 한국의 젊은 세대는 '역사상 처음으로 아버지 세대보다 못사는 세대'가 될 것이라는 전망이 많다. 그 와중에 베이비붐 시대에 태어난 앞 세대를 부양해야 하는 책임까지 짊어져야 한다. 아이를 낳아야 하는 연령대의 한국인들이 '내 아이가 (앞으로 더 나빠질 것 같은) 이 나라에서 힘들게 살게 하고 싶지 않다'는 생각들을 하니, 정부의 온갖 출산 장려 정책에도 불구하고 출산율이 올라갈 줄을 모르는 것이다. 같은 이유로 한국에서는 세대 갈등도 점차 고조되는 중이다.

이렇게 나열하다보니 한국이 정말로 '나쁜' 나라처럼 보일까봐 걱정이 된다. 사실 그렇게 나쁘지는 않다. 숫자로 설명하기는 어렵지만, 좋은 점도 정말 많다(이 책의 나머지 부분에서 좋은 점들을 숱하게 이야기하고 있지 않나). 사회의 거의 모든 시스템은 매우 효율적으로 돌아가고, 치안 수준도 매우 높으며, 사람들은 전반적으로 밝고 따뜻한 품성을 갖고 있다. 좁고 자원이 없는 나라에서 아등바등 사느라고 다들 좀 피곤에 절어 있지만, 놀 때는 없는 힘을 짜내어 신나게 잘 노는 민족이다. 고대의 역사책에도 '음주가무'에 능한 민족이라고 명시되어 있다. 그리고 무엇보다, 외국인에게 친절하다. 당신은 한국에 와서 좋은 것들만 경험하고 가면 된다. 골치 아픈 문제들은 우리가 어떻게든 해볼 테니까.

끝으로 재미있는 사실 두 가지만 더 언급한다. 한국은 도안이나 액면가 등이 새겨지지 않은 동전의 재료 생산에서도 세계 1위다. 40여 개국에 수출하며 세계 시장 점유율은 50퍼센트 수준이다. 미국, 유럽, 호주 등의 여러 나라에서 쓰이는 동전의 상당수는 알고 보면 한국 출신이다.

한국 여권의 파워도 굉장하다. 2022년 현재 한국 여권으로는 무려 192개 나라에 비자 없이 입국할 수 있다. 193개 나라에 무비자 입국이 가능한 일본에 이어 세계 2위다(1개 나라의 차이는 중국 때문이다. 중국은 아직도 한국인에게 비자 발급을 요구하고 있다. 중국에 대한 한국인의 부정적 인식에 이것도 아주 조금은 영향을 미칠 것이다. 아, 물론 중국인도 비자를 받아야만 한국에 들어올 수 있다). 반대로 한국에 무비자로 입국할 수 있는 국가의 수는 104개국이다. 192개국에 비하면 훨씬 적지만, 이는 전 세계에서 서른일곱번째로 많은 것이다.

9.

Why are Koreans #1 in these particular metrics?

You can't deny that genetics plays a part in shaping an ethnic group's customs and habits. But let's not forget the shared experiences of a people over many generations. The ups and downs of the last century have definitely left their mark on Koreans, shaping their unique folkways.

For centuries, from ancient times until the late 1800s, Koreans followed a Confucian tradition that placed a great emphasis on loyalty. Despite being a non-affluent nation, it remained stable with a richly individual language and culture. While the majority of commoners who did not belong to the gentry class("yangban") led difficult lives due to the caste system, they were somewhat resigned to their fate. The country was agrarian, and there was a strong sense of community among the people. The political system, represented by the king, was accepted (to a certain extent) as working for the benefit and happiness of the people.

In the late 19th century, turbulent times began, and in the early 20th century, the country was colonized. The people, who did nothing wrong, suffered greatly because of their incompetent leaders. After a dogged resistance, the country was eventually reclaimed, but it was followed by division and war. The people's faith in the government was shattered, and they were faced with destruction, chaos, and poverty. As a result, they realized that they could not rely on anyone else or any other country for their protection and survival, leading to a focus on practicality over idealism. "In the modern world, knowledge is power, which is why education is so important. If you don't empower yourself, you're powerless." This idea was prevalent on a personal level, and on a national level as well.

Two keywords that have emerged in Korean culture are "gakjadoseng" and "gukppong". "Gakjadoseng" means "finding one's own way to survive", reflecting a sense of individualism and competition that has replaced the conventional emphasis on community and collective identity. This phrase also carries a sense of melancholy or weariness, suggesting that navigating life independently can be challenging and burdensome. "Gukppong", on the other hand, combines the words for "country" and "methamphetamine" and signifies extreme and irrational patriotism. While patriotism has long been an important value in Korean society, "gukppong" carries a negative connotation.

Fortunately, the culture of self-reliance that prevailed in Korean society for a long time is gradually diminishing. With the country's increasing wealth, the once weak welfare system has significantly improved, leading to a more relaxed society and the emergence of a culture that values caring for the socially disadvantaged. People have come to realize that their own happiness is more important than competing with others, and they are paying more attention to values like distribution and equity, which were often overlooked in the past in favor of purely quantitative growth. (Although the culture of self-reliance is becoming less pervasive, it still exists to a notable extent in Korean society.)

The term gukppong has gained widespread use in the past decade to describe a specific kind of patriotism particular to Koreans. Korea is one of the few countries to have maintained its language and culture for over a thousand years with minimal ethnic mixing and few border changes. During times of national crisis, such as war, Koreans have come together to form armies and resist foreign powers. While Koreans may openly acknowledge their government's incompetence or criticize certain customs, they tend to react negatively when such criticisms come from outsiders. This attitude is reflected in the saying, "I can criticize my own country, but I cannot tolerate foreigners doing the same."

Koreans have a strong concern in how they are perceived by foreigners. Furthermore, they place a lot of importance on so-called "global standards" and are overly obsessed with numbers like "OECD average". This is probably due to the painful result of living in isolation for hundreds of years without foreign interaction until the end of the 19th century, like a 'babe in the woods.' Moreover, this desire may stem from the stunning progress they have achieved in recent decades. In other words, they want to objectively measure how far they have come. It's like a student who has studied very hard and is waiting for the next exam.

The tendency for Koreans to seek validation from foreigners is often manifested in their eagerness to ask the question, "Do you know OOO?" without providing any context. Common examples of "OOO" include PSY, Gangnam Style, Kim Yuna, and kimchi. More recently, "Parasite" and "Squid Game" have also been added to the list. (However, BTS is an exception to this rule, as Koreans assume that everyone already knows them.) When a foreigner responds positively, Koreans feel pleased, and if the foreigner expresses admiration for the mentioned item, Koreans become even more thrilled. It's important to note that this question is not limited to everyday interactions with foreigners on the street; even reporters interviewing foreign celebrities in front of TV cameras have been known to ask this question, although it is generally considered impolite.

Actually, this book has the potential to spark a controversy surrounding "gukppong." Some individuals who are wary of extreme patriotism might criticize my positive depictions of Korea, while those who strongly embrace it may criticize my negative portrayals. (However, I have made a conscious effort to maintain an objective perspective throughout the book.)

In any case, Koreans have a strong inclination towards monitoring their country's rankings across multiple categories. They strive to achieve higher rankings in areas where they excel and work diligently to improve in areas where they fall behind. Let's take a look at some of these rankings to help you understand how unique South Korea's culture is.

First, Korea boasts one of the world's lowest illiteracy rates and one of the highest university enrollment rates. The country's own language and script, known as Hangeul, which we'll examine further later, makes it remarkably easy for its citizens to read and write. It's safe to say that very few Koreans cannot read Hangeul, with a basic illiteracy rate that's nearly zero. Furthermore, South Korea's university enrollment rate stands at an impressive 70%, a figure significantly exceeding the OECD average of roughly 40%. As previously mentioned, Koreans historically staked their lives on their children's education as a means to escape poverty. The wage gap between college graduates and those without higher education was substantial, although it's gradually narrowing over time.

But let's not jump to conclusions about Korea's literacy rate just yet. While the ability to read and write may be widespread, there are concerns about functional literacy and critical thinking skills. According to the OECD's International Adult Literacy Surveys (IALS), which assess prose literacy, document literacy, and quantitative literacy, Korea ranks in the lower middle range in all three categories. Furthermore, when the survey focuses solely on university graduates, the results are even more disappointing. This could be attributed to the high rate of university enrollment, which might contribute to a lower overall average level of competency.

One possible explanation for these results is the education system in Korea, which has been criticized for its emphasis on rote learning and memorization rather than fostering critical thinking and practical skills. Another contributing factor could be the lack of a strong reading culture in the country. (It's a well-known fact that Koreans aren't big readers. Even books with a good reputation, like some I've written in the past, don't seem to fly off the shelves in Korea. That's why I decided to write a book aimed at foreigners instead.) Furthermore, the issue of an oversupply of college graduates exacerbates the problem by creating an imbalance in the job market. White-collar jobs are scarce. Blue-collar jobs, on the other hand, are more abundant. This creates difficulties for university graduates seeking suitable employment opportunities.

Secondly, Korea stands as a global leader in several industries that have been pivotal to its spectacular economic growth. To begin with, as a powerhouse in the realm of information technology, Korea takes the lead in internet speeds and smartphone adoption worldwide. Depending on the source and time of day, Korea's internet speeds are three to four times faster than the global average. Smartphone usage stands at around 95%, and the nation ranks among the most advanced globally in the commercialization of 5G technology.

Its online gaming industry is also very advanced, and its e-sports scene, where professional gamers compete, is among the best in the world. Moreover, it excels in memory semiconductors, commanding a substantial 70% combined market share through industry giants like Samsung Electronics and SK Hynix. The country's shipbuilding industry is also highly developed, dominating the global market with over 40% of the world's ships being constructed in Korea.

Korea's steel industry, while not the largest by market share, hosts the world's largest and second-largest steel mills. Additionally, the content industry, which you may be familiar with, is another arena where Korea has made noteworthy strides in recent years. The nation's influence in movies, dramas, pop music, and more is clearly evident.

Thirdly, Korea presents an compelling case when it

comes to carbon neutrality, showcasing both positive and negative indicators. On the positive side, Korea is on par with Germany in having the world's best waste separation system. This accomplishment can be attributed, in part, to the long-standing policy of using government-mandated and expensive garbage bags for non-recyclable waste. However, despite this success, Koreans still generate a considerable amount of plastic waste. In fact, the country ranks as the world's third-largest producer of plastic waste per capita (88kg), trailing behind only the United States (130kg) and the United Kingdom (99kg). This situation may be partly attributed to the absence of a cost associated with discarding recyclable waste. Additionally, a particularly developed delivery culture in Korea may also play a role.

Furthermore, Koreans are heavy users of electricity, ranking third in per capita electricity consumption among 34 OECD countries, surpassed only by Canada and the United States. As a result, Korea stands among the top 10 countries worldwide in terms of total carbon emissions, and its per capita emissions are more than double the global average. Although efforts are being made, achieving carbon neutrality in Korea remains a challenging goal due to several factors, including the country's export-oriented industrial structure.

Fourthly, Koreans work the longest hours in the world. According to the OECD, as of 2020, Koreans worked an average of 1,908 hours per year. Although this is significantly lower than in the past, it still ranks third globally, following Mexico (2,124 hours) and Costa Rica (1,913 hours). It is also 221 hours longer than the OECD average of 1,687 hours, meaning that Koreans work nearly an extra hour every day compared to workers in other OECD countries. Despite various factors like the percentage of part-time workers and self-employed individuals, it is evident that Koreans work longer hours compared to the United States and developed European countries. The long working hours are further exacerbated by the fact that Koreans also have the longest average commuting time of 58 minutes, compared to the OECD average of 28 minutes. Due to long working hours and extended commutes, there is little time for rest or leisure activities.

By the way, regrettably, labor productivity in Korea remains among the lowest in the OECD countries. Some attribute this to workers being less efficient due to their long work hours, which could be a possible explanation. It is noteworthy that most Korean workers take a solid one-hour lunch break, and it is commonly accepted to return to work a little over an hour later, as it is not uncommon for people to work past their official end of the work day. (But they don't take naps.) However, there is another crucial factor to consider. Labor productivity does not solely measure the quantity of goods a worker produces but rather the value added by the worker in terms of money, which is strongly related to the worker's wage level. If a worker earns twice as much for the same work, their productivity is measured as twice as high. Higher average wages in a country are typically associated with higher productivity rates, and Korea's high percentage of self-employed and service workers, whose average wages are low, contribute to the country's low labor productivity rate.

Fifthly, Korea's rankings in gender equality indices are disheartening. The country's position on the Gender Gap Index (GGI) from the World Economic Forum is 99th out of 146 countries, indicating significant gender disparities. Similarly, on the United Nations Development Program's (UNDP) Gender Development Index (GDI), Korea ranks 57th out of 62 countries. Additionally, Korea holds the lowest rank on The Economist's Glass-ceiling Index. Although the UNDP's Gender Inequality Index (GII) places Korea 11th out of 189 countries, it is important to note that this index heavily relies on healthcare and education infrastructure and may not adequately reflect gender discrimination. It may be fair to say that Korea is not a very good place to be a woman. Meanwhile, factors such as a patriarchal culture, laws related to sexual crimes and stalking, and the gender-specific military service further contribute to gender conflicts, particularly among the younger generation.

In addition to gender inequality, South Korea also grapples with a serious wealth disparity issue. The relative poverty rate, which indicates the percentage of households earning 50% or less of the median income, stands at 15%, making it the second highest among OECD countries, surpassed only by the United States. The situation is further exacerbated for the elderly population, as they experience an even higher poverty rate, compounding the social and economic challenges faced by the country.

Sixthly, South Korea is confronted with one of the world's lowest fertility rates and one of the highest rates of aging. The issue of low birth rates is particularly critical. Currently, Korea has the lowest fertility rate globally, with a total fertility rate (TFR) of only 0.78 in 2022. To provide a comparison, Japan, which also grapples with a persistent low birthrate, has a TFR of 1.26 in 2022. Korea implemented birth control policies in the past to curb population growth. Following the baby boom after the Korean War in the 1950s, the fertility rate exceeded 6.0. However, from the early 1960s to the early 1980s, stringent birth control measures were enforced, leading to a fertility rate below the replacement level of 2.1 by 1983. The decline has continued since then. Various factors have contributed to this decline, including the 1997 foreign exchange crisis, the 2009 global financial crisis, and the increasing participation of women in the workforce. However, the primary challenge lies in Korea being regarded as a "challenging country for parenting." Despite the government's efforts to promote childbirth starting in 2003, the fertility rate has steadily decreased, reaching 0.98 in 2018, marking the first time Korea had a fertility rate below 1.0 in the world. Over the course of the following four years, the rate further declined to 0.78, raising concerns about the prospect of "national extinction".

Korea is grappling with a concerning rate of population aging, stemming from a combination of low fertility and increasing life expectancy. Currently, 17.5% of the population is aged 65 or older, which may not appear alarming when compared to other nations. However, the underlying trend is worrisome. If this trend persists, Korea is projected to transition into an ultra-elderly society by 2025, with over 20% of the population aged 65 or older. Furthermore, by 2045, this proportion is anticipated to rise to 37%, establishing Korea as the world's oldest country.

Seventhly, on the other end of the spectrum from 'gukppong' is the term 'Hell-Joseon,' which depicts a perception that present-day Korean society is excessively challenging to live in. The addition of "hell" to the name of the Joseon Dynasty, a historical period in Korea, reflects a sense of self-mockery and discontent with the current state of the country. This sentiment arises from various factors, including long working hours, intense competition, a significant wealth gap, outrageously high real estate prices, and a shortage of desirable employment opportunities. Consequently, Korea faces one of the highest suicide rates globally, with 24.6 suicides per 100,000 people annually, more than double the OECD average.

Indeed, the term "Hell-Joseon" is predominantly used by young individuals who are yet to establish a solid footing in society. Given the prevailing economic circumstances, a multitude of predictions suggest that the current generation of young Koreans could be the first in history to experience a lower standard of living compared to their parents. Compounding their concerns, they also face the burden of supporting the older generations who were born during the baby boom era. As individuals of childbearing age contemplate the future, they express apprehension about the notion of bringing a child into a country they believe will only deteriorate further. Consequently, despite the government's concerted efforts to encourage childbirth, the birth rate remains stagnant. Consequently, generational conflicts are becoming more prominent in Korea.

The previous list may give the impression that Korea is a really bad country. However, it's actually not that bad. It's difficult to quantify, but there are many positive aspects to Korea. (They are abundantly covered in the rest of this book, right?) Many societal systems are highly efficient, safety and security are top-notch, and the people are generally welcoming and amiable. Although living in a small country with few resources can be exhausting, Koreans possess a vibrant energy and know how to enjoy life. In ancient history books, Koreans are described as a people skilled at drinking, singing, and dancing. Furthermore, they are known for their friendliness towards foreigners. If you visit Korea, you'll experience many good things, and the people here will take care of any potential problems.

Lastly, I'd like to share two more interesting facts. The first one is about coins (real coins, not bitcoin). Korea is the world's leading producer of coin blanks, which are coins without any design or denomination. These coin blanks are exported to over 40 countries, making up approximately 50% of the global market share. It's fascinating to know that many countries, such as the United States, Europe, and Australia, use coins that originate from Korea.

Another fascinating fact is related to passport power. As of 2022, the South Korean passport holds an impressive position among the most powerful passports in the world. It grants visa-free access to an astounding 192 countries. This places Korea in second place, just behind Japan, which enjoys visa-free access to 193 countries. It's worth mentioning a noteworthy difference between the Korean and Japanese passports: Korean citizens require a visa to enter China, whereas Japanese citizens do not. (This may have a slight influence on the negative perception of China among Koreans. It's important to note that Chinese citizens also require a visa to enter Korea.) Furthermore, South Korea is a welcoming destination for citizens of 104 countries, as they can enter without a visa, ranking the country as the 37th most welcoming in the world.

10.

오직 한국에만,
오직 한국인만

당신의 나라에서는 산모가 아이를 낳은 직후에 무엇을 먹게 하는지? 오랫동안 못 마셨던 맥주? 기운을 차려야 하니까 스테이크? 당신이 네덜란드 사람이라면 모이쉐스 비스킷(beschuit met muisjes)을 떠올릴 것이고, 당신이 튀르키예 사람이라면 로후사 서르베티(lohusa serbeti)를 떠올릴 것이다. 다른 나라에도 이와 같은 특별한 음식들은 제법 존재한다. 하지만 대부분의 경우 이런 음식들은 하나의 '상징'이므로, 한두 번 먹으면 그만이다. 한국은 다르다. 한국의 산모들은 출산 직후 약 2~3주 동안(!) 모든 끼니에서 같은 음식을 먹는다. 미역국이라는 음식이다.

당신의 나라에서는 생일날 먹는 특별한 음식이 있는지? 당신이 호주나 뉴질랜드 사람이라면 요정 빵(fairy bread)을 떠올릴 것이고, 당신이 스웨덴 사람이라면 공주 케이크(princess cake)를 떠올릴 것이다. 중국에서는 장수면이라 불리는 국수를 먹지만, 대부분의 나라에서 생일날 먹는 특별한 음식은 주로 디저트 계열이다. 한국은 다르다. 한국인들은 생일날 반드시 미역국을 먹어야 한다. '미역국도 못 먹었어'라는 말은 한국에서 '쓸쓸한 생일', '제대로 축하받지 못한 생일'을 보냈다는 관용적인 표현이다.

미역은 해조류의 일종이다. 전 세계의 바다에는 다양한 해조류가 있다. 그중 일부는 여러 나라에서 식용으로 사용된다. 하지만 한국인만큼 해조류를 많이 먹는 나라는 없을 것이다. 여러 종류를 먹고, 많이도 먹는다. 미역이 대표적이고, 그 외에도 여러 가지가 있다. 외국에 널리 알려진 또다른 한국의 해조류 중에는 김이 있다(김에 관해서는 나중에 다시 이야기한다).

미역으로 미역국만 끓이는 건 아니다. 미역은 바다에서 건진 후 바로 먹을 수도 있다. 고추장에 설탕과 식초를 섞은 초고추장이라고 하는 디핑 소스에 찍어 먹는 것이 보통이다(초고추장은 한국식 생선회를 먹을 때도 흔히 곁들여진다. 보기엔 케첩과 비슷하지만 맵다). 적당한 소스를 넣어 샐러드처럼 만들어 먹기도 한다. 하지만 가장 대표적인 방법은 미역국을 끓이는 것이다. 미역국은 생미역을 쓰는 게 아니라 말린 미역을 다시 불려서 만든다. 소고기를 같이 넣고 끓이는 것이 가장 일반적이지만, 조개, 전복, 굴, 생선 등을 활용하는 레시피도 있다.

출산 이후 몇십 번의 끼니 동안 내내 미역국을 먹는 것도 특이한 문화지만, 더욱 특이한 것은 이 음식을 먹는 장소다. 한국의 산모들도 대부분 병원에서 아이를 낳는데, 퇴원 후에 가는 곳은 집이 아니라 산후조리원이다. 대략 80퍼센트의 한국 산모들은 이곳에서 2~3주를 보낸 다음 집으로 간다.

산후조리는 출산 직후의 산모가 몇 주 동안 푹 쉬면서 몸을 추스르는 일련의 과정을 통칭하는 말이다. 한국에서는 전통적으로 이를 매우 중요하게 여겼다. 산후조리를 제대로 하지 않으면 산모의 몸이 망가져 나중에 여러 가지 질병에 시달리게 된다는 속설 때문이었다(과학적 근거는 별로 없다). 이 기간 동안 산모는 당연히 가사노동에서 해방되었고, 아이를 직접 돌볼 필요도 없었다. 아이와 산모를 돌보는 것은 가족들 모두의 몫이었다. 이런 풍습 때문에 산모들은 자신의 회복과 아이와의 유대관계 형성에 집중할 수 있었다(물론 모두가 그랬던 것은 아니다. 경제적 여유가 없거나 남편이나 시부모가 배려라고는 모르는 사람들일 경우엔 출산 후 며칠 만에 온갖 노동에 내몰리기도 했다).

하지만 핵가족 시대가 되면서 산후조리를 도와줄 사람을 찾기가 어려워졌고, 그 대안으로 등장한 것이 산후조리원이다. 산후조리원은 1990년대 중반에 처음 생겨난 이후 급속도로 확산됐다. 산모들은 여기에 머물면서 휴식도 취하고 아이에게 젖을 먹이고 운동도 하고 마사지도 받는다. 그리고 친구(역시 최근에 아이를 낳은 사람들)도 사귄다(이들은 나중에 산후조리원 동창회도 여는 등 관계를 지속한다. 그 관계가 아주 오래 지속되는 경우도 있다). 남편은 퇴근하고 이곳에 들러 아이와 산모를 만난다. 이 서비스는 당연히 유료이며, 정부 지원이나 보험 적용이 안 되므로 개인이 전액 부담해야 한다. 비용은 얼마나 들까? 숙박비, 하루 세끼 식비, 아이를 돌보는 비용, 추가적인 여러 서비스가 모두 제공되니, 호텔 숙박비보다는 당연히 비싸다. 2주간 이곳에 머무는 비용은, 지역이나 시설에 따라 편차가 크지만, 대체로 2천 달러 내외다. 스위트룸을 선택하면 3천 달러를 훌쩍 넘고, 아주 비싼 곳은 1만 달러를 넘어가는 곳도 있다.

당신도 한국에서 미역국을 맛볼 기회가 있을까? 이건 운에 달렸다. 여러 종류의 미역국을 주된 메뉴로 판매하는 독특한 식당들이 있기는 한데, 그 수가 많지 않고 그나마 서울이 아닌 해안가 도시들에 주로 위치하고 있기 때문이다. 대신 꽤 많은 식당에서 다양한 반찬 중의 하나로 미역국이 나오기도 한다(이 경우는 양이 많지 않고, 맛도 그리 훌륭한 편은 아니다). 아무튼, 미역국은 한국인이 매우 좋아하는 음식 중의 하나이고, 생일이 아닌 평소에도 즐겨 먹는 음식이다. 그 맛이 정말 궁금한데 먹어볼 기회가 없다면, 편의점에서 파는 즉석 미역국을 구입하는 방법도 있다. 뜨거운 물만 붓거나 전자레인지에 잠깐 돌리면 바로 먹을 수 있는 미역국 상품들이 편의점에 있다.

한국 산모들의 미역국 사랑은 특별하다. 평소에 좋아하지 않던 사람들도 꾸역꾸역 먹는다. 막 태어난 아기의 건강과 행복을 기원하는 일종의 의식과도 같은 행위일지도 모른다. 하나의 산부인과 클리닉에서 출발하여 지금은 여러 개의 대형 병원과 의과대학과 관련 기업 들까지 거느린 차병원 그룹의 성공 비결이 산모들에게 제공된 '맛있는 미역국'이었다는 전설과 같은 이야기도 있다(차병원은 미국 로스앤젤레스에도 분원이 있는데, 그곳에서도 산모들에게는 미역국을 제공한다).

그런데 산모들에게 왜 굳이 미역국을 그렇게나 많이 먹이는 것일까? 그러한 전통이 생겨난 이유는 불확실하지만, 요오드 함량이 높아서 산모와 아이 모두의 건강에 좋기 때문이라는 설명이 있기는 하다. 하지만 의사들은 과도한 요오드 섭취가 오히려 갑상선 질환 등을 유발하거나 악화시킬 수 있다고 경고한다. 어쩌면 몇 주 동안 산모의 밥상을 차려야 하는 누군가(주로 친정 엄마 아니면 시어머니)가 매번 새로운 반찬을 만들기 귀찮아서 지어낸 말일지도 모른다.

재미있는 것은, 시험을 앞둔 시기에는 절대로 미역국을 먹지 않는 문화도 있다는 사실이다. 미역은 미끈거리는 성상을 갖고 있는데, 한국어에서 '미끄러지다'라는 단어는 시험에서 떨어진다는 의미를 함께 갖고 있기 때문이다. 대신 시험을 앞두고는 입에 잘 들러붙는 음식인 찹쌀떡이나 엿을 먹는다. '붙다'라는 한국어 단어에는 시험에 합격한다는 의미가 있기 때문이다.

한국의 결혼식과 장례식 문화도 좀 독특하다. 일단 두 의식 모두, 참석자들이 돈을 낸다. 축하 혹은 위로의 뜻을 현금으로 전하는 것이다(직접 가지 못하는 경우에는 다른 참석자를 통해 전달하거나 온라인으로 돈을 부친다). 친소 관계나 경제적 여력에 따라 다르지만, 대체로 50달러 아니면 백 달러 정도를 봉투에 넣어 전달하는 것이 일반적이다. 참석 인원도 다른 나라에 비해 많은 편이다. 수백 명이 모이는 것은 보통이고, 신랑 신부의 부모나 고인 혹은 고인의 자제들의 사회적 지위가 높은 경우에는 천 명이 넘게 모이기도 한다. (결혼식은 한 시간 걸리는 행사이니 아주 넓은 공간이 필요하고, 장례식은 2박 3일에 걸쳐 진행되기 때문에 그렇게 큰 공간이 필요하지는 않다.) 예식의 규모가 크기 때문에 당연히 비용도 많이 드니, 보통 사람들에게는 큰 부담이 된다. 그래서 지인들이 그 비용을 조금씩 부담하는 문화가 생긴 것으로 생각된다(예식을 소규모로 하고 서로 주고받지 않는 방법도 있긴 한데, 한번 형성된 문화가 쉽게 바뀌지는 않는다).

결혼식과 관련해서 또다른 특이한 점으로는 '하객 알바'가 존재한다는 사실이다. 한국인들은 결혼식에 참석하는 손님이 너무 적은 것을 '체면이 깎이는 일'로 받아들이는 편이다. 그래서 (이런저런 사정으로) 초청할 사람이 너무 적을 경우, 약간의 돈을 지불하고 가짜 손님을 부르기도 한다. 아주 흔한 일은 아니지만, 아주 드문 일도 아니다. 영화 〈기생충〉에서도 배우 박소담이 과거에 '결혼식 하객 알바'를 많이 했었다는 대사가 나온다.

장례식과 관련해서 또다른 특이한 점도 있다. 대부분의 장례식장이 병원 내에 있다는 사실이다. 한국은 장례를 사흘에 걸쳐 치르는 나라이고, 앞에서 설명했듯이 많은 손님이 조문을 위해 찾아온다. 오래전에는 각자의 집에서 장례를 치렀지만 현대 사회에서는 그게 매우 어려운 일이니, 장례식만을 위한 별도의 시설이 생겨난 것이다. 그런데 대부분의 사람들이 병원에서 사망하는 시대가 되고 보니, 장례식장이 병원 내에 있는 것이 여러모로 가장 편리하다. 병원과 장례식장이 같은 공간에 있는 것을 기괴하다고 생각하는 외국인도 많지만, 한국인들은 매우 자연스럽게 받아들이고 있다(물론 눈에 잘 띄지 않는 곳에 숨어 있기는 하다).

한국에만 존재하는 아주 특이한 문화 중에는 '전세'라는 부동산 임대 방식도 있다. 한국에는 두 종류의 주택 임대 방법이 있다. 그중 하나는 월세인데, 이는 외국에도 흔한 방식이니 전혀 신기할 것이 없다. 하지만 전세는 집값의 절반이 넘는 큰돈을 보증금으로 집주인에게 맡겨놓는 대신 월세를 한 푼도 내지 않는 방식이다. 대체로 2년인 계약 기간이 끝나면 맡겨놓았던 보증금을 전액 돌려받는다. 집값이 백만 달러라면, 보증금은 50만~70만 달러 정도 된다(예를 든 집값 백만 달러가 너무 큰 금액으로 느껴지는가? 땅이 좁고 인구가 많은 한국은 부동산 가격이 높은 편이며, 특히 서울의 주택 가격은 어마어마하다. 백 제곱미터 정도 되는 작은 아파트의 가격이 백만 달러를 넘는 것은 매우 흔하며, 지역에 따라 3백만~4백만 달러인 집도 많다). 간단해 보이지만, 서울과 같이 주택이 부족하고 부동산 가격이 지속적으로 상승하는 곳에서는 여러 가지 복잡한 문제가 생긴다. 최근 수십 년 동안 한국 정부는 전세 관련 제도를 여러 차례 손보았지만, 논란은 끊이지 않고 있다.

부동산 분야에서 특이한 다른 한 가지는 '반지하'라는 주거 형태다. 영화 〈기생충〉의 주인공 가족이 살던 그 집, 바닥이 지면보다 1미터 이상 아래에 있지만 창문이 위에 있어서 바깥이 살짝 내다보이는 그런 집이 반지하다. 빈곤층이 거주하는, 축축하고 곰팡이가 피는, 그래서 특유의 '냄새'가 옷과 몸에 밸 수 있는 그런 집이 반지하다.

사실 반지하도 역사적·문화적 맥락이 있다. 1968년, 북한의 특수 부대원들이 대통령 암살을 목적으로 서울에 침투한 적이 있다. 31명의 공작원 중에 28명이 사살되었고 두 명은 북으로 도주했고 한 명은 생포되었다(그 사람은 나중에 한국으로 귀순했고, 목사가 되었다. 80세를 넘긴 지금도 한국에서 살고 있다). 작전은 실패했지만 이 사건은 한국 사회에 큰 충격을 주었다. 이후 남북한 사이의 긴장이 이어지던 1970년대(외국인들은 지금도 그러하다고 느끼겠지만, 당시는 지금보다 훨씬 긴장이 높았다), 한국 정부는 전쟁 발발 가능성을 대비해 주택마다 지하실을 만들 것을 법제화했다. 유사시에 방공호로 활용하기 위한 목적이었다. 당시에는 이 지하 공간을 따로 임대하는 것을 불법으로 규정했지만, 1980년대에 들어 주택 부족이 심해지자 규제를 완화했고, 그 이후 반지하는 가난한 사람들의 터전이 되었다.

반지하는 점차 감소하고 있지만, 여전히 한국에는 32만 가구에 달하는 반지하 주택이 있다. 그중 60퍼센트가 넘는 20만 가구가 서울에 있다. 2022년 여름에는 서울에 백여 년 만에 가장 많은 비가 내려 큰 피해가 발생했다. 반지하 주택들의 침수 피해가 특히 심해서, 사망자까지 발생했다. 영화 〈기생충〉에서 한국 사회의 양극화를 은유적으로 보여줬던 물난리 장면이 현실에서 발생한 것이다.

한국의 독특한 문화 중에 '대리운전'도 빼놓을 수 없다. 술을 마신 운전자를 대신해서 자동차를 운전해주는 서비스이다. 음주에 비교적 관용적인 한국에서 이 서비스는 매우 활성화되어 있다.

요금은 편도 택시요금보다는 비싸고 왕복 택시요금보다는 저렴한 것이 보통이다. 직장 앞에서 술을 마셨을 경우, 차를 세워놓고 택시로 퇴근했다가 다음날 아침에 택시로 출근하는 것보다는 대리운전 서비스를 이용하는 것이 경제적인 선택이 된다. 스마트폰이 없던 시절에는 전화로 기사를 호출했고, 지금은 대부분의 사람들이 앱을 이용한다. 밤 10시에서 자정 사이에는 수요가 몰려 기사를 구하기 어렵다. 대리운전 서비스는 일본의 오키나와를 비롯하여 일부 외국에도 존재하기는 하지만, 한국처럼 보편화된 나라는 없다.

음주와 관련한 독특한 풍속도 다양하다. 한국인들은 술은 반드시 서로에게 따라줘야 한다고 생각한다. 상대방 술잔이 비었는데 얼른 다시 채워주지 않는 행위나 스스로 자신의 잔에 술을 따르는 행위는 뭔지 모르게 예의 없는 행동으로 간주된다(술집에서 누군가가 상대방에게 갑자기 '바쁘냐?'라고 묻기도 하는데, 이럴 때 상대방은 곧바로 알아듣고 술병을 집어든다. '술 한잔 따라줄 시간이 없을 만큼 바쁘냐?'라는 농담이기 때문이다). 또한 누군가가 술을 따라줄 때는 반드시 술잔을 든 채 받아야 한다. 친구들끼리는 술을 따르는 사람이나 받는 사람이나 한 손으로 해도 되지만, 윗사람에게 술을 따르거나 윗사람으로부터 술을 받을 때는 두 손으로 해야 한다. 지금은 위생상의 문제로 점차 사라지고 있는 문화이지만, '술잔 돌리기'라는 관습도 있었다. 자신의 잔을 비우고 나서 (티슈 등으로 슥, 형식적으로 닦는 척을 한 다음) 그 잔을 상대방에게 내밀면서 술을 따라주는 행동이다. 친밀한 관계임을 확인하는 행위로 해석

되지만, 이를 극혐하는 사람도 많다.

놀랍게도 전 세계에서 한국인만 먹는 음식도 꽤 여러 가지다 (전 세계 어느 나라 사람들도 먹지 않는데 당신의 나라에서만 먹는 음식이 혹시 있을까? 대부분의 경우 단 한 개도 떠오르지 않을 텐데, 한국에는 이런 음식이 여러 개 있다. 한국의 식문화는 얼마나 다양한가!). 모양이나 맛이 꽤 특이하여 외국인이 도전하기 쉽지 않은 것도 있기는 하지만, 대부분은 처음 보는 사람도 별다른 거부감 없이 시도해볼 수 있는 것들이다.

우선, 과일 중에는 참외가 있다. 이건 한국의 멜론이다. 껍질은 노랗고 과육은 하얗다. 멜론보다는 조금 작고, 사과보다는 조금 크다. 먹어보면 멜론의 일종이라는 걸 느낄 수 있지만, 멜론과는 확실히 느낌이 다르다. 참외는 한국 외의 지역에서는 찾아보기 어렵고, 일부 국가에서 혹시 보인다면 한국이 수출한 것일 가능성이 높다. 당신이 여름철에 한국을 방문한다면 반드시 맛보아야 한다.

다음으로 깻잎이 있다. 참깨를 모르는 사람은 아마 없을 것이다. 천일야화 중 「알리바바와 40인의 도둑」 이야기에 나오는 "열려라 참깨"를 어릴 적에 한번쯤 외쳐보지 않은 사람은 없을 테니 말이다(전 세계적으로 히트한 어린이 프로그램 〈세서미 스트리트〉도 있다). 참깨는 인류가 기름을 얻기 위해 재배한 첫번째 작물로 추정될 만큼 오래전부터 이용됐다. 참기름은 서양에서는 그리 흔한 식재료가 아니지만, 동양에서는 꽤 많이 쓰이고, 특히 한국에서는 정말 중요한 향신료 중의 하나다(당신이 먹어볼 가능성이 제법 높은 비빔밥을 비롯한 수많은 한국 음식에 첨가된다).

한국인만 먹는 식재료 중에서 빼놓을 수 없는 것은 참깨와 비슷한 들깨다(모양이 비슷하고 한국어 이름도 비슷하지만, 분류학적으로는 상당히 다른 종류라고 한다). 일본에서 먹는 시소와도 다르고 동남아 음식에 흔히 들어가는 고수와도 많이 다르다. 들깨는 정말 특이한 식물이다. 참깨는 씨를 먹거나 기름을 짠다. 시소나 고수는 잎을 먹는다. 그런데 들깨는 씨도 먹고 기름도 짜고 잎도 먹는다. 볶은 들깨로 만드는 들기름은 참기름과 더불어 다양한 한국 요리에 쓰이며, 가루로 만든 들깨 역시 다양한 음식을 위한 향신료로 활용된다. 하지만 가장 중요한 들깨의 용도는 잎을 먹는 것이다. 깻잎이란 들깨의 잎을 의미한다. 한국인들은 다양한 방법으로 정말 많이 먹지만, 한국인 말고는 전 세계의 누구도 이걸 먹지 않는다(심지어 이런 사실을 아는 한국인도 많지 않다. 워낙 자주 먹는 풀이라, 당연히 외국에도 있으려니 생각한다. 또한, 많은 한국인은 깻잎이 들깨가 아니라 참깨의 잎이라고 잘못 알고 있기도 하다. 들기름보다는 참기름이 훨씬 더 많이 쓰이기 때문이리라. 하지만 참깨 잎은 한국인도 먹지 않는다).

깻잎이라는 단어를 어디선가 들어본 듯하다는 느낌이 든다면, 당신은 이 책을 정말 열심히 읽고 있는 것이다. 어느 부분에서 보았는지까지 생각이 난다면, 당신은 정말 훌륭한 기억력의 소유자다. 깻잎은 삼겹살에 흔히 곁들여 먹는 채소 중의 하나로 이미 언급됐다. 깻잎은 시소나 고수에 비하면 훨씬 향이 약하다(물론 일본인이나 베트남인은 다르게 생각할 수도 있다). 타임, 로즈마리, 파슬리,

바질 등의 서양 허브에 비해서도 향이 약하다(물론 서양인들은 다르게 생각할 수도 있다). 처음 먹어보면 그냥 나뭇잎을 씹는 것처럼 느껴질지도 모른다(이걸 왜 먹지?). 하지만 잘 음미해보면 약간의 민트 향과 약간의 쓴맛이 어우러진 오묘한 맛을 느낄 수 있다. 전혀 위험하지 않으니, 눈에 띄기만 하면 한번 시도해보길 바란다.

한국인들은 깻잎을 매우 다양한 방식으로 즐긴다. 일단 구운 고기나 생선회 등의 풍미를 더하기 위해 함께 먹는다. 샐러드나 국물 요리에 넣기도 하고, 김치나 장아찌 형태로 만들어 반찬으로 조금씩 먹기도 한다. 당신이 방문한 한국 음식점에서 우연히 접할 가능성도 꽤 된다.

이것 말고도 한국인만 먹는 특별한 음식은 더 많다. 골뱅이라는 것도 술안주로 꽤 인기가 있는데, 한국식 달팽이 요리라고 생각하면 된다. 외국에서는 다람쥐나 먹는 것으로 알려진 도토리도 한국인들은 묵으로 만들어서 즐겨 먹는다. 도토리묵은 반찬으로도 먹고 술안주로도 먹는다. 외국인들의 눈에는 갈색 푸딩처럼 보일 텐데, 한국인들은 이걸 젓가락으로 집어 먹는다(전 세계에서 한국인이 젓가락질을 가장 잘한다). 콩나물도 한국을 제외한 나라에서는 거의 먹지 않지만, 한국인들은 엄청나게 자주 먹는 음식이다. 제법 많은 나라에서 먹는 숙주나물과 비슷하지만 좀더 단단한 편이다. 물론 한국인은 숙주나물도 먹는다. 그 외에도 수없이 많은 풀이나 나뭇잎을 한국인은 음식으로 먹는다.

한국인이 가끔이라도 먹는 채소의 종류는 3백 가지가 넘는다. 한국인이 전혀 먹지 않는 풀은 독초라고 생각하면 된다는 농담도 있다. 종류만 많은 것이 아니라 채소의 섭취량도 많다. 고기도 상당히 많이 먹는 한국인의 비만율이 다른 나라에 비해 현저히 낮은 것도 이와 관련이 있을 것이다.

어쩌면 외국인들은 의아해할지도 모르겠다. 인간이 어떻게 그렇게 다양한 식물을 먹을 수 있느냐고. 비결은 채소와 함께 먹는 다양한 양념들에 있다. 평범하고 특별한 맛이 없는 채소도 앞에서 설명한 쌈장이나 고추장에 찍어 먹으면 이야기가 달라진다. (한국인은 심지어 삶은 양배추도 잘 먹는다. 쌈장만 있으면. 한국인은 심지어 브로콜리도 잘 먹는다. 초고추장만 있으면.) 거기에 참기름을 섞으면 더욱 맛있다.

여기서 '나물'이라고 하는 단어를 설명해야겠다. 나물은 사람이 먹을 수 있는 풀이나 나뭇잎 혹은 그것을 삶거나 볶거나 날것으로 양념하여 무친 음식을 통칭하는 단어다. 웬만한 채소는 살짝 데친 다음 된장 혹은 간장과 참기름을 넣고 버무리면 그럴듯한 반찬이 된다. (나중에 다시 설명할 비빔밥은 사실 여러 종류의 나물에 밥을 더한 다음, 거기에 다시 고추장이나 참기름을 추가하여 비벼 먹는 음식이다.)

끝으로 아마도 당신이 쉽게 접하기 힘들거나 혹시 발견하더라도 쉽게 먹기 힘든 '한국인만 먹는' 음식 몇 가지를 소개한다. 우선 미더덕이라는 것이 있다. 해안에 서식하는 무척추동물이며, 모양이나 식감은 별로지만 특유의 바다 냄새 때문에 좋아하는 사람이 제법 있다. 해물찜 등에 흔히 넣으며, 된장찌개에 넣기도 한다. 그리고 외국인들은 대개 질겁하지만 한국인들이 길거리 음식이나 술안주로 즐기는 번데기가 있다. 모든 곤충의 번데기를 다 먹는 것이 아니라 딱 한 종류, 누에나방의 번데기만 먹는다. 모양이 벌레 같아서 그렇지(뭐, 실제로 벌레이긴 하지만), 모르고 먹으면 맛은 꽤 좋다(하지만 한국인 중에도 안 먹는 사람이 꽤 있다).

영화 〈올드보이〉에 등장하여 유명해진 산낙지도 있다. 영화에서처럼 먹는 한국인은 아무도 없고, 잘게 잘라서 참기름과 소금을 적당히 뿌린 다음 먹는다. 실제로 살아 있는 것은 아니니, 움직이는 것을 먹기가 꺼려진다면 움직임이 멈출 때까지 기다렸다가 먹으면 된다(생각보다 금방 멈춘다). 낙지는 말하자면 작은 문어다. 문어를 '악마의 물고기'라고 부르며 기피하는 나라도 많지만, 한국에서 문어는 상당히 귀한 음식으로 취급된다. 심지어 이름 자체가 '문학 물고기'다. 오징어는 당연히 한국에서도 인기 있는 해산물이며, 크기가 아주 작은 주꾸미라는 것도 있다. 한국인들은 이걸 다 좋아한다. 문어와 낙지는 상당히 비싼 편이고, 오징어와 주꾸미는 훨씬 저렴하다. 산낙지는 굳이 도전하지 않아도 좋지만, 낙지를 매운 양념에 볶은 '낙지볶음'은 추천하고 싶다. 당신에게 멋진 추억(?)을 만들어줄 만큼 충분히 맵다.

진짜 마지막으로, 넷플릭스 시리즈 〈수리남〉(외교적 문제로 인해 영문 제목은 'Narco-Saints', 그러니까 '마약상 성자'로 바뀌었다)에 등장하는 홍어가 있다(실제로는 수리남이 아니라 칠레나 아르헨티나에서 많이 수입한다. 한국산 홍어는 정말 비싸서, 8킬로그램 한 마리에 수백 달러다). 홍어는 한국 음식 중에서 가장 강력하고도 독특한 향이 난다. 날로 먹어도 향이 강하지만, 이것을 발효시켜 향을 더 강하게 만들어서 먹기도 한다. 중국의 취두부, 동남아의 두리안, 북유럽의 루테피스크(lutefisk), 스웨덴의 수르스트뢰밍(surströmming) 등을 먹을 수 있는 사람이면 한국의 홍어도 먹을 수 있다. 한국인들은 삭힌 홍어를 삶은 돼지고기와 많이 숙성된 김치와 함께 먹는 것을 선호하며, 세 가지를 모았다는 의미의 '삼합'이라 부른다. 한국인의 40퍼센트는 삭힌 홍어를 좋아하고, 30퍼센트는 가끔 먹기는 하지만 즐기지는 않고, 30퍼센트는 한 번도 먹어보지 않은 것으로 추산된다(그냥 나의 짐작이다). 당신은 어디까지 도전해보고 싶은가?

10.

Only Korea,
Only Korean

What's the deal with the grub they serve up to new moms in your countries? A refreshing beer to celebrate their well-deserved break? A comforting steak to lift their spirits? Like, if you're in the Netherlands, you'll be enjoying beschuit met muisjes(rust with mice), and in Turkiye, it's all about that lohusa serbeti(postpartum sherbet). Other nations got their own sparkling food for the occasion. But those foods are usually just one-time deals, serving as symbolic gestures with blessings or well-wishes. In Korea, they take things to the next level. New moms get to slurp down the same dish for every meal, day in and day out, for two to three weeks straight. And what's this magical dish that Korean moms can't get enough of, you ask? None other than "miyeokguk", sea mustard soup.

Do people in your country have any particular foods they like to chow down on to celebrate birthdays? Now, if you're from the land down under or the Kiwi country, you probably think of fairy bread, and if you're Swedish, maybe you've got princess cake on your mind. And in China, there's a noodle called longevity noodle that's believed to bring good luck. For the most part, birthday specialties around the world tend to be desserts. However, Korea breaks the mold. On their birthdays, Koreans must slurp on some sea mustard soup. In Korea, the phrase "I didn't even get to eat sea mustard soup." is used as an idiom to describe a 'lonely birthday' or 'poorly celebrated birthday.'

Miyeok, also known as sea mustard, is a type of seaweed that holds sizable culinary importance in Korea. While many countries incorporate edible seaweed into their cuisine, none quite rival the consumption of seaweed in Korea. Koreans have a diverse range of seaweed dishes and consume it in substantial quantities. Miyeok is a prime example of the favored seaweed, but there are several others. One Korean seaweed variety that has garnered international recognition is "gim," also referred to as laver. (We will explore laver in more detail later on.)

Miyeok offers a variety of culinary possibilities beyond its usage in soup. In Korea, it can be enjoyed straight from the sea, often paired with a dipping sauce called "chogochujang." This spicy sauce is made with gochujang, sugar, and vinegar. This dipping sauce is also used as a condiment for Korean sashimi. Its appearance may resemble ketchup, but with a appealing spiciness. Another enticing way to savor miyeok is in the form of a salad when paired with the appropriate dressing. However, the traditional method of preparing miyeok in Korea is through making miyeokguk. This involves soaking and cooking dried miyeok instead of using fresh sea mustard. While beef is the most common ingredient used in miyeokguk, various types of seafood such as clams, abalone, oysters, and fish can also be used to create this flavorful soup.

While it may seem unusual to have sea mustard soup as a staple meal for several weeks after giving birth, what's even more unique is the location where it's consumed. In Korea, the majority of mothers give birth in hospitals and are then transferred to a "sanhujoriwon," or postpartum care center, instead of going home immediately. It is estimated that approximately 80% of Korean mothers spend two to three weeks at these centers to receive specialized postpartum care before returning home with their newborns.

The practice of "sanhujori" is a deeply ingrained tradition in Korea and is taken very seriously as part of the postpartum care routine. During this time, it is believed that the mother needs to rest and recover for a few weeks after giving birth. In Korea, there is a strong belief that proper postpartum care is essential for a mother's well-being, and a lack of it may lead to potential health problems in the future. However, it is important to note that there is limited scientific evidence to support these widespread beliefs.

In the past, during the postpartum period, the mother was often relieved of domestic duties and was not solely responsible for taking care of the child. Instead, it became the responsibility of the entire family to support and care for both the mother and the newborn. This practice allowed the mother to focus on her recovery and bonding with the baby. Unfortunately, not all women had access to such support and some may have been subjected to inconsiderate treatment from their husbands or in-laws, compelling them to undertake strenuous tasks shortly after giving birth.

However, in the age of the nuclear family, finding someone to help with postpartum care has become increasingly challenging, leading to the rise of postpartum care centers as an alternative. These centers emerged in the mid-1990s and have since become widespread. Mothers choose to stay at these centers to rest, breastfeed their babies, engage in exercise programs, receive massages, and form friendships with other mothers who have recently given birth. These newfound friendships often extend beyond the center, resulting in postpartum reunions that can last for years. Husbands typically visit after work to spend time with their children and wives.

These postpartum care centers are not government-funded or covered by insurance. Instead, individuals are required to pay for the services in full. The cost of staying at these centers is higher than that of a standard hotel stay, as it includes accommodation, three meals a day, childcare service, and a range of additional amenities. The price for a two-week stay usually amounts to around $2,000, varying depending on the location and facilities of the center. Opting for a suite can increase the cost to well over $3,000, with the most luxurious options reaching upwards of $10,000.

If you have a desire to taste sea mustard soup while in Korea, it can be a bit of a game of chance. While there are a few specific restaurants, primarily located in coastal cities, which specialize in different types of sea mustard soup, some restaurants in Seoul offer it as a side dish alongside many other options. In such cases, the portion size may not be substantial, and the flavor may not be particularly outstanding.

Anyway, despite its association with birthdays, sea mustard soup remains a beloved dish in Korea and is commonly enjoyed beyond special occasions. If you're eager to try it and don't have the opportunity to visit a restaurant that serves it, you can still experience the flavors by purchasing ready-made sea mustard soup from convenience stores. These pre-packaged options simply require you to add hot water or microwave them for a few minutes, providing a convenient way to enjoy this authentic Korean dish.

The love for sea mustard soup among Korean mothers is indeed special. It is said that even those who don't typically enjoy it find themselves consuming it, in spite of being boring. Sea mustard soup may hold a symbolic significance as a ritual, a way of praying for the health and happiness of a newborn baby. According to legend, the success of the Cha Hospital Group, which started as a single maternity clinic and has now expanded to include multiple large hospitals, medical schools, and related businesses, can be attributed to the "delicious sea mustard soup" served to new mothers. (Even the Los Angeles branch of Cha Hospital serves it to new mothers.)

The reason behind insisting on mothers to eat sea mustard soup is still not entirely clear, but there are some theories. One of them is that the soup's high iodine content is beneficial for the mother and the child's health. However, it's worth noting that excessive iodine intake can cause or exacerbate thyroid problems and other issues, as cautioned by doctors. Another likely but unfounded explanation is that it is a matter of convenience for the person responsible for cooking during the postpartum period, such as the mother or mother-in-law, who may find it laborious to prepare a new side dish for each meal.

It is indeed amusing to note that in Korea, there is a custom of avoiding sea mustard soup during exams. This is due to the slimy texture of sea mustard, as the Korean word for "slip" is associated with negative connotations related to exam failure. Instead, people often choose foods such as "chabssaltteog," a glutinous rice cake, or "yeot," a rice taffy, which have a sticky texture. This preference is influenced by the positive associations of the Korean word for "stick" with passing an exam.

Korean wedding and funeral customs differ from those of other cultures. In Korea, guests are expected to give money as a gift for both ceremonies and the amount varies depending on the relationship and financial means of the guest. Typically, it's common to give $50 or $100 in an envelope. (If someone is unable to attend the wedding or funeral in person, it's common for them to pass on their monetary gift to another attendee or to pay online.) Attendance is also much higher than in other countries, with hundreds of people often attending, and over a thousand people may attend if the individuals involved have high social status. (Weddings are generally an hour-long ceremony and require a large space, while funerals last for two nights and three days and require less space.) The scale of these events can make them quite costly, which can be a burden for most people. To alleviate the burden, there is a culture of acquaintances contributing little by little to the cost. Although there are ways to have a smaller ceremony and not exchange moneys, it's difficult to change the culture once it's formed.

Another intriguing aspect of Korean weddings is the concept of "guest jobs." In Korean culture, it is considered embarrassing to have a wedding with too few guests. Therefore, if the number of invitees falls short for any reason, people may opt to pay a small fee to bring in fake guests. While this practice is not very common, it is not unheard of either. In the movie "Parasite," actress Park So-dam's character mentioned her past experience with "hired wedding guest."

It is noteworthy to highlight another exceptional aspect of funerals in Korea: the common practice of locating funeral homes within hospitals. In Korea, funeral services typically span a period of three days, attracting a considerable number of guests who come to offer their condolences. In the past, funerals were often conducted in private homes. However, as societal dynamics have evolved, it has become increasingly challenging to host funerals at home, leading to the establishment of dedicated funeral facilities. Given that many individuals pass away in hospitals, having funeral homes in close proximity has become convenient. While the idea of having a funeral home within a hospital may seem unusual to some foreigners, Koreans view it as a natural arrangement. It is worth mentioning that these funeral facilities are usually situated in discrete areas of the hospital.

One of the distinguishing characteristics of the Korean real estate rental culture is the practice of "jeonse." In Korea, there are two primary types of housing rentals: monthly rentals, which are common in other countries, and jeonse, which involves paying a considerable deposit to the landlord and not paying any monthly rent for the duration of the contract, commonly two years. At the end of the contract, the tenant receives their deposit back in full. In the case of jeonse, the deposit amount is substantial, often exceeding half the price of the house. For example, for a $1 million house, the deposit would range between $500,000 and $700,000. (Is the price of $1 million for the house described in the example considered too high? Due to Korea's limited land area and dense population, real estate prices, particularly in Seoul, are generally high. It is not uncommon for a small 100-square-meter apartment to cost over $1 million, and homes in certain neighborhoods may range from $3 million to $4 million or even higher.) While the jeonse system may appear straightforward, it can be complex, especially in Seoul where the demand for housing is intense, and real estate prices are continuously rising. The Korean government has made efforts to address the issues associated with the jeonse system in recent decades, but the controversy surrounding it remains unresolved.

The "banjiha" or semi-basement housing is indeed a notable aspect of real estate in Korea. These homes are situated with their floors more than a meter below ground level, while the windows are positioned above ground, allowing occupants to have a view of the outside. Usually, these houses are occupied by low-income families. However, banjiha housing often faces issues such as dampness and mold, leading to a characteristic odor that can cling to clothes and skin. The portrayal of this type of housing in the movie Parasite brought attention to its unique characteristics and living conditions.

Semi-basement housing has a historical and cultural context that dates back to the late 1960s. In 1968, a group of North Korean special force operatives infiltrated Seoul with the aim of assassinating the president. Out of the 31 operatives, 28 were killed, two managed to escape to the North, and one was captured alive. The captured operative eventually returned to South Korea, became a pastor, and now lives in the country at the age of 80s. While the operation ultimately failed, the event left a deep impact on South Korean society. Later, in the 1970s, during a time when tensions between North and South Korea were high(much higher than they are now), the South Korean government made it mandatory for every home to have a basement as a precautionary measure in case of war. Originally, it was illegal to rent out these underground spaces, but in the 1980s, as the housing shortage became more severe, regulations were relaxed and semi-basement housing became home to many low-income families.

Although the number of semi-basement houses in Korea is decreasing, there are still around 320,000 of them, with over 60% of them located in Seoul. The severe flooding caused by the heaviest rainfall in over a century in the summer of 2022 resulted in significant damage, with a particularly devastating impact on these homes, causing deaths. The water flooding scene in Parasite, which served as an excellent metaphor for the wealth inequality in Korean society, tragically became a reality in 2022.

Surrogate driving is a unique practice in Korean culture where a person can hire a driver to operate their car after they have been drinking. The service is very popular in Korea, where drinking is relatively tolerated. The price is usually higher than a one-way taxi fare and lower than a round-trip taxi fare. If you've been drinking in front of work, it's more economical to use a surrogate driving service than to park your car, take a taxi home, and then take a taxi to work the next morning. However, it can be challenging to find drivers between 10 p.m. and midnight due to the high demand. In the pre-smartphone era, drivers were called by phone, and now most people use apps. Such services exist in some foreign countries, including Okinawa in Japan, but they are not as common as they are in Korea.

Koreans have characteristic customs surrounding alcohol. One such custom is the belief that alcohol should be served to each other. So, it is occasionally considered somewhat impolite or improper not to refill someone's glass after they have emptied it, or to pour a drink for oneself. In bars, it is common for someone to ask, "Are you busy?" out of the blue, which is a playful way of saying, "Are you so busy you don't have time to pour me a drink?" When someone pours a drink, it is important to accept it with a glass in hand. Between friends, one hand is acceptable for pouring or receiving drinks, but if pouring for someone in authority or receiving drinks from someone in authority, two hands should be used. There was also a custom of "sharing the glass", although this is gradually disappearing due to hygiene concerns. This is the act of emptying one's own glass (after pretending to wipe it formally with a tissue) and then holding it out to the other person to pour them a drink. It's interpreted as a sign of intimacy, but many people don't like this custom.

It's quite surprising that there are a number of unique Korean foods you won't find anywhere else in the world. (Think about it - can you name a food that's exclusive to your country and not enjoyed anywhere else on the planet? It's a rare find, but Korea has several such dishes. What a diversity of Korean food culture!) While a few of these might seem unconventional in looks or taste, making them somewhat challenging for foreign palates, most can be sampled by newcomers without much fuss.

One fruit that's worth trying in Korea is "chamoe", a type of Korean melon. This exotic fruit features a vibrant yellow skin and white flesh, falling between the size of a cantaloupe and an apple. While its flavor resembles that of a melon, chamoe possesses its own distinctive taste that sets it apart. It's not easy to find outside of Korea, and if you do spot it in some countries, chances are it was imported from Korea. If you visit Korea during the summer, be sure to give chamoe a try.

Next, we have "kkaennip," also known as perilla leaf. While sesame is a well-known ingredient, kkaennip must be less familiar. You probably don't know anyone who hasn't shouted "Open sesame" at least once as a child, inspired by the story of "Ali Baba and the Forty Thieves" from One Thousand and One Nights. (There's also the globally successful children's program Sesame Street.) Also, sesame has been around long enough to be one of the first crops humans cultivated for oil. Although it may not be as commonly used in the West, sesame oil is a crucial ingredient in East Asian cuisine, including Korean dishes like bibimbap, which you've most likely tried.

Perilla seeds, similar in appearance to sesame seeds but particularly distinct, have an exclusive place in South Korean cuisine. Despite their visual resemblance to sesame, these seeds belong to a different botanical category. While shiso is appreciated in Japan, and coriander or cilantro is commonly used in Southeast Asian dishes, perilla stands apart. This exceptional plant is versatile in its usage, setting it apart from its culinary counterparts. Sesame seeds can be enjoyed whole or pressed into oil. Shiso and cilantro are primarily cherished for their leaves. On the other hand, perilla offers a range of culinary possibilities. Its seeds can be consumed directly or pressed for oil, while its leaves are equally delectable. Roasted perilla seeds, when ground into a powder, serve as a characteristic spice in many Korean dishes. However, the crowning glory of perilla lies in its leaves, a culinary treasure unique to Korean traditions. Interestingly, many Koreans may not even be aware that these leaves are exclusive to Korean cuisine. In fact, some mistakenly believe they are eating sesame leaves. This confusion might arise because sesame oil is much more prevalent than perilla oil, but it's important to note that sesame leaves aren't a part of the Korean culinary repertoire either.

If the term "kkaennip" sounds familiar, you're certainly diving deep into this book. If you can even pinpoint where you encountered it, your memory is quite outstanding. It was introduced earlier as one of the vegetables commonly paired with pork belly. While it might not boast the same level of fragrance as shiso or cilantro (a point Japanese and Vietnamese individuals might contest), or the robust aroma of Western herbs like thyme, rosemary, parsley, and basil (though Westerners may have a different perspective), perilla leaves are certainly worth a try. At first bite, you might think you're just chewing on a leaf and wonder why you're eating it. But, as you savor the experience and take your time, you will discover a subtle flavor with a hint of mint and a gentle bitterness. Rest assured, perilla leaves are perfectly safe to consume. So go ahead and give them a try!

Koreans have a wide range of culinary applications for

perilla leaves. They are commonly paired with grilled meats and sashimi, adding a fresh and aromatic element to the dishes. Perilla leaves are also used in salads, stews, and soups, enhancing the overall flavor profile. Additionally, perilla leaves are utilized in the preparation of kimchi or pickles, serving as a flavorful and aromatic side dish. When dining at a Korean restaurant, you'll frequently find perilla leaves used in a variety of dishes.

Besides, Koreans enjoy a variety of exclusive dishes not found elsewhere. One such delicacy is "golbaengi," also known as moon snail. Golbaengi is a well-liked drinking snack and can be compared to the Korean version of escargot. Another unusual ingredient is "dotori," which translates to acorn. In Korea, acorns are transformed into "muk," a type of jelly that serves as a side dish or snack, often enjoyed with alcohol. Dotori-muk resembles brown pudding and is commonly eaten using chopsticks, showcasing the dexterity of Koreans who are known for their excellent chopstick skills. "Kongnamul," or soybean sprouts, is another unique food in Korean cuisine. While similar to the mung bean sprouts consumed in many other countries (of course including Korea), kongnamul has a slightly firmer texture. Koreans also have a tradition of incorporating various grasses and leaves into their meals.

Koreans have a remarkably diverse palate when it comes to vegetables, with more than 300 types being consumed at least occasionally. There's a lighthearted joke that goes: 'If Koreans don't eat a type of grass, it must be poisonous.' Not only do Koreans eat a wide variety of vegetables, but they also consume them in substantial quantities. Despite a considerable meat consumption, the obesity rate in Korea is lower compared to other countries. This could be attributed to the abundance and variety of vegetables in their diet.

Maybe, it can be hard for foreigners to understand how humans can eat so many different plants. The key to understanding the consumption of such a diverse array of vegetables lies in the variety of condiments used to enhance their flavors. Even plain, unremarkable vegetables can be transformed by dipping them in the aforementioned ssamjang or gochujang. Koreans will even enjoy boiled cabbage (as long as they have a ssamjang) or broccoli (as long as they have a gochujang). The addition of sesame oil further enhances the taste.

At this point, it's important to clarify the meaning of the word 'namul'. Namul refers to a wide range of human-edible grasses and leaves, as well as foods that are boiled, stir-fried, or served raw and seasoned. Most vegetables can be quickly blanched and dressed with doenjang or soy sauce and sesame oil to create a delicious side dish. Bibimbap, which we'll discuss later, consists of rice mixed with a variety of vegetables and seasoned with gochujang and sesame oil.

Lastly, here are a few "only Koreans eat" foods that you probably don't come across very often, or if you do, they're not easy to eat. Among these foods is "mideodeok," which is a stalked sea squirt found in coastal areas. It's a coastal invertebrate that doesn't look or taste great, but some people love it for its distinctive sea smell. Mideodeok is commonly used in steamed seafood dishes and doenjang jjigae, a traditional fermented soybean paste stew. Then there's "beondegi" which often puts off foreigners but enjoyed by Koreans as street food or as a snack with alcohol. Beondegi refers to silkworm pupae. It's worth noting that Koreans consume the pupae of a specific species, the silkworm, and not any other insects. Although they may resemble worms (it's natural because they are indeed worms), they have a pleasant taste if one can ignore what it is. However, not all Koreans enjoy this particular food.

There is a Korean dish called "san-nakji," which refers to

live small octopus, that gained global awareness through the movie "Oldboy." However, it's important to note that Koreans do not consume it in the manner depicted in the movie. Instead, the small octopus is typically chopped up, seasoned with sesame oil and salt, and eaten. Although it may seem alive due to its movement, it is not. If you're hesitant to try it because of its appearance, you can wait until it stops moving, which usually happens quickly. Octopus, which is referred to as "mooneo" in Korean, is highly regarded in Korean cuisine, despite being referred to as a "devil fish" in some countries. In fact, its Korean name translates to "literature fish." Squid is of course a popular seafood in Korea, and there's also a very small version called "jukkumi" (web-foot octopus). Koreans enjoy all of these seafood delicacies, but octopus and small octopus tend to be more expensive, while squid and jukkumi are relatively affordable. If you're not inclined to try live small octopus, I recommend sampling the spicy stir-fried small octopus dish called "nakji-bokkeum." It is known for its fiery spiciness and is sure to leave an impressive memory to you.

Lastly again, there is a Korean delicacy called "hongeo," which refers to skate, featured in the Netflix series "Narco-Saints"(although it is actually imported from Chile and Argentina, not Suriname). Skate caught off the coast of Korea is particularly expensive, with an 8-kilogram fish costing hundreds of dollars. Hongeo has one of the most distinguishable and powerful flavors among all Korean foods. When consumed raw, it possesses a strongly pronounced taste, but it is also fermented to intensify its flavor. If you can handle stinky tofu in China, durian in Southeast Asia, lutefisk in Northern Europe, and surströmming in Sweden, then you can certainly give Korean skate a try. Koreans often enjoy it with boiled pork and aged kimchi, which they refer to as "samhap," meaning three things together. It is estimated that approximately 40% of Koreans enjoy hongeo, 30% consume it occasionally but do not necessarily enjoy it, and 30% have never tasted it (this is just my estimation). Are you willing to go the extra mile and give it a try?

11.
한글, 발명자가 알려진 유일한 알파벳

알파벳은 누가 만들었나? 세르게이 브린(Sergey Brin)과 래리 페이지(Larry Page)가 창고에서 함께 만들었다고? 그 알파벳 말고 진짜 알파벳을 처음 고안한 사람은 누구일까? 당연히 우리는 그게 누군지 모른다. 아주 오래전에 페니키아(Phoenicia) 문자의 영향을 받아 그리스문자가 생겨나고, 그것이 영어를 비롯한 여러 언어 알파벳의 기원이라는 것을 알 뿐이다.

그럼 중국의 문자인 한자는 누가 만들었나? 이 질문도 복잡한 한자의 모양처럼 어려운 것이다. 아주 오래전에 상형문자가 있었고, 그것이 점차 발전하여 복잡한 문자 체계가 만들어졌다고 짐작할 뿐이다. '가나'라고 부르는 일본의 문자 역시 한자의 획 일부를 활용하여 만들어진 것이라는 사실을 알 뿐, 언제 누가 개발했는지는 알 수가 없다. 다른 여러 언어권의 문자나 아라비아 숫자도 마찬가지다.

한글이라고 부르는 한국어 알파벳만이 예외다. 한글은 1443년에 세종대왕이 창제한 문자다. 물론 혼자 해낸 일은 아니고, 세종의 지시를 받은 여러 학자가 오랜 기간 노력한 끝에 만든 것이긴 하다. 그러나 새로운 문자 체계를 만든다는 혁명적인 시도는 왕의 결단과 후원이 없이는 불가능한 일이기에, '세종대왕이 한글을 발명했다'는 표현은 결코 과장이 아니다. 실제로 세종은 한글의 개발 과정에 깊숙이 관여한 것으로 전해진다.

한국인은 아주 오래전부터 고유의 언어를 사용했지만, 고유의 문자를 갖지는 못했다. 그럼 15세기까지는 어떤 문자를 썼을까. 소수의 지식인은 한자를 사용했고, 나머지 대다수 백성은 문자를 사용하지 못했다. 하지만 한자를 공부한 사람들도 그것을 이용하여 한국어를 그대로 표기할 수 있었던 것은 아니다. 중국어와 한국어는 완전히 다른 언어이기 때문이다. 당연히 모든 한국인의 언어생활은 대단히 불편했다.

당시의 지식인들은 현대인이 외국어를 공부하듯 어릴 때부터 한자를 배웠고, 한자로 쓰인 문장을 해독하고 한자로 자신의 생각을 기록할 수 있는 능력을 갖추고 있었다. 즉 말하기와 듣기는 한국어로 하고, 읽기와 쓰기는 중국어로 했다고도 할 수 있다. 하지만 중국어로 대화를 할 수 있는 사람은 소수에 불과했다. 한자로 기록된 문서를 읽을 때는 한국식 발음으로 읽었다. 모든 한자에는 (중국인의 발음과는 다른) 한국식 발음이 정해져 있었던 것이다. 관리를 뽑는 시험도 한자로 치러졌고, 국가의 모든 문서는 한자로 기록되었다. 시도 중국 문자로 썼고, 소설도 중국 문자로 썼다. 한자를 배울 기회를 얻지 못한 대다수 백성은 무언가를 새로 배우기도 쉽지 않았고, 자신의 생각을 다른 사람에게 전달하기도 쉽지 않았다.

조선왕조의 네번째 왕인 세종대왕은 이런 상황을 타개하고자 했다. 모든 백성이 쉽게 읽고 쓸 수 있는 문자를 새로 만들 생각을 한 것이다. 하지만 당시의 지식인들 대부분은 이러한 시도에 격렬하게 저항했다. 언제나 눈치를 보며 살았던 중국의 심기를 거스르지 않을까 하는 외교적(?) 고려도 없지 않았겠지만, 다른 이유도 있었을 것이다.

읽기와 쓰기를 할 수 없는 대다수 백성은 매우 불편했겠지만, 한자를 아는 지식인들의 불편은 사실 그리 크지 않았다. 오히려 한자를 이해하는 능력은 일종의 특권이었고, 한자 사용 능력은 지배계급의 상징인 동시에 신분 사회의 질서를 유지하는 장치였던 것이다. 모든 사람이 문자를 알게 되어 지식수준이 높아지면, 자신들이 누리고 있는 기득권을 조금이나마 내려놓아야 할지도 모른다는 불안감이 저항의 이유였다.

그러나 세종은 강력한 추진력을 발휘했고, 마침내 한국어에 가장 잘 어울리는 새로운 문자를 만들어냈다. 당시의 이름은 '훈민정음'이었는데, '백성을 가르치는 바른 소리'라는 뜻이다. 당시 왕의 이름으로 발표된 창제의 이유는 세종의 정신을 잘 드러내고 있다.

"나라의 말이 중국과 달라서 (중국의) 문자와는 서로 맞지 아니하여, 백성들이 말하고자 하는 바가 있어도 자신의 뜻을 제대로 펼치지 못하는 경우가 많다. 내가 이를 안타깝게 생각하여 새로 스물여덟 글자를 만드니, 모든 사람이 쉽게 익혀서 날마다 편안하게 사용하기를 바란다."

그렇다. 한글은 처음 만들어질 때는 스물여덟 글자였다. 자음이 17개, 모음이 11개였다. 이후 네 개의 글자는 사용하지 않게 되어, 지금은 자음 14개에 모음 10개, 총 스물네 글자로 이루어져 있다. 영어 알파벳보다 글자 수가 두 개 적지만, 이것을 조합하여 정말 다양한 소리를 표기할 수 있다. (자음을 두 개 붙여서 쓰거나 모음을 두 개 이상 붙여서 쓰는 방식이 존재하기 때문에, 실제 사용되는 자음과 모음의 개수는 좀더 많다.)

한국어는 외국인이 배우기 쉽지 않은 언어다. 영어권 사람들에게는 특히 어렵다. 하지만 한글은 의외로 쉽다. 당신도 일주일만 공부하면 한글을 읽을 수는 있게 된다. 진짜다. (물론 그 의미를 이해할 수는 없고, 그저 발음을 할 줄 알게 된다는 뜻이다.)

이게 가능한 이유는, 한글은 모든 글자가 똑같은 구조를 갖고 있기 때문이다. 자음과 모음을 결합하여 하나의 글자를 만드는 방식인데, 둘 중 하나다. 자음 더하기 모음, 아니면 자음 더하기 모음 더하기 자음. 그래서 모든 글자가 네모반듯하다. 네모반듯한 것은 한자와 비슷하지만, 그보다 훨씬 간단하다. 외국인들의 눈에 한자가 복잡한 그림이나 암호처럼 느껴진다면, 한글은 기호나 로고처럼 느껴진다고나 할까.

10여 년 전, 브리트니 스피어스가 한글이 새겨진 드레스를 입은 모습이 한국인들 사이에서 큰 화제가 된 적이 있는데, 아마도 그녀의 눈에는 한글이 독특한 디자인 요소로 보였기 때문이지 싶다(그 옷에 적힌 일곱 글자의 내용이 아주 독특해서 더욱 화제가 되었다. 억지로 비유하자면 이런 뜻이었다. '할리우드에 사는 플로리다 태생들의 친목 모임.' 물론 실제로는 할리우드나 플로리다가 아니라 한국의 지명이었다. 외국에도 이런 모임이 많이 있는지는 모르겠으나, 출신 지역이 같은 것을 큰 인연으로 생각하는 경향이 있는 한국인들은 이런 종류의 모임을 많이 만드는 편이다). 최근에는 한글이 디자인 요소로 들어간 패션 아이템을 찾는 외국인들이 점차 늘어나는 추세이다.

또한 한글은 컴퓨터나 스마트폰에 글자를 입력할 때 아주 편리하다. 알파벳을 이루는 글자 수가 24개밖에 되지 않고, 자음과 모음이 계속 반복되는 방식을 가졌기 때문이다. 먼저 키보드를 생각해보자. 영어 알파벳 26개 자리에 각각 한글의 자음이나 모음을 하나씩 배열하고 나면 두 자리가 남는다. 그 자리에는 모음을 두 개 붙여서 쓰는 경우 중에서 가장 자주 쓰이는 것을 배치해놓았다. 입력을 할 때는 그냥 필요한 글자들을 고르기만 하면 된다. 한글은 대문자 소문자 구별이 없고, 유럽 문자들에 흔히 등장하는 복잡한 첨가 기호가 전혀 없어서 더욱 편하다. 키보드의 한정된 공간에 모든 주요 문자들을 전부 대응시킬 수 없어서 자국의 문자를 영어식으로 발음하면서 여러 번 변환키를 눌러야 하는 언어들에 비하면 한글은 키보드 입력 분야에서는 거의 최고의 효율을 자랑한다.

자음과 모음을 반복해서 입력하는 것도 타이핑 속도를 높이는 요소가 된다. 한글 키보드에서 자음은 대부분 왼손으로, 모음은 대부분 오른손으로 입력하게 되어 있다. 때문에 한글 타자에서는 왼손 혹은 오른손을 세 번 이상 연속해서 사용하는 경우가 거의 없다. 다른 문자를 입력할 때는 왼손과 오른손의 사용 빈도가 불규칙적인 것이 보통이고, water나 million과 같이 한쪽 손만 써서 입력하는 단어도 제법 있다(영어 단어 중에는 무려 열두 번이나 연속해서 한쪽 손을 사용해야 하는 단어도 있다. stewardesses).

스마트폰을 이용할 때는 한글의 이러한 장점이 더욱 빛난다. 키보드 입력과 비슷한 방식으로 입력하는 것도 물론 가능하지만, 다른 방법도 있다. 자음은 그대로 14개가 필요하지만, 기본만 10개이고 실제로는 훨씬 여러 개인 모음 모두를 단 세 개의 자판만 사용해서 입력할 수도 있기 때문이다. 그것은 세종대왕이 한글을 처음 만들 때부터 모음은 점, 가로선, 세로선, 이렇게 세 가지 요소를 조합하여 만드는 방식을 택했기 때문이다(점은 하늘, 가로선은 땅, 세로선은 사람을 뜻한다). 처음 보면 한글의 모음은 가로선과 세로선의 복잡한 조합으로 이루어져 있는 것처럼 보이지만, 사실 짧은 선과 긴 선이 있다. 가로 혹은 세로로 그어진 하나의 긴 선을 제외한 나머지 짧은 선들은 사실은 '점'이라고 할 수도 있다. (쉽게 설명하려고 정말 열심히 노력하고 있지만, 외국인들은 도대체 이게 뭔 소린가 싶을 것 같긴 하다. 궁금한 분들은 알파벳의 자회사 구글에 접속하여 'korean alphabet'을 검색해보기 바란다.) 실제로 많은 한국인은 단 세 개의 자판만으로 모든 모음을 만들어내면서 놀랍도록 빠른 속도로 문자메시지를 보낼 수 있다.

한글은 한국인들이 매우 자랑스럽게 생각하는 문화유산 중의 하나다. 세종대왕이 한글을 창제하지 않았더라면, 한국인들은 지금도 듣기와 말하기에 사용하는 언어와 쓰기와 읽기에 사용하는 문자가 서로 맞지 아니하여 큰 불편과 혼란을 겪었을 가능성이 크다. 아마도 거기에 영어까지 배워야 하는 삼중고에 시달렸을 것이고. 그래서 세종대왕은 한국인이 가장 존경하는 두 인물 중의 하나다. 다른 한 사람은 16세기 일본의 침략을 막아내는 데 혁혁한 공을 세운 이순신 장군이다. 한국에서 아주 중요한 장소라 할 수 있는 광화문 광장에는 이렇게 딱 두 사람의 동상이 있다(장군은 서 있고, 왕은 앉아 있다). 2009년에 5만 원권 지폐가 등장하기 전까지 오랫동안 가장 고액의 지폐였던 만 원권 지폐에 그려져 있는 인물도 세종대왕이다. 이순신 장군은 지금은 쓰이지 않는 5백 원권 지폐의 도안에 사용됐다.

말이 나온 김에 다른 지폐에 등장하는 인물도 잠시 살펴보자. 천 원권에는 조선시대의 학자 퇴계 이황, 5천 원권에는 역시 조선시대의 학자인 율곡 이이, 5만 원권에는 한국 역사상 최고로 훌륭한 어머니로 손꼽히는 신사임당의 얼굴이 그려져 있다. 신사임당은 시인이자 화가이자 서예가로 이름을 떨쳤으며, 율곡의 어머니로 더욱 유명하다. 어머니와 아들이 모두 지폐의 도안으로 활용된 사례는 전 세계에서 유일하다[어머니와 아들이 모두 노벨상을 받은 경우도 없다. 어머니와 딸이 모두 노벨상을 받은 경우는 마리 퀴리(Marie Curie)와 그녀의 딸 이레네 졸리오 퀴리(Irène Joliot-Curie)

가 있다]. 당신이 혹시 한국의 배우 소지섭의 팬이라면, 천 원권 지폐를 기념으로 하나쯤 챙겨도 좋겠다. 퇴계의 초상화가 소지섭과 제법 닮은 것으로 화제가 된 적이 있기 때문이다(특히 눈 부분은 정말 닮았다).

세종대왕의 업적은 한글 창제만 있는 것이 아니다. 32년의 재위 기간(1418~1450) 동안 정말 어마어마하게 많은 일을 했다. 북쪽으로 영토를 조금 확장하여 지금의 한반도 전체에 해당하는 국경을 확정했고, 다양한 법령을 정비하였으며, 농업과 과학기술의 발전에도 상당한 기여를 했다. 세계 최초의 측우기도 세종 시절에 만들어졌고, 한국의 독특한 부동산 임대 제도인 전세 제도도 세종 때에 확립되었다. 국민 전체를 상대로 설문조사를 실시하기도 하는 등 백성들의 인권 신장에도 크게 기여했다. 한마디로 건국 초기였던 조선이라는 나라의 수준을 한 번에 여러 단계 끌어올린 왕으로 평가받고 있다. 많은 한국인이 세종대왕과 같은 왕이 한두 명만 더 있었더라면 조선의 역사가 크게 달라졌을 것이라 생각한다.

때문에 '세종'이라는 이름은 매우 중요한 의미를 지니며, 지금도 여러 곳에 쓰인다. 광화문 앞 넓은 도로의 이름이 세종로이고, 그곳에 있는 대형 극장의 이름도 세종문화회관이며, 한국의 주요 정부기관이 여럿 밀집해 있는 신도시의 이름 역시 세종특별자치시다. 그 외에도 대학, 호텔 등의 이름에 널리 쓰인다.

그런데 이처럼 훌륭한 세종대왕도 미처 생각하지 못한 것이 하나 있었다. 그것은 바로 띄어쓰기였다. 단어와 단어 사이에 여백을 둘 생각을 하지 못한 것이다. 아마도 여백이란 것이 거의 없는 중국어의 영향이었을 것이다. 한글이 창제 이후 수백 년 동안 세종의 기대만큼 널리 쓰이지 못한 이유 중에는 띄어쓰기가 없었던 것도 한몫했을 것이다(다른 중요한 이유는 지배계급의 의도적 무시였다). 한글 표기에서 띄어쓰기가 시작된 것은 창제 이후 4백 년 이상의 시간이 흐른 19세기 후반이고, 그 이후 한글은 모든 한국인에게 널리 사용되기 시작했다.

한글에 대한 이야기를 마치기 전에, 한국어의 중요한 특징 한 가지만 더 언급한다. 한국어는 존댓말이 매우 발달했다. 다른 언어에도 존댓말이 없지 않지만, 한국어만큼 그것이 발달한 언어는 없을 것이다. 우선 사용하는 단어 자체가 달라지는 경우가 매우 많다. 예를 들어 나이, 이름, 생일, 식사 등 수많은 단어에서, 반말과 존댓말 어휘는 완전히 다르다. 명사만 그런 것도 아니다. 먹다, 묻다, 자다, 주다, 죽다, 말하다 등의 동사도 마찬가지이고, 배고프다와 같은 일부 형용사도 그렇고, 인칭대명사나 호칭도 상대에 따라 다르게 써야 한다. 심지어 같은 단어에 대한 경어 표현이 여러 개인 경우도 있다. 조선시대에는 왕에게만 쓸 수 있는 특별한 경어가 별도로 존재하기도 했고, 지금도 상대방이 얼마나 높은 사람이냐에 따라(회장님이냐 부장님이냐, 할아버지냐 삼촌이냐 등등) 적절한 경어 표현이 달라진다.

별개의 단어가 존재하지 않는 경우에도 경어 표현은 다양하게 가능하다. 명사 뒤에 흔히 따라오는 조사도 경어가 있고, 동사나 형용사의 뒷부분을 조금씩 변화시키는 방법으로도 경어를 만들 수 있다. 한마디로 엄청나게 어렵다(물론 한국인들은 어려워하지 않는다). 그래서 한국인들은 존댓말을 완벽하게 사용하는 외국인을 보면 깜짝 놀란다.

한국인들은 아주 가까운 관계일 때만 반말을 사용하고, 그렇지 않은 대부분의 관계에서는 서로가 존댓말을 사용하는 것이 일반적이다. 처음 만난 사람에게 반말을 쓰는 것은 나이나 지위의 차이가 클 경우에도 무례한 행동으로 받아들여진다. 낯선 사람에게 반말을 쓰는 경우는 불량배가 시비를 걸 때, 강도질을 할 때, 평생의 원수를 맞닥뜨렸을 때 등 극히 제한적이다. 때문에 여행 가이드북 등에 나와 있는 간단한 한국어 표현들도 대부분 존댓말이다. 안녕하세요, 감사합니다, 주세요 등이 다 그렇다(하지만 외국인이 반말을 쓰면, 그 말을 들은 한국인들은 대체로 즐거워한다. 싸우자는 뜻이 아니라 한국어가 서툰 것임을 충분히 알기 때문이다).

존댓말이 이렇게 발달한 것은 위계질서를 중시하는 한국 문화의 특징 때문으로 보인다. 한국은 오랫동안 신분제 사회였고, 같은 신분이라도 나이에 따른 서열을 매우 중시해왔다. 좀 과장해서 말하면, 한국인들은 낯선 사람을 만나면 일단 나이를 확인함으로써 서열을 정하려 하는 경향이 있다. 나이가 많은 사람은 반말을 해도 되고, 나이가 어린 사람은 존댓말을 해야 하기 때문이다. 물론 현대 사회에서는 나이 차이가 나더라도 아주 가까운 사이이거나 나이가 어린 쪽이 먼저 허락했을 때가 아니면 서로가 존댓말을 사용한다.

끝으로, 간단한 인사말을 제외하고, 한국을 여행하는 외국인이

한 번쯤 써보면 재미있을 것 같은 한국어 표현 몇 개만 소개한다(앞에서 이미 '테슬라'와 '아무거나' 등의 표현도 알려준 바 있다).

먼저, '여기요'라는 단어가 있다. '여기'는 'here'이며, '요'는 존댓말을 만들 때 흔히 덧붙이는 말이다. 이 표현은 식당에서 직원을 부를 때(왜 불러야 하는지는 다음 글에서 자세히 설명한다), 혹은 낯선 사람에게 말을 걸 때 'Excuse me'와 비슷한 느낌으로 쓸 수 있는 표현이다. '여기 있는 나에게 관심 좀 가져달라'는 의미가 되겠다.

다음으로 '맛집'이라는 단어가 있다. 직역하면 'taste-house'가 되는 이 표현은, '맛있는 음식을 판매하는 식당'을 지칭한다. 당신이 식당에서 먹은 음식이 매우 맛있을 때, 종업원에게 '여기 맛집이네'라고 말하면 주변의 한국인들이 당신의 한국어 실력에 놀라면서 활짝 웃을 것이다. 엄지손가락을 치켜들면서 말하면 더욱 좋겠다. 이것이야말로 한국에서의 미식 경험을 가장 즐겁고도 완벽하게 표현하는 수단이다.

'대박'이라는 표현도 써볼 수 있겠다. 이 단어는 '대단하다' '잭팟' '놀랍다' 등의 뜻을 담고 있는 말이니, 한국 여행중 뭔가 멋진 경험을 했을 때 사용하면 적절하다. '대'를 길게 끌면서 발음하면 더욱 강력한 표현이 된다. 당신이 맛있게 음식을 먹은 다음 식당을 나설 때, 평범한 인사말(이게 더 암기하기 어렵다) 대신 '대박 나세요'라고 말하면서 떠날 수도 있겠다(장사가 아주 잘되기를 바란다는 뜻이다).

모쪼록 당신이 한국에서 매우 많은 맛집을 방문하기를, 매우 여러 번 '대박'이라고 외치게 되기를 희망한다. 또한 당신의 인생에 여러 번의 '대박'이 찾아오기를 기원할 터이니, 당신은 이 책이 '대박' 나기를 기원해주기 바란다.

11.

Hangeul: The Only Alphabet with a Known Inventor

Who on Earth invented the alphabet? Did Sergey Brin and Larry Page team up in some secret warehouse to create it? And if that wasn't the alphabet we're referring to, who was the genius that came up with the first (English) alphabet? Well, that remains a mystery for the ages! What we do know is that in ancient times, the Greeks drew great inspiration from the Phoenicians, which eventually led to the development of the alphabets we utilize today in some languages such as English.

Then, who invented Chinese characters? It's a question as intricate as the characters themselves. What we can gather is that rudimentary hieroglyphics existed in ancient times and gradually evolved into the complex writing system we know today. While it's clear that the Japanese kana script drew inspiration from Chinese characters, the exact origin story and timeline remain elusive. A similar enigma surrounds the scripts of many other languages and even the fascinating history of Arabic numerals.

The Korean alphabet, Hangeul, stands out as an amazing exception. It was created during the reign of King Sejong the Great in 1443, within the Joseon Dynasty. King Sejong didn't accomplish this monumental task single-handedly; it required years of dedicated effort from a group of talented scholars under his guidance. When we say 'King Sejong invented Hangeul,' we're not just paying him lip service, as his unwavering determination and support were instrumental in bringing this revolutionary and phonetic writing system to life. In fact, it is widely believed that King Sejong himself actively participated in its development.

Since ancient times, Koreans had their own language, but they encountered a major obstacle—they lacked a writing system of their own. Before the 15th century, only a small group of intellectuals relied on Chinese characters, while the majority of the population grappled with their ineffective use. Even those who devoted themselves to studying Chinese characters found it challenging to apply them to the Korean language. The fundamental differences between Chinese and Korean were apparent. As a result, the language experience for all Koreans was marked by discomfort and inconvenience.

Before the invention of Hangeul, intellectuals in Korea dedicated themselves to the study of Chinese characters from a young age, much like how individuals today engage in learning foreign languages. They possessed the ability to decipher sentences written in Chinese characters and express their thoughts through writing using the same script. While their spoken language was Korean, their reading and writing skills revolved around Chinese characters.

However, only a select few were proficient in conversing in Chinese. When reading texts written in Chinese characters, they would pronounce the characters using Korean readings. Each Chinese character had its own Korean pronunciation, separate from its Chinese counterpart. Official examinations for government officials were conducted in Chinese characters, and all official documents were written using the same script. Poetry and novels were also composed in Chinese characters. Unfortunately, the majority of

Koreans who were unable to learn Chinese characters faced significant challenges in acquiring new skills and effectively expressing their thoughts.

King Sejong the Great, the visionary fourth king of the Joseon Dynasty, had a profound desire to transform the linguistic landscape of Korea. His ambitious goal was to create a new writing system that would provide all citizens with easy access to literacy. However, this audacious undertaking encountered strong opposition from the intellectual circles of the time. There may have been diplomatic considerations, as it could potentially offend China, a nation that had exerted considerable influence over Korea for centuries, and there were also other reasons as below.

While the plight of the illiterate majority posed burdensome challenges, it should be noted that intellectuals well-versed in Chinese characters faced relatively fewer inconveniences. In fact, their command of Chinese characters conferred a sense of privilege to the intellectuals themselves, symbolizing their belonging to the ruling class and serving as a mechanism for upholding the existing social hierarchy. Their vehement resistance to the creation of a new writing system was precisely due to these vested advantages. The fear was prominent among the intellectual elite: a more educated populace, empowered by the acquisition of this new script, might lead to the erosion of their privileged positions, necessitating the relinquishment of some of their vested rights.

Undeterred by the resistance, King Sejong persevered and ultimately devised a new script that harmoniously complemented the Korean language. This revolutionary writing system was aptly named "Hun-min-jeong-eum," meaning "the correct sounds for the instruction of the people." The purpose behind its creation, proclaimed in the name of the king himself, encapsulated the very essence of King Sejong's spirit. "The language of Korea differs from that of China, rendering the written language incompatible and limiting the people's ability to effectively convey their thoughts and desires. This lamentable situation has moved me to create a fresh set of twenty-eight characters, designed to be easily learned and comfortably utilized by all individuals in their daily lives."

Indeed, when Hangeul was initially devised, it consisted of 28 letters—17 consonants and 11 vowels. Over time, four of these letters fell out of use, resulting in the current composition of 14 consonants and 10 vowels, totaling 24 letters. Although this may seem slightly fewer than the English alphabet, Hangeul's letters can be ingeniously combined to represent an extensive range of sounds, with specific methods for combining two consonants or including more than two vowels to represent certain sounds, resulting in a more extensive set of characters.

Korean is undeniably a challenging language for foreigners to learn, particularly for English speakers. However, amidst its complexity, Hangeul surprisingly emerges as a beacon of simplicity. Believe it or not, after just a week of dedicated study, one can grasp the ability to read Hangeul. Yes, you read that correctly! (However, this proficiency is limited to pronunciation itself and doesn't guarantee comprehension of meaning.)

The amazing simplicity of Hangeul arises from its consistent structure. Each letter in Hangeul is formed by combining a consonant and a vowel in one of two ways: either a consonant followed by a vowel or a consonant followed by a vowel and another consonant. This consistent combination method results in all Hangeul letters having a square shape. While these squares may bear some resemblance to Chinese characters, they are much simpler in nature. For foreigners, Chinese characters can often appear as intricate drawings or cryptic codes, whereas Hangeul takes the form of recognizable symbols or even logos.

A decade ago, Britney Spears made waves among Koreans when she donned a dress adorned with Hangeul, causing quite a stir. Perhaps, it's because in her eyes, Hangeul held a unique and distinct appeal as a design element. The fact that the seven characters on the dress were so unusual made it even more amusing. To draw an analogy, it could be likened to conveying 'a social group of Florida-born people living in Hollywood.' It wasn't actually referring to Hollywood or Florida, but rather a specific place name in South Korea. While I'm uncertain if such groups exist in abundance in other countries, Koreans have a propensity for forming such associations, as they often find a strong sense of connection in shared origins. Recently, there has been an increasing trend among foreigners to seek out fashion items incorporating Hangeul as a captivating design element.

Hangeul also offers great convenience when it comes to typing on computers or smartphones. With just 24 letters in the alphabet, which are repeated in assorted combinations of consonants and vowels, the typing process becomes straightforward. After placing one consonant and one vowel in each of the 26 spots in the English alphabet, you have two spots left. These two spaces are dedicated to the two most common complex vowels, which are written using two vowels. To type, you simply select the appropriate letters you need.

Hangeul's user-friendliness stems from its lack of case sensitivity and the absence of complex add-on symbols commonly found in European scripts. In comparison to many other languages that struggle to accommodate all their essential characters within the limited keyboard space and require multiple keystrokes or conversion keys for proper input, Hangeul emerges as one of the most efficient languages for keyboard input.

The repetition of consonants and vowels in Hangeul not only contributes to the ease of typing but also enhances typing speed. On the Hangeul keyboard layout, the majority of consonants are conveniently typed with the left hand, while most vowels are efficiently typed with the right hand. As a result, it is uncommon for a Hangeul typist to use either hand more than three times consecutively. In contrast, when typing in other languages, the use of the left and right hands can be irregular, and there are countless words that can be typed with only one hand, such as "water" and "million." Interestingly, there is one English word, "stewardesses," that requires using one hand a staggering twelve times in a row!

The advantage of Hangeul becomes even more pronounced when using a smartphone. While it is possible to type on a smartphone keyboard in a similar way to a regular keyboard, there are additional options available. This is because, while you still need 14 keys for 14 consonants, all of the vowels can be typed using just three keys!

King Sejong the Great, when creating Hangeul, designed the vowels using a combination of three elements: a dot, a horizontal line, and a vertical line. The dot represents the sky, the horizontal line represents the earth, and the vertical line represents the human. Although Hangeul's vowels may appear complex with their combination of horizontal and vertical lines, they can actually be simplified into short and long lines. Apart from one long line, which can be either horizontal or vertical, the other short lines can be considered as dots. (Although I'm trying to make it easy to explain, this may seem a bit perplexing for foreigners. For more information, you can search "Korean alphabet" on Alphabet's subsidiary, Google.) In practice, many Koreans can effectively type all of the vowels using just three letters, enabling them to text at an astonishingly high speed.

Hangeul is a source of immense pride for Koreans. If King Sejong the Great hadn't created Hangeul, Koreans would indeed still have to contend with the challenges of using a writing system that didn't align well with their spoken language. This would have made their linguistic situation even more complicated, especially considering the additional burden of learning English. That is why King Sejong the Great holds a revered place in Korean history, alongside General Yi Sun-sin. General Yi Sun-sin's remarkable achievements in defending against a Japanese invasion in the 16th century have made him another highly respected figure in Korean culture. The statues of both King Sejong and General Yi Sun-sin in Gwanghwamun Square, one of Korea's most significant locations, serve as powerful symbols of their importance. (The general stands, and the king sits behind.)

Additionally, King Sejong's contribution is commemorated by featuring him on the 10,000-won bill, which remained the highest denomination for an extended period until the introduction of the 50,000-won bill in 2009. Similarly, General Yi Sun-sin was honored on the now-discontinued five-hundred-won bill.

Speaking of which, let's explore some other Korean

banknotes. The 1,000-won bill features the face of Joseon Dynasty scholar Lee Hwang (pen name Toegye), while the 5,000-won bill showcases Yi I (pen name Yulgok), another esteemed Joseon Dynasty scholar. On the 50,000-won bill, you'll find the face of Shin Saimdang, an influential figure in Korean history and celebrated poet, painter, and calligrapher. What's special about Shin Saimdang is that she is also celebrated for being the mother of Yulgok. This makes it the only banknote in the world to feature both a mother and son. (Interestingly, no mother and son have ever won a Nobel Prize, although Marie Curie and her daughter, Irène Joliot-Curie, were the first mother and daughter to receive a Nobel Prize.) If you're a fan of Korean actor So Ji-sub, you might find it intriguing to collect a 1,000-won bill as a souvenir, as there has been buzz about the striking resemblance between Toegye's portrait and So Ji-sub, particularly in the eyes.

Indeed, the creation of Hangeul was not the only remarkable achievement of King Sejong. Throughout his 32-year reign (1418-1450), he accomplished much more. He expanded the territory slightly to the north, establishing the borders of what is now the entire Korean Peninsula. King Sejong implemented various legal reforms and made significant contributions to agriculture and science. Notably, his reign witnessed the creation of the world's first rain gauge and the establishment of Korea's unique real estate leasing system, the Joense. King Sejong's dedication to improving the human rights of the people is exemplified by his comprehensive survey of the entire nation. In short, King Sejong is highly regarded as a transformative king who propelled Joseon, a budding nation, to multiple levels of progress simultaneously. Many Koreans believe that if there had been one or two more kings like King Sejong, the history of Joseon would have taken a drastically different path.

The name "Sejong" holds great prominence across the nation, being widely used in various contexts. Sejongno (Sejong Street), the expansive road in front of Gwanghwamun Gate, stands as a notable landmark bearing the name. Adjacent to it is Sejong Center, a large theater that showcases a wide array of cultural performances. Additionally, Sejong's legacy extends to the establishment of Sejong Special Self-Governing City, a new city that accommodates many of Korea's major government agencies. Moreover, the name "Sejong" finds its place in an array of institutions, including universities, hotels, and more.

However, one aspect that King Sejong the Great did not incorporate into Hangeul was the use of spacing between words. This omission could be attributed to the influence of the Chinese language, which customarily lacks clear spacing between characters. The absence of word spacing in Hangeul may have hindered its adoption in the centuries following its creation, beside the deliberate disregard for Hangeul by the ruling class of that time. It wasn't until the late 19th century, more than 400 years after the creation of Hangeul, that the practice of using spacing between words became widely embraced by Koreans. The introduction of word spacing greatly enhanced readability and played a pivotal role in facilitating Hangeul as a writing system.

Now, let's delve into another fascinating aspect of the Korean language – their intricate system of honorifics. While other languages incorporate honorifics, the Korean system is incredibly comprehensive. Hold on as we explore it – not only do they employ additional words for age, names, birthdays, and meals when speaking formally, but even common verbs like eat, ask, sleep, give, die, and say have varying forms. And that's not all; adjectives like hungry, personal pronouns, and titles are also part of this system.

Here's the entertaining part – they don't just have one or two honorifics for a given word, but a range of them! In the Joseon Dynasty, they even had a specific honorific reserved exclusively for the king. And the complexities continue in contemporary Korean society, where appropriate honorifics vary across different levels of hierarchy, ranging from top positions like chairman to managerial roles, from wise elder figures to friendly uncles, and many more.

Even in situations where there isn't a dedicated term, the Korean language provides multiple methods to convey honorifics. Honorific expressions are frequently found in postpositions that follow nouns, and you can even adjust verb and adjective endings to create honorific forms. I must say, it can be quite a challenge. (Although for us Koreans, it's not so difficult.) That's why it always impresses Koreans when they hear a foreigner expertly using honorific language.

In Korean culture, casual speech is predominantly reserved for very close relationships, while honorifics are commonly used in most other interactions. It is considered impolite not to use honorifics when meeting someone for the first time, irrespective of the age or status difference. However, there are a few situations where one might choose to use more casual language or speak without honorifics. Picture this: a bully picking a fight, a rogue mugger ready to snatch your wallet, or the dramatic encounter with a lifelong enemy. That's why many of the basic Korean phrases found in travel guidebooks are presented in honorific form - greetings, expressions of gratitude, requests, and so on. (Nevertheless, when foreigners don't use honorifics, Koreans are often amused to hear them because they understand that it's not an indication of hostility, but rather a limitation in their Korean language proficiency.)

The development of honorifics in the Korean language can be attributed to the cultural emphasis on hierarchy, which has been prevalent throughout Korea's history. A caste system has played a significant role, placing great importance on age-based hierarchy, even within the same caste. To exaggerate slightly, when Koreans encounter a stranger, there is a tendency to establish a hierarchy by first determining their respective ages. This is because the older individual has the liberty to speak casually, while the younger person is obligated to show respect. In modern society, however, even with an age difference, it is generally expected for individuals to maintain a respectful demeanor unless they share a close relationship or the younger person explicitly grants permission to use informal language.

Lastly, besides basic greetings, let me share a few entertaining Korean expressions that I believe foreigners traveling to Korea might find enjoyable to use. We've already covered phrases like "tesla" and "amugona," so here are a few more to add to your linguistic repertoire.

First, let's delve into the word 'yeogiyo.' It's formed by combining two words: 'yeogi,' meaning "here," and 'yo,' which is often added to express respect. This phrase proves useful when you want to call out to a staff member in a restaurant (I'll explain the reason behind this in the next chapter) or when you seek the attention of a stranger, similar to saying 'Excuse me.' By using 'yeogiyo,' you are essentially conveying the message, "Please pay attention to me here."

Let's move on to the word 'matjip.' Translated literally as 'taste-house,' it refers to a restaurant that serves mouthwatering, delectable food. Imagine this: you're dining at a restaurant, and the flavors tantalize your taste buds, leaving you thoroughly impressed. In that moment, you can turn to the waiter and exclaim, 'Yeogi matjibine!' The Koreans around you will be amazed at your Korean language skills and break into smiles. For an extra touch of excitement, don't forget to accompany your words with a thumbs-up gesture. It's the perfect way to express your satisfaction and share in the joy of experiencing exceptional cuisine.

Here's another expression for you to try out: 'daebak.' This versatile word carries the meaning of 'awesome,' 'jackpot,' or 'amazing,' making it the perfect choice when you want to convey your excitement about an extraordinary experience during your travels in Korea. Picture this: you've just finished an incredible meal at a restaurant, and it has left you thoroughly impressed. Instead of bidding a regular goodbye in Korean (which can be a bit harder to remember), you can leave with a memorable parting phrase: 'Daebak naseyo!' This phrase conveys the well-wish of 'May your business be successful,' showing your appreciation and goodwill to the establishment.

May you have the opportunity to explore and indulge in the finest restaurants in Korea, uttering the word "daebak" with great frequency. May your life be brimming with extraordinary and awe-inspiring moments, much like the essence of "daebak." And lastly, I hope you will extend your support and blessings to this book, allowing it to achieve its own "daebak."

12.

알고 보면 신기한

한국의 식당 문화

한국 식당에 존재하는 특이한 점 중에서 몇 가지는 이미 말했다. 식당의 테이블 아랫면에 부착된 서랍에 숟가락과 젓가락이 숨어 있다거나, 테이블 가운데에 숯불이나 버너를 두고 음식을 직접 구워 먹는다거나, 주문하지도 않은 다양한 음식들이 반찬이라는 이름으로 무제한 제공된다거나 하는 것만 해도 충분히 신기하지만, 여기서 끝이 아니다. 한국의 식당 문화는 정말 독특하다. 이제부터 하나씩 살펴보자.

한국인은 오랫동안 유교적 전통을 지키며 살아왔다. 학문이자 철학이면서 종교이기도 한 유교는 동양 문화 전반에 큰 영향을 끼쳤지만, 사람들의 실생활에 미친 영향은 발상지인 중국보다 오히려 한국에서 더 컸다고 할 수 있다. 5백 년 넘게 지속된 조선왕조가 유교를 국가의 통치 이념으로 삼은 것과 관련이 있다.

유교는 인본주의를 근간에 두고 있는 이념이지만, 가부장적 특성이 매우 강했고, 각종 의식(ritual)을 매우 중요하게 생각했다. 결혼식이나 장례식과 같은 예식을 치르는 절차와 방식이 까다롭게 정해져 있었고, 조상의 영혼을 기리는 제사를 1년에 몇 번씩이나 지내야 했다. 그 외에도 왜 그렇게 해야 하는지는 아무도 모르지만 '이럴 때는 이렇게 해야 한다', '저럴 때는 저렇게 해야 한다'는 식의 규율이 엄청나게 많았다. 하지만 이러한 규율 중에서 대부분은 현대 사회에서 불필요하고 불합리했다. 때문에 20세기 중반 이후 한국 정부는 불필요한 각종 절차들을 '허례허식'이라 규정하며, 이를 줄이기 위한 여러 가지 정책을 펴기도 했다. 점차 줄어들고는 있지만, 이런 전통은 아직 한국 사회 곳곳에 꽤 많이 남아 있다.

하지만 유교적 전통에 따른 의식을 철저히 지키는 것은 지배계급(이들을 '양반'이라 불렀다)에 국한되었던 것도 사실이다. 백성의 대다수를 차지했던 평범한 사람들은 그렇게까지 엄격하게 규율에 얽매이지 않았다. 각종 의식을 제대로 치르는 데 필요한 경제적 여유가 없기도 했고, 법률이 아닌 관습으로 요구되는 각종 규칙들을 굳이 지켜야 할 이유가 없기 때문이기도 했다. 유교적 전통에 매몰되어 있던 지배계급과 달리 평범한 한국인들은 지극히 실용주의적 관점을 견지했다고 할 수 있다. 오히려 보통의 한국인들은 '왜 안 되는데?' 정신을 발휘하여, 새로운 생활양식을 만들어냈고 필요한 도구들을 만들어 사용했다.

한국인이 개발한 도구 중에 가장 널리 알려진 것은 '호미'다. 호미는 정원을 가꾸는 데 아주 유용한 도구이다. 가장 빨리 데워지고 빠르게 식는 양은냄비나, 정반대로 천천히 데워지지만 한번 달궈지면 오랫동안 열을 품고 있는 돌솥도 한국인이 만들어서 점차 해외로 퍼지고 있는 도구이다. 유명해지지 않았을 뿐, 자신의 작업에 가장 적합한 도구를 스스로 만들어 사용하는 한국인은 의외로 많다. 한국인은 리얼 호모 파베르다.

한국인들이 그렇게 다양한 채소들을 먹게 된 것도, 외국에 비해 훨씬 많은 종류의 해산물을 먹게 된 것도, 부족한 식량 사정을 타개하기 위해 스스로 찾아낸 방편이었을지도 모른다(이건 순전히 나의 개인적인 견해이며, 아무런 학문적 근거가 없는 주장이다). 즉 한국인의 유전자에는 좋게 말해 실용주의적 태도가, 나쁘게 말하면 생존에 필요한 각종 꼼수를 발휘하는 능력이 내재되어 있다는 뜻이다.

한국의 독특한 식당 문화는 '효율성'을 높이기 위한 수많은 술책의 누적으로 형성된 결과라는 말이다. 앞에서도 여러 번 설명했지만, 한국은 수십 년 전만 해도 무척이나 가난한 나라였다. 한 끼를 해결하기 위해 지불할 수 있는 금액이 그리 크지 않았던 시절이 길었다는 뜻이다. 사람들은 낮은 가격에 상대적으로 질 높은 식사를 원했고, 식당 주인들은 같은 음식이라도 최대한 싸게 팔아야 더 많은 손님을 끌어올 수 있었다.

생각해보라. 손님이 올 때마다 포크, 나이프, 스푼을 근사하게 배열하는 것보다 그것들을 미리 테이블에 잔뜩 놓아두고 손님이 알아서 필요한 도구들을 사용하게 하는 것이 당연히 비용이 적게

드는 방법이다. 실제로 한국의 식당들은 수저를 플라스틱이나 나무로 만든 상자에 여러 개 넣어두는 방식을 주로 택했다. 뚜껑이 없는 길쭉한 원통에 수저를 여러 개 세로로 꽂아두는 경우도 있었다. 이 방식은 효율적이긴 한데, 두 가지 문제가 있다. (특히 뚜껑이 없는 용기에 담아두었을 때는) 위생 측면에서 나쁘고, 커다란 수저통이 놓여 있으니 테이블이 복잡해진다. 누군지는 모르지만, 어떤 한국인이 어느 날 묘수를 찾았다. 테이블 밑면에 수저통을 숨기는 방법 말이다. 처음에는 숟가락과 젓가락만 테이블 아래에 있었지만, 굳이 그래야 할 이유는 없다. 또 누군가의 아이디어로, 테이블 아래 박스가 커졌고, 거기에는 냅킨이나 병따개 같은 것들이 함께 자리를 잡기 시작했다. 한국인들은 좋은 아이디어를 수용하는 데 적극적이다. 순식간에 이런 방식이 널리 퍼졌고, 지금은 허다한 식당에서 이렇게 생긴 테이블을 사용한다.

　가위를 사용하는 것도 효율성을 위해서다. 커다란 삼겹살덩어리를 불에 구운 다음, 우리가 선택할 수 있는 방법들을 생각해보자. 한국인들은 숟가락과 젓가락을 주로 쓰기에, 고기를 자르기 위해 별도의 포크와 나이프를 사용하는 건 별로 좋은 생각이 아니다. 워낙 많은 반찬이 놓여 있기 때문에 그럴 만한 여유 공간도 없다. 적당히 익은 고기를 종업원이 가져가서 주방에서 자른 다음 다시 가져다주는 건 어떤가? 이것도 매우 번거롭다. 처음부터 한입에 먹을 수 있을 정도로 잘게 잘라서 내놓는 건 어떤가? 일부 삼겹살집에서는 이런 방식을 택하기도 하지만, 작은 고기 조각들을 일일이 뒤집어가며 익히려면 귀찮다.

가위를 쓰면 모든 문제가 해결된다. 적당히 익은 큰 고깃덩어리를 가위를 사용해서 자른 다음 조금 더 익혀서 먹으면 간편하다. 고급 식당에서는, 또한 불 위에 놓인 고기가 상당히 비싼 것일 때는, 손님이 아니라 종업원이 (전문가의 솜씨로) 가위질을 해주며, 저렴한 대중식당에서는 손님이 직접 가위질을 하는 것이 보통이다.

가위만 있다고 고기를 자를 수 있는 것은 아니니, 당연히 집게도 사용된다. 가위는 헝겊이나 종이를 자를 때나 쓰는 도구라는 생각에서 벗어나면, 그 용도는 다른 차원으로 확장된다. 한국인들이 하나의 가위로 가죽도 자르고 철사도 자르고 삼겹살도 자르는 것은 물론 아니다. 음식을 자르는 가위로는 음식만 자른다. 심지어 음식을 자르기에 가장 적합하게 가위의 모양도 살짝 변형되어 있다. 끝이 뾰족하지 않고 뭉툭하게 처리되어 있으며, 날이 약간 휘어져 있는 경우가 많다. 그러니 당신이 한국의 고깃집을 방문했을 때, 조금도 주저하지 말고 가위로 고기를 자르는 모험을 즐기면 된다.

효율성을 추구하는 문화가 만들어낸 최고의 작품은 호출 벨이다. 전부는 아니지만 상당히 많은 식당에는 테이블 위 어딘가에 (혹은 벽면 어딘가에) 작은 버튼이 설치되어 있다. 고기를 추가로 주문하고 싶을 때, 소주를 더 시키고 싶을 때, 김치 그릇이 비었을 때, 그걸 누르면 종업원이 온다. 손님도 편하고 종업원도 편하다.

식당의 손님은 밥을 먹는 동안 종업원에게 요청할 일이 많다. 그래서 고급 음식점에서는 서빙을 하는 사람들이 수시로 자신이 담당한 테이블의 상황을 체크한다. 그러다가 알아서 물이나 와인을 따라주기도 하고, 포크를 떨어뜨리는 손님이 있으면 즉시 새것을 가져다준다. 빈 접시가 생기면 얼른 치우고, 테이블 위에 떨어진 빵 부스러기가 있으면 그것도 치워준다. 눈만 마주쳐도 다가오고, 요청하지 않아도 수시로 찾아온다. 음식 맛은 괜찮은지, 불편한 것은 없는지, 더 주문할 것은 없는지 반복해서 묻는다. 물론 환하게 웃으면서. 그게 좋은 서비스이기 때문이기도 하고, 그렇게 해야 자신이 받을 수 있는 팁의 액수가 늘어나기 때문이기도 하다. 하지만 이런 훌륭한 서비스는 결코 공짜가 아니다. 팁의 형태로든 비싼 음식 가격의 형태로든, 대가를 지불해야 한다.

하지만 한국의 식당들은 호출 벨을 설치함으로써 인력 운용의 효율을 높인다. 종업원들이 손님들을 자주 쳐다보는 시간을 아껴서 다른 일을 할 수 있다. 손님들은 종업원들과 눈을 맞추기 위해 애쓸 필요가 없고, 필요한 것이 생기면 벨을 누르는 방법으로 종업원을 쉽게 부를 수 있다. 호출 벨이 설치되어 있지 않은 곳이면 어떻게 하느냐고? 앞의 글에서 이미 알려주었다. '여기요'라고 하면 된다.

한국은 팁 문화가 없다(어쩌면 그래서 종업원들이 손님을 계속 주시하지 않는 것인지도 모른다. 닭이 먼저냐 달걀이 먼저냐 하는 문제이긴 하지만). 식당에서도 팁을 줄 필요가 없고, 택시에서도 팁을 줄 필요가 없다. 과거 현금을 사용하던 시절에는 "거스름돈은 가지세요"라고 말하는 것이 흔한 일이기는 했지만, 그 액수는 대체로 적어서 기껏해야 50센트 내외의 소액이었다. 지금은 현금을 거의 사용하지 않으니 이런 소액의 팁도 거의 사라졌다. 호텔 방에서 나올 때 메이드를 위해 1달러를 놓아두는 문화도 없다. 호텔에서 짐을 옮겨준 직원에게 팁을 주는 경우도 별로 없다(물론 줘도 된다). 결혼식이나 장례식에 참석할 때는 반드시 현금을 주고받는 것이 한국인인데, 팁 문화는 생겨나지 않았다. 내 생각엔 그냥 복잡한 것을 싫어하는 성향이 반영된 게 아닐까 싶다.

팁을 주는 행위는 사실 복잡하다. 얼마를 줄지 미리 생각해야 하고, 지갑을 열어 돈을 꺼내야 하고, 너무 적게 줘서 무언의 비난을 받지 않을지, 너무 많이 줘서 쓸데없이 돈을 낭비하지 않을지 고민스럽다. 15퍼센트든 18퍼센트든 비율을 정해놓고 주려 하면 계산이 복잡해져서 또 싫다. 그냥 업주들이 미리 정해놓은 액수를 딱 그대로 지불하는 게 깔끔하다. 받는 입장에서도 기대보다 팁이 적어서 속상할 일도 없고, 팁을 더 받기 위해 손님의 눈치를 살피는 피곤함을 감수하지 않아도 된다.

팁 문화가 없는 한국의 식당에서는 손님과 담당 종업원이 정확하게 지정되어 있지 않으니, 상황에 따라 누구든 필요한 서비스를 제공할 수 있어서 효율이 더 올라간다. 팁의 전부 혹은 대부분을 전적으로 담당 서버가 가져가는 나라의 경우를 생각해보면 쉽다. 그런 나라의 식당에서는 내 옆에 아무리 많은 직원이 오가더라도(심지어 그들이 매우 한가하더라도), 내 담당 서버가 나타나지 않으면 문제 해결이 안 되지 않나. 하지만 한국의 식당에서는 모든 종업원들이 하나의 팀으로 유기적으로 움직인다. 필요한 것을 누구에게 말해도 다 해결이 된다는 뜻이다.

물론 한국인들도 팁 문화가 있는 외국에 나가면 팁을 준다. 로마에 가면 로마법을 따라야 하니까. 하지만 언제나 낯설어한다. 메뉴판에 있는 가격을 보고 대략 환율 계산을 한 다음 거기에 다시 팁을 추가해야 하니, 내가 주문할 음식의 가격이 얼마인지 파악하기가 쉽지 않아서다. 신용카드 영수증에 자신이 지불할 팁의 액수를 직접 적어 넣는 방식도 썩 내키지 않는다. 계산도 복잡할 뿐더러, 한국에는 없는 팁을 많게는 20퍼센트까지 지불하게 되면 뭔지 모르게 바가지를 쓰는 기분을 느끼기 때문이다.

아무튼, 당신은 한국 여행중에 단 한 번도 팁을 주지 않아도 된다. 하지만 한국에 팁 문화가 아예 없는 것은 아니다. 특급 호텔 식당을 비롯한 소수의 식당은 10퍼센트 정도의 팁을 반드시 지불하도록 아예 메뉴판에 명기해놓았다. 그 외에는 다음과 같은 경우에 드물게 팁을 주기도 한다(팁 문화가 없는 나라이기 때문에 받는 사람이 매우 고마워한다). 고급 미장원에서 마음에 드는 서비스를 받았을 때, 매우 비싼 고깃집에서 종업원이 예술적으로 고기를 구워줄 때, 고급 스시 레스토랑에서 오너 셰프가 직접 찾아와서 정중히 인사를 건넬 때, 음식이나 서비스가 정말로 감동적이어서 그것을 표현하고 싶을 때, 그리고 데이트나 비즈니스 미팅을 할 때 자신을 좀더 친절하고 너그럽고 부유한 사람으로 포장하고 싶을 때 등등(물론 이런 목적으로 팁을 줄 때 너무 거만한 태도를 보이면 오히려 감점이다).

한국의 일부 식당에는 테이블 위에 두루마리 휴지가 놓여 있기도 하다. 화장실에 놓여 있어야 할 물건이 음식들과 나란히 존재하는 것이 매우 어색하기는 한데, 이것은 과거 한국이 매우 가난하던 시절의 흔적이 아직도 남아 있는 것이다. 몇십 년 전의 한국인들은 화장실에서는 신문지 따위를 쓰고 두루마리 휴지를 거실이나 식탁에 두고 사용하곤 했다. 지금은 가정집이라면 이런 일이 거의 없지만, 원가를 절감하려는 일부 저렴한 식당들은 아직도 냅킨 대신 두루마리 휴지를 비치해놓고 있다(그러니 혹시 발견하더라도 너무 놀라지 마시라).

역시 원가 절감의 차원에서, 한국의 식당에서는 '셀프 서비스' 방식이 제법 많이 남아 있다. 음식은 가져다주지만 물은 손님이 알아서 정수기를 이용해야 하는 경우는 꽤 흔하고, 김치와 같은 반찬들은 뷔페 방식으로 알아서 가져다 먹게 하는 식당도 많다. 식사를 마친 후에 커피나 아이스크림 등을 알아서 챙겨 먹도록 하는 경우도 제법 있다. 다른 손님들의 행동을 잘 관찰하여, 당신도 눈치껏 가져다 먹으면 된다.

당신이 스스로 해야 하는 일들 중에 가장 중요한 것은 숟가락과 젓가락 세팅이다. 서양 음식을 파는 식당에서는 포크와 나이프 등의 도구가 가지런히 놓여 있는 것이 일반적이다. 한국 음식을 파는 고급 식당에도 숟가락과 젓가락이 미리 세팅되어 있다. 하지만 그 외 대부분의 음식점들, 그러니까 테이블 아래 숨어 있는 박스 안에 숟가락과 젓가락이 비치되어 있는 경우라면, 그것을 꺼내어 정리하는 것은 당신의 몫이다. 그냥 꺼내놓기만 하면 될까? 아니다. 99퍼센트 이상의 한국인들은 냅킨을 한 장 뽑아서 테이블에 놓은 다음 그 위에 수저를 놓는다. 한식당에서는 손님이 바뀔 때마다 테이블보 혹은 테이블 매트를 바꾸는 경우가 드물고, 주로 행주로 닦는 것이 전부다(알코올 스프레이 등을 함께 사용하는 집도 많다). 뭔지 모르게 테이블이 깨끗하게 느껴지지 않기 때문에, 냅킨을 일회용 테이블 매트처럼 사용하는 것이다. 당신도 그렇게 하면 된다.

그런데 재미있는 것은 여러 사람이 식당에 갔을 때 최연소자가 모든 사람의 수저 세팅을 도맡아 하는 경우가 흔하다는 사실이다. 반드시 그래야 하는 것은 아니지만, 많은 한국인이 이를 자연스럽게 받아들인다. 연장자를 공경하는 유교적 전통이 현대에 남긴 문화라 할 수 있다(하지만 연장자는 이를 너무 당연한 것으로 여기면 안 된다. 그러면 '꼰대' 소리를 듣는다. 본인이 스스로 하려는 척이라도 하든지, 신경써줘서 고맙다는 표시는 해야 한다). 고깃집에서 고기를 굽고 자르는 것도 주로는 막내의 몫이다(물론 자신이 굽는 것을 좋아하는 꼰대도 있다. 그럴 때는 "부장님, 정말 고기를 잘 구우시네요"라고 옆에서 한마디 해줘야 한다).

자, 당신도 한국에서는 한국식 식당 문화를 모두 체험해보자. 테이블에 앉자마자, 주문을 하기도 전에, 테이블 아래에 숨어 있는 냅킨과 숟가락과 젓가락을 꺼내어 예쁘게 놓아보자. 그리고 가위로 음식을 자르는 경험도 해보자. 소주 한 병을 추가 주문하기 위해 호출 벨도 눌러보자(정말 순식간에 사람이 나타난다). 식당을 나올 때 팁은 안 줘도 된다. 팁을 주고 싶을 만큼 만족스러운 식사였다면, 팁 대신, 앞에서 배운 한국어를 써먹으면 된다. "대박! 여기 맛집이네!"

12.

Unveiling the Marvels of Korean Restaurant Culture

We've already revealed some of the intriguing aspects you'll encounter in Korean restaurants. From the sneaky spoons and chopsticks hidden in secret compartments beneath the table to the blazing charcoal grills or sizzling burners at the center of your table, ready for your food-grilling adventures. And of course, the astonishing array of never-ending "side dishes" that appear without you even ordering them. But buckle up, because Korean restaurant culture is about to take you on a culinary journey like no other. Get ready for a truly unique dining experience!

For centuries, Koreans have embraced the profound traditions of Confucianism, a comprehensive philosophy, discipline, and religion. Confucianism has had a huge impact on Eastern culture as a whole, but its impact on people's real lives has been exceptionally deep-rooted, even surpassing its birthplace, China. This enduring influence can be attributed to the Joseon Dynasty, which upheld Confucianism as the nation's governing ideology for over five centuries.

While Confucianism espoused humanistic values, it also embraced strong patriarchal characteristics and placed great emphasis on rituals. Ceremonies, such as weddings and funerals, followed strict protocols, and ancestral rites were performed multiple times a year to honor departed spirits. Countless other rules dictated when and how certain actions should be performed, often lacking clear explanations. Nevertheless, as time progressed, many of these rules came to be seen as unnecessary and impractical in the modern world. So, since the mid-20th century, the Korean government has recognized these superfluous practices as "empty formalities and vanity," taking steps to reduce their prevalence. While their influence has gradually waned, remnants of this tradition still linger in a multitude of aspects of Korean society.

However, it is important to note that the strict adherence to Confucian rituals was primarily limited to the ruling class known as the "yangban." The common people, who made up the majority of the population, were not as bound by these rigid rules. Due to economic constraints, they often couldn't afford the elaborate rituals and saw little incentive to conform to customs that lacked legal requirements. Unlike the privileged ruling class deeply entrenched in Confucian tradition, ordinary Koreans exhibited an eminently pragmatic mindset. With a "why not?" mentality, they forged their own path and devised practical solutions for their daily lives.

One remarkable example of their ingenuity is the creation of singular tools. For instance, the "homi" is a Korean hand plow that is widely recognized for its efficiency in gardening. Koreans have also developed and introduced other innovative tools, such as the nickel-silver pot, which heats up quickly and cools down rapidly, and the "dolsot," a stone pot that heats up slowly but retains heat for an extended period. Despite not gaining widespread fame, there are many individuals who craft their own specialized tools tailored to their specific needs. Koreans truly embody the spirit of "homo faber," the maker of things.

It is conceivable that Koreans have developed a penchant for consuming a diverse range of vegetables and seafood compared to their foreign counterparts, potentially as a response to historical food shortages. While this notion is speculative and lacks scholarly support, it suggests that pragmatism runs deep in their cultural DNA, enabling them to adapt and employ various tactics and strategies for survival, whether through resourceful measures or the occasional gimmick.

Korea's distinctive restaurant culture has evolved through the accumulation of a variety of tricks aimed at enhancing efficiency. As previously emphasized, Korea experienced significant economic challenges in the not-so-distant past. During this period, individuals were reluctant to spend exorbitant amounts on meals. The populace sought a balance between high-quality dining experiences and affordability, prompting restaurant proprietors to devise ways to offer their guests at competitive prices, thereby attracting a larger customer base.

Consider this: It is undeniably more cost-effective to pre-set a multitude of forks, knives, and spoons on the table, allowing customers to conveniently utilize the utensils they require, rather than meticulously arranging them before each patron's arrival. In the past, Korean restaurants used to store their cutlery in plastic or wooden containers, sometimes vertically positioned in elongated cylinders without lids. While this approach proved efficient, it posed two predicaments. Firstly, it compromised hygiene, particularly when using uncovered containers. Secondly, it cluttered the table with a conspicuous bin of cutlery.

Then, an ingenious Korean innovator, whose identity remains unknown, devised a solution: hiding the cutlery bin beneath the table's surface. Initially, only spoons and chopsticks found their discreet abode there. However, it soon became evident that this innovative concept could accommodate additional items. Napkins, bottle openers, and more discovered their rightful place in the concealed compartment. Koreans have an admirable openness to embracing exceptional ideas, and it didn't take long for this trend to gain traction. Now, countless restaurants feature tables adorned with this clever setup.

Consider the aspect of efficiency once more, this time in relation to the utilization of scissors. Imagine a sizable slab of succulent pork belly sizzling on the grill, and ponder the available alternatives. Given that Koreans predominantly employ spoons and chopsticks during their meals, resorting to a separate fork and knife for cutting the meat proves less than ideal. Additionally, with an array of delectable side dishes adorning the table, there is scarce space to accommodate such additional utensils. One could propose the notion of having a diligent waiter transport the cooked meat from you, subsequently slicing it in the kitchen, and finally returning it to your table. However, this approach proves laborious and impractical. So, why not endeavor to pre-cut the meat into bite-sized portions from the outset? Indeed, certain pork belly establishments adopt this practice. Yet, one may find it tiresome to incessantly flip over the diminutive meat pieces for thorough cooking.

Scissors come to the rescue, solving all your dilemmas. It's a breeze to wield a pair of scissors, effortlessly snipping through a moderately cooked slab of meat, allowing it to continue cooking to perfection. In upscale establishments, where the sizzling meat commands a higher price tag, the skilled staff expertly handles the cutting duties. However, in more casual eateries, it's common for patrons to take matters into their own hands and wield the scissors themselves.

In the realm of meat-cutting, scissors alone do not reign supreme; tongs also play a vital role. It is crucial to dispel any misconceptions that scissors are solely reserved for fabric or paper, for in the culinary world, their purpose takes on a different dimension. Koreans understand the significance of specialized tools, as they do not employ the same pair of scissors to conquer leather, manipulate wire, and slice succulent pork belly. Scissors designed explicitly for culinary endeavors are solely dedicated to the art of food cutting. Moreover, a subtle variation in their shape enhances their efficacy in this domain. The tips, intentionally blunted rather than pointed, and the blades, often subtly curved, epitomize the utmost convenience when it comes to the precise act of food cutting. So, next time you find yourself at a Korean barbecue restaurant, don't hesitate to grab those scissors and embark on a culinary adventure of meat-cutting mastery.

A true testament to our culture of efficiency is the ingenious invention known as the call bell. Found in many, though not all, restaurants, this small button discreetly positioned on the table or wall holds the power to fulfill your every desire. Whether you yearn for an additional serving of tantalizing meat, crave another round of invigorating soju, or find your kimchi bowl lamentably empty, a simple press of the button beckons a diligent server to your aid. The call bell effortlessly bridges the gap between customer and staff, ensuring a seamless and convenient dining experience for all.

Diners often find themselves with a myriad of requests to make while indulging in their meal. This is precisely why, in esteemed establishments, diligent servers make periodic visits to each table. They graciously attend to your needs, be it replenishing your water or wine, promptly replacing a dropped fork, swiftly clearing away empty plates, or even tidying up bread crumbs that may have found their way onto the table. Their attentive presence is not limited to your beckoning; they actively ensure your satisfaction by regularly checking in, even when unbidden. With a warm smile adorning their faces, they inquire about the quality of your dishes, your comfort level, and whether your desire additional orders. This exceptional level of service is driven by a twofold motivation: the pursuit of excellence in customer experience and the desire to maximize potential gratuities. That is to say, such exceptional service is not bestowed without its associated costs. Whether through gratuities or slightly elevated prices, you are offered the opportunity to appreciate and reciprocate the efforts of these dedicated individuals.

Restaurants in Korea have adopted an additional measure to enhance their workforce efficiency by implementing call bells. This ingenious system alleviates the need for staff members to constantly monitor customers and enables them to attend to other tasks. With call bells at their disposal, patrons no longer face the challenge of making eye contact with the staff. If assistance is required, a simple ring of the bell summons the attentive service of the staff. However, what if you find yourself in a dining establishment without a call bell? Fear not, for we have already addressed this in a previous chapter: a straightforward and widely used solution is to call out "yeogiyo" to get the attention of the staff.

It is true that South Korea does not have a widespread tipping culture. Perhaps that's the reason why the staff doesn't have their peepers glued to customers like a hawk. It's like pondering the age-old dilemma of which arrived on the scene first, the clucking chicken or the elusive egg. Unlike some other countries, tipping in restaurants or taxis is not customary in Korea. In the past, when cash transactions were more common, people occasionally said "keep the change," but the amounts were typically small, usually around 50 cents or less. With the shift towards cashless transactions, these small tips have become less common. In the realm of Korean customs, leaving a dollar for the hotel maid or tipping the luggage carrier is not the norm, though it remains an option. While cash exchanges are customary at weddings and funerals, the practice of tipping has not gained traction. This could be attributed to a preference for simplicity and a general aversion to needless complexities.

Tipping can indeed be a rather intricate affair. It requires careful consideration of the appropriate amount to give, rummaging through one's wallet for cash, and the constant worry of striking the right balance between being perceived as stingy or overly generous. The thought of calculating percentages like 15% or 18% can be quite bothersome, adding unnecessary complexity to the equation. How refreshing it is to simply pay the predetermined amount set by the business owner. As a recipient, there's no need to fret over receiving a smaller tip than expected or exhaust oneself in the pursuit of securing more.

In Korean restaurants, where the concept of tipping is not prevalent, the distribution of responsibilities among the staff is not rigidly defined. This flexibility allows anyone to attend to your needs based on the situation, leading to a more efficient system. Contrast this with the image of a restaurant in a country where a much larger portion of your tip goes directly to your designated server. In such cases, regardless of how many bustling staff members come and go around you (even when they are not so busy), if your server happens to be absent, it can cause inconvenience. In the absence of a designated server, you have the freedom to approach any staff member for assistance, knowing that your requests will be promptly attended to.

Indeed, when Koreans visit foreign countries with a tipping culture, they adhere to local customs and tip accordingly. "When in Rome, do as the Romans do" is a well-known maxim to all the Koreans. However, the process can feel unfamiliar and perplexing. It involves scrutinizing the menu prices, estimating the currency exchange rate, and factoring in the gratuity, making it challenging to determine the total cost of the food being ordered. The act of writing the tip amount on a credit card receipt can feel unsettling, too. Not only is the calculation process complex, but the notion of paying an additional 20% gratuity, which is non-existent in Korea, can leave one with a sense of being overcharged.

In most cases, tipping is not expected during your trip to Korea. However, it's worth noting that tipping is not entirely absent in the country. Some high-end restaurants, particularly those in upscale hotels, may include a 10% tip expectation on their menus. Moreover, in the following situations, tipping is sometimes expected (and recipients are usually very appreciative for the unexpected tips): when you receive exceptional service at a high-end beauty salon, when the staff at a premium beef restaurant skillfully prepares and grills your meat, when the owner-chef personally visits your table at a top-notch sushi restaurant and greets you with utmost politeness, when you're genuinely impressed with the food or service and wish to express your appreciation, or when you want to convey a generous and affluent image during a date or business meeting. It's important, however, not to be overly arrogant when tipping for any of these purposes, as it can have a negative impact.

In certain restaurants in Korea, it is not uncommon to find a roll of toilet paper placed on the table. While it may initially seem unusual to have restroom items alongside the food, it has a historical context rooted in economic hardships. Several decades ago, Koreans would use newspapers as makeshift toilet paper and keep the rolls of actual toilet paper in the living room or on the dining table for convenience. Although this practice is now rare in Korean households, some budget-friendly restaurants choose to provide rolled tissues instead of standard napkins as a cost-saving measure. So, if you happen to encounter this unique setup, there's no need to be surprised or concerned.

To keep costs down, many Korean restaurants adopt a "self-service" approach. It is not uncommon for these establishments to require customers to help themselves to water while serving the main dishes. Additionally, a notable feature is the availability of "side dishes," like kimchi, which are often offered as a self-serve buffet with unlimited refills. In certain cases, diners may be encouraged to enjoy self-served ice cream or coffee after the meal. By observing the behavior of others, you can easily navigate and adapt to these practices.

The most crucial step for diners in Korean restaurants is to set their own spoon and chopsticks. Unlike Western restaurants that commonly lay out utensils like forks and knives in a neat row, Korean restaurants (except high-class establishments) often hide spoons and chopsticks in a box beneath the table, leaving it to customers to retrieve and arrange them. However, simply leaving the utensils on the table is not the norm in Korean dining culture. It is ingrained in Korean etiquette that the majority of Koreans will grab a napkin, place it on the table, and then position their cutlery on top of it. This practice serves a purpose, as tablecloths or mats are seldom changed between diners and are usually wiped down with a dishcloth, sometimes even sanitized with alcohol spray. Due to this, the tables may not always feel completely clean, so using napkins as makeshift disposable mats is a common practice. By following these practices, you can fully immerse yourself in the Korean dining culture.

Interestingly, it is quite common for the youngest person in a group to take on the responsibility of setting everyone's cutlery when dining at a restaurant in Korea. While it is not a strict requirement, many Koreans consider it a natural gesture rooted in the Confucian tradition of showing respect to elders. However, it is important for elders not to take this for granted. And then, they may be playfully referred to as "ggondae" or "boomer." It is advisable to either make an effort to set your own cutlery or express gratitude to the person who takes on the task. Similarly, when visiting samgyeopsal restaurant, it is often the duty of the youngest person to handle the grilling and cutting of the meat. (Of course, there may be exceptions, with some ggondae who particularly enjoys grilling taking charge. In such cases, it is appropriate to commend their grilling skills by saying something like, "Hey, manager, you're really good at grilling meat.")

Now that you're immersed in the Korean restaurant culture, you can fully embrace the experience. As soon as you take your seat at the table, even before placing your order, gracefully retrieve the napkins, spoons, and chopsticks from under the table and arrange them neatly. Don't forget to engage in the unique practice of cutting your food with scissors—it adds a touch of authenticity to your dining experience. And if you find yourself craving an extra bottle of soju, simply ring the bell, and a prompt and attentive staff member will swiftly come to your aid. Remember, tipping is not customary in Korean restaurants, but if you truly enjoyed your meal and wish to show appreciation, you can utilize the Korean phrases you've learned earlier. To express your satisfaction, shout out something like, "Daebak! Yeogi Matjibine!"

13.
한국인이 못 말리는 국수와 국물 사랑

2022년 6월, 한국의 신문들에 다음과 같은 내용의 기사가 실렸다. "한국인의 1인당 라면 소비량이 세계 2위로 나타났다. 세계라면협회(World Instant Noodles Association, WINA)의 2021년 자료에 따르면, 한국인은 연간 1인당 73개의 라면을 먹는다. 1위는 87개의 베트남이고, 3위는 55개의 네팔이다. 한국은 관련 통계가 시작된 2013년 이후 줄곧 1위였으나, 이번에 2위로 내려앉았다."

　재미있는 것은 이 기사에 달린 댓글들이다. '이상하게 열받네', '오늘부터 반 개씩 더 먹겠다', '분하다', '분발해야겠다', '오늘 점심은 라면이다' 등등. 한국인들에게 라면이 얼마나 중요한 음식인지 잘 보여주는 사례다. 한국인들은, 라면에 관해서라면, 누구나 할말이 아주 많다. 한국인은 라면에 진심이다.

라면은 중국에서 출발했지만 일본에서 변형되며 큰 인기를 끌었다. 주로 전문 식당에서 만들어 팔던 라면은 1958년에 처음으로 인스턴트로 나오면서 집에서도 간편하게 끓여 먹을 수 있는 음식이 되었다. 1960년대에는 한국의 한 회사가 일본의 기술을 들여왔고, 저렴하게 한끼를 해결할 수 있는 방법으로 엄청난 인기를 끌었다. 이후 한국의 인스턴트 라면은 맛과 다양성 측면에서 지속적으로 발전했다. 한국인의 입맛에 맞게끔 변화를 거듭한 결과, 한국의 인스턴트 라면은 일본의 그것보다 훨씬 덜 느끼하고 대체로 더 매운 쪽으로 진화했다(자 이제부터 일본의 것은 '라멘'으로, 한국의 것은 '라면'으로 표기한다. 실제로 한국인들은 일본의 것은 라멘이라 부르고, 한국의 것은 라면이라 부른다).

한국은 인스턴트 라면의 천국이다. 단종된 것을 제외하고 현재 시중에 팔리고 있는 것만 해도 5백 종류가 넘는다. 면의 굵기도 다양하고, 수프의 맛은 더욱 다양하고, 국물의 양도 천차만별이고, 중국이나 동남아 요리의 풍미가 더해진 것들도 있다. 4분 내외의 시간 동안 끓여 먹는 것이 표준이지만, 뜨거운 물만 부어서 3분 정도 기다리면 바로 먹을 수 있는 컵라면의 종류도 부지기수다. 전혀 맵지 않은 것부터 어마어마하게 매운 것까지 매운 정도도 제각각이다.

한국 라면은 해외로도 많이 수출되고 있다. 2021년에는 7억 달러 가까이 수출됐고, 2023년에는 9억 달러를 넘었다. 몰라서 그렇지 한번 먹어보면 은근히 중독성이 있기 때문이기도 할 것이고, 한국 콘텐츠가 세계적 인기를 끌면서 한국 음식에 대한 관심이 점차 높아지기 때문이기도 할 것이다. 라면은 여러 가지로 변형도 가능한데, 영화 〈기생충〉에 등장한 '짜파구리'처럼, 두 가지 종류의 라면을 섞어서 조리함으로써 독특한 풍미를 만들어내는 경우도 있다.

한국인이 라면을 사랑하는 것은 어쩌면 당연한 결과다. 한국인이 정말 좋아하는 요소들이 전부 포함되어 있기 때문이다. 일단, 한국인은 원래 국수를 좋아한다. 나중에 다시 자세히 설명할 냉면을 포함해서, 수많은 종류의 면요리가 존재한다. 한국인은 '국물'을 너무도 사랑하는 사람들이다. '국물'은 BTS 멤버 진이 키우는 다람쥐의 이름으로도 유명하지만, 원래는 국에 물이 더해진 말로, 찌개나 국과 같이 수분이 많이 포함된 음식에서 건더기를 뺀 물을 가리키는 말이다.

한국인은 식사를 할 때 국물이 전혀 없으면 뭔가 허전함을 느낀다. 서양인들과 달리 식사 도중에 물을 거의 마시지 않는 것도(물론 술은 마실 수 있지만), 대부분의 한국 음식에는 많든 적든 국물이 곁들여지기 때문이다. 또한 서양의 수프에 비해 한국인이 즐기는 국의 염도가 낮은 편이지만(실제로 많은 한국인이 해외여행 중에 먹게 되는 서양식 수프가 짜다고 느낀다), 전체 소금 섭취량이 오히려 많은 것도 워낙 국물을 많이 마시기 때문이다(한국인의 소금 섭취량은 WHO 권장량의 두 배 이상으로, 세계 최고 수준이다).

'국물이 맛있는 국수'라는 사실에 더해, 라면이 가진 최고의 장점은 값이 싸고 조리 시간이 매우 짧다는 데 있다. '빨리빨리'라는 말을 입에 달고 사는 성격 급한 한국인들에게 매우 잘 어울리며, 가난한 사람들도 라면 덕분에 굶지 않을 수 있었다. 또한 라면은 봉지에 들어 있는 면과 수프만 넣어 끓여도 맛있지만, 기호에 따라 계란, 파, 햄, 치즈, 떡, 만두 등 다양한 재료를 첨가하여 먹을 수 있다. 김치와 매우 환상적인 궁합을 보이기도 한다. 면을 전부 건져 먹은 후 남은 국물에 약간의 밥을 넣어 먹는 것도 많은 한국인이 라면을 즐기는 방법이다.

한국인들은 가끔씩 라면을 끓이지 않고 그냥 먹기도 한다. 면위에 수프를 살짝 뿌려서 간식이나 술안주로 먹는 것이다. 사실라면은 공장에서 한번 익힌 다음 말려서 판매하는 것이므로, 그냥먹어도 된다. 드라마 〈오징어 게임〉에서 배우 이정재와 오영수가편의점 앞에서 소주를 마실 때 함께 먹던 것이 바로 이것이다.

영어의 "넷플릭스 같이 볼래?(Do you want to Netflix and chill?)"의 한국어 표현에도 라면이 들어간다. 그건 "(우리 집에 가서) 라면 먹고 갈래요?"다. 드라마 〈대장금〉과 영화 〈친절한 금자씨〉 등으로 유명한 배우 이영애가 영화 〈봄날은 간다〉에서 이 말을 한 이후에 유명해졌다(이 말을 들은 사람은 영화 〈올드보이〉에 나오는 배우 유지태. 그 두 사람은 결국 라면만 먹지는 않았다).

당신이 한국에 머무르는 짧은 기간 동안 맛보아야 할 한국 음식이 너무도 많기에, 굳이 그중 한끼를 라면으로 해결하라고 조언하고 싶지는 않다. 그러니 치킨을 야식으로 먹는 것처럼, 숙소로 돌아가는 길에 편의점에서 컵라면을 하나 사서 야식으로 맛보는 것이 좋겠다. 편의점에 라면 종류가 너무 많아서 고르기 힘들다면, 한국 라면 중에서도 최고의 판매량을 보이는 '신라면'을 선택하면 된다(정말 한국인처럼 먹고 싶으면 가장 작은 사이즈의 미니 김치도 함께 구입하면 좋다). 마음에 들거든, 당신이 모국으로 돌아간 후에 잘 찾아보시라. 꽤 큰 슈퍼마켓이나 아시안 푸드 마켓 같은 곳에 가면 한국 라면이 제법 있을 것이다(신라면은 조금 매운 편이니, 당신이 매운 음식을 못 먹는 편이라면 두번째로 잘 팔리는 '진라면'을 택하면 되겠다).

라면 외에 한국인이 사랑하는 국수 요리나 국물 요리는 정말로 많다. 그중에서도 가장 중요한 것은 '냉면'이다. 냉면은 차가운 육수와 메밀로 만든 국수로 이루어진 음식이다. 전 세계에 정말 다양한 면요리가 있지만, 차갑게 먹는 국수는 흔하지 않으며, 냉면처럼 대중에게 사랑을 받는 경우는 없다고 해도 과언이 아니다(물론 일본에서 소바나 우동을 차갑게 먹는 경우가 흔하기는 하지만, 그 경우는 '국물'이 없다. 동남아에서 볼 수 있는 몇몇 차가운 국수 요리도 마찬가지다).

냉면을 파는 식당은 정말 많다. 냉면만 파는 식당도 없지는 않지만 고기를 비롯한 다른 음식을 함께 파는 경우가 많아서 정확한 숫자는 파악하기 어려운데, 냉면을 비롯한 국수 요리를 파는 식당은 전국에 2만 개가 넘는 것으로 추산된다. 그들 중 상당수는 '공장'에서 만들어서 공급되는 육수를 사용하지만, 장사가 잘되는 유명한 냉면집들은 대부분 각자의 비법으로 육수를 만들고 면을 뽑아낸다. 냉면 육수를 만드는 데는 소고기가 가장 중요한 재료이지만, 일부 식당은 닭고기, 닭뼈, 돼지고기 등을 조금 섞기도 한다. 고기류 외에 다양한 채소나 과일이 부차적인 재료로 활용되기도 하며, 고춧가루를 넣지 않고 무를 주재료로 만든 물김치의 국물이 첨가되기도 한다. 그래서 식당마다 맛이 다 다르고, 냉면을 사랑하는 많은 사람에게 다양한 미식 경험을 제공한다.

사실 냉면이라는 음식은 여러 종류다. 앞에서 길게 설명한 냉면의 정확한 명칭은 '평양냉면'이다. 맞다. 평양은 북한의 수도 이름이다. 그곳에서 처음 탄생했기 때문이다. 평양냉면의 가장 큰 특징은 국물이 '밍밍하다'는 것이다. 한국인들도 처음으로 이 음식을 먹으면 '아무 맛도 느껴지지 않는다'거나 '만들다 만 것 같은 맛'이라고 느낄 정도다. 식당마다 맛이 다르다고 했는데, 특히 어떤 식당들은 그 밍밍함의 정도가 놀라울 정도다. 하지만 자꾸 먹다보면 이 옅은 국물에 점점 빠져들게 되고, 결국에는 냉면 마니아가 된다. 거의 매주 한두 번씩은 냉면을 먹는 사람도 많고, 전국의 유명 냉면집을 순례하는 것을 취미로 갖고 있는 사람도 많다. '당신은 어느 식당의 평양냉면을 가장 좋아하느냐?'라는 질문은 한국인들 사이에 아이스 브레이킹을 위한 유용한 질문으로 활용되며, 서로 다른 취향을 가진 사람들끼리 치열한(?) 논쟁을 벌이기도 한다. 아마도 한 번만 먹어서는 그 맛을 충분히 느끼기 어렵겠지만, 원래 면요리를 좋아한다면 한번쯤 시도해보길 바란다. 특히 유명한 냉면집 목록은 이 책의 뒷부분에 따로 정리해놓았다.

다른 종류의 냉면들도 있다. 대표적인 것은 비빔냉면이다. 국물 없이 메밀 면 위에 매운 양념을 얹은 것으로, 면과 양념을 골고루 비벼 먹으면 된다. '비빔'은 '비빔밥'에 쓰이는 바로 그 단어로, 섞고 문지른다는 뜻이다. 회냉면이라고, 양념에 버무린 생선회를 추가한 비빔냉면의 변형도 있다. 이런 것들은 당신이 한국을 두번째 방문했을 때 맛보아도 된다.

한국인이 즐겨 먹는 또다른 국수 요리로는 칼국수가 있다. 이 단어는 칼과 국수가 더해진 것인데, 기계로 만든 것이 아니라 사람이 칼로 잘라서 만든 국수라는 의미를 담고 있다(물론 요즘은 기계로 만든 국수가 더 많이 쓰인다). 밀가루를 반죽해서 넓게 편 다음 밀가루를 묻혀가며 적당히 접은 다음 칼로 자르는 방식이라, 면의 굵기가 조금 굵은 편이다. 국물의 재료로는 소고기, 닭고기, 조개류가 가장 흔히 쓰인다.

칼국수와 비슷한 듯하지만 한국인들은 완전히 다른 음식으로 생각하는 수제비라는 것도 있다. 이것은 엄밀히 말하면 국수가 아니다. 두 시간 이상 숙성시킨 밀가루 반죽을 손으로 얇게 펴면서 적당한 크기로 떼어내 끓는 물에 바로 넣고 익히는 음식이다. 라자냐를 손으로 만든다고 생각하면 비슷하겠다(반죽에 달걀을 넣지 않는다는 점에서는 라자냐와 다르다). 매끈매끈한 식감이 독특하며, 국물은 칼국수를 만들 때와 거의 같은 방식으로 만든다. 하지만 칼국수는 면에 묻어 있는 밀가루가 국물에 섞여 들어가기 때문에 수제비에 비해 국물이 걸쭉한 편이다.

콩국수라는 것도 한국인만 먹는 아주 특이한 국수다. 면은 평범하지만, 국물이 특별하다. 콩을 삶아서 소량의 물과 함께 믹서(과거에는 맷돌)에 갈아서 만든 것이기 때문이다. 역시 처음 먹으면 당황스러운 맛이지만, 많은 한국인은 오랜 전통을 가진 이 음식을 별미로 생각한다. 차갑게 먹는 국수라서 특히 여름철에 높은 인기를 누린다.

국물 요리도 매우 많다. (앞에서 설명한 김치찌개나 된장찌개에도 국물이 있지만, 여기서 말하는 국물 요리는 국물의 양이 좀더 많은 것들이다.) 대표적인 것은 곰탕과 설렁탕이다. 둘 다 소고기를 오랫동안 삶아서 우려낸 국물에 밥을 말아 먹는 것인데, 곰탕은 소고기만 사용하고 설렁탕은 소고기, 소의 내장, 소뼈 등 여러 가지를 모두 사용하는 것이 다르다. 그래서 곰탕은 국물이 맑고 설렁탕은 탁하다. 소의 꼬리나 양과 같이 특정한 부위만을 이용해서 끓인 곰탕도 있다.

또다른 대표적인 국물 요리는 해장국이다. 이름부터 '숙취 해소를 위한 국'이라서, 음주 다음날에 먹기 좋은 음식이다. 해장국은 어떤 재료로 끓였느냐에 따라서 매우 다양한 종류가 있는데, 흔히 쓰이는 재료로는 콩나물, 우거지, 선지 등이 있다(그렇다. 한국인은 소의 피도 굳혀서 먹는다. 당황스러울지 모르지만, 꽤 맛있다. 의외로 외국인들도 좋아하는 사람이 많다).

해산물을 넣고 끓여서 먹는 음식도 여러 가지다. 꽃게를 넣고 끓이면 꽃게탕이고, 조개를 넣고 끓이면 조개탕이며, 여러 종류의 해물을 넣고 끓이면 해물탕이다. '해물'은 해산물을 통칭하는 단어다. 복어, 대구, 명태 등 다양한 물고기를 주된 재료로 하는 국물 요리도 별미다. 해산물을 넣고 끓이는 국물 요리에는 비린내를 없애기 위하여 다양한 채소들이 활용되는데, 그중 대표적인 것이 미나리다. 영화 제목에 쓰인 그 단어 맞다. 미나리는 영어로 dropwort, water parsley, water celery 등으로 번역되는데, 한국인 외에는 이 풀을 즐겨 먹는 사람들이 별로 없다.

그 외에도 여러 국물 요리가 있다. 감자탕은 돼지의 척추뼈와 감자와 채소를 넣고 끓인 음식이고, 삼계탕은 닭과 인삼을 넣고 끓인 음식이다. 감자탕은 소주에 정말 잘 어울리는 음식이니 당신이 소주를 사랑하게 되었다면 한번 시도해볼 만하다. 삼계탕은 작은 크기의 닭 한 마리가 통째로 뚝배기라고 불리는 돌솥에 담긴 채로 전달되기 때문에, 처음 보면 놀랄 수도 있다. 하지만 닭이 원래 그렇게 생겼다는 것은 당신도 이미 알고 있는 사실이지 않나(다행히 머리는 없다). 맛은 정말 끝내준다. 한국인들은 이 음식을 1년 내내 먹지만, 특히 지치기 쉬운 한여름에 많이 먹는다. 원기 회복에 도움이 된다고 생각하기 때문이다.

순두부찌개도 빼놓을 수 없다. 보통의 두부보다 훨씬 부드러운 순두부를 주재료로 매콤하게 끓인 찌개다. 한국인들이 가장 사랑하는 찌개를 세 가지 꼽으라면, 김치찌개와 된장찌개에 이어 세 번째 순위를 차지할 정도로 대중적인 음식이다. 순두부 외에 어떤 재료가 들어가느냐에 따라 여러 종류가 있는데, 소고기, 돼지고기, 새우, 굴, 조개, 낙지 등이 주로 활용된다. 한국의 다른 찌개들과 구별되는 것은 달걀을 넣어서 먹는다는 점이다. 한국 음식점에서는 주요리가 나오기 전에 여러 가지 반찬들이 먼저 제공된다고 이미 말했는데, 순두부찌개 전문점에서는 그때 날달걀을 하나 가져다준다. 삶은 달걀인 줄 알고 깨뜨리면 안 되고, 그냥 먹어도 안 된다. 뚝배기에 담겨 펄펄 끓고 있는 상태의 찌개가 나오면, 그때 깨뜨려 넣어야 한다. 뜨거운 국물에 달걀이 살짝 익으면서, 원래 맛있는 순두부찌개가 더욱 부드러운 맛으로 업그레이드된다.

육개장도 한국인들이 사랑하는 국물 요리 중의 하나다. 소고기와 여러 채소를 넣고 맵게 끓인 음식인데, 육개장에 반드시 들어가는 채소 중의 하나가 고사리다. 고사리도 오직 한국인만 먹는 채소 중의 하나로, 독성이 있기 때문에 아주 어린 줄기만 골라서 반드시 익혀 먹어야 한다. 한국인은 나물로도 먹고, 비빔밥이나 육개장에 넣기도 한다.

너무 많은 음식을 한꺼번에 소개하여 혼란스러울 것이다. 그러나 이것도 줄이고 줄여서 대표적인 것들만 고른 것이다. 짧은 한국 방문 중에 모두 다 먹어볼 수는 없을 테고, 이들 중 과연 무엇을 맛봐야 할까. 핵심을 말하자면 다음과 같다.

이 글에 등장한 수많은 음식 중에서 최우선적으로 맛보아야 하는 음식은 아무래도 '냉면'이다. 이왕이면 유명한 곳에 가서 제대로 된 냉면을 맛보길 바란다. 그다음으로는 뭘 먹을까? 당신이 비프 콘소메를 좋아한다면 곰탕을 맛보시길. 당신이 포크 스튜를 좋아한다면 감자탕을 맛보시길. 당신이 국수 마니아인데 여름에 한국을 방문했다면 콩국수를 맛보시길. 당신이 어제 소주를 너무 많이 마셨다면, 해장국을 맛보시길. 한 번도 먹어보지 않은 특이한 재료를 경험하고 싶다면, 그중에서도 '선지'가 들어간 해장국을 맛보시길. 당신이 매운 음식을 좋아한다면, 육개장이나 순두부찌개를 맛보시길. 인스타그램에 올리기 좋은 특이한 음식 사진을 원하신다면, 삼계탕을 맛보시길(삼계탕은 한국인이 외국인에게 가장 많이 추천하는 한국 음식이기도 하다). 아, 라면은 언제 먹지?

이미 먹고 싶은 음식이 너무 많아서 뭘 골라야 할지 모르는 상태겠지만, 아직 이 책에 등장하지 않은 멋진 한국 음식들은 더 많다(그중 일부는 뒤에 설명할 것이다). 결정 장애에 빠진 당신에게 충고한다. 한국 체류 기간을 하루만이라도 늘리시라. 그럼 최소 세 가지 음식은 더 맛볼 수 있다.

13.

Noodlicious Obsession: Koreans' Passion for Noodles and Pot Liquor

In June 2022, South Korean newspapers highlighted a fascinating piece of information as follows. "South Koreans are the world's second-largest consumers of ramen noodles per capita. The World Instant Noodles Association (WINA) reported that in 2021, South Koreans consumed an average of 73 ramen noodle servings per person per year, placing them just behind Vietnam, which claimed the top spot with 87 servings. Nepal followed closely in third place with 55 servings. Remarkably, South Korea has been the number one position since 2013, when the statistics began, but it dropped to second place."

What caught the attention even more were the colorful comments from readers on the article. Expressions like "I'm weirdly pissed off," "I'm going to have one and a half servings from now on," "I'm furious," "I need to get my act together", and "I'm having ramen for lunch today" were just a few examples of the passionate responses. It's clear that ramen holds a special place in the hearts and stomachs of South Koreans, evoking a range of emotions and sparking enthusiastic discussions about personal ramen consumption habits. Without a doubt, Koreans take their ramen seriously.

Ramen, originally from China, found its true calling in Japan with a fascinating twist. While initially enjoyed in specialized restaurants, the advent of instant ramen in 1958 transformed it into a convenient meal that could be easily prepared at home. In the 1960s, the Korean peninsula caught wind of this culinary sensation when a South Korean company imported the Japanese technology, catapulting instant ramen to newfound popularity as an affordable and time-saving meal option. Since then, Korean ramen has undergone a flavor revolution, adapting to suit the discerning Korean palate. As a result, it has emerged as a bolder, spicier counterpart to its Japanese cousin, boasting a tantalizing array of flavors and varieties. So from now on, when we mention ramen, we're talking about the Japanese version, while "ramyun" takes center stage as the beloved Korean twist on this noodle sensation. (Actually, Koreans call the Japanese version "ramen" and the Korean version "ramyun".)

Korea is truly a paradise for instant ramyun enthusiasts. With a staggering selection of over 500 varieties available on the market today (and that's excluding discontinued ones), the options are virtually limitless. You'll find an array of noodle thicknesses, an assortment of soup base powders with different flavors, varying levels of pot liquor, and even influences from Chinese and Southeast Asian cuisines. While the standard cooking time is around four minutes of boiling, there's a whole range of ready-to-eat cup noodles that can be effortlessly prepared by adding hot water and waiting a mere three minutes. The spiciness spectrum of Korean ramyun knows no bounds, ranging from mild and non-spicy to tongue-scorchingly fiery.

The popularity of Korean ramyun extends far beyond the borders of Korea, with significant exports to international markets. In 2021 alone, the export value reached nearly $700 million, increasing to over $900 million in 2023. The allure of Korean ramyun can be attributed to its addictive nature, capturing the taste buds of people around the globe. Additionally, the rising global popularity of Korean content, including movies, music, and dramas, has also contributed to the increased demand for Korean ramyun overseas. In some instances, the creativity surrounding Korean ramyun knows no bounds. A prime example is the iconic dish Jjapaguri, featured in the critically acclaimed movie Parasite, where two different types of ramyun, Jjapaghetti and Neoguri, are ingeniously mixed together to create a peculiar and flavorful combination.

Koreans' deep affection for ramyun comes as no surprise, as it embodies several elements that resonate with their culinary preferences. Foremost, Koreans have an insatiable love for noodles, which is evident in the plethora of noodle dishes available, including the beloved cold noodles, "naengmyeon" that we'll delve into later. Additionally, Koreans have a special fondness for "gukmul," a term combining "guk" (soup) and "mul" (water). This refers to a watery part of stews of soup, besides the solid ingredients. It's worth noting that "gukmul" is also the name of BTS member Jin's pet sugar glider.

Koreans have a strong affinity for "gukmul" as an integral part of their meals. In contrast to Western dining practices, Koreans rarely consume water alongside their meals (although they do enjoy alcoholic beverages), choosing instead to incorporate varying amounts of soup. Notably, Korean soups tend to have a more subtle level of saltiness compared to their Western counterparts. In fact, when Koreans sample Western soups while traveling abroad, they often find them to be overly salty. However, despite the relatively lower salt content in Korean soups, the overall salt intake among Koreans remains high due to their much consumption of soup. In fact, Koreans have the highest salt intake globally, surpassing the recommended levels set by the World Health Organization by more than double.

Ramyun offers a multitude of advantages beyond its delectable taste. One of its greatest appeals is its affordability and swift cooking time, catering perfectly to the fast-paced lifestyle embraced by Koreans who live by the mantra "pali-pali" (quickly). Additionally, ramyun serves as a valuable resource for preventing hunger among those with limited means. While the noodles and soup alone provide a delightful culinary experience, you can further enhance your meal by incorporating additional ingredients such as eggs, green onions, ham, cheese, rice cakes, dumplings, and more, tailored to your personal preferences. It also pairs exceptionally well with the beloved Korean staple, kimchi. Moreover, it is not uncommon for many Koreans to add a small portion of rice to the soup after consuming all the noodles, elevating the dining experience to another level.

Occasionally, Koreans enjoy eating ramyun without boiling. That is, dry noodles are lightly seasoned with the soup powder and consumed as a snack or with alcoholic beverages. It's worth noting that the noodles are cooked once in the factory and then dried, allowing them to be eaten without additional cooking. This particular way of enjoying ramyun was depicted in the well-received drama "Squid Game," where actors Lee Jung-jae and Oh Young-soo were shown enjoying this style of ramyun while drinking soju in front of a convenience store.

The Korean expression for 'Do you want to Netflix and chill?' involves ramyun, which translates to 'Do you want to (come over my house and) eat ramyun?' This phrase gained popularity after actress Lee Young-ae, known for her roles in the drama 'Dae Jang Geum' (Jewel in the Palace) and the movie 'Sympathy for Lady Vengeance,' said it in the film 'One Fine Springday.' In the movie, the actor Yoo Ji-tae from 'Old-boy' was the recipient of the phrase. (Of course, their plans didn't end up being solely about eating ramyun.) While you may not have the opportunity to use this phrase in Korea, who knows what may happen in the world. Therefore, I wanted to share this magical expression with you in Korean. (How kind of me!) The pronunciation might not be perfect, but it can effectively convey your intention. Let's memorize it: "Ramyun meokko gallaeyo?"

With the abundance of delicious Korean food to try during your limited time in Korea, I wouldn't recommend relying solely on ramyun for your one meal. However, just like grabbing a late-night chicken snack, you might consider picking up some cup noodles from a convenience store on your way back to the hotel. If you find yourself overwhelmed by the extensive variety of ramyun options at the store, I suggest going for Shin Ramyun, which happens to be the top-selling Korean ramyun. Shin Ramyun is a bit on the spicy side, so if you're not a fan of spicy food, you can go with the second best-selling product, Jin Ramyun. (If you truly want to embrace the Korean experience, you can even grab the smallest size of kimchi.) If you enjoy it, be on the lookout for Korean Ramyun when you return to your home country; most large supermarkets and Asian food markets will have a selection of Korean ramyun available.

In addition to ramyun, there is a wide variety of noodle

and broth dishes that Koreans hold dear. One of the most beloved among them is "naengmyeon", which translates to "cold noodles." Naengmyeon features a refreshing cold broth accompanied by noodles made from buckwheat. While there are various noodle dishes found worldwide, cold noodles are not common, and it's safe to say that none have achieved the same level of fame as naengmyeon. (Although it's worth mentioning that cold soba or udon noodles are consumed in Japan, they are typically enjoyed without a broth. The same goes for some noodle dishes that are widespread in Southeast Asia.)

Korea features a plethora of restaurants specializing in naengmyeon. While it can be challenging to determine an exact count due to many establishments serving a diverse range of dishes, including meat, that serve noodles too, it is estimated that there are over 20,000 restaurants nationwide that offer naengmyeon and other noodle delicacies. While some restaurants rely on factory-made broths, the most renowned and successful naengmyeon establishments prepare their own broth recipes and craft their noodles. Beef holds a pivotal role in naengmyeon broth, although some places incorporate chicken, chicken bones, pork, and other ingredients. Alongside meat, a variety of vegetables and fruits are commonly used as complementary components, and certain establishments even incorporate a broth made from water kimchi, a radish-based concoction without chili powder. The flavor profiles of naengmyeon can vary significantly from one restaurant to another, providing diners with a diverse and enticing culinary experience.

Indeed, there exist various types of naengmyeon, and the specific dish we have been discussing at length is called "pyeongyang naengmyeon." Its name is derived from Pyongyang, the capital city of North Korea, where it was originally created. The defining characteristic of pyeongyang naengmyeon is its "bland" broth. When Koreans try it for the first time, it is not uncommon for them to be taken aback by the apparent lack of flavor. Some even humorously describe it as if the chef decided to quit in the middle of cooking. The taste can vary from one restaurant to another, with some establishments emphasizing a particularly mild flavor profile. However, with repeated consumption, individuals often develop an appreciation for the subtle nuances of the light broth, eventually becoming avid fans of pyeongyang naengmyeon. Many people enjoy naengmyeon on a regular basis, with some even embarking on pilgrimages to celebrated naengmyeon restaurants throughout the country. In Korea, the question "Where is your favorite pyeongyang naengmyeon restaurant?" serves as a useful conversation starter and can lead to lively debates among individuals with differing taste preferences. It may be difficult to fully grasp the flavor after just one bite, but if you are a fan of the noodle dish, it is certainly worth a try. A list of particularly famous naengmyeon restaurants can be found at the end of this book.

There are other variations of naengmyeons worth mentioning. One notable type is "bibim naengmyeon", which consists of buckwheat noodles served without broth. Instead, they are topped with a spicy seasoning and enjoyed by mixing and rubbing the noodles with the seasoning, ensuring an even distribution of flavors. The term "bibim" is the same as the one used for "bibimbap," signifying the act of mixing and rubbing ingredients together. Another variation is "hoe naengmyeon", which incorporates slices of raw marinated fish tossed in spices alongside the noodles. These unique variations of naengmyeons are definitely worth trying during your second visit to Korea.

Another beloved Korean noodle dish is "kalguksu", which derives its name from the combination of the words "kal" (knife) and "guksu" (noodle). This signifies that the noodles are originally handmade and cut with a knife, rather than being produced by a machine (although machine-made noodles have become more prevalent in recent times). The process of making kalguksu involves kneading flour, rolling it out, folding it with flour, and then cutting it with a knife, resulting in slightly coarse noodles. The soup for kalguksu commonly features ingredients such as beef, chicken, and shellfish, providing a flavorful and satisfying dining experience.

In addition to kalguksu, there is another Korean dish called "sujebi," which is similar in some ways but considered a seperate culinary creation. Sujebi is not technically a noodle dish. To make sujebi, you knead flour, let it rest for at least two hours, then roll it out by hand, cut it into small pieces, and drop it directly into boiling broth to cook. Think of it like making lasagna by hand, although sujebi does not contain eggs in the dough. The resulting texture of sujebi is smooth and charming. The broth for sujebi is prepared in a similar manner to kalguksu. However, kalguksu usually has a thicker broth due to the incorporation of flour from the noodles during the noodle-making process.

Kongguksu, or soy milk noodle soup, is another unique noodle dish that is exclusive to Korean cuisine. While the noodles themselves are plain, the soup is what sets it apart. To make the soup, soybeans are boiled and then ground in a blender (or traditionally using a millstone) with a small amount of water. The resulting mixture creates an exceptional and somewhat surprising taste. Despite its initial unfamiliar flavor (it's a little bit similar to but definitely different with soy milk), many Koreans consider kongguksu a delicacy with a long-standing tradition. The noodles are served cold, making it a particularly favored dish during the summer months.

There are several popular broth-based dishes in Korean cuisine. While kimchi-jjigae and doenjang-jjigae also have broth, the focus here is on dishes that have a significant amount of broth. Two well-known examples are "gomtang" and "seolleongtang". Both dishes are prepared by simmering beef for extended hours and served with rice, but they differ in their ingredients and resulting broth. Gomtang features a clear broth made solely from beef, while seolleongtang incorporates a combination of beef, beef organs, beef bones, and other elements, resulting in a cloudy broth. Additionally, some kind of gomtang can be prepared using specific parts of the cow, such as the tail or rumen.

"Haejangguk", also known as hangover soup, is a popular broth dish in Korean cuisine, specifically enjoyed as a remedy for hangovers. There are varying types of haejangguk, each with its own set of ingredients. Common components include bean sprouts, "ugeoji" (outer leaves of napa cabbage), and "seonji" (coagulated cow's blood). While the idea of consuming coagulated blood may sound unfamiliar to some, it is a flavorful element in the soup, and surprisingly, many foreigners also appreciate its taste.

There are several seafood broth dishes in Korean cuisine that are prepared by boiling and enjoyed for their flavors. When blue crab, known as "kkotge" in Korean, is added, it becomes "kkotgetang". Similarly, the addition of clams, known as "jogae", results in "jogaetang". And when various types of seafood are combined, it is called "haemultang", with "haemul" referring to seafood in general. Some other dishes commonly feature fish such as blowfish, cod, pollock, and others as the main ingredients. To enhance the flavors and reduce any fishy odors, a variety of vegetables are added, including "minari". Yes, that's the word in the movie title. In English, minari is translated as dropwort, water parsley, or water celery, but it is not widely appreciated outside of Korea.

There are a few more notable broth dishes in Korean cuisine. "Gamjatang" (pork back-bone stew) is prepared using pork vertebrae, potatoes, and veggies. On the other hand, "samgyetang" is a chicken soup infused with ginseng, where a whole small chicken is presented in a stone pot called "ttukbaegi". It may be surprising to see the chicken served whole, but you've known for a long time that chickens look like that. And rest assured, it does not include the head. The flavors of these dishes are truly marvelous. Gamjatang pairs exceptionally well with soju, making it a tempting combination worth trying if you have developed a fondness for the drink. Samgyetang is enjoyed throughout the year, but it holds particular popularity during the hot summer months when individuals seek a revitalizing boost for their bodies.

One more dish that should not be forgotten is "sundubu-jjigae", a spicy stew made with soft tofu. Sundubu-jjigae ranks third on the list of Koreans' favorite stews, just behind kimchi-jjigae and doenjang-jjigae. The key ingredient that sets it apart is the soft tofu (silken tofu), which has a wonderfully delicate texture. Sundubu-jjigae comes in diverse variations, with additional ingredients such as beef, pork, shrimp, oysters, clams, and octopus. What makes sundubu-jjigae truly absorbing is the way it is served. Typically, in Korean restaurants, you are served a variety of side dishes before the main course. However, in restaurants specializing in sundubu-jjigae, a raw egg is brought to the table. It's important to resist the temptation to crack the egg too soon or mistake it for a hard-boiled egg. When the piping hot stew arrives, still bubbling and simmering, you crack the raw egg into it and mix it in. The heat of the stew gently cooks the egg, creating a creamy and delicious addition to the already flavorful dish.

Yukgaejang, a spicy beef soup with vegetables, is another beloved Korean soup dish. This flavorful stew features tender beef and a medley of vegetables, including a staple ingredient called "gosari", which refers to fernbrake or bracken fiddleheads. Gosari is a unique vegetable primarily enjoyed by Koreans, and due to its poisonous nature, only the youngest stalks are harvested and cooked. In Korean cuisine, gosari is commonly consumed as "namul" and is also incorporated into dishes such as bibimbap and yuk-gaejang.

Introducing too many food options all at once may be overwhelming. Although I've tried to make it simple, it seems that I have confused you with too many food names. Given the limited time of your visit to Korea, it's impossible to try them all. Without further ado, here are some tips help your choice.

Of all the foods mentioned in this article, your first priority should be trying naengmyeon. If possible, visit an eminent restaurant to taste the authentic version. Wondering what to try next? If you enjoy beef consommé, venture into gomtang. For fans of pork stew, gamjatang is a must-try. If you're a noodle aficionado visiting Korea in the summer, kongguksu should be on your list. Had a bit too much soju yesterday? Haejangguk is your remedy. To experience exceptional ingredients you've never tried before, opt for haejangguk with seonji. Craving spice? Give yukgaejang or sundubu-jjigae a shot. If you're seeking an unconventional and Instagram-worthy food photo, samgyetang is a great choice. (Samgyetang is undoubtedly one of the top Korean dishes that Koreans enthusiastically recommend to foreigners.) Oh, the agony of a life devoid of precious ramyun time!

You might already be overwhelmed with the multitude of food options you want to try, leaving you indecisive about what to choose. However, there are still numerous incredible Korean dishes that haven't been mentioned yet (some of which will be discussed later). Here's my advice for the hesitant ones: consider extending your stay in Korea by at least one more day, allowing yourself the opportunity to savor three additional culinary wonders.

14.

비빔밥과
길거리 음식들

한국 음식에 대해 조금은 알고 있는 독자라면 의아해할 수도 있겠다. 지금까지 그렇게 많은 음식 이야기를 했는데, 정작 가장 유명한 한식인 불고기, 갈비, 비빔밥이 등장하지 않았기 때문이다. 사실 이들을 먼저 소개하지 않은 것은 이유가 있다. 불고기, 갈비, 비빔밥은 자세한 설명이 필요 없을 정도로 외국인들에게 널리 알려져 있고, 세계 곳곳에 퍼져 있는 한국 식당에 가면 손쉽게 먹을 수 있기 때문이다. 굳이 한국에서 먹을 필요가 없다는 뜻이다(물론 한국에서 먹는 것이 외국의 한국 식당에서 먹는 것보다 맛있지만). 이번 글에서는 그것들을 포함하여, 아직도 남아 있는 한국 음식 이야기들을 마무리해보자.

먼저 불고기. 불고기는 이름 자체가 불에 구운 고기라는 뜻이다. 불에 고기를 굽는 것은 세계 어디에서나 사용하는 방법일 터이니 특별할 것이 없다. 하지만 한국의 불고기는 얇게 썬 고기를 '간장 베이스의 양념'에 재워놓았다가 먹는다는 점이 특징이다. 짠맛과 단맛이 절묘하게 어우러지기 때문에 외국인들이 선호하는 한국 음식 중의 하나다.

원래는 소고기로 만들지만 돼지고기로 만들기도 하는데, 이때는 혼동을 피하기 위해 돼지불고기라고 부르며 양념도 고추장을 베이스로 하는 경우가 보통이다. 대중적인 식당에서 제육볶음이라는 메뉴를 발견할 수 있는데, 이것이 돼지불고기와 매우 비슷하다(제육볶음은 한국인에게는 싼 가격에 한끼를 때우는 데 적당한 평범한 음식이지만, 몇몇 외국인은 의외로 이 음식에 열광하는 경우가 있다. 이걸 자신이 먹어본 한식 중 최고로 꼽는 사람도 있었다).

재미있는 것은 음식 이름 앞에 '불'이라는 말이 붙어 있는 한국 음식이 여러 가지가 있지만, 맵지 않은 것은 불고기 외에는 거의 없다는 사실이다. 불고기의 불은 불에 굽는다는 의미이지만, 다른 음식에서 불은 '입에 불이 날 정도로 맵다'는 뜻이다. 정말 상당히 맵기 때문에 한국인 중에도 이런 음식은 피하는 사람이 적지 않다. 그러니 메뉴판에서 '불'로 시작하는 음식을 발견하고 이것도 불고기와 비슷한 것이려니 하고 주문했다가는 소방차를 불러야 할지도 모른다(한국의 화재 신고 전화번호는 119다). 하지 말라고 하면 더 하고 싶은 것이 인간의 마음이니, 당신이 '불'로 시작하는 음식에 도전하고 싶을 수도 있겠다. 도전하는 것은 말리지 않지만, 그전에 의료비가 보장되는 여행자보험에 꼭 가입하기를 바란다.

갈비는 사람이나 동물의 신체 부위 이름인 동시에 음식의 이름이다. 엄밀히 말하면 갈비는 뼈의 이름이지만, 음식을 말할 때는 갈비뼈 근처의 고기를 뜻하고, 많은 경우에 뼈와 고기가 붙어 있는 모양 그대로 서빙된다. 대부분은 전혀 익히지 않은 고기가 나오고, 삼겹살집에서 그렇게 하듯 테이블 위의 불판에서 구워 먹는다.

그냥 갈비라고만 하면 소갈비를 뜻하는 경우가 많고, 돼지나 양이나 닭 등의 다른 동물의 갈비는 그 앞에 동물 이름을 붙여서 구별한다. 갈비는 크게 생갈비와 양념갈비로 나뉘는데, 상대적으로 더 좋은 품질의 고기는 양념을 하지 않고 그냥 구워 먹는 편이다. 때문에 대부분의 식당에서 생갈비가 조금 더 비싸다. 하지만 외국에 널리 알려진 한국의 갈비는 주로 양념갈비로, 소갈비나 돼지갈비 모두 한국인이 사랑하는 구이 요리이다.

갈비는 안심이나 등심에 비하면 조금 질기지만, 특유의 커팅 방법과 칼집 내기를 통해 먹기에 적당한 식감을 만들어낸다. 또한 양념에 재우는 과정에서 연육 작용이 일어나기 때문에 양념갈비는 조금 더 부드럽다.

한국에서 소갈비는 정말 비싸다(안심과 등심도 물론 비싸다). 비교적 저렴한 식당도 없지 않지만, 고급 식당의 경우는 정말 놀랄 정도로 비싸다(저렴한 식당은 미국이나 호주산 소고기를 쓰고, 비싼 식당은 한국산 소고기를 쓴다). 한 사람이 먹기에 조금 부족한 1인분의 가격이 40~70달러인 경우가 흔하며, 최고급 식당에서는 백 달러 이상의 가격이 책정되기도 한다. 정말 비싸지만, 정말 입에서 살살 녹는다. 이렇게 비싸기 때문에, 삼겹살과 달리 고급 소고기 구이의 경우 종업원이 조심스럽게 구워주는 경우가 많다. 양념갈비는 양념 때문에 쉽게 타버리므로, 대부분은 종업원이 구워준다(전문가가 구워도 고기 일부분이 타는 경우가 흔한데, 이때도 가위가 유용하게 사용된다. 버리는 부분이 최소화되도록, 못 먹게 된 부위만을 화려한 가위 기술로 잘라내는 것이다). 삼겹살과 마찬가지로, 그냥 고기만 먹는 것이 아니라 여러 채소와 다양한 반찬들과 함께 먹으며, 고기를 다 먹은 다음에는 냉면이나 찌개로 마무리하는 것이 일반적이다.

비빔밥은 밥 위에 다양한 음식들을 예쁘게 올린 다음 골고루 비벼 먹는 음식이다. 비빔밥을 만들 수 있는 재료는 무궁무진한데, 가장 기본적인 것이 나물이다. 고기나 달걀이 포함되는 경우도 아주 흔하다. 그 외에도 취향에 따라 다양한 재료가 첨가될 수 있다. 약간의 고추장이나 간장을 넣어서 먹는 경우가 많지만, 넣지 않을 수도 있다. 참기름은 거의 반드시 들어가는 재료다. 즉 비빔밥의 조리법은 하나로 정해져 있는 것이 없다. 그런 면에서는 샌드위치와도 비슷하다고 하겠다.

사실 비빔밥은 '일종의' 패스트푸드라고도 할 수 있다. 상당히 많은 재료가 들어가고 각각의 재료를 따로따로 조리해야 한다는 점을 생각하면 패스트푸드와 정반대 성격을 갖고 있지만, 그 재료 중 다수가 한국인들이 반찬이라고 부르는 것들, 그러니까 한 번에 많이 만든 다음 냉장고에 보관하며 여러 번에 걸쳐 조금씩 먹는 음식들이기 때문이다. 그러니 가령 혼자 사는 사람이 집에서 식사를 준비할 때, 주요리를 만들 만한 재료가 없거나 시간이 없을 때, 피곤하고 귀찮아서 요리를 하고 싶은 마음이 전혀 들지 않을 때, 냉장고에 있는 몇 가지 반찬을 대충 모아서 밥에 올린 다음 참기름과 고추장을 넣고 비벼 먹으면 그게 바로 비빔밥이다. 달걀프라이를 하나 추가하면 더 좋다. 밥은 어디 있느냐고? 한국인의 가정에는 냉동실에 얼려놓은 밥이나 진공포장 상태로 판매되는 즉석 밥이 언제나 있다. 전자레인지에 데우면 끝이다. (집에서 가족들이 함께 밥을 먹는데 메뉴가 비빔밥이라면, 엄마 혹은 식사 담당자의 그날 컨디션이 별로 좋지 않아서일 수도 있다.)

물론 비빔밥은 고급 음식의 성격도 갖고 있다. 정말 좋은 재료들로 정성껏 만들면 매우 훌륭한 주요리가 될 수 있다. 게다가 매우 아름답다. 처음부터 배열까지 고려하여 재료를 선택하고 손질하는 경우가 많아서, 미적 측면에서만 보면 한국 음식 중에 최고라 할 수도 있다. 하지만 아름다운 모양을 망가뜨리지 않고 먹을 방법은 없다. 얼른 스마트폰을 꺼내 사진부터 찍은 다음, 용감하게 모두 섞어서 먹으면 된다.

비빔밥이 집에서 만들어 먹는 '패스트푸드'라면, 식당에서 사먹는 한국인의 진짜 패스트푸드는 김밥이다. 김은 한국인이 엄청나게 많이 먹는 해조류 중에서도 미역, 다시마와 더불어 가장 중요하다. 김은 바다에 서식하는 해조류의 이름이기도 한데, 음식 이름으로 사용될 때는 그것을 건져서 종이와 같이 얇고 넓게 펴서 말린 것을 말한다. 한국인들이 워낙 김을 좋아하기 때문에, 양식을 통해 대규모로 생산된다. 주로 한반도의 남쪽 해안에서 양식하는데, 김·미역·다시마 양식장은 위성사진에서도 보일 정도로 큰 규모다. 김을 양식하는 나라는 한국·중국·일본 세 나라뿐인데, 한국산 김의 품질이 특히 좋아서 연간 7억 달러 정도를 외국에 수출하고 있기도 하다. (한국인들은 김밥의 재료로 쓰거나 기름을 바르고 소금을 살짝 뿌려서 구운 다음 주로 반찬으로 먹지만, 외국인들은 이를 술안주나 스낵으로 많이 먹는다.)

해조류는 대기에서 탄소를 제거하고 바닷물의 산성도를 낮춰서 환경보호에 매우 큰 도움이 된다고 알려져 있다. 플라스틱과 에너지 소비량에서 세계 최고 수준인 한국인들은 해조류를 많이 먹음으로써 지구에 대한 미안한 감정을 조금이나마 상쇄하고 있는 셈이다(세계에서 가장 낮은 한국의 출산율도 한국에는 나쁜 일이지만 지구에게는 좋은 일이다).

김밥은 김 위에 밥을 얇게 편 다음 여러 가지 재료를 놓고 돌돌 말아서 원기둥 모양을 만든 다음 한입 크기로 썰면 완성된다. 일반적으로 대여섯 가지 정도의 재료를 넣지만, 더 다양한 재료를 쓰기도 한다. 역시 샌드위치처럼 수많은 변형이 가능해서, 한국의 음식점에서 판매하는 김밥의 종류는 수십 가지에 달한다. 밥과 반찬이 합쳐져 있는 형태이고, 젓가락이 없으면 손으로 집어먹을 수도 있어서 매우 편리하다. 자동차나 기차에서도 먹을 수 있고, 사무실에서 일하면서도 먹을 수 있다.

김밥은 사 먹을 때는 매우 편리하지만 집에서 직접 만들려고 하면 상당히 많은 시간이 걸린다(엄청난 슬로푸드다). 그래서 한국인들은 자녀들이 학교에서 소풍을 갈 때, 아니면 온 가족이 멀리 여행을 떠날 때와 같이 특별한 날에만 집에서 김밥을 만든다. 김밥은 한 줄에 3~4달러 정도면 먹을 수 있다. 여러 사람이 조금씩 나눠 먹기도 편리한 음식이니, 혹시 김밥을 판매하는 식당을 방문하게 되거든 여러 종류를 시켜서 모두 맛보기를 권한다.

김밥은 마키 혹은 노리마키라고 부르는 일본의 음식과 비슷하지만 차이가 좀 있다. 마키는 밥 외에 한 가지 혹은 두세 가지 재료만 들어가서 크기가 작지만 김밥은 훨씬 여러 종류가 들어가고 크기도 좀 크다. 마키에는 참치나 연어를 비롯한 다양한 생선이 주로 들어가지만, 김밥에는 생선이 들어가는 경우가 많지 않다(참치김밥이라는 게 있기는 한데, 일본은 생참치를 사용하지만 한국에서는 익혀서 통조림에 담아 판매하는 참치를 사용한다). 그럼 어느 쪽이 원조일까? 두 나라 모두 오래전부터 김을 먹었던 나라라서 우연히 비슷한 음식이 생겨났다는 설도 있고, 일본의 마키가 한국에 소개된 이후에 변형되었다는 설도 있다. 하지만 일본의 마키가 아주 오래전에 한국에서 전파된 것이라는 설도 있다. 어쨌든 지금은 김밥과 노리마키가 상당히 다른 음식이다(캘리포니아롤은 노리마키가 미국식으로 변형된 것이다).

한국은 채식주의자가 살기 힘든 나라다. 엄격한 비건은 더 힘들다. 식당에서 파는 음식들 중에 고기가 전혀 들어가지 않는 음식이 드물기 때문이다. 눈으로 보기에는 고기가 없어도 국물을 내는 재료로 고기가 사용된 경우도 매우 많다. 김밥과 비빔밥은 채식주의자들이 선택할 수 있는 좋은 옵션이 된다. 여러 가지 김밥 중에는 고기가 들어가지 않은 김밥이 꽤 있다(고기는 없어도 달걀은 대부분 들어간다). 또한 비빔밥 중에도 고기가 없는 것들이 꽤 있으며, 비빔밥을 주문할 때 '고기를 빼달라'고 말하면 그렇게 해 준다. 따라서 채식주의자들이 꼭 알아야 할 한국어로는 '고기 빼 주세요'가 있겠다.

길거리 음식의 종류도 엄청나게 많다. 가장 대표적인 것은 떡 볶이다. 떡은 곡식의 가루를 찌거나 삶아서 모양을 빚어 먹는 음 식으로, 간식이나 디저트로 먹기도 하고 주요리의 재료로도 사용 된다. 떡의 종류는 굉장히 많은데, 그중에서 가장 단순한 가래떡 으로 만드는 것이 떡볶이다. 고추장과 설탕 등을 이용한 양념에 볶는 것이라 외국인이 먹기엔 매운 편이지만, 특별히 매운 맛으로 유명한 가게가 아닌 이상 못 먹을 정도는 아니다. 떡 외에 어묵이나 채소, 삶은 달걀 등이 곁들여지는 경우가 많다(라면을 넣기도 한다. 수프는 빼고).

순대라는 음식도 있다. 이건 아이스크림이 아니고 한국식 소시 지다. 돼지의 창자에 채소와 당면 등을 돼지 피와 함께 넣어서 만 든다. 수증기에 쪄서 그냥 먹는 것이 가장 흔하며, 볶음이나 국의 형태로 먹기도 한다.

호떡은 녹인 설탕과 잘게 부순 견과류가 속에 들어 있는 팬케 이크라고 할 수 있는데, 특히 겨울철에 한국인들이 정말로 사랑 하는 간식이다. 역시 겨울철에 인기 있는 간식 중에는 붕어빵이 라는 것도 있다. 생선이 들어가는 것이 아니라 생선 모양의 틀에 구워내기 때문에 이런 이름이 붙었다. 밀가루 속에 들어 있는 것은 주로 팥을 설탕과 함께 으깬 것이다.

당신이 여름철에 한국을 방문하여 무더위에 직면한다면, 꼭 먹어보아야 할 간식은 팥빙수다. 물 혹은 우유를 얼린 다음 곱게 갈고, 그 위에 설탕을 넣어 끓인 팥을 올린 간식이다. 빙수는 얼음물이라는 뜻인데, 팥 대신 과일이나 다른 재료를 이용한 빙수들도 있지만, 그래도 최고의 인기를 누리는 것은 역시 팥빙수다. 팥은 대부분의 나라에서 흔히 먹는 곡식이 아니지만, 한국인들은 매우 다양한 방식으로 즐겨 먹는다. 얼음 위에 팥만 올리면 당연히 맛이 없겠지만, 팥빙수에 올라가는 팥은 엄청나게 많은 설탕과 함께 오랫동안 졸인 것이라 달콤한 맛이 일품이다.

아직 끝이 아니다. 호두과자는 밀가루 반죽에 호두와 팥을 넣어 호두 모양의 틀에서 구워내는 일종의 쿠키 혹은 빵이다. 과거에는 고속도로 휴게소에서 주로 팔리는 간식이었지만, 지금은 전국 곳곳에서 쉽게 먹을 수 있다. 식은 것보다는 갓 구운 호두과자가 훨씬 맛있지만, 한 번에 크게 베어 물면 화상을 입을 수 있으니 조심해야 한다. 호두과자, 붕어빵, 호떡 등은 모두 서양식 빵 문화가 없던 한국에서 생겨난 간식들로, 한국식 빵이라고 해도 크게 틀리지 않는다.

당신이 한국에서 맛보면 좋은 음식 중의 하나는 회다. 소고기를 날것으로 먹기도 하지만, 날것으로 먹는 가장 대표적인 음식은 생선회. 앞에서 한국의 간장과 일본의 간장이 다르다고 했다. 두 나라 모두 간장 문화가 매우 발달하여, 만드는 방법과 숙성 기간에 따라 상당히 많은 종류의 간장이 있다. 하지만 근본적인 차이는 콩만을 이용해서 만드는 한국의 간장과 달리, 일본의 간장은 콩 외에 밀이나 보리를 함께 사용하여 만든다는 데 있다. 또한 한국의 간장은 메주를 이용하지만 일본의 간장은 메주 대신 특유의 곰팡이균을 넣어준다는 점도 다르다. 한국은 간장을 만들고 나서 남는 것이 곧 된장이 되지만, 일본은 간장 제조 후에 남는 것은 그냥 버린다. (한국 간장은 기계를 쓰지 않아도 되기에 가정에서도 만들 수 있지만, 일본 간장은 압축 과정이 필요해서 특별한 설비를 갖춘 공장에서 만드는 점도 다르긴 하다. 압축을 하기 때문에 남는 것이 별로 없는 것이다.) 하지만 일본에도 '미소'라고 불리는 된장이 있다. 이건 기본 재료인 콩에다 쌀, 보리, 밀가루 등을 적당히 섞어서 별도로 만든다.

비슷해 보이지만 한국과 일본의 간장이나 된장이 제법 다른 것처럼, 생선을 날로 먹는 방법 역시 한국과 일본이 비슷하면서도 다르다. 일본의 사시미와 한국의 생선회의 가장 큰 차이는 숙성 여부다. 한국의 회는 살아 있는 생선을 잡아 회를 뜬 후 '즉시' 먹는 것이고, 일본의 사시미는 하루나 이틀 정도 숙성시킨 다음 먹는 것이다. 이런 차이로 인해 한국의 회는 훨씬 쫄깃쫄깃한 식감을 보이고, 일본의 사시미는 부드럽고 풍부한 맛이 느껴진다. 일본의 사시미는 간장과 고추냉이 외에는 아무것도 첨가하지 않고 먹는 것이 일반적이지만, 한국의 회는 간장(이건 일본 간장이다)과 고추냉이 외에 초고추장, 쌈장 등 여러 가지 양념에 찍어 먹고, 깻잎이나 상추 등의 채소와 함께 먹는 경우가 더 많다(한국의 회는 소주와 어울리고 일본의 사시미는 사케와 어울린다).

앞에서 한국인이 사랑하는 다양한 면요리를 소개했지만, 사실 하나 빼놓은 것이 있다. 그것은 한국의 중국 식당에서 판매하는 짜장면이다. 짜장면은 잘게 자른 돼지고기와 양파를 비롯한 여러 채소에 중국의 첨면장과 비슷한 춘장이라는 소스를 넣고 센 불에 볶은 다음 삶은 국수에 비벼 먹는 음식이다. 짜장면은 중식당에서 팔지만, 사실 한국인의 솔 푸드 중의 하나다. 김치찌개나 된장찌개나 라면을 이길 수는 없겠지만, 최소한 10등 안에는 들어가는 음식이다. 음식 배달의 원조가 중식당이라 짜장면은 이삿날 배달시켜 먹는 음식으로도 유명하고, 지금보다 훨씬 가난했던 시절에는 서민들의 대표적인 외식 메뉴이기도 했다. 영화 〈올드보이〉에서 주인공이 15년간 군만두가 아니라 짜장면만 먹었다면, 역시 조금은 긴장감이 덜했을 것이다(갇혀 있는 주인공의 상황에는 물론 '만두'가 더 어울린다).

짜장면은 1905년에 인천 차이나타운의 한 중국 식당에서 처음 만들어서 팔기 시작한 것으로 알려져 있다. 중국 음식이라기보다는 한국에서 개발된 중국풍 음식이라는 뜻이다. 실제로 비슷한 것은 있어도 짜장면과 완전히 똑같은 음식은 중국에 아예 없다.

짜장면만 그런 것이 아니다. 한국에 있는 대부분의 중국 식당은 전통적인 중국 음식을 파는 것이 아니라 한국인의 입맛에 맞게 변형된 음식들을 판매한다. 물론 중국 현지의 음식을 거의 똑같이 만들어내는 식당도 없지 않지만, 한국에 있는 2만 개가 넘는 중국 식당 대부분은 한국식 중국 식당이다. 당신이 만약 평소 중국 음식을 즐긴다면, 그리고 한국 영화나 드라마에 흔히 등장하는 시커먼 국수가 어떤 맛인지 궁금하다면, 한 번쯤은 중국 식당을 방문해도 좋겠다. 아무래도 한국 체류 기간을 하루 더 늘려야 하지 싶다.

14.

Bibimbap and Street Food Extravaganza

You might think you already know a thing or two about Korean food, don't you? You might be scratching your head, wondering why I haven't talked about the big dogs yet: bulgogi, galbi, and bibimbap. Well, let me tell you, there's a method to our madness. These dishes are so well-known by foreigners and are available in Korean restaurants worldwide, so I figured, why bore you with something you already know? (Of course, indulging in Korean cuisine directly in Korea surpasses the experience of dining at a Korean restaurant abroad.) In this post, I'll dive into these classics and unravel the fascinating stories behind various Korean foods.

Let's kick things off with bulgogi, a dish whose name simply means grilled meat(gogi) over a fire(bul). While grilling meat is a universal practice, what sets Korean bulgogi apart is the magic that happens when thin slices of meat marinated in a savory soy sauce-based concoction. This perfect marriage of salty and sweet flavors has turned it into a darling among foreigners and one of the most sought-after Korean dishes.

Bulgogi is commonly crafted with beef, but it can also be prepared with pork, known as dwaeji-bulgogi, to avoid any confusion. In the case of pork bulgogi, the seasoning often incorporates gochujang, adding a spicy kick. Another kindred dish you might encounter in humble restaurants is "jeyuk bokkeum", closely resembling pork bulgogi. While jeyuk bokkeum is considered a simple and satisfying meal by Koreans, it has surprisingly garnered enthusiastic praise from some foreigners, with claims of it being the best Korean food they've ever tasted.

It's worth noting that while there are several Korean dishes with the prefix "bul," most of them are known for their fiery spiciness, except for bulgogi. While bulgogi refers to grilling over fire, in other dishes, "bul" signifies a level of spiciness that can burn your mouth. Those are indeed quite fiery, and many Koreans opt to avoid them. So, if you encounter a menu item starting with "bul" and order that assuming it's similar to bulgogi, be prepared for potential fire in your mouth. In extreme cases, you might even need to call the fire department (Korea's emergency number is 119). It's human nature to be tempted when told something is off-limits, so if you choose to try it, ensure your travel insurance covers any potential medical expenses.

Galbi, translating to ribs, is a term that carries a delightful duality, representing both a body part and a scrumptious culinary treasure. Strictly speaking, it refers to the bone itself, but in the culinary realm, it signifies the meat adjacent to the ribs, often served with the bone intact. In many instances, the meat isn't pre-cooked but is instead grilled directly on a tabletop grill, reminiscent of the practices observed in pork belly establishments.

When the term galbi is used without any specific mention, it often refers to beef ribs, while ribs from other animals like pork, lamb, or chicken are distinguished by prefixing the animal's name. Within Korean cuisine, there are two main types of galbi: saeng galbi (fresh ribs) and yangnyeom galbi (marinated ribs). The superior quality meat of saeng galbi is typically grilled without any marinade, making it slightly pricier and exquisite choice at most restaurants. However, internationally, Korean galbi is commonly known as marinated ribs, and both beef and pork ribs are beloved grilled dishes among Koreans.

While galbi may be slightly chewier compared to tenderloin or sirloin cuts, it employs a particular cutting and sheathing method that enhances its texture, resulting in a truly satisfying eating experience. Furthermore, marinated ribs, whether crafted from beef or pork, tend to be more tender owing to the marinating process, effectively tenderizing the meat.

In Korea, beef galbi, alongside tenderloin and sirloin cuts, can command hefty prices, particularly at upscale restaurants. Cheaper establishments may opt for American or Australian beef, while more luxurious venues favor the premium quality of Korean beef. A single serving, though not always sufficient for one person, can range from $40 to $70 and even surpass $100 at extravagant establishments. Despite the considerable cost, the undeniable melt-in-your-mouth goodness of galbi makes it an unparalleled delicacy.

Due to its expense, high-end grilled beef is often meticulously prepared by the staff, a departure from the casual ambience of samgyeopsal restaurants. Grilling yangnyeom galbi presents its own set of challenges, as the seasoning can easily burn. Even in the hands of professionals, certain parts may char, necessitating impressive scissor skills to remove only the inedible portions and minimize waste. As previously mentioned in the pork belly story, the enjoyment of galbi extends beyond the meat itself. It is commonly accompanied by a variety of vegetables, side dishes, and often complemented with cold noodles or stew.

Bibimbap is an enticing dish that showcases a harmonious arrangement of various ingredients atop a bed of rice, resulting in a flavorful ensemble when mixed together. While vegetables, known as "namul," form the basic foundation of bibimbap, it can also feature meats, eggs, and an array of other additions tailored to individual preferences. A dash of gochujang or soy sauce is commonly added, although it can be adjusted or omitted according to personal taste. Almost always present is the touch of sesame oil, contributing to the characteristic of bibimbap. Similar to a sandwich, there is no fixed recipe for bibimbap, allowing for endless possibilities for customization and personalization.

In a way, bibimbap can be considered a kind of fast food. While it may require individual cooking of each ingredient, many of these components fall under the category of "banchan", which are dishes prepared in larger quantities and stored in the refrigerator for multiple meals. This makes bibimbap a convenient choice for individuals living alone or in situations where time or energy for cooking a main dish is limited. By combining an assortment of side dishes from the fridge, adding sesame oil and gochujang, and mixing it with rice, a satisfying bibimbap can be created. Adding a fried egg on top further enhances the overall experience. As for rice, Korean households often have frozen rice stored in the freezer or convenient vacuum-sealed packages of instant rice available. Simply heating it up in the microwave provides the rice component for bibimbap. So, if bibimbap happens to be on the menu for a family meal at home, it could be because the person responsible for cooking, such as your mom, may not be feeling well that day.

Of course, bibimbap can also be enjoyed as a luxurious main dish when made with high-quality ingredients. Its beauty is undeniable, with carefully selected and artfully arranged ingredients that render it one of the most visually appealing Korean dishes. However, once served, there's no avoiding the inevitable act of mixing it all together, potentially disrupting its pristine presentation. So, before indulging, don't forget to quickly snap a photo with your smartphone to capture its beauty, and then bravely embrace the delightful chaos of blending all the flavors together.

If bibimbap represents the homemade fast food, then "gimbap" takes the crown as the true Korean fast food available in restaurants. Gim, also known as laver, holds a significant place among the various seaweeds that Koreans consume in abundance, including miyeok (sea mustard) and dashima (kelp). Gim refers to both the seaweed that grows in the sea and the dried and thinly stretched seaweed sheets resembling paper. To meet the high demand, gim is extensively cultivated through aquaculture on the southern coast of the Korean Peninsula, where sprawling farms of laver, sea mustard, and kelp can even be seen on satellite images. Among the three countries engaged in laver farming—South Korea, China, and Japan—South Korean laver stands out for its exceptional quality, resulting in annual exports worth approximately $700 million. While Koreans commonly use gim as an ingredient in gimbap or enjoy it as a side dish after grilling with oil and a sprinkle of salt, many foreigners also relish it as an enjoyable snack on its own.

Seaweed is recognized for its substantial environmental benefits, such as absorbing carbon dioxide from the atmosphere and helping to mitigate seawater acidity. South Koreans, with their high levels of plastic and energy consumption, may find solace in their consumption of seaweed, viewing it as a way to offset their environmental impact. (Interestingly, South Korea's extremely low fertility rate, while posing challenges for the country, can be considered a positive factor for the planet in terms of population control and resource sustainability.)

Gimbap, a culinary marvel, is crafted by layering a thin sheet of seaweed with rice, adding a variety of ingredients, rolling it into a cylindrical shape, and then slicing it into bite-sized pieces. While typically featuring around five or six ingredients, the variations are practically limitless. Much like the versatile sandwich, gimbap opens up a world of possibilities, with Korean restaurants offering dozens of creative types. It combines the flavors of rice and side dishes into a convenient and portable package. Gimbap can be enjoyed without chopsticks and easily eaten by hand, making it a practical choice for on-the-go consumption, whether in the car, on the train, or even while working at the office.

While purchasing gimbap is incredibly convenient, making it at home can be quite time-consuming, earning it the label of a "slow food." As a result, Koreans tend to prepare gimbap at home on special occasions, like when their children have school picnics or when the entire family embarks on a long journey. The cost of gimbap can range from as little as $3 to $4 per roll. Due to its shareable nature, it is often advisable to order a variety of gimbap when dining at a restaurant, allowing your group to sample different flavors and ingredients.

While purchasing gimbap is incredibly convenient, crafting it at home can be quite time-consuming, earning it the label of a 'slow food.' Consequently, Koreans often reserve the preparation of gimbap for special occasions, such as school picnics for their children or when the entire family embarks on a long journey. The cost of gimbap can range from as little as $3 to $4 per roll. Due to its shareable nature, it is often advisable to order a variety of gimbap when dining at a restaurant, allowing your group to sample different flavors and ingredients.

Gimbap and the Japanese dish maki or norimaki have similarities, but they also have distinct differences. Maki usually contains one, two, or three ingredients along with rice, whereas gimbap incorporates a wider variety of ingredients. In terms of size, gimbap is generally larger than maki. Maki commonly includes different types of fish like tuna and salmon, whereas gimbap generally does not include fish as a filling. However, there are variations of gimbap, such as tuna gimbap, which uses cooked and canned tuna, while maki typically uses raw tuna.

The origins of gimbap and maki/norimaki are subjects of debate. One viewpoint suggests that both Korea and Japan have a long history of consuming seaweed, leading to the independent development of similar dishes. Another perspective proposes that Korean gimbap was influenced by Japan's maki after its introduction to Korea. Additionally, there is a theory that Korean gimbap was introduced to Japan in ancient times. Despite the debate surrounding their origins, gimbap and norimaki have diverged into individual dishes with their own characteristics. (It is evident that California rolls, in particular, represent an Americanized adaptation of norimaki.)

Visiting South Korea can pose challenges for vegetarians, and adhering to a strict vegan diet can be even more difficult. Vegetarian options are often limited in restaurants, with meat commonly used as an ingredient, even if it's not immediately apparent, such as in broths. However, there are some viable choices for vegetarians, notably gimbap and bibimbap. Gimbap offers several meatless varieties (though eggs are usually included), and there are also meatless options available for bibimbap. By tactfully requesting "gogi ppejuseyo" (without meat please) when ordering bibimbap, vegetarians can effectively communicate their dietary preferences.

Street food in South Korea offers a plethora of options, and one of the hottest choices is "tteokbokki," consisting of simmered rice cakes. "Tteok" refers to steamed or boiled grain flour that is molded and enjoyed as a snack, dessert, or an ingredient in main dishes. Among the various types of tteok, "garae-tteok" stands out as a simple, long, white, cylinder-shaped rice cake. Tteokbokki is commonly made by stir-frying garae-tteok with gochujang (red pepper paste) and sugar, resulting in a flavorful and spicy dish. However, the spice level is usually moderate and not overwhelming for foreigners, unless specifically seeking out a restaurant known for its spiciness. Accompanying the rice cakes, you'll often find "eomuk" (fishcake), vegetables, and boiled eggs. Sometimes, ramyun noodles are also included, but without the soup.

Indeed, "sundae" (or soondae) is a unique Korean dish that might be misleading for those expecting ice cream. Sundae refers to Korean sausage made by filling pig's intestines with a mixture of vegetables, "dangmyeon" (glass noodles), and pig's blood. It is a ubiquitous street food item and can be prepared in different ways. The most common method is steaming the sausage, which is then enjoyed plain. However, sundae can also be stir-fried or used as an ingredient in soups.

"Hotteok" is a beloved Korean snack. It is a pancake that is filled with melted sugar and crushed nuts, creating an irresistible combination of flavors and textures. Koreans savor hotteok for its warmth and comforting taste on chilly days. Similarly, "bungeo-ppang", also known as carp bread, is a popular winter treat. Despite its name, it does not contain fish. Instead, bungeo-ppang is baked in a fish-shaped mold, giving it its recognizable appearance. The filling consists primarily of red beans that are mashed with sugar, resulting in a sweet and satisfying treat.

If you're sweating like a pig in Korea during the summer, you gotta treat yourself to some "pat-bingsoo" (red bean bingsoo). This icy dessert is crafted with meticulously shaved water or milk, and crowned with boiled red beans soaked in sugar. Bingsu literally means "ice water", and although there are other bingsu flavors that use fruits, teas, or coffees instead of red beans, red bean bingsu stands out as the most preferred choice. While red beans may not be a common pantry staple in most countries, the Koreans are onto something with the versatile ingredient. True, plain red beans on ice might sound unexciting, but the red beans in pat-bingsu are slow-simmered with tons of sugar, granting it a satisfyingly sweet flavor.

Hold on to your taste buds, because we're about to dive into the world of "hodugwaja," the Korean walnut pastry. This intriguing treat is like a cookie or bread, but with a twist. Crafted using a special mold shaped like a walnut, it cradles a heavenly combination of flour dough, walnuts, and red beans. Once exclusively found at highway rest stops, these goodies have now spread across the country, ready to satisfy your cravings. Trust me, nothing surpasses the taste of a freshly baked walnut bun that's still warm and gooey. Just a word of caution, though: take small bites because these treats can be piping hot and leave you with a burn to remember. Korean snacks like hodugwaja, bungeo-ppang, and hotteok are true originals, hailing from a land that didn't have a strong Western bread culture.

One of the culinary highlights you must not miss in Korea is "hoe", which refers to raw food. While you can enjoy raw beef, the most common choice is "saengseon-hoe", raw fish. Earlier, I mentioned the distinction between Korean and

Japanese soy sauce. Both countries have well-developed soy sauce cultures, offering various types based on production methods and aging. However, the key difference lies in the ingredients. Korean soy sauce is made exclusively from soybeans, while Japanese soy sauce incorporates wheat or barley along with soybeans. Another notable contrast is the use of "meju" in Korean soy sauce, whereas Japanese soy sauce employs a specific mold instead of meju. In Korea, leftover soy sauce is used to make doenjang, while in Japan, it is simply discarded. Korean soy sauce can be made at home without machinery, but Japanese soy sauce requires specialized factories and a compression process, resulting in fewer leftovers. Interestingly, Japan also has its own doenjang called "miso," which is made separately from soybeans and includes ingredients like rice, barley, and flour.

Just as the distinction between soy sauce and doenjang/ miso in Korea and Japan reveals culinary variations, the preparation and consumption of raw fish also showcase notable differences. The key disparity lies in the aging process of raw fish. Korean hoe is relished "immediately" after the fish is caught and filleted, while Japanese sashimi is allowed to age for a day or two before being savored. This contrast contributes to the varying textures and flavors. Korean hoe tends to be chewier, while Japanese sashimi offers a softer, more indulgent taste. In terms of serving, Japanese sashimi is typically enjoyed with minimal accompaniments such as soy sauce and wasabi, whereas Korean hoe is often dipped in various sauces like chogochujang and ssamjang, accompanied by vegetables like perilla leaves and lettuce. It's worth noting that Korean hoe is commonly paired with soju, while Japanese sashimi finds its perfect match in sake.

While we've explored a variety of beloved Korean noodle dishes, one notable omission is "jjajangmyeon", a staple found in Korean Chinese restaurants. Jjajangmyeon features a delectable combination of shredded pork, onions, and assorted vegetables stir-fried with "chunjang", a savory black bean sauce similar to China's Tianmian sauce. This tantalizing mixture is then tossed with boiled noodles to create a truly satisfying dish. Although commonly associated with Chinese cuisine, jjajangmyeon holds a special place in the hearts of Koreans as one of their favorite comfort foods. While it may not surpass the popularity of kimchi-jjigae, doenjang-jjigae, or ramyun, it certainly ranks among the top 10. Notably, Chinese restaurants are well-known for pioneering food delivery, and jjajangmyeon has become a representative moving day food. In the past, when people faced greater financial hardships, it was a frequent meal for the working class when dining out. To add a cinematic twist, in the movie "Oldboy," had the protagonist subsisted on jjajangmyeon for 15 years instead of fried dumplings, the tension may have been slightly alleviated. (Of course, considering the circumstances, "dumplings" were a more fitting choice.)

Legend has it that 'jjajangmyeon' originated from a Chinese restaurant nestled in Incheon's Chinatown back in 1905. While it may bear Chinese influences, 'jjajangmyeon' is heralded as a distinctively Korean creation rather than an authentic Chinese dish. Actually, there isn't an exact counterpart to 'jjajangmyeon' in China, although there are variations that share some similarities.

Jjajangmyeon is not an isolated example. Many Chinese restaurants in Korea have adeptly adapted their dishes to cater to Korean preferences rather than strictly serving authentic Chinese cuisine. While there are indeed some Chinese restaurants that excel at preparing genuine Chinese food, the majority of the over 20,000 Chinese restaurants in Korea specialize in Korean-style Chinese cuisine. If you have an appreciation for Chinese cuisine and are intrigued to taste the black noodles often featured in Korean movies and dramas, it's worth visiting a Korean-style Chinese restaurant at least once. Why leave when there's still so much more to explore in Korea? Stay one more day and let's see what other adventures await you.

15.
서울, 잠들지 않는 도시

한국에서는 카페에서 노트북이나 휴대폰을 테이블에 두고 자리를 비워도 아무 문제가 없다는 이야기를 앞에서 했다(어떤 사람은 이를 두고 'K-양심'이라고 하고, 다른 어떤 사람은 'K-CCTV'라고 말한다). 양심 때문이든 CCTV 때문이든, 한국의 치안 수준은 매우 높다. 낮이든 밤이든.

인생은 짧고, 여행자의 시간은 특히 빠르게 흐른다. 당신의 여행 스타일이 수면 시간을 최소한으로 하면서 최대한 많은 경험을 하는 걸 좋아하는 쪽이라면, 서울은 당신에게 최적의 관광지다. 24시간 불이 꺼지지 않는 도시이기 때문이다.

일단 밤새도록 문을 여는 식당과 상점이 정말 많다(24시간 편의점들은 당연히 24시간 열려 있다. 극소수의 예외는 있지만). 24시간까지는 아니더라도, 자정 혹은 새벽 한두 시까지 문을 여는 식당이나 술집은 더 많다. 당신의 숙소가 아주 특별한 지역에 위치한 것이 아니라면, 적어도 서울에서는 걸어갈 수 있는 거리에 반드시 한밤중에도 영업하는 음식점이 있다(그러니 다이어트 생각일랑 잠시 미뤄두고, 한국에서는 하루에 네 끼를 먹자).

재미있는 것은 '24시간 영업'이라는 표시를 걸어놓았지만 실제로는 24시간 문을 열지 않는 식당도 가끔 있다는 사실이다. '24시간 영업'을 '맛집' 혹은 '장사 잘되는 집'의 상징으로 생각하는 식당 주인들이 있기 때문이다. 인기가 없고 손님도 없는 식당이 그렇게 오랫동안 문을 열어놓지는 않을 테니, '24시간 영업'이라는 문구가 어느 정도는 품질을 보증하는 것도 사실이긴 하다. 하지만 어떤 가게에는 '24시간 영업'이라는 커다란 글자 아래 작은 글씨로 이렇게 적혀 있다. 브레이크 타임 02:00 ~ 07:00(웃기려고 일부러 그러는 것일까?).

코로나19 팬데믹 이후에 영업시간이 단축되긴 했지만, 서울에는 24시간 운영되는 시장도 있다. 대표적인 곳이 남대문시장이다. 남대문시장은 서울에서 가장 오래되고 큰 전통 시장이다. 6백 년 넘는 장구한 역사를 자랑하며, 무려 만 개 이상의 작은 가게가 밀집되어 있다. 상인과 쇼핑객과 관광객 들을 상대하는 음식점도 많다. 숭례문이라고도 불리는 남대문은 조선왕조 당시 도심으로 들어가는 가장 중요한 문이었고, 한국의 국보 1호로 지정되어 있다. 남대문시장에서는 정말 온갖 것들을 판매하는데, 낮에는 소매 위주로 밤에는 도매 위주로 영업이 이뤄지기 때문에

24시간 많은 사람이 오간다(물론 모든 가게가 24시간 문을 여는 것은 아니다). 하지만 솔직히 당신이 이곳에서 살 만한 물건은 많지 않을 것이다. 당신이 지갑을 열어야 할 더 중요한 장소는 동대문시장이다.

동대문시장은 그 규모가 어마어마하다. 1905년에 한국 최초의 근대식 시장으로 출발한 이곳은 서울 시민들도 어디서부터 어디까지가 정확히 동대문시장인지 말할 수 없을 정도다. 각기 이름이 다른 여러 개의 시장이 밀집해 있기 때문이다. 평화시장, 광장시장, 방산시장, 중부시장 등이 모두 1·4호선 동대문역과 2·4·5호선 동대문역사문화공원역 인근에 모여 있다. 영국의 건축가 자하 하디드가 설계한 동대문디자인플라자도 인근에 있다.

동대문시장은 특히 의류 분야에 특화된 시장으로, 세상에 존재하는 거의 모든 의류가 놀라울 정도로 싼 가격에 팔리고 있다. 어떤 스타일이든 어떤 사이즈든, 다 있다. 이 넓은 시장 중에 도대체 어디를 가야 할지 모르겠다면, 일단 두타몰 혹은 밀리오레를 가면 된다. 코로나19 팬데믹 이전에는 새벽까지 영업을 했지만, 팬데믹 기간 동안에는 자정 혹은 새벽 2시까지만 문을 열기도 했다. 지금은 대부분의 시장이 예전처럼 새벽까지 문을 열지만, 정기휴일은 있다.

서울에는 한밤중에 갈 수 있는 공원이나 언덕도 많다. 서울 시내를 동서로 지나는 한강의 남쪽과 북쪽 강변 모두에는 공원이 조성되어 있다. 날씨가 좋다면 강변에 있는 공원으로 가서 서울의 야경을 바라보며 맥주를 마셔도 좋겠다(한국에서는 공공장소에서 음주가 가능하다고 이미 말했다). 공원 곳곳에 위치한 24시간 편의점에서 다양한 주류와 간단한 스낵과 컵라면 등을 구입할 수 있다. 한강시민공원 중에서 특히 인기가 많은 곳은 여의도, 이촌, 반포 지구 등이다. 여의도나 이촌 지구에서 보이는 원효대교는 봉준호 감독의 영화 〈괴물〉의 주요 촬영지다. 여의도에서는 유람선을 탈 수도 있는데, 주간보다는 야간에 타는 것이 훨씬 아름답다(저녁 식사가 포함된 옵션도 있다). 이촌 지구에서는 강 건너편에 보이는 야경이 아름답고, 반포 지구에서는 분수가 설치되어 있는 반포대교와 플로팅 아일랜드인 세빛둥둥섬이 근사하다.

하지만 야간에 산책을 하기에 가장 특별한 장소는 낙산공원이다. 이곳은 옛 서울에 존재했던 성곽의 일부를 따라 조성된 공원이다. 언덕 위에 있지만 걸어 올라가기에 그리 높지는 않다. 지하철 4호선 혜화역에서 10분을 걸어가면 되고, 동대문시장에서 30분 정도 성벽을 따라 걸어갈 수도 있다. 수백 년 전에 건설된 성곽에서 서울 도심의 마천루들을 바라보면, 서울의 과거와 현재를 동시에 느낄 수 있다. 낮에 방문해도 근사하지만 야간에 방문하면 더욱 운치가 있다. 그야말로 인스타그래머블한 장소다.

젊은이가 많이 모이는 힙한 동네는 서울 곳곳에 여러 곳이 있다. 그런 지역에 있는 레스토랑과 카페와 바 들은 대부분 밤늦게까지 영업을 한다. 인사동이나 이태원과 같이 가이드북에 나오는 오랜 명소는 물론이고, 비교적 근래에 떠오른 동네인 경리단길, 한남동, 성수동, 상수동, 익선동, 신용산역 뒷골목, 경복궁 양쪽에 있는 북촌과 서촌 등에는 분위기 좋은 가게들이 즐비하다. 숙소와 가까운 곳을 한두 곳 골라서 방문해봄직하다. 대부분은 좁은 골목이 많아서 길을 잃기 십상이지만, 걱정할 필요는 없다. 당신에게는 스마트폰이 있고, (아주 운이 나쁘지만 않으면) 잠시 길을 잃는다 해도 머지않아 지하철역이 나타나기 마련이다.

당연히 금요일과 토요일 밤에 가장 사람이 많지만, 다른 날에도 서울 시내 곳곳에서는 자정이 넘도록 적지 않은 사람이 먹고 마시고 논다. '한국인들은 잠이 없나?' 이런 의문을 가질지도 모르니, 사실을 알려준다. 실제로 한국인들은 잠을 적게 잔다. 통계에 따라 다르지만 한국인의 평균 수면 시간은 일곱 시간 내외로 매우 짧은 편이다. 공부 부담이 큰 청소년들은 더 짧다. 한국인은 다른 나라 사람들에 비해 대략 매일 30분씩은 잠을 덜 자는 셈이다(어쩐지 피곤하더라).

그것 말고도, 야간에 서울 거리를 돌아다니다보면 생길 수 있는 의문이 하나 더 있다. '저 많은 붉은 십자가는 뭐지?'라는 것이다. 정말 많다. 한국인들은 익숙해서 이상하다는 생각을 하지 않지만, 외국인이 처음 보면 당황스러울 정도로 많다. 공동묘지가 동네마다 있는 것일까? 아니면 한국인은 온 국민이 적십자 회원인가? 이런 생각을 할지도 모르겠다.

당황하지 마시라. 그건 모두 교회다. 가톨릭 성당은 그렇지 않은데, 개신교 교회들은 흔히 붉은색 십자가 네온사인을 건물 꼭대기에 매단다. 그것도 최대한 크게, 최대한 높게. 다른 나라 교회들은 이러지 않는데, 한국의 교회들은 왜 이러는 걸까?

한국의 기독교는 그리 오랜 역사를 갖고 있지 않다. 천주교는

18세기 후반, 개신교는 19세기 후반이 되어서야 들어왔다. 개신교는 주로 미국을 통해 들어왔는데, 당시 개신교를 전파한 종파들은 대체로 교회 건물과 같은 외형보다는 신앙심 자체를 중시하는 계열이었다. 나중에는 엄청나게 많은 신도를 거느린 초대형 교회도 많이 생겨났지만, 초창기 교회들은 주로 일반 용도의 건물 혹은 건물의 일부를 사용했다(지금도 전국 곳곳에는 상가 건물의 한두 개 층을 사용하는 작은 교회가 많다). 여기가 교회라는 사실을 드러낼 만한 상징이 별로 없었던 것이다.

평범한 교회 건물에 십자가 네온사인을 다는 유행이 퍼지기 시작한 것은 1960년대의 일이다. 붉은색이 선택된 이유는 여러 가지 네온사인 중에서 붉은색이 가장 저렴했기 때문이라는 설이 있는데, 확인된 바는 없다. 이후 개신교도가 크게 늘어나고 교회도 엄청나게 늘어나면서 많은 교회가 서로 경쟁하는 관계가 되었고, 점점 더 크고 눈에 잘 띄는 상징을 내세우기 시작한 것으로 보인다. 현재 한국에는 약 천만 명이 개신교를, 약 4백만 명이 천주교를 믿는 것으로 추산된다(불교를 믿는 사람은 약 8백만 명이며, 전 국민의 절반 이상은 종교가 없다).

붉은 십자가가 점점 많아지고 커지고 밝아지자, 10여 년 전부터는 빛 공해에 관한 논란도 생겨났다. 도시의 야경을 해칠뿐더러 숙면에도 방해가 되니 규제가 필요하다는 목소리가 나온 것이다(어떤 곳에서는 한눈에 10개 이상의 붉은 십자가가 눈에 들어오기도 한다). 이후 광고 등 야간 조명을 규제하는 법률이 제정되었지만, 지금도 교회의 십자가는 규제 대상에서 제외되어 있다(개신교를 믿는 사람들의 표를 의식한 결과이리라). 작은 교회가 많다보니 한국에는 최소한 5만 개 이상의 교회가 있는 것으로 추산된다(치킨집보다는 적지만, 스타벅스나 맥도날드보다는 훨씬 많다). 그러니 수만 개의 붉은 십자가가 한국의 밤하늘을 밝히고 있는 셈이다. 아무튼, 붉은 십자가는 공동묘지가 아니라 교회일 뿐이니, 너무 놀라지 마시라.

야간에 방문하면 좋은 또다른 장소로는 대형 마트가 있다. 전세계 어느 나라를 가든 현지의 시장을 둘러보는 일은 즐거울 테지만, 한국에서는 전통시장 못지않게 즐거운 곳이 대형마트다. 이마트, 롯데마트, 홈플러스 등의 3대 체인이 있는데, 아무 곳이나 가도 된다. 다른 나라의 슈퍼마켓보다 훨씬 크고 훨씬 다양한 제품이 판매되고 있다. 까르푸나 월마트하고도 분위기가 완전 다르다(까르푸와 월마트 모두 한국 시장에 진출했지만 실패하고 철수했다. 두 기업의 실패는 수없이 많은 경영학 책에서 '현지화 실패 사례'로 다뤄지고 있다. 해외의 거대 유통기업 중 한국에서 살아남은 것은 코스트코가 유일하다).

한국의 대형 마트에는 정말 다양한 종류의 공산품이 있고, 과일, 채소, 육류, 생선 등의 신선식품도 있으며, 의류, 완구, 침구, 가전제품 등을 파는 곳도 많다. 대형 마트에서 팔지 않는 품목을 나열하는 것이 오히려 빠를 정도다(여기에 없는 아이템들을 잘 모아서 판매하는 유통업체는 따로 있다). 앞에서 수없이 등장한 다양한 한국 음식들의 재료는 물론이고 집에 가서 데우기만 하면 되는 즉석식품도 상상을 초월할 정도로 많다.

한 달에 이틀 정도를 빼면 매일 문을 열고(정부가 전통시장을 보호하는 차원으로 휴업을 강제하고 있다) 밤 11시 전후까지 영업하는 것이 일반적이니, 그냥 구경 차원으로라도 잠시 들어가볼 만하다(하지만 아마도 빈손으로 나오지는 못할 거다). 당신이 구매하기 적당한 아이템들로는 라면, 김(김밥에 도전할 것이라면 그냥 김을, 스낵으로 먹기를 원한다면 기름을 바르고 소금을 뿌려 살짝 구운 김을 사야 한다), 스틱형 커피(인스턴트커피와 설탕과 크림이 모두 섞여 있어서 뜨거운 물만 부으면 한국 스타일의 달달한 커피가 된다), 최근 한국에서 큰 인기를 끌고 있는 바프 아몬드(H는 묶음이다. 엄청 종류가 많은데, 베스트셀러는 허니버터 아몬드다), 쌈장 등이 있다. 한국에서는 엄청나게 많이 팔리지는 않지만 의외로 수출이 많이 되는 배 음료도 맛볼 수 있겠다. 한국어 상품 이름은 '갈아만든 배'인데, '배'라는 한글을 흘려서 쓰면 영어의 IdH와 비슷하게 보이기 때문에 외국인들은 IdH 드링크라고 부른다. 숙취 해소에 효과가 있어서 주당들이 특히 좋아한다고 한다. 원래는 한국의 음료 회사가 개발하여 판매하던 음료인데, 지금은 코카콜라가 판권을 갖고 있으며, 최근에는 숙취 해소 기능을 더욱 강화한 제품을 출시하면서 아예 이름을 '아이디에이치(I.d.H)'로 붙여서 화제가 됐다. 대형 마트는 전국에 4백 개 넘게 있으니 조금만 검색하면 쉽게 찾을 수 있다.

뷰티 제품이나 그루밍에 관심이 있는 사람이라면, 대형 마트보다 우선하여 찾아갈 곳이 있다. 전국에 무려 1,200개나 매장이 있는 '올리브영'이라는 가게다. 올리브영은 건강 및 뷰티 관련 제품을 파는 한국형 드러그스토어다. 백화점에서 팔기엔 가격이 싸고 대형 마트에서 팔기엔 부피가 작고 소량 구매에 적합한, 온갖 물건들이 다 있다. 국내외 다양한 브랜드의 화장품들이 있고, 건강·미용·그루밍 등과 관련된 소품이 매우 많다. 남자들을 위한 제품도 꽤 있다. 프랑스의 세포라가 화장품에 집중한다면, 올리브영은 화장품 비중이 상대적으로 적은 대신 건강 및 위생과 관련된 다양한 제품들을 구비해놓았다. 일본의 마츠모토 키요시와도 비교되는데, 마츠모토 키요시는 약국에서 출발한 가게라 아무래도 의약품의 비중이 높은 반면, 올리브영에는 의약품이 거의 없다. 올리브영에는 식품도 꽤 있으며, 무엇에 쓰는 물건인지 알아차리기 힘든 아이디어 상품도 많다. 하다못해 마스크팩이라도 구매할 수밖에 없을 거다.

외국인들도 많이 찾아서, 일부 점원은 영어나 일본어, 중국어를 구사할 수 있다(계산할 때 '멤버십 카드'가 있느냐는 질문을 받을 텐데, 관광객인 당신은 이런 게 있을 리가 없다. 구매 금액의 겨우 1퍼센트 정도를 적립해주는 것이니 너무 아까워하지 말고, 특가 상품을 노리면 되겠다). 올리브영도 밤 10시나 11시까지 영업하는 것이 일반적이다.

쇼핑과 관련해서 몇 가지 할 이야기가 더 있다. 한국에서 유난히 비싼 아이템과 반대로 유난히 저렴한 아이템들이 따로 있기 때문이다. 한국, 특히 서울은 물가가 비싼 편이지만, 그중에서도 과일의 가격은 상상을 초월할 정도로 비싸다. 날씨가 좋은 유럽 국가들과 비교하면 3~4배 비싼 것은 보통이고, 어떤 것은 열

배쯤 비쌀 수도 있다. 대형 마트에서 과일들의 가격을 보아도 놀라겠지만, 고급 백화점에 가면 거기에서 다시 두 배쯤 비싸지는 경우가 흔하다. 고급 백화점을 기준으로 하면 딸기 한 알(주의, 한 팩 아님)에 2달러, 사과나 배 한 개에 5~7달러, 멜론 한 개에 20~25달러, 복숭아 한 개에 4~5달러, 뭐 이 정도가 기본이다. 수입 과일도 결코 싸지 않아서, 블루베리나 체리와 같이 한국에서 많이 생산되지 않는 과일들도 미국이나 유럽에 비해 몇 배는 확실히 비싸다. 한국인이 가격에 큰 부담을 느끼지 않고 먹을 수 있는 과일은 바나나가 거의 유일하지 싶다. (하지만 한국에서 생산되는 과일들이 비싼 만큼 엄청나게 달고 맛있는 것도 사실이다. 대부분의 한국인은 외국에 나가면 과일이 맛이 없다고 느낀다.)

반대로 엄청나게 싼 아이템 중에 대표적인 것은 굴이다. 유럽이나 미국에서는 레스토랑 가격으로 굴 한 개에 4~5달러가 기본이고, 품종에 따라 더 비싼 것도 있다. 시장에서도 굴은 개수를 세서 판매하는 것이 일반적이다. 하지만 한국에서는 굴을 개수로 판매하지 않고 무게를 달아서 판매한다. 마트에서는 껍질을 제거한 굴 20마리쯤을 담아서 5달러 내외에 판매한다. 물론 한국의 굴이 크기가 좀 작긴 하지만, 굴이 비싼 나라의 10분의 1이 채 안 되는 가격이라 할 수 있다. 한국의 해산물 식당에서는 굴 한 접시(주의, 한 개 아님)에 15불 내외에 판매하고, 좀더 고급 식당에서는 굴을 한 사람에 두어 개 씩은 공짜로 준다(일종의 반찬으로 취급된다).

한국에서 굴이 이렇게 저렴한 것은 남해안을 비롯한 여러 지역에서 대규모로 양식을 하기 때문이다. 한국인들은 싱싱한 굴은 당연히 날로 먹고, 조금 선도가 떨어지는 굴은 밀가루와 계란옷을 입힌 다음 굽거나 튀겨서 먹고, 그래도 미처 다 못 먹은 굴은 얼려놓았다가 국이나 찌개에 넣어서 먹는다. 평소 비싼 가격 때문에 굴을 마음껏 먹지 못한 사람이라면, 한국에서 최대한 많이 먹고 가기를 바란다. 참, 한국인들은 굴에 레몬을 뿌려 먹기도 하지만, 대부분은 초고추장에 찍어 먹는 것을 좋아한다.

굴 이외에 한국에서 유난히 싸게 구입할 수 있는 제품은 무엇이 있을까? 아무리 생각해봐도, 안타깝지만 굴 말고는 없는 듯하다. 굳이 찾자면 '제품'이 아니라 '서비스' 중에는 있다. 미용실에 가서 머리를 자르거나 펌을 하는 비용은 미국이나 유럽에 비해 확실히 싸다. 남성 커트는 10~20달러, 여성 커트도 20~30달러 수준이고, 염색이나 펌 역시 40~80달러 정도면 가능하다(더 비싼 곳이 없지는 않지만, 대체로 그렇다. 위의 가격보다 다섯 배 이상 비싼 특별한 미용실들도 서울 강남에 있기는 한데, 일부러 찾아가려 해도 어려울 것이니 걱정할 필요 없다). 한국의 미용실은 가격만 저렴한 것이 아니다. 매우 친절하고, 매우 빠르며, 엄청 스타일리시하게 만들어준다. 한번 방문해볼텨?

마지막으로 좋은 소식과 나쁜 소식이 하나씩 있다. 먼저 좋은 소식. 앞에서 말했듯이 한국은 택시 요금이 매우 싼 편이다. 그러니 지하철과 버스가 운행을 멈추는 자정 무렵을 훌쩍 넘겨서 놀아도, 택시 요금 걱정 없이 숙소로 편안하게 돌아갈 수 있다. 이번엔 나쁜 소식. 원래는 그렇지 않았는데 최근에는 여러 가지 이유로 인해 특히 밤 10시부터 1시 사이에는 택시 잡기가 매우 어렵다. 그러니 두 가지 선택지가 있다. 적당히 즐기다가 지하철을 이용하거나, 아니면 왕창 늦게까지 놀거나(새벽 5시까지 놀다가 지하철 첫차를 타는 세번째 방법도 있긴 하다).

15.

Seoul: The City That Never Sleeps

As I mentioned before, in South Korea, you can casually leave your laptop or phone on the cafe table and it magically stays put. (Some people call it 'K-moral', others call it 'K-CCTV'.) Whether it's the power of conscience or the watchful eye of CCTV, South Korea takes security to a whole new level, 24/7.

Life is short, and time flies, especially for travelers. If your style of travel is to cram in as many experiences as possible with as little sleep as possible, Seoul is the perfect destination for you. Seoul is a city where the lights never go out.

To kick things off, Seoul offers an abundance of restaurants and shops that keep their doors wide open throughout the night. (Convenience stores, understandably, are the real night owls, open 24/7 with only rare exceptions.) Even if not operating around the clock, you'll find numerous eateries and bars that stay open until midnight or even until the early hours of the morning. Unless you're staying in an ultra-exclusive neighborhood, you'll always find a restaurant within a leisurely stroll, especially in Seoul, that satisfies your late-night cravings. So, let go of any thoughts about dieting for a moment, in Korea, please indulge in four meals a day!

It's quite amusing to discover that certain restaurants proudly display a sign that boldly claims "open 24 hours," yet they don't quite live up to that promise. It appears that for some owners, having the label "open 24 hours" serves as a symbol of prestige or success for their establishment. Undeniably, the phrase itself carries a sense of assurance, as it suggests that a restaurant staying open for such extended hours must be prosperous and thriving. However, it can be a source of amusement to find the small print beneath the grand proclamation stating something along the lines of "Break time 02:00 - 07:00." (Are they doing it on purpose to be funny?)

In Seoul, you can find a few markets that remain open round the clock, although their operating hours have been slightly adjusted during the pandemic. One notable example is Namdaemun Market, the oldest and largest traditional market in the city, boasting a rich history spanning over 600 years. With its vast array of more than 10,000 small shops, the market caters to both locals and tourists alike. Additionally, a multitude of eateries are available, catering to the needs of vendors, shoppers, and visitors. Namdaemun (Gate), also known as Sungnyemun, holds great significance as the primary entrance to the city center during the Joseon Dynasty and proudly bears the title of Korea's National Treasure No. 1. At Namdaemun Market, you can find virtually anything your heart desires. As a retail hub during the day and a wholesale center at night, it sees bustling activity around the clock, although not all shops operate 24/7. However, it's worth noting that while the market offers a diverse range of goods, you might find Dongdaemun Market to be a more suitable destination for satisfying your shopping cravings.

Dongdaemun Market is a sprawling and monumental destination. It first emerged in 1905 as Korea's inaugural modern market, and its sheer scale can perplex even the locals when it comes to pinpointing its exact boundaries. Comprising several interconnected markets, each with its respective name, Dongdaemun Market has become an intricate tapestry of commerce. Notable market sections such as Pyeonghwa Market, Gwangjang Market, Bangsan Market, and Jungbu Market are clustered around Dongdaemun Station, accessible via Lines 1 and 4, as well as Dongdaemun History and Culture Park Station, which is served by Lines 2, 4, and 5. A stone's throw away from the bustling markets lies the iconic Dongdaemun Design Plaza (DDP), an architectural marvel envisioned by the celebrated British architect Zaha Hadid.

Dongdaemun Market, a haven for fashion enthusiasts, is renowned for its extensive range of clothing offerings, where you can discover an astonishing array of styles and sizes at incredibly affordable prices. Whatever you're seeking, be it any style imaginable, you'll find it within the market's sprawling expanse. If you find yourself overwhelmed by the sheer size of this bustling marketplace, make your way to Dutamall or Miliore, two popular destinations that offer a more focused shopping experience. Prior to the pandemic, these establishments pleased shoppers by staying open until the early hours of the morning, but their operating hours had since been adjusted to close around midnight or 2 am. But, currently, almost every market has resumed their full late-night operations once again, while some sections still close their doors regularly.

Seoul offers a diverse range of parks and hills that are equally captivating during the late hours. The city is blessed with parks located on both the southern and northern banks of the Han River, which flows through the heart of downtown Seoul. This abundance of green spaces provides plentiful opportunities for nighttime adventures. On pleasant evenings, you can head to one of the riverside parks, unwind with a refreshing beer, and immerse yourself in the enchanting night views of Seoul. (Remember, I mentioned earlier that public drinking is legal in Korea.) Within these parks, you'll find 24-hour convenience stores that offer a selection of alcoholic beverages and light snacks, including cup noodles.

Among the notable sections of the Han River Citizen Park are the vibrant districts of Yeouido, Ichon, and Banpo. Yeouido and Ichon offer splendid views of the iconic Wonhyo Bridge, which gained fame as a filming location in Bong Joon-ho's film, The Host. In Yeouido, you can also embark on a nighttime boat ride, where the allure is heightened under the cover of darkness, and enjoy a charming dinner while cruising the river. The Ichon district presents breathtaking vistas across the river, while the Banpo district captivates with the Banpo Bridge adorned with its enchanting fountains and floating islands (Sebitseom).

But, a truly enchanting spot for a nocturnal wander is Naksan Park, nestled along a section of Seoul's historic castle wall. Perched atop a gentle hill, Naksan Park provides a pleasant ascent that doesn't require arduous climbing. You can easily reach the park with a mere 10-minute stroll from Hyehwa Station on Subway Line 4, or you can embark on a scenic 30-minute walk along the city walls from Dongdaemun Market. From this vantage point, gazing upon the modern skyscrapers that adorn downtown Seoul while standing within the remnants of a centuries-old castle is a remarkable juxtaposition of the city's past and present. Naksan Park proves to be a splendid destination both during the day and at night, where its allure is heightened. However, the park's enchanting beauty truly shines under the starry sky, making it an Instagrammable hotspot for capturing stunning moments of Seoul's past and present in perfect harmony.

Seoul is brimming with vibrant neighborhoods that are buzzing hangouts for young people, offering a wide range of options for late-night dining, cozy cafes, and trendy bars.

In addition to well-known areas like Insadong and Itaewon, there are also emerging districts to explore, such as Gyeongridan-gil, Hannam-dong, Seongsu-dong, Sangsu-dong, Iksun-dong, the hidden alleys near Sinyongsan Station, and the charming neighborhoods of Bukchon and Seochon, located on either side of the majestic Gyeongbokgung Palace. Choose a couple of these lively enclaves that are conveniently located near your accommodation and embark on an exploration of their unique offerings. While the labyrinthine streets may occasionally confuse you, there's no need to worry. Your trusty smartphone will guide your way, and even if you happen to wander off track for a while, you can be confident that stumbling upon a metro station is only a matter of time (unless luck plays an unexpected trick).

Naturally, Friday and Saturday nights take center stage with their vibrant energy, but Seoul never fails to provide a lively atmosphere, even on other days of the week. People can be found drinking, dining, and enjoying themselves well past midnight. You might wonder, "Do Koreans ever sleep?" Well, it is true that Koreans tend to get less sleep. According to statistics, the average Korean gets around 7 hours of sleep, which is notably shorter than in other countries. This sleep deprivation is particularly prevalent among teenagers who carry heavy study loads. On average, Koreans sleep approximately 30 minutes less per day compared to their counterparts in other countries. (Perhaps that's the reason behind my constant fatigue?)

Aside from that, there's one more question that may arise while wandering the streets of Seoul at night: What are all those red crosses? You'll notice an abundance of them, as red crosses adorn multiple locations. While Koreans are accustomed to their presence and don't find it peculiar, it can be quite perplexing for a foreigner encountering them for the first time. Do they imply the existence of a cemetery in every neighborhood? Or perhaps every Korean is a member of the Red Cross? These thoughts might cross your mind.

No need to worry, those are actually churches. While Catholic churches may not have them, it's quite common for Protestant churches in Korea to proudly display neon red crosses atop their buildings, as large and high as possible. While churches in other countries don't do this, why do churches in Korea?

Christianity in South Korea has a relatively short history, with Catholicism arriving in the late 18th century and Protestantism in the late 19th century. The introduction of Protestantism was largely influenced by American missionaries, and the denominations that brought it to Korea often prioritized faith over extravagant church buildings. While mega-size churches with an enormous number of believers emerged later in South Korea, the earliest churches found their humble beginnings in general-purpose buildings or shared spaces within existing structures. Even today, you can find a lot of small churches occupying a floor or two of commercial buildings across the country. As a result, there were limited symbols or visual cues to indicate the presence of a church.

It wasn't until the 1960s that the trend of adorning plain church buildings with neon crosses began to gain prevalence. The exact reason behind the choice of red as the predominant color remains speculative, with one theory suggesting that it was selected for its affordability among the various neon color options. Nevertheless, as the Protestant population in South Korea experienced substantial growth, accompanied by a significant increase in the number of churches, a sense of competition emerged, prompting the adoption of larger and more prominent symbols. Presently, South Korea is home to an estimated 10 million Protestants and 4 million Catholics. (Around 8 million follow Buddhism, while over half of the country's population does not have a religious affiliation.)

Over the past decade, the increase in the number, size, and brightness of red crosses on churches has ignited controversy, particularly in relation to light pollution concerns. It's not uncommon to spot more than 10 red crosses in a single glance in some areas. While regulations have been implemented to control nighttime lighting and advertising, church crosses have received an exemption, possibly due to political considerations, including the influence of Protestant votes. (South Korea boasts an estimated 50,000 churches, surpassing the number of Starbucks or McDonald's locations but falling short of chikin restaurants.) As a result, the South Korean night sky is illuminated by the brilliance of tens of thousands of red crosses. Rest assured, these crosses symbolize churches, not cemeteries, so there's no cause for alarm.

Another exciting destination to experience at night is a hypermarket. No matter where you find yourself in the world, exploring local markets is always a delight, and in Korea, hypermarkets offer an equally captivating experience compared to traditional markets. The three major chains - E-Mart, Lotte Mart, and Homeplus - are worth a visit. These hypermarkets surpass the scale of supermarkets found in other countries and display a vast array of products. The atmosphere within is distinctively different from that of Carrefour or Walmart. (Carrefour and Walmart made unsuccessful attempts to enter the Korean market and eventually withdrew. Their failures have been extensively discussed in numerous business books as "localization failures." Costco stands as the sole foreign retail giant to survive in Korea.)

Korean hypermarkets offer a wide array of products, ranging from manufactured goods to fresh produce such as fruits, vegetables, meat, and fish. Additionally, they provide clothing, toys, bedding, appliances, and a plethora of other items. It is challenging to identify specific products that Korean hypermarkets do not sell, as their offerings are comprehensive. (There are specialized retailers that focus on curating and selling unique items not generally found in hypermarkets, and I will discuss these stores later.) The assortment of ingredients for various Korean dishes, as well as the extensive selection of ready-made meals for convenient home heating, is truly impressive.

These hypermarkets operate every day, except for a few days mandated by the government to protect traditional markets. They usually close around 11 p.m., so it's worth stopping by for a quick browse. And chances are, you won't leave empty-handed. Ideal items for foreigners to buy at

Korean hypermarkets include ramyun noodles, laver (plain for making gimbap, lightly toasted for snacking), coffee on a stick (a sweetened Korean-style coffee made with instant coffee, sugar, and cream), and Hbaf almonds (with the H silent, and Honey Butter Almonds being the top-selling flavor among various options). You can also try a pear drink, known as 'crushed pear,' which, although not a major seller in Korea, is surprisingly exported. Foreigners often refer to it as the IdH drink due to the resemblance of the Korean word for 'pear (bae)' in a running style to the English letters IdH. This drink is especially in demand among those seeking hangover relief. Initially developed and sold by a Korean beverage company, Coca-Cola now holds the rights and has recently launched an even more potent hangover-relieving version called "I.d.H.," gaining big popularity. With over 400 hypermarkets scattered throughout the country, a little searching will make it easy to find one nearby.

If you're interested in grooming or beauty products, there's a place you should visit before heading to the hypermarkets - Olive Young. With 1,200 stores nationwide, Olive Young is a Korean drugstore specializing in health and beauty products. They have everything that is cheap enough to be sold in a department store and small enough to be bought in bulk at a hypermarket. You'll find cosmetics from various brands, both domestic and foreign, as well as a plethora of accessories related to health, beauty, and grooming. Olive Young also caters to men with a decent selection of products. Unlike France's Sephora, which focuses primarily on cosmetics, Olive Young has a relatively smaller collection of cosmetics, but abundant health and hygiene products. It can be compared to Japan's Matsumoto Kiyoshi, which originated as a pharmacy and thus stocks a higher proportion of medicines, although Olive Young has fewer medicinal products. Additionally, you'll find a variety of food items and unique products that might leave you wondering their purpose. Anyway, you can't help but buy something, even if it's just a face mask sheet.

The store is popular among foreigners, and you'll find that some of the staff can speak English, Japanese, and Chinese. At the checkout, they may ask if you have a "membership card," but as a tourist, it's unlikely that you have one. The membership card only offers about a 1% mileage on your purchase, so it's not worth obtaining unless you plan to make frequent visits. Instead, keep an eye out for any special promotions or discounts available. It's worth noting that Olive Young often has extended operating hours, with some stores staying open until 10 or 11 pm, allowing for convenient shopping even in the evenings.

When it comes to shopping in South Korea, there are a few things to keep in mind. While the country, especially Seoul, has a high cost of living, some items are exceptionally expensive, while others are surprisingly cheap. For example, the price of fruit in Korea is notoriously high. Compared to sunny European countries, you can expect to pay three to four times as much, and sometimes even ten times as much. Prices for fruit in large supermarkets might surprise you, but they can be double in high-end department stores. To give you an idea, a single strawberry can cost around $2 (note, not per pack), while an apple or pear can cost between $5 and $7, a cantaloupe can go for $20 to $25, and a peach might be $4 to $5. Even imported fruits are not cheap, and blueberries and cherries, for example, can cost several times more than in the US or Europe. Bananas are one of the few affordable fruits in Korea. However, it's worth noting that Korean fruits are incredibly sweet and delicious, which is why many Koreans find fruit tasteless when they travel abroad.

On the other hand, oysters are a prime example of an incredibly affordable item in Korea. In Europe and the United States, oysters can cost between $4 and $5 per piece in restaurants, with some varieties being even more expensive. Even at markets, oysters are commonly sold by the dozen. However, in Korea, oysters are sold by weight rather than by number. In supermarkets, a bag of 20 shucked oysters costs around $5. While Korean oyster may be smaller, they're still less than a tenth of the price of oysters in other countries where they are more expensive. At seafood restaurants in Korea, a plate of oysters (note, not a single one) usually costs around $15, and at more upscale restaurants, a couple of oysters per person are often provided for free as a side dish.

Why are oysters so cheap in South Korea? Well, turns out they're farmed in huge quantities in many parts of the coast, especially in the south. And although Koreans love them raw, the slightly less-than-fresh ones get thrown into a batter of flour and egg and baked or fried. Any leftovers? No worries, they're frozen and later thrown into soups and stews. So if you're an oyster lover who's been held back by the steep prices elsewhere, it's time to hit up Korea and chow down on all the shelled goodness you can handle. And speaking of chowing down, while some Koreans may give their oysters a squeeze of lemon, most prefer to dip them in choguchujang (red chili pepper paste with vinegar) for a real kick in the taste buds.

Besides oysters, what else can you buy in Korea that's exceptionally cheap? I've racked my brain, but I'm coming up empty-handed. If there's something in Korea that's exceptionally cheap besides oysters, it's probably not a product, but a service. Like, for instance, getting your hair done at a salon. Trust me, compared to the US or Europe, you're getting a steal here. Guys can get a trim for just $10-20, and ladies can expect to shell out $20-30. And if you're feeling particularly brave, you can even score some color or a perm for just $40-80. Now, there are some uppity salons in Gangnam that'll charge you a small fortune, but they're pretty well-hidden, so don't worry too much. And the cherry on top? Korean salons are not only affordable, but they're also super friendly, super fast, and super stylish. So why not treat yourself to a little pampering?

Finally, I've got some good news and some bad news for you. First, the good news: Taxis in Korea are dirt cheap! So even if you stay out until midnight when the buses and subways stop running, you won't have to worry about breaking the bank on a taxi ride back to your hotel. Now for the bad news: Due to multifaceted reasons, it has become quite a challenge to snag a taxi, particularly between 10 p.m. and 1 a.m. So, you have two options. Either you can pace yourself and stick to moderate fun, opting for the subway instead, or you can go all out and party by 1 or 2 a.m. (Or there's always option three: stay out until 5 a.m. and hop on the first subway).

16.

한국 여행 전에 보면 좋은 영화와 드라마들

한국 영화나 드라마를 보다보면 교도소 출소 장면이 흔히 나온다. 재소자 신분에서 막 해방된 사람은 건달일 수도 있고 정치인일 수도 있고 평범한 주부일 수도 있다. 공금을 횡령한 회사원일 수도 있고 마약사범일 수도 있고 살인범일 수도 있다. 그들이 복역한 기간은 짧게는 한두 달부터 길게는 수십 년에 이른다. 간혹 마중 나온 사람이 아무도 없을 때도 있지만, 대부분은 누군가가 기다리고 있다. 교도소 앞에서 기다리고 있던 지인들은 애틋한 포옹, 담백한 악수, 혹은 깍듯한 90도 인사를 건넨 다음, 반드시 이것을 건넨다. 일회용 접시 혹은 비닐봉투에 담긴 하얀 직육면체. 그것을 건네받은 사람은 크게 한입 베어 문다. 두부다.

　감옥살이를 하고 나온 사람에게 두부를 먹이는 문화가 언제부터 생겨났는지는 모른다. 왜 이런 문화가 생겼는지도 확실하지 않지만, 여러 가지 설이 있기는 하다. 하얀 두부처럼 앞으로는 깨끗하게 살라는 뜻을 담고 있다는 해석이 있는가 하면, 교도소에 있는 동안 부족했던 영양 보충을 위해 단백질이 풍부한 두부를 먹인다는 해석도 있고, 출소하자마자 과식을 하기 쉬우니 포만감이 있고 소화가 잘되는 두부를 먼저 먹게 한다는 해석도 있다. 하지만 내가 가장 좋아하고 가장 그럴듯하다고 생각하는 다분히 문학적인 해석은 이렇다. 두부는 콩으로 만든다. 콩으로 두부를 만들 수는 있지만, 두부를 다시 콩으로 만들 수는 없다. 즉, 두부를 먹이는 행위는 '죄를 짓는 과거의 삶'으로 다시는 되돌아가지 말라는 뜻을 담고 있다는 것이다.

이런 해석이 억지처럼 들릴 수 있다. 스테이크를 다시 소로 만들 수 없고, 치즈를 다시 우유로 만들 수 없고, 포도주를 다시 포도로 만들 수 없고, 김치를 다시 배추로 만들 수는 없으니 말이다. 그럼 뭐든 먹어도 되는데 왜 하필 두부를? 하지만 스토리가 더 있다. 콩은 한국에서 수감 생활을 상징하는 곡식이다. '콩밥을 먹는다'라는 말은 감옥살이를 의미하는 관용적인 표현이다(한국 영화에서 "너, 콩밥 먹고 싶냐?"라는 대사를 발견한다면, 그건 메뉴를 고르라는 뜻이 아니라 감옥에 갈 만한 행동을 하지 말라는 뜻이다). 실제로 한국의 감옥에서는 '콩밥'을 준다(내가 아직 들어가보지 않아서 확신할 수는 없는데, 모든 끼니는 아니더라도 꽤 자주 주는 것은 사실인 듯하다). 재소자에게도 어느 정도 균형 잡힌 식사를 제공해야 하는데, 가장 낮은 비용으로 공급할 수 있는 가장 양질의 단백질원이 콩이기 때문이다. 즉 한국에서 콩은 감옥을 상징하고 두부는 감옥 밖의 세상을 상징한다.

한국 영화에서 매우 흔히 볼 수 있는 또다른 특이한 장면은 직장인들이 퇴근 후에 단체로 식당이나 술집에 모여서 먹고 마시고 떠드는 장면이다. 이건 '회식'이라고 부르는, 실제로 한국 사회에서 매우 흔한 문화다. 영어로 옮기자면 company dinner, 혹은 team dinner 정도가 될 텐데, 이렇게 번역해서는 한국의 회식을 정확히 표현할 수가 없다.

외국에서는 직장 동료들끼리 가볍게 맥주 한두 잔 혹은 피자 한두 쪽 먹고 각자 계산한 다음 헤어지는 것이 일반적이다. 하지만 한국의 회식은 어느 정도의 '강제성'이 존재한다는 점, 술을 (반강제로) 상당히 많이 마신다는 점, 한 장소에서 끝나지 않고 여러 음식점과 술집 등으로 옮겨가며 밤늦게까지 이어진다는 점, 대부분의 비용이 회사 자금으로 지불된다는 점, 그래서 이건 단순한 친목 모임이 아니라 '업무의 연장'으로 받아들여진다는 점 등이 독특하다.

물론 이런 걸 모두가 좋아하지는 않고, 과도한 회식으로 인한 여러 가지 문제도 있다. 그래서 지금은 과거에 비해 많이 달라지긴 했다. 하지만 여전히 회식에 불참하는 사람은 (그 회식이 퇴근 두 시간에 전에 갑자기 결정됐다 하더라도) 회사 혹은 팀장에 대한 충성심이 부족한 사람, 사회생활의 기술이 부족한 사람 취급을 받을 수 있다. 술을 싫어하거나 잘 못 마시는 사람이 직장 상사의 강권으로 억지로 술을 마셔야 하는 일도 여전히 벌어진다.

여러 사람이 모여서 크게 취한 상태로 어울리다보니 성추행이나 성희롱과 같은 불미스러운 사건이 발생하기도 하고, 너무 심하게 취한 사람이 계단에서 넘어지거나 해서 부상을 당하는 경우도 종종 생긴다(업무의 연장으로 받아들여지기 때문에, 이런 경우에도 산재보험에서 보상을 해주는 경우가 많다. 업무의 연장이 아니라 차라리 그냥 업무로 인정하여 근무시간중에 하든지). 회식을 주도하는 사람(가장 직급이 높은 사람이자 자신의 법인카드로 돈을 내는 사람)이 필요 이상으로 말을 많이 하고, 툭하면 술잔을 높이 들고 뭔가 교훈적인 이야기(물론 본인 생각에 그렇다는 의미일 뿐, 듣는 사람 입장에서는 개소리)를 하면서 모두가 동시에 술잔을 비워야 한다고 주장한다. 그래서 모든 참석자들은 최대한 회식의 주도자와 멀리 떨어져 앉기 위해 애쓴다.

회식이 밤늦게까지 계속될 경우 흔히 등장하는 장소는 '노래방'이다. '비어 있는 오케스트라'라는 뜻의 가라오케는 일본에서 시작된 문화로 세계 곳곳에 퍼져 있지만, 노래방이라고 불리는 한국의 가라오케는 조금 독특하다. 대부분의 나라에서 가라오케는 넓은 홀에 무대가 있고, 사람들이 돌아가며 무대에 올라가 노래를 부르는 장소다. 서로 모르는 사람들이 섞여 있기 때문에, 너무 소리를 지르거나 과도한 퍼포먼스를 보이는 것은 실례다. 이 장소는 '노래를 부를 수 있는 술집'에 가까우므로, 노래를 부르겠다는 사람이 없을 때는 평범한 술집과 비슷한 모습으로 바뀔 수 있다.

하지만 한국의 노래방은 노래를 부르는 것이 주된 목적인 장소다. 술을 마실 수 있는 노래방도 있지만, 대개의 노래방에서는 술을 전혀 팔지 않고 공간만 빌려준다. 주로 4~5명이 들어가면 적당한 크기지만, 어떤 방은 열 명 이상이 들어가도 넉넉할 정도로 넓고, 혼자 노래 부르고 싶은 사람을 위한 아주 작은 방도 있다. 아는 사람들끼리만 모여 있으니, 다른 손님들 눈치보지 않고 최대한(?) 즐겁게 논다. 회식중인 회사원들이라면 (이미 많이 취해서, 혹은 팀장을 비롯한 선배들을 즐겁게 해주기 위해서) 넥타이를 풀어 머리에 두르기도 하고, K팝 스타들의 안무를 그대로 흉내내기도 하며, 노래방에 비치된 탬버린을 신들린 솜씨로 흔들기도 한다. 그러니 한국 영화나 드라마에 나오는 노래방 장면은 전혀 과장이 아니다.

노래방은 남녀노소 모두가 즐기는 장소다. 술을 전혀 마시지 않은 상태에서도 간다. 기쁠 때도 가고 슬플 때도 간다. 대낮에도 간다. 청소년도 간다. 가족들끼리도 간다. 심지어 진짜 가수도 간다(노래를 다 부르면 기계가 매긴 점수가 공개되는데, 전문 가수가 자신의 노래를 부른다고 해서 백 점이 나온다는 보장이 없다. 변별력이 별로 없다는 이야기다). 한국인은 노래를 부르고 춤을 추면서 스트레스를 푼다. 한국인은 스스로 '음주가무에 능한 민족'임을 자랑스러워한다(중국의 고대 문헌에 나오는 표현인데, 한국에 대한 중국의 서술 중에서 한국인이 거의 유일하게 좋아하는 표현이다).

한국 영화에 가끔 나오는 공간 중에 '찜질방'이라는 곳도 외국인들이 신기해하는 곳이다. 찜질방을 설명하려면 한국 가옥의 전통적인 난방 방식부터 이야기해야 한다. 한국은 '온돌'이라는 고유의 난방 방식을 수천 년 전부터 발전시켜왔다. 아궁이라고 부르는 공간에 나무 등을 이용해 불을 때면 그 열기가 거실이나 방의 아래에 마련된 공간을 타고 흐르면서 바닥을 데운 다음 굴뚝으로 연기가 빠져나가는 방식이다(아주 간단해 보일지 모르지만 온돌은 매우 다양한 유형이 있고, 수많은 과학적 원리가 숨어 있다. 현대 건축가들도 감탄한다고 들었다). 불을 피웠는데 바닥만 데우면 아까우니, 아궁이의 열기는 당연히 취사에도 사용되었다(여름에는 방을 데울 필요가 없으니, 바닥과 연결되지 않은 아궁이도 따로 있다). 바닥이 갈라지거나 깨지면 연기가 올라와서 일산화탄소 중독을 일으킬 수 있다는 단점이 있지만, 열효율이 매우 높고 실내 공기가 탁해지지 않는 훌륭한 난방법이다.

온돌은 한국인의 좌식 문화와 밀접한 관련이 있다. 벽난로가 없고 바닥이 따뜻한 공간에서 추운 겨울날 잠을 잔다고 생각해보라. 당신 같으면 바닥에서 1미터쯤 떠 있는 침대에서 자겠는가, 바닥에 이불을 펴고 자겠는가. 밥을 먹을 때나 휴식을 취할 때도 마찬가지다. 한국인은 (적어도 겨울에는) 최대한 바닥에 붙어 있어야 유리하다. 그러니 의자나 침대 문화가 발달하는 대신 방석을 깔고 바닥에 앉아서 생활하는 문화가 생긴 것이다. 밥상도 놓아야 하고 이불도 깔아야 하는 공간이니, 당연히 신발은 밖에 벗어두고 들어가게 된 것도 설명이 된다.

물론 현대의 한국인은 아궁이에서 밥을 짓지 않고, 난방을 위해 나무를 때지도 않는다. 하지만 온돌 문화는 고스란히 남아서, 한국에 있는 거의 모든 주택은 바닥을 데우는 것을 기본적인 난

방법으로 채택하고 있다.

찜질방은 기본적으로 아주 커다란 온돌방이라 할 수 있다. 쾌적한 온도의 가장 넓은 공간은 쉬거나 수다를 떨거나 간식을 먹는 공간이다. 그 외에도 다양한 공간들이 배치되어 있는데, 실내 온도가 섭씨 70도 내외의 아주 뜨거운 공간도 있고, 이글루와 같이 아주 차가운 공간도 있다. 벽면의 재료로는 나무, 흙, 소금, 돌 등이 다양하게 활용된다. 땀을 많이 흘리는 곳이니 손님들은 모두 업소에서 제공하는 가벼운 옷을 입고 휴식을 취한다. 샤워나 목욕을 할 수 있는 공간 외에는 남녀 구분이 없다. 찜질방에서 가장 인기 있는 간식은 '식혜'라고 불리는, 쌀로 만든 한국의 전통 음료와 '구운 계란'이다.

찜질방은 휴식의 공간이기도 하지만, 24시간 문을 열기 때문에 밤에는 '저렴한 숙박업소'의 역할도 한다. 가난한 여행자나 막차를 놓친 직장인들은 이곳에서 하룻밤을 보내기도 한다. 비용도 매우 저렴해서, 낮에는 시간 제한 없이 5~10달러, 밤에는 그보다 몇 달러 높은 정도가 대부분이다.

재미있는 것은 한국인들은 찜질방에만 가면 수건을 접은 뒤 모자처럼 만들어 머리에 쓴다는 사실이다. 누가 처음으로 수건을 이렇게 활용했는지는 알 수 없지만, 〈내 이름은 김삼순〉이라는 2005년 드라마 때문에 유행하기 시작한 것은 확실하다. 이 로맨틱 코미디는 한국에서 가장 히트한 드라마들 중의 하나다. 한국인들은 '양머리'라고 부르는데, 만드는 방법은 유튜브에 'jjimjilbang head towel'이라고 검색하면 많이 있다. K팝 팬이라면, 블랙핑크 멤버들이 찜질방에서 양머리 수건을 머리에 쓰고 즐겁게 노는 영상을 찾아봐도 좋을 것이다(이 영상은 조회수가 2,500만을 넘겼다). 혹시 찜질방을 방문하게 되면, 양머리 수건을 머리에 쓰고 식혜와 구운 계란을 먹으며 셀카를 찍지 않을 수는 없을 것이다. 한국에 오면 한국 스타일로!

한국 영화나 드라마를 보는 외국인들이 가장 이해하기 힘든 장면 중의 하나는 거의 모든 학생들이 다니는 '학원'이다. 한국의 학생들은 학교만 다니는 것이 아니라 학원도 다닌다. 학교가 파하면 거의 대부분의 학생들은 학원에 간다. 한 곳만 가면 다행이고, 하루에 두 곳 이상의 학원을 가는 경우도 흔하다. 학교와 학원 두세 곳을 거치고 나면 대개는 밤 9~10시가 된다.

학원은 '뭔가를 배우는 장소'라는 의미로 폭넓게 쓰이는 단어다. 배움의 대상은 외국어, 악기, 스포츠, 요리, 컴퓨터, 미술, 노래, 댄스, 자동차 운전 등 매우 다양하다. 어린이부터 노인들까지, 학원에서 뭔가를 배우는 사람들의 연령대도 다양하다. 대학생들도 많이 다니는데, 이들은 주로 토플이나 토익과 같은 영어 시험 점수를 올리기 위해서, 혹은 취업 준비를 하기 위해서 다닌다(대부분의 학원들은 영어 표기에서 academy, school, institute 등의 단어를 쓰고 있다. 외국인의 눈에는 온 나라가 무슨 연구소처럼 보일지 모르지만, 이들 대부분이 학원이다. 한국에 있는 진짜 연구소들은 관광객들의 눈에 잘 띄지 않는 곳에 있다).

한국에서 가장 중요한 학원은 입시학원이다. 청소년들은 대부분 입시를 위해 학원에 다닌다. 한국은 교육열이 매우 높고,

학벌이 매우 중요한 나라다. 학교 수업만으로는 경쟁에서 이기기 힘들다고 느끼는 학생과 학부모들이 어쩔 수 없이 (남들도 다다니니까) 학원을 선택한다. 분명히 학교는 아닌 것 같은 장소, 즉 평범한 상가 건물 같은 곳에서 학생들이 우르르 나오는 장면이 한국 영화에 나온다면, 그건 백 퍼센트 학원이다. (학교 교사보다 학원 선생님이 더 잘 가르친다고들 한다. 학교는 딱 정해진 커리큘럼이 있고 모든 학생들의 수준을 고려해야 하지만, 학원은 입시에 중요한 내용에 집중하며 수업의 난도를 자유롭게 조절할 수 있기 때문이기도 하다. 소위 '잘나가는' 학원 선생님들은 학교 교사보다 훨씬 돈도 많이 번다.)

이처럼 많은 사람이 학원을 다니니 사교육 시장 규모도 엄청나서, 한국인들은 매년 2백억 달러를 학원에 쓴다(이는 교육부 예산의 30퍼센트 수준이다). 한 조사에 의하면, 한국의 초등학생, 중학생, 고등학생 들은 평균적으로 매월 약 3백 달러를 사교육에 쓰고 있다. 사정이 이렇다보니 학부모도 힘들고 학생들도 힘들다. 한국에서 부모와 자녀 사이의 가장 큰 갈등 요인은 공부와 학원이다. 한국 청소년의 자살률과 우울증 유병률이 높은 것도 이런 문화와 관련이 높을 것이다.

당신은 이제 한국에 대해서 이전보다 훨씬 많이 알게 됐다. 과거에도 한국 영화나 드라마를 재미있게 보았겠지만, 앞으로는 더 재미있게 볼 수 있을 것이다. 당신이 한국 여행 전에 미리 보면 좋을 영화와 드라마 열 편의 목록을 만들어보았다(열 편만 고르느라 힘들었다). 물론 지극히 주관적인 것이고, 당신이 이미 본 것들도 있을 것이다. 아직 안 본 작품은 꼭 보고, 이미 본 작품은 다시 보라. 분명히 처음 봤을 때와는 다른 것들이 보일 것이다. 1인치의 장벽만 넘으면 된다.

- 기생충(Parasite): 봉준호 감독의 2019년 영화. 말이 필요 없는 유명한 작품. 이 책에도 이미 여러 번 등장했다. 그 유명한 '짜파구리'는 원래 두 가지 라면을 따로 구매한 다음 한꺼번에 조리하는 것이지만, 영화가 히트한 이후 같은 이름의 컵라면이 출시되어 편의점에서 판매하고 있다. 집에서 만드는 것과 완전히 똑같지는 않지만, 궁금하면 한번 먹어보길.

- 오징어 게임(Squid Game): 황동혁 감독의 2021년 넷플릭스 드라마. 9부작. 3화에 등장하는 '뽑기(혹은 달고나)'라는 게임은 실제로 한국 어린이들이 즐겨 하는 놀이라서, 초등학교 주변을 잘 찾으면 발견할 수도 있다. 6화에 등장하는 '깐부'라는 단어는 '같은 편'을 뜻하는 용어인데, 같은 이름의 치킨집 체인도 있다.

- 올드보이(Oldboy): 박찬욱 감독의 2003년 영화. 산낙지는 한국에서 흔히 먹을 수 있는 음식이지만 영화에서와 같이 먹으면 안 된다. 주인공이 15년간 먹었던 군만두는 한국의 수많은 중국 식당에서 판매한다. 짜장면을 맛보기로 결심했다면, 군만두도 먹어보면 좋겠다.

• 살인의 추억(Memories of Murder): 봉준호 감독의 2003년 영화. 실화를 바탕으로 만들었으며, 1980년대의 한국 사회를 잘 그려냈다. 연쇄살인범을 쫓는 형사 이야기지만 봉준호 감독 특유의 유머감각이 곳곳에서 빛난다. 사건의 범인은 2019년에야 밝혀졌다.

• 1987(1987: When the Day Comes): 장준환 감독의 2017년 영화. 한국 현대사에서 가장 중요한 연도라 할 수 있는 1987년의 민주화 투쟁을 영상으로 옮겼다. 당연히 대부분의 내용이 실화다. 한국인 대부분이 너무도 잘 아는 내용이지만 흥행에도 성공했다. 당신이 한국의 현대사를 잘 모르더라도, 흡인력 있는 이야기를 충분히 즐길 수 있을 것이다.

• 극한 직업(Extreme Job): 이병헌 감독(배우 이병헌과 동명이인)의 2019년 영화. 역대 한국 영화 중에서 두번째로 많은 관객을 동원한 영화다. 한국의 인구가 5천만 명인데, 이 영화를 극장에서 본 사람만 1,626만 명이다. 거의 모든 한국인이 다 봤다고 할 수 있다. 경찰 마약반이 잠복 수사를 위해 치킨집을 위장 창업하는 설정이다. 영화를 보면 한국식 치킨이 더욱 먹고 싶어질 것이다.

• 나의 아저씨(My Mister): 김원석 감독의 2018년 드라마. 16부작. 최고의 K팝 가수이자 배우인 아이유(배우로 활동할 때

는 이지은)와 〈기생충〉의 배우 이선균 주연의 휴먼 드라마. 많은 한국인이 인생 드라마로 꼽는 명작. 제각기 상처를 가진 여러 사람이 서로의 관계 속에서 치유를 경험하는 놀라운 이야기. 당신도 결국 눈물을 흘릴 것이다.

• 나의 해방일지(My Liberation Notes): 김석윤 감독의 2022년 드라마. 16부작. 〈나의 아저씨〉와 〈나의 해방일지〉의 대본은 모두 박해영이 썼다. 현재 한국의 20~30대들의 피곤한 삶을 가장 현실적으로 보여준다는 평가를 받았다. 초반에는 스토리 전개가 느린 편이지만, 계속 보다보면 빠져든다. 출퇴근, 직장 생활, 회식 등 한국인의 일상이 매우 사실적으로 묘사된다.

• 도깨비(Guardian: The Lonely and Great God): 이응복 감독의 2016~2017년 드라마. 16부작. 한국에서 가장 유명한 드라마 작가 중 한 사람인 김은숙의 작품. 9백 년 넘게 살고 있는 불멸의 도깨비와 죽은 사람의 영혼을 볼 수 있는 능력을 가진 여고생이 주인공. 리얼리티라고는 전혀 없는 드라마이지만, 작가의 세계관을 기꺼이 받아들인 한국인들이 열렬히 사랑한 작품이다.

• 헤어질 결심(Decision to Leave): 박찬욱 감독의 2022년 영화. 칸영화제에서 감독상을 받았다. 〈살인의 추억〉에서 살인 용의자였던 배우 박해일이 이 영화에서는 변사 사건을 추적하

는 형사 역할을 맡았다. 중국 배우 탕웨이의 출연도 화제가 됐다. 박찬욱 영화 중에서는 가장 '순한 맛'으로 꼽힌다.

16.

From Screen to Korea: Must-Watch Movies and Dramas Before Your Trip

It's not uncommon to see someone being released from prison in Korean movies and dramas. It could be a thief, a politician, or an ordinary person, such as a housewife. It could be an office worker who embezzled public funds, a drug dealer, or even a murderer. The length of their sentence can vary from a few months to several decades. Sometimes, they are left without anyone to greet them, but more often than not, someone is there waiting for them. After exchanging greetings, whether it be an affectionate hug, a cordial handshake, or a respectful bow, the person waiting outside the prison usually hands them a white cube in a disposable plate or plastic bag. The recipient takes a big bite of it. It's tofu.

It's unclear when the practice of serving tofu to those returning from prison began, and it's also unclear why, but there are several theories. Some say that the white color of the tofu signifies a clean life ahead, others that the protein-rich tofu is meant to replenish the nutrients they lacked while in prison, and some suggest that the filling and easily digestible nature of tofu is meant to prevent those released from prison from overeating suddenly and causing digestive issues. However, my favorite and most plausible literary interpretation is this one. Tofu is made from soybeans. You can make tofu out of soybeans, but you can't make soybeans out of tofu, which means that the act of feeding them tofu is meant to prevent them from going back to their sinful past lives.

Now, I know what you're thinking. We cannot turn a steak back into a cow, cheese back into milk, wine back into grapes, kimchi back into napa cabbage, etc. So, of all occasions, why tofu? But hold on, there's more to this story. See, soybeans are like the grain version of a ball and chain in Korea - they symbolize imprisonment. The term "eating kong-bap (rice with soybeans)" is a figure of speech that means prison in Korean culture. For instance, if you come across the line "Do you want to eat kongbap?" in a Korean movie, it doesn't mean that the characters are discussing a restaurant menu, but rather that they are warning one another not to engage in activities that could lead to incarceration. Interestingly enough, Korean prisons do serve kongbap (I can't speak from personal experience, but I'm fairly certain that it's a staple dish and is served regularly, if not at every meal). Prisoners also should be provided with a somewhat balanced diet, and soybean is the most affordable and nutritious protein source available. This is why soybeans have come to be associated with imprisonment, and why tofu has become a symbol of life outside of prison, at least in Korea.

Another frequent scene that might appear unusual to Western audiences but is commonplace in Korean movies is the "hoesik," where coworkers gather at a restaurant or bar after work to eat, drink, and chat. In Korean culture, this is a regular occurrence, extending beyond a simple company or team dinner, as it may be translated in English.

In some other countries, it's typical for colleagues to grab a couple of drinks or a slice of pizza, settle the bill, and go their separate ways. However, in Korea, work parties take on a different dynamic. There's a certain level of persuasion (sometimes coercion) involved, alcohol is often consumed in excess (sometimes under duress), and the night doesn't conclude at just one venue. It involves hopping from one restaurant to another, one bar to another, lasting until the midnight or even wee hours of the morning. Moreover, the majority of the expenses are covered by the company, turning it into an "extension of work" rather than a pure social gathering.

Of course, not everyone enjoys this kind of work culture, and excessive drinking can lead to many problems. Nowadays, the landscape is different from what it was in the past. However, if you happen to miss a work dinner, even if it's a last-minute decision made two hours before, it may be perceived as a lack of loyalty to your company or team leader, or even a deficiency in social skills. Additionally, it remains common for individuals who either don't enjoy drinking or aren't proficient at it to be compelled by their bosses to partake.

Unfortunately, there are instances where excessive drinking leads to unpleasant incidents such as sexual harassment, molestation, or injuries resulting from falling down stairs. Surprisingly, such injuries are often covered by workers' compensation because they are considered an extension of work, even though they are not inherently part of the job itself. (One might wonder, if it's an extension of work, why not conduct it during business hours?) Additionally, the person leading the dinner, typically the one with the most seniority who pays with their corporate card, tends to be overly talkative, often sharing didactic stories that are often meaningless to the listeners. They also insist, holding their drink high in the air, that everyone empties their glasses simultaneously, leading people to strategically sit as far away from the leader as possible.

When Korean work parties continue into the late night, a commonly enjoyed venue is the "noraebang" (Korean karaoke). Karaoke, derived from the Japanese words 'kara' (meaning empty) and 'oke' (short for orchestra), is a form of entertainment that has spread around the world and is widely embraced. Karaoke is commonly more of a "bar" than a dedicated space for singing, often referred to as "a bar where you can also sing." It is commonly found in a large hall with a stage where people take turns singing. Since it's a mix of people who don't know each other, it's considered rude to shout or over-perform. When there are no singers, it can simply function as a regular bar.

In contrast to karaoke venues in other countries, noraebang in Korea has a primary focus on singing. While some noraebangs serve alcohol, many of them are solely for renting out space to sing and do not sell alcohol. The rooms are typically designed for a small group of four or five people, although larger rooms for groups of ten or more, as well as smaller rooms for solo singing, are also available. As the venue is usually filled with people who know each other well, it becomes a place to let loose and have fun without the fear of judgment - either because they're already quite drunk or to entertain their team leader and seniors). There, attendees may find themselves loosening their ties, mimicking the dance moves of K-pop stars, or skillfully playing the tambourine. The noraebang scenes often depicted in Korean movies and TV dramas are not exaggerated at all.

Noraebang is a popular activity in Korea enjoyed by people of all ages and backgrounds. It can be experienced sober or not, during the day or night, alone or with family and friends. Even professional singers sometimes join in. After someone finishes singing, the machine-generated score is revealed, and there's no guarantee that a professional singer will get a perfect score, even if singing their own song (it's not very discriminating). Singing and dancing at noraebang serve as a way for Koreans to release stress, and they take pride in their reputation as a people who excel in drinking, singing, and dancing. (It's a phrase from ancient Chinese literature, and it's almost the only thing Koreans like about Chinese descriptions of Korea.)

Korean-style saunas, known as 'jjimjilbang,' are cultural spaces frequently featured in Korean movies but may be unfamiliar to foreigners. To comprehend jjimjilbangs, we first need to delve into Korea's traditional heating method called 'ondol,' a practice spanning thousands of years. In this method, a fire is lit in a specially designed firebox known as 'agungi,' and the heat circulates beneath the living room or room, warming the floor and channeling smoke up the chimney. Despite its seemingly simple appearance, ondol heating systems come in various types, with a significant amount of scientific knowledge and engineering behind their design—something even modern architects often admire. The heat generated by the firebox was also utilized for cooking purposes, maximizing its utility beyond floor heating. (Separate fireboxes exist that are not connected to the floor, allowing for use without heating the room in the summer.) While this method is efficient and does not pollute indoor air, a downside emerges if the floor is cracked or broken, as smoke can rise and potentially cause carbon monoxide poisoning.

Ondol is deeply intertwined with Korea's sedentary culture, placing great value on the warmth of the floor during the cold winter season. Envision yourself on a chilly winter day, seeking comfort in a room without a fireplace but featuring a heated floor. Faced with the choice, would you opt for a bed raised about a meter from the ground or a snug futon on the cozy floor? This cultural preference extends beyond sleeping to dining and leisure activities, where Koreans often gather on the floor with cushions. Furthermore, it's customary to remove shoes before entering a Korean home, as the floor space is commonly utilized for dining and sleeping arrangements, featuring a low table and futon.

Indeed, while the ancestral methods of cooking and heating with fire pits and wood have been replaced by modern technologies, the cultural influence of ondol has persisted in South Korea. Today, the majority of homes in South Korea are equipped with heated floors as the main source of heating.

A jjimjilbang can be envisioned as a spacious ondol room, commonly found in Korean-style spas or saunas. The main area is maintained at a comfortable temperature, creating a space for relaxation, conversation, and enjoying snacks. Alongside the main room, diverse other chambers offer different temperatures, ranging from very hot (around 70 degrees Celsius, 160 degrees Fahrenheit) to very cold (resembling an igloo). These rooms feature walls constructed from diverse materials, including wood, dirt, salt, and stone. To accommodate guests who are likely to perspire, lightweight clothing is provided by the establishment. Gender division is generally absent, except in the shower or bath area. Popular snacks available in jjimjilbangs include "sikhye", a traditional Korean rice drink, and baked eggs.

Jjimjilbangs not only offer a relaxing experience but also serve as affordable accommodation for travelers or office workers who miss their last train, as they operate 24 hours a day. The cost of staying at a jjimjilbang is usually very low, ranging from $5 to $10 during the day with no time limit and a slightly higher rate at night. This provides a convenient and budget-friendly option for overnight stays.

It's interesting to note that when Koreans visit a jjimjilbang, they often fold their towels into hats and wear them on their heads. Although it's unknown who first utilized towels in this way, the trend gained fame after the 2005 Korean drama, My Lovely Sam Soon, a romantic comedy that remains one of the most beloved Korean dramas of all time.

Koreans affectionately call the towel hat 'yangmeori' (sheep head), and there are plenty of tutorials on how to make one available by searching 'jjimjilbang head towel' on YouTube. Even K-pop stars like Blackpink have been spotted having fun in a jjimjilbang with sheep head towels on their heads (with over 25 million views of the video). If you ever find yourself at a jjimjilbang, taking a selfie with a sheep head towel on your head while snacking on sikhye and baked eggs is a must. When in Korea, do as the Koreans do!

For foreigners watching Korean movies and dramas, one of the most challenging concepts to grasp is the idea of a 'hagwon,' which almost all Korean students attend. In Korea, students not only attend regular school but also go to hagwons. After the regular school day concludes, it's common for almost all students to visit a hagwon. Being fortunate might mean attending only one, and it's not unusual for students to participate in two or more hagwons in a single day. By the time they finish two or three hagwons, it's usually around 9-10 pm.

The term 'hagwon' refers to a place of learning, covering a wide range of subjects, including foreign languages, music, sports, cooking, computing, art, driving, and more. People of all ages, from children to the elderly, attend hagwons.

University students also frequently enroll in hagwons, often to enhance their English language test scores (e.g., TOEFL or TOEIC) or to prepare for their future careers. Many hagwons use terms like 'academy,' 'school,' or 'institute' in their English translations, creating a landscape that might make the whole country seem like a research cluster to a foreigner, as hagwons can be found on nearly every street corner. However, most of them are not actual academic institutions, and the genuine academic institutes in Korea are often not visible to tourists.

Among hagwons, cram schools play a pivotal role in Korea, particularly for teenagers preparing for university entrance exams. In Korea, where education holds high value, having a solid educational background is crucial. Students and parents often feel that regular school classes alone are insufficient to compete with others, compelling them to choose hagwons (because everyone else is doing it). In Korean movies or dramas, if you see a group of students in a place that doesn't resemble a school, like an ordinary commercial building, it's most likely a hagwon. There's a prevailing belief that hagwon teachers are superior to school teachers as they can focus on content crucial for entrance exams and have the flexibility to adjust the difficulty level of their classes. In contrast, schools follow a set curriculum that must consider the varying levels of all students. Consequently, top-tier cram school teachers often earn considerably more than their counterparts in schools.

With a substantial number of people attending hagwons, the market for private education in South Korea is immense, with an estimated $20 billion being spent on hagwons each year (equivalent to about 30% of the Ministry of Education's budget). On average, South Korean elementary, middle, and high school students spend around $300 per month on private education, creating a significant financial burden for parents and posing mental and emotional challenges for students. The pressure to excel in exams and attend multiple hagwons can lead to conflicts between parents and their children, contributing to high rates of suicide and depression among Korean youth.

Now that you've learned more about Korea, you might find watching Korean movies and dramas even more enjoyable than before. To assist you in preparing for your trip to Korea, I've curated a list of 10 movies and TV dramas worth considering. It was challenging to narrow it down to just 10, and of course, the selection is subjective. You may have already seen some of them, but I encourage you to watch the ones you haven't seen yet and revisit the ones you have. Upon rewatching, you might notice new things. As the saying goes, sometimes all you need to do is cross the one-inch barrier to discover something new and wonderful.

• "Parasite", a film by Bong Joon-ho that took the world by storm in 2019, needs no interpreter—it's a masterpiece. The famous "jjapaguri" dish, made by mixing two different types of ramyun noodles, gained popularity thanks to the film. Its success even led to a cup noodle version of jjapaguri being sold in convenience stores. While it may not quite match the homemade version, if you're feeling curious, why not give it a shot?

• "Squid Game", the 2021 Netflix drama directed by Hwang Dong-hyuk, is a nail-biting thrill ride that will keep you on the edge of your seat for all nine episodes. In episode 3, the game 'ppopgi' (also known as 'dalgona') is a beloved pastime among Korean children—you might even spot some kids playing it around elementary schools if you keep your eyes peeled. In episode 6, you'll come across the term 'kkanbu' (or 'gganbu'), which translates to 'same side'—also the name of a well-known chain of chicken restaurants in Korea.

• "Oldboy", the 2003 film directed by Park Chan-wook, features iconic scenes that have become well-known among Korean movie lovers. While sannakji, a dish made with live small octopus, is a common food in Korea, it's crucial to remember that it shouldn't be consumed like it was in the movie. The dumplings that the main character ate for 15 years are also a common dish found in many Chinese restaurants in Korea. If you're planning on trying jjajangmyeon, a Korean-Chinese noodle dish, you might also want to indulge in some 'gunmandu' (fried dumplings).

• "Memories of Murder", a 2003 film directed by the talented Bong Joon-ho, unfolds a gripping narrative based on a true story that took place in Korea during the 1980s. It follows the journey of a detective on the trail of a notorious serial killer, with Bong Joon-ho's trademark humor sprinkled throughout. In a twist of fate, the killer wasn't actually caught until 2019.

• "1987: When the Day Comes", is a 2017 blockbuster directed by Jang Joon-hwan that narrates the noteworthy story of South Korea's democratization struggle in 1987, a pivotal year in the country's modern history. This gripping film is primarily based on true events and has deeply resonated with Korean audiences. Even if you're not familiar with Korean history, this movie is a must-watch for anyone who appreciates a well-crafted, engaging story.

• "Extreme Job" is a 2019 film that tells the story of a police narcotics unit that goes undercover by opening a chicken restaurant. Directed by Lee Byung-heon (who coincidentally shares the same name as actor Lee Byung-heon), the film has achieved the remarkable feat of becoming the second most watched Korean movie of all time. Out of South Korea's population of 50 million, a whopping 16.26 million people watched it in theaters. Almost every South Korean has seen it, and it's not hard to see why. This movie is guaranteed to leave you craving Korean-style chicken!

* "My Mister" is a 2018 Korean drama directed by Kim Won-seok. It spans 16 episodes and features K-pop sensation and actress IU (real name Lee Ji-Eun) and "Parasite" actor Lee Sun-Kyun in the lead roles. This emotional-

ly-charged human drama is widely regarded as a Korean classic, with a deeply moving story about a group of people with struggles who find solace and comfort in their connections with each other. Get ready for a rollercoaster of emotions that will have you shedding tears!

- "My Liberation Notes" is a 2022 TV drama directed by Kim Seok-yoon. It's a 16-episode drama written by Park Hae-young, who also penned the acclaimed series "My Mister". Both viewers and critics have praised it for its unflinching portrayal of the exhaustion and ennui faced by young Koreans in their 20s and 30s. While the story starts slowly, if you stick with it, you will be hooked. The show paints a highly realistic picture of daily life in Korea, from the daily grind of commuting to the trials and tribulations of work and drinking culture including "hoesik".

- "Guardian: The Lonely and Great God" is a 2016-2017 TV drama directed by Lee Eung-bok and written by Kim Eun-sook, a legendary Korean drama writer. The show follows the tale of an immortal goblin who has lived for over 900 years and a high school girl who can see the souls of the dead. It's a fantasy drama that defies reality, but it captivated the hearts of Koreans ready to immerse themselves in the writer's imaginative world.

• "Decision to Leave" is a 2022 movie from the acclaimed director Park Chan-wook, who recently won the Palme d'Or for Best Director at the Cannes Film Festival. Actor Park Hae-il, who was a murder suspect in "Memories of Murder," plays a detective who tracks down the case of unnatural death in this movie. Tang Wei, a prominent Chinese actress, also appears in the movie and adds to its star power. It is considered to be the most "mildly flavored" of the Park Chan-wook movies.

17.

K팝 명소를 찾아서

지난 2012년, 싸이의 〈강남스타일〉이 세계적인 히트를 쳤을 때, 한국인들은 무슨 생각을 했을까? '우리 싸이, 드디어 외국인들도 가치를 알아보는구나' '우리 싸이, 언젠가는 저렇게 성공할 줄 알았다' '역시, 멋진 노래는 누구에게나 근사하게 들리는구나' 이런 생각을 했을까? 아니다. 보통의 한국인들은 이렇게 생각했다. '왜?' '도대체 왜?' '가사도 못 알아들을 텐데?' '한국 남자가 다 저렇게 생긴 줄 알면 어떡하지?' 등등.

싸이는 〈강남스타일〉 이전에도 한국에서는 많은 이에게 사랑을 받는 톱스타였다. 그는 데뷔곡을 발표하자마자 스타가 됐고, 〈강남스타일〉 이전에도 10년 이상 활동하며 여러 노래를 히트시켰다. 독특한 창법에 가려졌지만 가창력도 좋고, 겸손한 몸매에 가려졌지만 춤도 잘 추고, 가수로 유명하지만 수많은 노래를 만든 작곡가이자 프로듀서이기도 하다. 심지어 유머감각도 탁월하다(그리 유창하지 않은 영어로도 그 정도 웃기지 않나. 한국어로는 훨씬 잘 웃긴다).

하지만 그의 노래가 전 세계에 울려퍼질 줄은 아무도 몰랐다. 전 세계 수십억 명이 그의 춤을 따라 추게 될 줄은 아무도 몰랐다(본인도 몰랐을 거다). 싸이가 어느 날 갑자기 글로벌 셀럽이 되었을 때, 한국인들은 솔직히 좀 당황했다(본인도 그랬을 거다).

물론 싸이보다 앞서서 외국인들을 사로잡은 한국의 가수나 배우들은 제법 있었다. 한국의 영화, 드라마, TV 쇼 들이 외국에서도 큰 인기를 끌고 있다는 사실도 잘 알려져 있었다. '한류'라는 용어는 1990년대 중반 무렵에 이미 생겼다. 하지만 싸이 이전엔 누구도 그렇게까지 커다란 성공을 거두지는 못했다. 한류는, 한국과 그래도 외모와 정서가 비슷한 동양권에서나 통용되는 말로 취급됐다. 때문에 싸이가 터뜨린 '대박'을 처음엔 한국인들이 잘 믿지 못했다. 오죽하면 만나는 외국인들 모두에게 '두 유 노우 싸이?'라고 물어보며 확인하고자 했을까.

그로부터 몇 년이 흐르는 동안 싸이의 '국제적' 인기는 조금씩 사그라들었고 (물론 그는 한국에서는 여전히 톱스타다), 〈강남스타일〉은 '극히 예외적인' 사례로 여겨졌다. 적어도 BTS 이전까지는 그랬다. 싸이의 사례를 경험했음에도, BTS의 놀라운 성공은 다시 한국인들에게 약간의 당혹감을 안겼다. BTS 팬들은 인정하지 않을지 모르지만, BTS가 해외에서 큰 인기를 끌기 시작할 무렬 BTS의 한국 내 위상은 〈강남스타일〉 직전 싸이의 한국 내 위상보다 높지 않았기 때문이고, BTS 바람은 싸이 때보다 훨씬 더 강하게 훨씬 더 오랫동안 지속됐기 때문이다. 아무튼 한국인들은 BTS의 세계적 성공 이후에 확신을 갖게 됐다. 싸이의 경우가 극히 예외적인 게 아니었구나. 이게 진짜 되는구나. K팝이 전 세계 사람들에게 먹히는구나. 같은 시기에 한국의 영화와 드라마들이 큰 인기를 끌면서 K콘텐츠에 대한 확신은 더욱 굳어졌다(나도 그런 확신 속에서 이 책을 쓰고 있다).

비틀스의 팬이라면 리버풀을 방문해보고 싶을 것이다. 엘비스 프레슬리의 팬이라면 멤피스를 방문해보고 싶을 것이다. 아바의 팬이라면 스톡홀름을, 모차르트의 팬이라면 잘츠부르크를, 가우디의 팬이라면 바르셀로나를, 뭉크의 팬이라면 오슬로를, 셰익스피어의 팬이라면 스트랫퍼드 어폰 에이번을 가고 싶을 것이다(피카소의 팬이라면 가고 싶은 곳이 너무 많아서 문제일 것이다). 당신이 K팝 팬이라면 당연히 한국 방문을 꿈꿀 것이고, 그중에서도 당신이 좋아하는 스타의 숨결을 조금이라도 더 느끼고 싶을 것이다. 그래서 준비했다. K팝을 사랑하는 당신이 방문하면 기뻐할 만한 장소들을 소개한다.

본격적인 소개에 앞서 먼저 양해를 좀 구하고 싶다. 한국에는 앞에서 나열한 도시들에 존재하는 것과 같은, 거의 모든 방문객을 매혹시킬 어마어마한 핫 스폿은 없다. K팝이 세계적인 관심을 끌기 시작한 지 오래되지 않았기 때문일 것이다. BTS 뮤지엄, 블랙핑크 제니의 생가, 싸이 아트홀, 트와이스 빌리지, 뭐 이런 건 없다는 말이다.

그래도 한국에 거주하는 K팝 팬들은 특별히 아쉽지 않다. 티켓을 구하는 것이 엄청나게 어렵기는 하지만 끊임없이 노력하다 보면 콘서트 현장에 가볼 수 있다. 티케팅에 실패하더라도 다음에 다시 도전할 수 있다는 희망이 있다. 좋아하는 가수의 스케줄을 미리 체크할 정성과 밤새도록 줄을 설 수 있는 체력이 있다면 음악 프로그램이 제작되는 방송국 내부의 극장에 입장할 수도 있다. 같은 가수를 좋아하는 팬들끼리 힘을 모아서 지하철역이나 신문 등에 광고를 게재할 수도 있다. 자신이 사랑하는 스타에게 선물을 보낼 수도 있다. 한정판으로 출시되는 '굿즈'를 구입하는 것도 가능하다(물론 어떤 한정판은 돈이 있어도 살 수가 없긴 하지만, 외국인보다야 가능성이 높다).

당신이 '성지순례'를 하는 마음으로 찾아가야 할 단 하나의 명소는 없지만, 외국인 관광객이 가볼 만한 장소가 아예 없지는 않다. 먼저 BTS 멤버들의 옛 숙소를 개조한 서울 논현동의 카페 '휴가'가 있다. 판매하는 빵이나 음료는 특별할 것이 없지만, 곳곳에 BTS의 흔적이 남아 있다. BTS의 팬들이 남겨놓은 쪽지도 많다. 그곳에서 걸어서 15분 거리에는 BTS가 지금처럼 유명해지기 전에 자주 들러 밥을 먹었다는 유정식당이 있다. 삼겹살을 비롯한 다양한 한국 음식들을 판매하는 유정식당에는 더 많은 BTS의 흔적이 남아 있다. 당신이 아미라면, BTS가 밥을 먹던 자리에서 밥을 먹고 BTS가 잠을 자던 공간에서 커피를 마실 수 있는 기회를 놓치지 말기 바란다.

아미들이 지갑을 열게 될 장소로는 BTS 멤버들이 캐릭터 개발에 참여한 것으로 알려진 '라인프렌즈 스퀘어'도 있다. 한국의 구글이라 할 수 있는 네이버가 운영하는 캐릭터 숍인데, 홍대, 강남, 명동 등에 있다(이태원 지점은 문을 닫았다).

서울대학교 내부에 있는 옛 수영장도 최근 BTS 팬들이 많이 찾아가는 장소다. 이곳은 서울대학교 학생들과 인근 주민들이 실제로 사용한 야외 수영장이었지만 지난 30여 년간 방치됐던 곳이다. 하지만 BTS가 2015년에 발표한 〈Intro: 화양연화〉라는 곡의 뮤직비디오를 여기서 찍은 이후 방문객이 늘기 시작했다. 서울대는 2019년에 이 수영장을 완전히 철거하기로 했고, 실제로 수영장의 네 벽 중 세 개는 사라졌다. 하지만 날로 높아지는 BTS의 인기와 BTS 관련 연구를 하는 홍석경 교수의 노력에 힘입어 서울대는 이곳을 보존하기로 했고, 아예 복합문화공간으로 탈바꿈시키는 프로젝트를 진행하고 있다. 아직 이름도 없는 이 장소는 서울대학교 유전공학연구소 근처에 있다.

BTS 멤버들이 여름휴가를 함께 보내면서 예능 프로그램을 촬영했던 장소를 구경할 수 있는 기회도 있다. 〈인더숲〉('In The Soop'에서 'Soop'은 forest에 해당하는 한국어를 영어로 표기한 것이다)이라는 TV 예능 프로그램의 두번째 시즌 촬영지가 관광 상품으로 변신한 것이다. 아쉽게도 이곳만 돌아볼 수는 없고, 인근에 있는 휘닉스 호텔앤드리조트에서 숙박하는 특별한 패키지 상품을 구매한 사람만 한 시간 30분 동안 관람할 수 있다. 2인 기준 하루 숙박 요금이 객실에 따라 220~400달러에 달하고, 서울에서 자동차로 두 시간을 가야 하는 곳이라 외국인이 가기는 쉽지 않아 보인다(게다가 이 패키지 상품이 언제까지 존재할지 아무도 모른다).

한국이 K팝의 고향임을 확실히 느낄 수 있는 의외의 장소는 일부 지하철역이다. 2호선 삼성·강남·합정·잠실·홍대입구, 3호선 압구정, 7호선 청담 등 여러 지하철역 내부에는 K팝 스타의 팬들이 돈을 모아서 게시한 광고물이 쉽게 눈에 띈다. 스타들의 소속사와 가까운 지하철역이나 유동 인구가 많은 지하철역에 광고가 많은데, 역마다 다르긴 하지만 한 달 동안 광고를 게시하는 비용은 2천~5천 달러에 달한다. 그럼에도 불구하고 한 해에 2천 건 넘는 광고가 내걸린다(거의 언제나 서울 시내 지하철역 곳곳에 최소한 백 개 이상의 이런 광고가 붙어 있다는 의미다). 주로 K팝 스타의 생일이나 데뷔 기념일 무렵에 게시되며, 멋진 사진과 함께 팬들이 보내는 응원과 사랑의 메시지가 적혀 있다. 당연히 많은 사람이 이 앞에서 기념사진을 찍는다. 이런 광고는 2호선 삼성역에 특히 많고, 단가도 그곳이 가장 비싸다. 만약 삼성역 지하에서 광고들을 구경했다면, 지상으로 올라가서 〈강남스타일〉 조형물까지 확인하면 좋겠다. 〈강남스타일〉을 부르며 춤을 추는 싸이의 손 모양을 본뜬 조형물이 있다.

도심 한복판에 자리한 롯데백화점 본점에는 '스타의 거리'가 있다. BTS를 비롯한 몇몇 K팝 스타의 핸드프린팅과 대형 사진들로 장식된 공간이다(핸드프린팅에 손을 대고 잠시 기다리면 해당 스타의 영상이 나타난다). 압구정동 갤러리아백화점 인근에는 'K-스타 로드'라는 이름의 거리가 있다. 유명 K팝 스타들을 모티브로 만든 곰 인형이 스무 개쯤 줄지어 서 있다(이 두 곳은 일부러 찾아 갈 필요는 없지만, 백화점에 갈 일이 있으면 잠시 시간을 내도 좋겠다).

용마랜드라는 특이한 장소도 K팝과 관련이 있다. 서울의 동북쪽 끄트머리에 있는 이곳은 원래 규모가 작은 놀이공원이었다. 1980년대부터 10여 년 동안 운영되다가 운영난으로 문을 닫은 후 한동안 버려진 공간이었다. 하지만 '버려진 놀이공원'만이 풍기는 독특한 분위기 때문에 언젠가부터 드라마, 영화, TV 쇼, 뮤직비디오 등의 촬영지로 조금씩 활용되다가, 최근에는 아예 촬영을 위한 '스튜디오'가 되어버린 곳이다. 입장료를 비롯한 몇 가지 부대 비용도 있다(야간에 가서 10달러 정도를 내면 회전목마에 한 시간 동안 조명을 켜준다). 하지만 공원 전체를 빌려서 영화라도 찍는 날이면 입장 불가다. 가장 가까운 지하철역에서 2킬로미터 정도 떨어져 있을 만큼 외진 곳이라 접근성이 매우 나쁘지만, BTS, EXO, 트와이스, 아이유, 아이즈원 등 수많은 가수가 촬영을 위해 다녀간 곳이다. 서울에 체류하는 기간이 열흘쯤 되는 K팝 팬이라면 가볼 수도 있겠다.

이처럼 아직은 K콘텐츠에 관심 있는 관광객을 위한 특별한 장소는 부족한 편이다. SM엔터테인먼트가 한동안 코엑스에서 운영하던 SM타운이라는 곳도 문을 닫았고, BTS의 팝업 스토어 '하우스 오브 BTS'는 2019년에 잠시 운영되어 큰 인기를 끌었지만, 영구적인 공간은 아니었다(80일 동안의 운영 기간 동안 18만 명이 모였는데, 왜 다시 안 생기는 걸까?). 2022년 가을에는 두 달여 기간 동안 BTS 소속사인 하이브 건물 내 '하이브 인사이트'라는 전시

공간에서 BTS 특별 전시회가 열렸지만, 역시 영구적인 것은 아니었다(하이브 사장님, 결단을 내리십시오! BTS 멤버들이 군대에 가 있는 동안 팬들의 아쉬움을 달랠 수 있도록 대규모이자 영구적인 뭔가를 만들어주세요!).

하지만 계속해서 뭔가가 만들어지고는 있다. 2022년 여름에는 한국관광공사가 서울 도심에 '하이커그라운드'라는 복합문화 공간을 만들었다. 이곳에 가면 유명 K팝 뮤직비디오의 주인공이 되어보는 체험을 할 수 있고, K팝 관련 전시도 볼 수 있다. 사진 찍기 좋은 곳이고, 입장료도 없다. 또한 2025년에는 서울 북부에 '서울아레나'라고 하는, K팝 콘서트 전용 극장이 완공될 예정이다. 공간 활용에 따라 만 8천 명에서 2만 8천 명까지 들어갈 수 있는 큰 규모다. BTS 멤버 모두가 군대에 다녀올 무렵에는 서울 아레나가 개관할 수 있을까? 그럴 수 있기를.

BTS의 열혈 팬이라서 BTS의 흔적을 찾아가는 것이 한국 방문의 가장 중요한 목적이라면, 갈 곳은 더 많다. 물론 대부분 서울 밖으로 나가야 한다. 서울에서 2백 킬로미터 넘게 떨어진 동해안에 가면 '향호해변' 버스 정류장이 있다. 2017년 발매된《유 네버 워크 얼론》의 타이틀곡 〈봄날〉의 뮤직비디오가 촬영된 곳이다. 자동차로 가면 두 시간 반 정도, 기차를 타고 가면 좀더 많은 시간이 걸린다. 하지만 '인생 사진' 한 장을 얻기 위해서라면 이 정도 투자를 못 할 것도 없다. 재미있는 것은 이 버스 정류장은 원래 촬영을 위해 만들었다가 철거했는데, 관광객들이 자꾸 찾아오자 강릉시에서 뮤직비디오에 나오는 것과 같은 모습으로 다시 만든 것이다(다시 안 만들었으면 시장이 쫓겨났을지도 모른다). 그곳에서 멀지 않은 삼척 맹방해변은 BTS의 〈버터〉 앨범의 재킷을 촬영한 곳이니, 동해안까지 찾아간 아미라면 그곳에 들를 만하다. 그보다는 훨씬 가깝지만 외국인이 대중교통을 이용해 찾아가기는 만만치 않은 곳 중에는 일영역이 있다. 지금은 쓰이지 않는 기차역인데, 역시 〈봄날〉의 뮤직비디오 촬영지다. 당신이 눈 내린 겨울날 서울에 머물고 있다면, 눈 덮인 철로에 무릎을 꿇고 앉아 있는 뷔의 모습 그대로 사진을 찍을 수 있겠다.

BTS의 흔적이 남아 있는 공간은 한국 전체로 보면 수십 곳 넘게 있다. 고궁, 박물관, 해변, 테마파크, 맛집, 뮤직비디오나 화보 촬영지, 심지어 멤버들이 어릴 적 놀았다는 동물원까지 한국의 아미들은 이런 장소들을 찾아다니며 'BTS 투어'를 즐긴다. 당신도 아미라면, 어디라도 한두 군데쯤은 방문해보길. 찾아가기 어렵더라도, 막상 가보면 생각보다 근사하지 않더라도, 추억은 오래 남을 것이다.

K팝 이야기를 마치기 전에, 당신에게 알려주고 싶은 또다른 K팝이 있다. 그것은 당신이 알고 있는 K팝과는 전혀 다르지만, 한국에서 매우 인기 있는 가요 장르인 '트로트'다. 얼마나 인기가 있느냐고? 2020년의 경우, BTS는 '한국 내 유튜브 조회 수' 순위에서 한국 가수 중 2위였다. 1위는 임영웅이라는 남자 가수였다. 당신은 누군지 전혀 모를 가능성이 높지만, 한국인 중에 임영웅을 모르는 사람은 없다. 그가 바로 '트로트 가수'다. 그 외에도 매우 인기 있는 트로트 가수가 많다.

한마디로 설명하기는 참 어렵지만, 트로트의 원류는 '1930년대의 K팝'이라고 할 수 있다. 음반 산업이 활성화되고 라디오가 보급되기 시작하던 시절, 전국적으로 유명세를 얻었던 가수들이 부른 노래의 장르가 트로트였다. 서양 음악과 일본의 대중음악과 한국의 민요가 적당히 섞인 독특한 노래였다. 트로트는 1960년대까지 한국 대중음악의 주류를 이뤘지만, 1970년대 이후 포크, 록, 발라드, 힙합 등 다양한 장르의 음악들이 쏟아지면서 한동안 침체기를 겪었다. 물론 1980년대 이후에도 인기 있는 트로트 가수들은 있었지만, 주로 50대 이상의 사람들이나 듣는 음악이라는 이미지가 강했다. 하지만 한국의 트로트는 2019년부터 화려하게 부활했다. 한 TV 방송사가 실시한 트로트 가수 오디션 프로그램이 큰 인기를 끈 것이 계기였다.

물론 지금도 젊은이들보다는 장년층이 좋아하는 장르이고, 촌스러운 B급 음악이라는 이미지가 강하긴 하다. 하지만 유명 트로트 가수의 콘서트에는 수만 명이 족히 몰리고, 관련 굿즈를 구매하거나 스타들과 관련된 장소를 찾아가는 등의 팬덤도 상당하다.

트로트라는 이름은 춤곡 장르의 하나인 폭스트롯에서 유래한 것으로 전해지는데, 현재 한국의 트로트는 원래의 폭스트롯과는 상당한 차이가 있다. 거의 백 년 동안 다양하게 변주되어 지금은 '정통' 트로트 외에 블루스, R&B, 록, 댄스, 포크 등이 가미된 것까지, 다양한 스타일이 존재한다. 직설적인 가사, 4분의 4박자 위주의 단순한 멜로디, '꺾기'라고 하는 독특한 창법 등을 특징으로 한다[꺾기는 클래식 음악의 '그루페토(gruppetto)' 장식과 유사한 점이 있어서, 하나의 음이 두 개 또는 네 개의 보조음으로 나뉜 것처럼 표현된다. 말로 설명하기는 매우 어렵지만, 한번 들어보면 쉽게 이해가 될 것이다. 다른 장르의 K팝에 비해 따라 부르기가 쉬워서, 노래방에서는 젊은이들에게도 드물지 않게 선택된다.

당신이 택시, 음식점, 고속도로 휴게소와 혹은 라디오나 TV에서 '뭔지 모르게 특이한 노래'를 듣게 된다면 그것이 바로 트로트일 확률이 매우 높다. 어떤 음악인지 궁금하면 유튜브에서 임영웅, 장윤정, 심수봉, 태진아, 송대관, 나훈아, 주현미 등의 가수 이름을 검색해보면 된다. 이들은 한국의 대표적인 트로트 가수들로, 모든 한국인이 그 이름을 다 안다.

한국인들은 트로트를 좋아하든 싫어하든, 이 장르가 매우 '한국적'이라는 사실에는 동의한다. 그래서 외국인이 트로트 노래를 부르는 걸 보면 엄청나게 신기해한다. 혹시라도 당신이 비즈니스 등의 이유로 한국인들과 노래방에 가서 트로트 노래를 하나 부른다면, 엄청난 박수갈채가 쏟아질 것이다.

BTS부터 임영웅까지, K팝의 폭은 꽤나 넓다(당신이 모르는 엄청나게 훌륭한 뮤지션이 많은데, 다 소개하지 못해서 아쉬울 뿐이다).

17.

Discover K-pop Spots

When PSY's "Gangnam Style" went viral worldwide in 2012, what were the thoughts among the Korean population? Were they pondering, "Finally, the world recognizes PSY's awesomeness," or "I always knew PSY would achieve great success one day," or "Seems like this catchy tune has universal appeal"? Well, not quite. The typical reaction among Koreans was more along the lines of, "What on earth is this?", "Why is this happening?", "They don't even understand the lyrics!", and "What if people start assuming that all Korean men look like PSY?" and so on.

PSY was already a beloved superstar in South Korea long

before the world went crazy for Gangnam Style. He had achieved immense popularity with his debut song and continued to release several hit songs throughout his career spanning over a decade. While he possesses a great voice, it is often overshadowed by his unique vocal style. Similarly, despite being a skilled dancer, his modest physique often takes the spotlight over his dance moves. PSY is not only a talented singer and dancer, but also a prolific songwriter and producer, having crafted a great many songs. In addition to his many talents, he possesses a great sense of humor, which shines through, even in his less-than-fluent English. (His humor is even more captivating in the Korean language.)

Nevertheless, no one could have predicted that his music would become a worldwide sensation, with billions of people dancing to his tunes. (PSY himself probably didn't see that coming either.) When PSY rose to global stardom out of the blue, it left many Koreans genuinely puzzled. (Even PSY himself was probably taken aback by his sudden global stardom.)

There were certainly other Korean singers and actors who had already captured the hearts of foreigners before PSY. Korean movies, dramas, and TV shows were prevalent overseas, and the term "Hallyu" (Korean Wave) had been coined by the mid-1990s. However, nobody had achieved the same level of worldwide success as PSY did. Koreans initially found it hard to believe that PSY had broken through, as the term "Hallyu" had been reserved for people in the Asia who shared similar looks and feelings to Koreans. (How unbelievable it was, they would approach every foreigner they met, asking "Do you know PSY?" just to confirm their doubts.)

As time went by, PSY's "international" fame dwindled (although he remains a major star in Korea), and Gangnam Style was seen as a one-off phenomenon. That is, until BTS came along. BTS's incredible success has once again caused some awkwardness for Koreans, who are aware that, although BTS fans might not admit it, BTS's status in Korea was no higher than PSY's in Korea just before Gangnam Style. However, BTS's wave was much more powerful and sustained than PSY's. In any case, Koreans have been convinced by BTS's global triumph that PSY's success was not a fluke, and that K-pop has universal appeal. Concurrently, Korean movies and dramas have also gained immense popularity, further strengthening the faith in K-content. (And it is with this same faith that I am writing this book.)

If you're a die-hard fan of The Beatles, then Liverpool is a must-visit destination. Similarly, fans of Elvis Presley flock to Memphis, while ABBA enthusiasts make their pilgrimage to Stockholm, and Mozart lovers head to Salzburg. For Gaudi admirers, Barcelona is a must-see destination, while Munch fans find solace in Oslo, and Shakespeare aficionados flock to Stratford-upon-Avon. (If you love Picasso, you'll be torn between all the places associated with his life and work that you want to explore.) And if you're a K-pop fan, there's no better place to experience the genre than in its birthplace of Korea. To help plan your ultimate K-pop adventure, I've compiled a list of must-visit destinations for any true fan.

Before we dive into the details, I have to confess something: South Korea doesn't have the kind of iconic attractions that can captivate almost any tourist, like the ones found in the cities mentioned above. This is partly because K-pop is a relatively new phenomenon that has yet to generate the same level of global allure as the Beatles, Elvis Presley, or Abba. Unlike Liverpool, Memphis, or Stockholm, there is no BTS Museum, Blackpink's Jenny's House, PSY Art Center, or Twice Village that fans can pilgrimage to.

Despite the lack of iconic K-pop attractions in South Korea, K-pop fans living in the country still have some advantages. While getting tickets to concerts can be challenging, persistent fans can still manage to attend. And even if you fail to get tickets, there is always the possibility of trying again in the future. If you are dedicated enough to check your favorite singer's schedule in advance and have the stamina to stand in line all night, you may even be able to get into the theater inside the broadcasting station where music programs are produced. Fans of the same singer can also band together and place ads in subway stations and newspapers. Additionally, you can send gifts to your favorite stars or purchase limited edition merchandise. Although some editions may be out of reach, even with money, chances of getting the merch are much higher than those of foreigners.

While there isn't a single K-pop "pilgrimage" spot, there are still plenty of places for foreign fans to visit in Korea. One such place is "Hyuga", a cafe in Seoul's Nonhyeon-dong neighborhood that was converted from the former home of BTS members. The baked goods and drinks may not be anything special, but there are traces of BTS everywhere and plenty of notes left by ARMYs. Just a 15-minute walk away from Hyuga, there is "Yujung Sikdang", a restaurant where BTS used to eat before they became famous. Here, you'll find even more signs of BTS, as well as a variety of Korean dishes including pork belly. If you're an ARMY, don't miss the chance to eat where they ate and drink coffee where they slept.

Another place where ARMYs will be opening their wallets is the Line Friends Store, where BTS members are known to have participated in character development. Run by Naver, Korea's Google, these character shops are located in Hongdae, Gangnam, and Insadong. (The Itaewon location is closed.)

The old swimming pool at Seoul National University has become a frequented spot among BTS fans. The pool, which was previously used by university students and nearby residents, had been neglected for the past 30 years. However, after BTS filmed a music video for "Intro: Hwayangyeonhwa" in 2015, the number of visitors increased. Although the university had initially planned to demolish the pool entirely in 2019, and in fact, three of the pool's four walls are gone. But, thanks to the growing popularity of BTS and the efforts of Professor Hong Seok-kyung, who researches BTS, the university decided to preserve it and is working on a project to turn it into a multicultural space. The as-yet-unnamed site is located near Seoul National University's Institute of Molecular Biology & Genetics.

You'll also have the chance to see where the members of BTS spent their summer vacations and filmed their entertainment programs. There's a TV show called "In The Soop" (Soop is the Korean word for forest) that features BTS members on vacation, and the filming location for the second season has been turned into a tourist attraction. Unfortunately, it's not open to the public, but only to those who purchase a special package deal that includes a stay at the nearby Phoenix Hotels & Resorts and a one and a half hour tour of the filming location. With nightly rates ranging from $220 to $400 for two people, depending on the room, and a two-hour drive from Seoul, it may not be a practical or budget-friendly option for most foreign visitors. Additionally, it's unclear how long this package deal will be available.

An unexpected place where you can experience K-pop culture in Korea is in some subway stations. Several subway stations, including Samsung, Gangnam, Hapjeong, Jamsil, and Hongik Univ. on Line 2, Apgujeong on Line 3, and Cheongdam on Line 7, feature advertisements posted by fans of K-pop stars who have raised money to support them. Subway stations close to the star's agency and those with high foot traffic tend to have the most ads. The cost of posting an ad for a month can range from $2,000 to $5,000. But, with over 2,000 of these ads a year, there are almost always at least 100 of them in many subway stations in Seoul. The ads are usually posted around the K-pop star's birthday or debut anniversary and feature stunning photos and messages of support and love from fans. Many people take pictures in front of them, and Samsung Station on Line 2 has the most ads and is the most expensive. Once you've seen the advertisements in the basement of Samsung Station, head upstairs to check out the "Gangnam Style" sculpture. The sculpture is modeled after PSY's hands as he dances while singing Gangnam Style.

In the heart of Seoul's city center, the main store of Lotte Department Store features Star Avenue, a space decorated with handprints and large photos of several K-pop stars, including BTS. If you touch a handprint and wait a moment, a video of the star will appear. Another must-visit location is K-Star Road, a street lined with about 20 teddy bears modeled after famous K-pop stars, located near the Galleria Department Store in Apgujeong-dong. You don't have to go to these two places on purpose, but it's worth taking a moment if you have a trip to the mall.

"Yongma Land" is an unconventional but noteworthy spot associated with K-pop. Located in the northeast corner of Seoul, it used to be a small amusement park that operated for a decade in the 1980s before shutting down due to operational issues. The park was abandoned for some time, but due to its peculiar atmosphere, it has become an unconventional filming location for dramas, movies, TV shows, and music videos. Recently, it has also been utilized as a "studio" for filming. There is an entrance fee and a few other charges. For example, if you go at night, they'll light up the carousel for an hour for about $10. However, if the park is entirely rented out for a movie, entry might not be possible. The park is relatively remote and inaccessible, about two kilometers away from the nearest subway station, but it has been used for filming by many K-pop stars, including BTS, EXO, TWICE, IU, IZ*ONE, and more. If you're a K-pop enthusiast visiting Seoul for around 10 days, Yongma Land could be a unique and exciting place to explore.

As you can see, there is still a lack of specialized venues for tourists interested in K-content. SM Entertainment's SM Town, which used to operate at COEX, has closed down, and pop-up place "House of BTS" was a massive success in 2019, but unfortunately, it wasn't a permanent space. (It attracted 180,000 people during its 80-day run, so why hasn't it returned?) In the fall of 2022, a special BTS exhibit was held for two months in an exhibition space called "Hybe Insight" in the HYBE building, but again, it wasn't permanent. (Mr.

President of Hybe, we urge you to build something large and permanent to help fans fill in the gaps while BTS members are away in the military!)

But, there's still some hope for K-pop fans out there! The Korea Tourism Organization just finished building a cultural complex in the heart of the city called HiKR Ground. Not only can you see K-pop exhibits there, but you can also live out your dream of being the star of your own music video - talk about a great photo op! The best part? No admission fee! And get this, in 2025, there's a new theater in town called Seoul Arena, dedicated solely to K-pop concerts. It's gonna be massive, fitting anywhere from 18,000 to 28,000 folks depending on how they configure the space. But here's the million-dollar question: will it be ready in time for when all the BTS boys are off serving in the military? Only time will tell! Fingers crossed!

If you're a die-hard BTS fan and your sole reason for visiting Korea is to catch a glimpse of the sensational group, then fear not - there are plenty of places to quench your thirst for all things BTS. But, most of these spots are located outside of Seoul. You could make the journey to the east coast and drive over 200 kilometers to reach the Hyangho Beach bus stop. This location is where the music video for

"Spring Day," the title track from the 2017 album "You Never Walk Alone", was filmed. It takes about two and a half hours to reach this spot by car, and slightly longer if you take the train, but trust me, the effort will be worth it when you get that 'life photo' that you've been dreaming of. Interestingly, this bus stop was initially constructed for the purpose of filming and was later demolished, but when tourists continued to flock there, Gangneung City decided to rebuild it to look exactly like the one in the music video. (The mayor would have been in big trouble if they didn't!) Another must-visit location is Samcheok Maengbang Beach, which is not far from the Hyangho Beach bus stop and is where BTS shot the jacket for their "Butter" album. While it might be a little trickier for foreigners to reach via public transportation, the Ilyeong station is another spot worth checking out. This disused train station was used to film the "Spring Day" music video, so if you happen to be in Seoul on a snowy winter day, you might just get a chance to snap a same photo of "V" kneeling on the snow-covered tracks.

Korea is filled with countless other locations that hold a special significance for BTS fans. From palaces and museums to beaches, theme parks, restaurants, music video sets, and even the zoo where the members played as children -

all are popular stops on "BTS tours" for Korean fans. As an ARMY, you're sure to come across at least one or two places that will excite you. While some of these locations may be challenging to reach, the memories you'll make there will last a lifetime - even if they don't quite live up to your expectations.

Before we conclude our K-pop story, there's another genre of K-pop in Korea that's worth mentioning: trot. This style of music is very different from the K-pop you're familiar with, but it's incredibly popular in Korea. In fact, in 2020, BTS was only ranked second among Korean singers in terms of "YouTube views in Korea". The top spot was claimed by a male trot singer named Lim Young-woong, who is virtually unknown outside of Korea but is a household name in the country. There are many other talented trot singers who enjoy immense popularity in Korea as well.

Although it's really hard to explain in a nutshell, trot, a widely embraced genre of music in Korea, can be traced back to the roots of K-pop in the 1930s. During a time when the record industry was booming and radio was beginning to gain traction, trot became the genre of choice for singers who achieved nationwide fame. These songs were a unique blend of Western music, Japanese pop music, and traditional Korean folk songs. Although trot remained a staple in Korean pop music until the 1960s, it experienced a period of stagnation in the 1970s as other genres like folk, rock, ballads, and hip-hop took over. Despite popular trot singers still existing in the 80s and beyond, the genre became primarily associated with those over 50 years old. However, in 2019, trot made a resurgence in popularity thanks to a television station's audition program for trot singers that became a hit with audiences.

Despite its reputation as "tacky" B-grade music and its appeal to older generations, trot has a devoted fan base that cannot be ignored. Concerts featuring famous trot singers often attract tens of thousands of attendees, and fans show their support by purchasing merchandise and visiting places associated with their favorite stars.

The name "trot" is said to have originated from the foxtrot, a genre of dance music, but the current Korean trot has evolved quite differently from its origins. With a history spanning nearly 100 years, there are now many different styles of trot, ranging from the "authentic" trot to blues, R&B, rock, dance, folk, and more. Trot songs are characterized by straightforward lyrics, simple melodies in four-quarter time, and a distinctive singing style called "kkeokk-ki." (This technique has some similarity with the grup-petto ornament of classical music. A note is figured as if it had been split into two or four subsidiary notes. But, it's very hard to explain in words. Just listen to it and you'll understand.) Compared to other genres of K-pop, trot is easier to sing along to, making it a frequent choice for noraebang, even among younger generations.

If you happen to come across a peculiar song while riding a taxi, dining at a restaurant, taking a break at a highway rest area, or tuning in to the radio or TV in Korea, there's a high chance that it's a trot song. To learn more about this genre, you can search for well-known trot singers such as Lim Young-woong, Jang Yoon-jeong, Sim Soo-bong, Tae Jin-ah, Song Dae-kwan, Na Huna, and Joo Hyun-mi on You-Tube. These are household names in Korea and highly recognized for their contributions to the trot music scene.

Whether Koreans are fans of trot or not, they all agree that the genre is definitely 'Korean'. As such, hearing a foreigner sing a trot song can be quite appealing and amusing. If you were to join Koreans at a noraebang for a business outing or similar occasion and perform a trot song, you would likely receive enthusiastic applause for your unexpected choice.

From global superstars BTS to talented trot singer Lim

Young Woong, the range of K-pop is incredibly wide and diverse. (And believe it or not, there are even more incredible musicians that you might not be familiar with yet! I apologize for not being able to include all of them in our discussion.)

18.

매우 주관적인 서울의 핫 플레이스 목록

여기까지 읽어온 당신은 이제 한국에 대해 제법 많이 알게 됐고, 한국에 오고 싶은 마음이 전보다 훨씬 커졌을 것이다. 그리고 이렇게 말하고 싶을 것이다. "오케이. 알겠다고. 한국이 얼마나 매력적인 곳인지 충분히 알았다고. 근데, 어디에 가면 그 매력을 가장 잘 느낄 수 있는지를 알려줘. 설마, 구체적인 명소 목록은 『론리 플래닛』을 참고하시오, 이렇게 말하고 끝낼 건 아니지?"

불친절한 책이라는 비판을 피하기 위해서, 비록 이 책이 전형적인 가이드북은 아니지만, 외국인이 서울에서 방문하면 좋을 것 같은 장소 목록을 제공한다(앞에서 이미 자세히 언급한 장소는 다시 언급하지 않았다). 아주 유명한 곳도 있고 덜 유명한 곳도 있다. 당연히 매우 주관적인 목록이며, 당신의 만족을 보장하지는 않는다. 백 명의 한국인에게 목록을 만들라고 하면 백 가지 다른 목록이 나올 것이다. 나는 그저, 내가 아는 외국인 친구들에게 추천하고 싶은 장소들과 추천의 이유를 짧게 정리했을 뿐이다. 부디 당신의 여행 스타일이 나와 조금이라도 비슷하기를 빈다.

먼저, 당신이 한국의 역사와 전통문화에 관심이 있다면, 국립중앙박물관을 가야 한다. 괜히 '국립' 박물관이 아니다. 짧게는 백여 년, 길게는 수천 년 전에 만들어진 수많은 '국보'가 전시되어 있고, 외국어 설명도 잘되어 있다. 상설 전시 품목만 해도 꽤 많아서, 제대로 보려면 최소 서너 시간은 잡아야 한다. 흥미로운 특별전이 열리는 시기에 방문한다면 한두 시간을 더 잡아야 할 수도 있다. 국립중앙박물관 바로 옆에는 국립한글박물관이 있다. 당신이 이 책의 11장을 읽으며 한국어와 한글에 관한 관심이 높아졌다면, 이곳까지 방문하기를 추천한다. 비교적 근래에 생긴 박물관이라 유물 자체는 많지 않지만, 한두 시간 동안 독특한 문자 '한글'의 매력을 충분히 느낄 수 있다.

한국의 전통 예술품과 한국 및 외국 유명 작가의 현대미술품을 동시에 볼 수 있는 훌륭한 미술관은 '리움'이다. 리움은 '리(Lee)'와 '뮤지엄(museum)'을 합친 단어다. 삼성의 창업자 고 이병철과 아들 고 이건희는 모두 미술품 수집에 큰 애정을 쏟았는데, 그들의 컬렉션 중에서 극히 일부가 리움에 전시되어 있다. 리움은 세 개의 건물로 이루어져 있는데, 한국의 고미술품을 전시하는 M1은 스위스의 마리오 보타(Mario Botta)가, 현대미술품을 전시하는 M2는 프랑스의 장 누벨(Jean Nouvel)이, 아동교육문화

센터는 네덜란드의 렘 쿨하스(Rem Koolhaas)가 설계했다. 리움은 소장 미술품의 수준도 매우 높지만 건물 자체도 아름답기 때문에 건축에 관심이 있는 사람에게도 추천할 만한 곳이다.

고 이건희 회장은 2020년에 사망했는데, 이후 유족들은 2만 3천여 점의 미술품을 국가에 기증했다. 무려 12조 원에 달하는 거액의 상속세 납부를 위해 매각할 것이라는 추측도 있었지만, 삼성 패밀리는 감정가액이 최소 3조 원에 이르는 방대한 컬렉션을 기부하기로 했다. 그중 일부는 한국의 여러 미술관에서 이미 전시되고 있으며, 주요 기증품들을 전시하기 위한 이건희미술관이 2027년에 지어질 예정이다.

한국의 전통문화 중에서도 고궁에 관심이 있다면, 창덕궁과 경복궁을 가면 된다. 창덕궁은 가장 오랜 기간 조선의 왕이 기거했던 궁이며, 최고의 아름다움을 자랑한다. 단풍이 물든 가을에 방문하면 가장 좋고, 더 좋은 것은 일부 기간에만 시행하는 야간 관람을 하는 것이다. 입장객 수를 제한하기 때문에 사전 예약이 필수이며, 야간 관람은 어마어마하게 인기 있기 때문에 예약이 쉽지 않지만 외국인을 위한 특별한 옵션도 있으니 시도해볼 만하다.

경복궁은 조선왕조의 궁궐 중 처음으로 지어졌지만, 16세기 일본 침략 당시 파괴되어 오랫동안 방치되어 있다가 19세기에 중건되었다. 지금도 원래의 모습이 완전히 복원되어 있는 상태는 아니지만, 조선 궁궐의 아름다움을 느끼는 데는 부족함이 없다. 역시 일부 기간에는 야간에도 문을 연다. 외국인은 상대적으로 입장이 편리하다.

창덕궁이나 경복궁을 관람할 때의 팁은, 궁궐 근처의 대여점에서 '한복'이라 부르는 한국의 전통 의상을 빌려 입고 들어가는 것이다. 오랫동안 추억이 될 근사한 사진을 백만 장 정도 찍을 수 있다.

작은 미술관 중에서는 환기미술관이 가장 근사하다. 김환기는 한국 추상미술의 선구자이자 20세기를 대표하는 화가로, 그림 가격이 가장 비싼 것으로도 잘 알려져 있다. 지하철을 타고 가기 어려운 곳에 있지만, 미술 애호가라면 반드시 가볼 만한 장소다. 환기미술관까지 갔다면, 근처의 석파정까지 돌아보면 좋다. 석파정은 한국 역사에서 왕이 아니지만 왕과 같은 권력을 누린 유일한 인물인 흥선대원군의 별장이었던 장소로, 매우 아름다운 한국식 정원이다. 영화 〈기생충〉에서 캠핑을 떠났다가 갑자기 돌아온 주인집 가족을 피해 송강호와 그 가족들이 도망치는 장면을 촬영한 장소도 바로 인근에 있다. 당신이 영국 사람이라면 '스코프'라는 빵집까지 방문하기를 권한다. '영국식 빵집'으로 한국에서 매우 인기 있는 가게인데, 진짜 영국식 빵을 파는지 확인해보길 바란다('영국식'을 내세우고 영업을 하는데 장사가 매우 잘되는 다른 곳은, 적어도 음식점 중에는 없다. 당신의 나라에는 혹시 있는지? 한국에도 어쩌면 없진 않을 텐데, 나는 모른다. 하지만 영국 음식이라고 하기는 힘든 베이글을 파는 빵집 중에 '런던 베이글 뮤지엄'이라는 곳은 몇 시간씩 줄을 서야 할 만큼 인기가 높기는 하다. 이름에 왜 '런던'이 들어갔는지는 모르겠다).

한국의 근대사에 관심이 있다면, 대한민국역사박물관을 추천한다. 19세기 말부터 현재까지, 일제강점기와 전쟁과 가난을 겪은 한국이 지금과 같은 발전을 이루기까지의 과정이 잘 정리되어 있다. 경복궁과 아주 가깝다. 격동의 한국 근대사 중에서 1950년대의 한국전쟁에 관한 전시에 집중하고 있는 곳은 전쟁기념관이다.

일제강점기와 관련이 있는 장소로는 서대문형무소역사관이 있다. 이곳은 1908년에 지어진 감옥으로, 일제강점기 동안 수많은 독립운동가가 고문을 받고 수감 생활을 하고 사형을 당했던 곳이다. 해방 이후에도 1987년까지 감옥으로 사용되었으며, 독재에 저항하여 민주화운동을 했던 사람들도 이곳에 수감된 바 있다(그중에는 김대중, 김영삼 두 전직 대통령도 있다). 1998년에 박물관으로 개장했다.

현대미술에 관심이 있다면 국립현대미술관이 가장 중요한 장소로, 총 네 곳이 있다. 가장 규모가 큰 과천관은 서울시 경계 바깥에 있지만 지하철 4호선을 타면 쉽게 갈 수 있고, 서울관은 경복궁 인근에 있다. 서울 시청 근처에 있는 서울시립미술관(SeMA)에서는 흥미로운 기획 전시를 많이 여는데, BTS 멤버이자 미술 애호가인 RM이 데이비드 호크니 전시회에 다녀가서 화제가 된 곳이다(RM이 방문한 미술관은 하도 많아서, 당신이 그 모든 곳을 방문할 수는 없을 것이다). SeMA도 여러 개의 분관이 있는데, 그중 SeMA 벙커라는 특이한 장소도 있다. 여의도에 있는 이곳은 2005년에 환승센터 건립을 위한 현지 조사중에 발견된 지하 벙커를 미술관으로 바꾼 곳이다. 1970년대에 비밀 방공호로 만들어진 것으로 추정되는 이 장소는 수십 년 동안 존재조차 알려지지 않았던 곳이다. IFC몰 바로 옆에 입구가 있다. 화장품 회사가 운영하는 아모레퍼시픽 미술관은 소장품은 별로 없지만 흥미로운 기획 전시를 꾸준히 개최하고 있다.

이마트, 롯데마트, 홈플러스 등의 대형 마트를 방문하는 것이 즐거울 것이라는 이야기는 이미 했지만, 몇몇 백화점도 방문할 가치가 있다. 신세계백화점 강남점은 한국에서 가장 높은 매출을 올리는 백화점으로, 2022년 매출이 거의 25억 달러에 이른다. 백화점이 다 비슷할 것이라고 생각하면 오산이다. 일단, 사람이 엄청나게 많다. 주말과 세일 기간에는 특히 더 많다. 영업을 시작하기 전부터 문 앞에 사람들이 몰려 있는 백화점은 흔하지 않다. 주차하는 데만 30분 이상 걸릴 수도 있다. 물건을 공짜로 나눠주는 것도 아닌데 그렇다(구매 실적이 좋은 고객에게 가끔씩 선물을 주기는 하지만). 이렇게 비싼 물건을 이렇게 복잡한 곳에서, 전혀 럭셔리하지 않은 분위기에서 구매한다는 사실에 놀랄 것이다. 그 결과, 이곳은 전 세계에서 가장 매출이 높은 백화점이다.

더욱 놀라운 것은, 초고가 럭셔리 브랜드 매장에 들어가기 위해 전날 밤이나 이른 새벽부터 대기하는 사람들이 있다는 사실이다. 외국의 부자들은 에르메스, 루이비통, 샤넬 등의 제품을 살 때 백화점이나 플래그십 스토어에 가서 에비앙이나 페리에를 마시며 우아하게 쇼핑을 하는데, 한국인들은 왜 이러는 것일까? 사실 침낭 속에서 하룻밤을 보내는 사람들은 진짜 부자가 아니다. 고급 핸드백을 구매한 다음 포장도 뜯지 않은 채 웃돈을 붙여 되팔려는 사람들이다. 만 달러짜리 핸드백을 사서 만 천 달러에 팔

수 있다면, 즉 하룻밤 고생해서 천 달러를 벌 수 있다면, 나름 괜찮은 장사가 아닐 수 없다(물론 모두가 되팔려는 사람은 아니고, 특히 인기가 높아서 돈 주고도 살 수 없는 제품을 반드시 구매하기 위해 밤을 새는 사람도 없지는 않다). 그럼 진짜 부자들은 이런 제품을 어떻게 구매할까? 아예 해외로 나가서 구입하기도 하고, 각 브랜드의 플래그십 매장에 예약을 하거나 초대를 받아 방문한다(이런 일은 상당한 '실적'이 있는 사람에게만 일어난다).

한국의 대표적인 부촌 중 하나인 압구정동에 있는 갤러리아백화점도 빼놓을 수 없다. 두 개의 건물로 이뤄진 이 백화점은 면적이 작아서 연매출은 10억 달러에 채 못 미치지만, 단위 면적당 매출은 세계에서 가장 높은 것으로 유명하다. 특히 서관에서는 주로 최고급 물건만 팔기 때문에 혼잡도는 다른 백화점들에 비해 낮은 편이다. 동관 지하 1층에 있는 식품관만 방문해도 이 백화점이 어떤 곳인지 잘 알 수 있다. 과일, 생선, 소고기 등의 가격이 상상을 초월할 정도로 비싸기 때문이다. 한국의 부자들은 어떤 옷을 입고 어떻게 스타일링을 하는지 구경하고 싶다면 이곳이 최적의 장소다.

규모가 크고 세련된 쇼핑몰에 관심이 있다면, 코엑스가 대표적인 장소다. 너무 넓어서 길을 잃을 수 있으니, 곳곳에 비치된 지도를 잘 보면서 다니는 것이 좋다. 건물 외부에는 엄청난 해상도를 자랑하는 초대형 LED 스크린이 있고, 내부에는 수많은 상점과 식당, 독특한 도서관, 적당한 규모의 아쿠아리움, 호텔, 백화점 등이 밀집해 있다.

여의도에 있는 IFC몰도 유명한데, 바로 옆에 붙어 있는 더현대 서울도 함께 돌아볼 수 있다. 잠실에 있는 롯데월드몰도 빼놓을 수 없다. 이곳은 한국에서 가장 높은 건물인 롯데월드타워, 서울 시내에 있는 것 중에서는 가장 훌륭한 테마파크인 롯데월드, 역시 적당한 규모의 아쿠아리움 등이 모여 있다.

서울에 있는 허다한 시장 중에서 해산물을 좋아하는 외국인이 가장 즐거워할 만한 곳은 노량진수산시장이다. 한국은 1인당 수산물 소비량이 세계 1위다. 노르웨이나 일본보다 많고, 미국보다는 두 배 이상 많이 먹는다(그래서 비만 인구가 적은지도 모르겠다). 당연히 수산시장에는 엄청나게 많은 손님과 엄청나게 다양한 해산물이 있다. 건물을 완전히 새로 지어서 과거에 비해 '이국적인' 느낌이 조금은 줄어들긴 했지만, 이곳은 여전히 독특하고 매력적인 장소다. 도매와 소매가 모두 이뤄지는 시장으로, 경매 방식의 도매는 주로 한밤중이나 새벽에, 소매 위주의 영업은 그 나머지 시간에 이뤄진다. 재미있는 것은, 1층에서 살아 있는 생선을 선택하여 구매한 다음 2층에서 곧바로 그것을 먹을 수 있도록 되어 있는 시스템이다. 1층에 있는 가게에서 생선값을 지불한 다음, 2층에 있는 식당 중 아무 곳이나 들어가면 그 생선을 손질하여 회와 매운탕으로 만들어주고, 함께 먹을 수 있는 채소와 반찬들도 준다. 물론 2층에서도 약간의 돈을 지불해야 하지만, 두 번에 걸쳐 지불한 돈을 합쳐도 평범한 식당에서 먹는 것보다 비싸지는 않다.

대도시에 가면 반드시 그 도시에 가장 높은 곳에 위치한 전망

대에 오르는 사람이 많은데, 그런 사람들에게는 세 가지 정도의
선택지가 있다. 우선 앞에서 언급한 롯데월드타워의 전망대이
다. 그곳은 해발 5백 미터 높이를 자랑하지만, 서울의 외곽에 위
치해 있어 서울 전체를 조망하는 데는 상대적으로 불리하고 입장
료가 비싸다. 수십 년 동안 한국에서 가장 높은 건물이었던 63빌
딩에 있는 전망대는 야경이 특히 아름답다. 서울 도심 한가운데
에 있는 남산 정상 부근의 N타워는 그 자체의 높이는 약 240미
터에 불과하지만 남산의 높이(약 240미터)까지 더할 경우 롯데월
드타워와 비슷하게 높아진다. 서울의 중심부에 있어서 거의 모든
방향을 다 조망할 수 있으며, 낮이나 밤이나 다 아름다운 곳이다.
남산은 그리 높지 않아서 여러 방향에서 걸어 올라갈 수도 있고,
케이블카를 타고 갈 수도 있다.

　높이가 아니라 어떤 전망이 보이는지를 더 중요하게 생각하는
사람이라면, 네번째 선택지도 있다. 서울 시청의 별관에 해당하
는 서소문청사의 13층에는 무료로 들어갈 수 있는 작은 전망대
가 있는데, 이곳은 주요 고궁 중의 하나인 덕수궁 바로 옆에 있기
때문에 서울의 과거와 현재를 동시에 조망할 수 있다(서울시립미
술관도 바로 옆에 있다).

　걷기를 좋아한다면, 갈 곳은 무궁무진하다. 우선 가장 유명한
관광지인 인사동이 있고, 인사동의 동쪽에는 익선동이 있으며,
인사동의 북쪽에는 북촌이라 불리는 오래된 동네가 있고, 북촌에
서 서쪽 방향으로 붙어 있는 곳이 삼청동이다. 삼청동의 옆이자
경복궁의 북쪽에는 오랫동안 대통령 집무실로 쓰였던 청와대가

있으며, 경복궁의 서쪽에는 서촌이라 불리는 오래된, 그리고 매력적인 동네가 있다. 서촌에서 더 서쪽에는 인왕산이 있는데, 산 중턱에 위치한 카페 겸 서점인 '더숲초소책방'을 방문하면 놀라운 풍경을 감상할 수 있다. 이 카페는 원래 서울을 지키는 군인들이 보초를 서던 초소였다가 오랫동안 방치됐던 장소를 리모델링한 곳이다.

당신이 마음만 먹는다면, 그리고 날씨가 너무 덥거나 춥지 않다면, 경복궁에서 출발하여 서촌을 구경한 다음 환기미술관에 들렀다가 〈기생충〉 촬영지와 더숲초소책방을 거쳐 다시 경복궁까지 돌아오는 도보 여행을 할 수도 있다. 미술관이나 카페에서 보내는 시간을 빼고 순수하게 걷는 시간은 두 시간이 채 안 걸린다.

오래된 동네도 좋지만 젊은이가 많이 모이는 힙한 동네를 걷고 싶다고 해도 갈 곳이 많다. 2호선 성수역 인근에는 근사한 카페와 음식점과 상점 들뿐 아니라 작은 미술관이 많고, 2호선 홍대입구역과 6호선 상수역 인근에는 거기에 더해 다양한 스타일의 클럽도 많다. 2022년 10월 29일 핼러윈 데이에 불행한 참사가 발생한 이태원 주변은 오래전부터 유명한 곳이지만, 지금은 그 범위가 더 넓어져서 다양한 종류의 핫 스폿들이 6호선 녹사평, 이태원, 한강진역의 남쪽과 북쪽 곳곳에 흩어져 있다(10. 29 참사 희생자 여러분의 명복을 빈다). 아무런 계획 없이 그냥 다녀도 재미있겠지만, 제법 넓은 지역이고 길이 상당히 꼬불꼬불하니, 최소한 두세 곳 정도는 목적지를 정해놓고 돌아다니기를 권한다.

서울 근교에도 외국인들의 관심을 끌 만한 장소들은 꽤 있다.

가장 대표적인 곳은 DMZ다. 정작 한국인들에게는 그리 인기 있는 관광지가 아니지만, 많은 외국인이 이곳을 궁금해한다. 이곳을 방문하는 외국인들은 DMZ가 서울과 너무도 가까운 곳에 있다는 사실에 깜짝 놀란다. 서울 도심에서 자동차로 한 시간밖에 안 걸리기 때문이다. DMZ는 군사분계선에서 남북으로 각각 2킬로미터씩 설정되어 있다. 1953년 휴전 이후 70년 동안 사람의 손길이 닿지 않았기에, 길이 248킬로미터, 폭 4킬로미터의 거대한 자연생태공원이 만들어져 있는 셈이다. 개별적인 관광은 어렵고, 외국인들을 위한 DMZ 투어 프로그램을 이용하면 된다.

여기서 흥미로운 사실 한 가지. 당신이 뉴스 등에서 보았던, 그리고 DMZ 투어에서 볼 수 있는 철조망은 군사분계선이 아니라 그보다 2킬로미터 남쪽에 있는 남방한계선 혹은 그보다 더 남쪽에 있는 민간인출입통제선이다. 군사분계선에는 철조망 같은 건 없고, 약 2백 미터 간격으로 총 1,292개의 작은 말뚝만 박혀 있다.

한국 최고의 놀이공원인 에버랜드도 서울 근교에 있다. 당신이 올랜도, 로스앤젤레스, 도쿄, 파리, 상하이 같은 도시에 살고 있다면, 에버랜드에 대해서는 관심을 꺼도 되겠다. 하지만 다른 대부분의 지역에서 온 관광객이라면, 그리고 한국에 머무는 기간이 4박 5일 이상이라면, 어릴 때부터 롤러코스터를 너무나 사랑했다면, 에버랜드에서 하루를 보내는 것은 매우 좋은 선택일 것이다.

에버랜드 바로 옆에는 '캐리비안 베이'라는 이름의 워터파크도 있는데, 이름은 좀 생뚱맞지만 '세계 최대 규모의 워터파크'다.

당신이 여름철에 한국에 온다면 에버랜드 대신 여기를 방문하는 것도 훌륭한 선택이 된다(아마 평생 가장 혼잡한 물놀이 경험을 하게 될 것이다). 그리고 중요한 한 가지. 당신이 아무리 놀이공원을 좋아한다고 하더라도, 5월 5일에는 절대로 에버랜드에 가서는 안 된다. 그날은 한국의 어린이날로, 에버랜드는 전국에서 가장 인구밀도가 높은 장소가 된다. 그리고 이왕이면 주말은 한국인들에게 양보하고, 비교적 덜 복잡한 평일을 택하기 바란다. 서울에서 에버랜드까지 지하철을 타고 갈 수도 있지만, 그건 좋은 선택이 아니다. 일반 버스 혹은 셔틀버스를 타는 게 훨씬 빠르고 편하다.

매우 주관적인 목록을 마무리하며, 한마디만 덧붙이고 싶다. 많은 여행자가 흔히 하는 실수는 가이드북에 나와 있는 유명한 관광지 목록에 얽매이는 것이다. 유명하다고 해서, 다른 사람들이 좋아한다고 해서, 당신도 좋아하리라는 보장은 없다. 어차피 다 못 본다. 좋은 곳이 좋은 게 아니라 당신이 좋아하는 곳이 좋은 곳이다. 가이드북에 너무 의존하지 마라(그런 면에서 가이드북만 읽지 않고 이 책을 고른 당신은 정말 훌륭한 여행자이지만, 내 말도 다 믿지는 마라). 여러 자료와 여러 사람의 의견을 참고하되, 당신이 최고로 즐거울 수 있는 당신만의 여행 계획은 당신이 직접 짜는 수밖에 없다. 그리고 계획했던 것을 모두 이뤄야 한다고 생각하지도 마라. 인생이 원래 계획대로 흘러가지 않는다는 것을, 하지만 가끔씩 뜻하지 않은 행운이 찾아온다는 것을 당신도 잘 알지 않나. 부디 당신이 세운 한국 여행 계획의 최소한 절반쯤은 멋지게 이뤄지기를, 그리고 나머지 절반쯤은 예기치 못한 즐거움으로 가득 채워지기를 진심으로 소망한다.

18.

Curated Collection of Seoul's Hottest Spots

If you've followed along so far, you've already become quite the Korea aficionado. I bet you're itching to pack your bags and head over to experience all that this fascinating country has to offer. But before you do, you might be thinking, "Enough with the generalities, buddy. Give me the details. Where should I go to get the authentic Korean experience? And please, spare me the 'check Lonely Planet' cop-out."

To avoid any accusations of lacking kindness, even though this book isn't your run-of-the-mill "guidebook," I'll go ahead and share a list of Seoul destinations that, in my opinion, any foreigner worth their salt should check out. (I won't repeat the places I've already raved about.) This list includes both well-known spots and hidden gems. Remember, it's entirely subjective, and I can't guarantee it will cater to your preferences. If you asked a hundred Koreans for their recommendations, you'd likely get a hundred different lists. Here, I've compiled a quick list of places I'd suggest to my out-of-town friends and explained why. Hopefully, our tastes in travel align.

First things first, if you're a history-and-heritage-culture buff, a visit to the National Museum of Korea is a must. Considered the OG (original gangster) of national museums, it houses countless 'national treasures' dating back hundreds and thousands of years. Clear explanations in multiple foreign languages enhance your understanding of the extensive permanent exhibitions. Allocate at least three to four hours to cover everything, and if you're lucky enough to catch a special exhibition, be prepared to spend an additional hour or two. For fans of Hangeul, the National Hangeul Museum next door is a must-visit. Despite having a relatively new space and a smaller artifact collection, it offers an excellent opportunity to spend a couple of hours delving into the wonderful alphabet, especially if Chapter 11 of this book has inspired you.

For those with an eye for art, both traditional and contemporary, the Leeum (Samsung Museum of Art) is an absolute must-see. The museum cleverly combines 'Lee' and 'museum' to pay tribute to the art collection of Samsung's founder, the late Lee Byung-chul, and his son, the late Lee Kun-hee. At Leeum, you can marvel at a small but impressive portion of their extensive collection, showcased across three buildings: M1, designed by Swiss architect Mario Botta, features Korean antiquities; M2, designed by French architect Jean Nouvel, showcases contemporary art; and the Samsung Child Education & Culture Center, designed by Dutch architect Rem Koolhaas. Leeum stands as a remarkable architectural masterpiece in its own right. Whether you're an art enthusiast or an architecture buff, the quality of the artwork and the beauty of the buildings at Leeum will undoubtedly leave you in awe.

After the passing of Chairman Lee Kun-hee in 2020, his family made a monumental contribution to the country by donating over 23,000 pieces of art. Initially, many Korean people speculated that the family would sell the collection to settle the colossal $10 billion inheritance tax bill. However, to everyone's surprise, the Samsung family decided to donate the massive art collection to the country instead. The collection, valued at a minimum of $3 billion, is already on display at diverse museums across South Korea. Additionally, the Korean government plans to construct the Lee Kun-hee Museum in 2027 to showcase these significant donations.

If you're interested in Korean historical culture and ancient palaces, two must-visit locations are Changdeokgung and Gyeongbokgung. Changdeokgung Palace stands as one of the most beautiful and enduring residences of the Joseon kings. For a truly captivating experience, it is recommended to visit in the fall when the foliage displays a breathtaking array of colors. Even more enchanting is the opportunity to explore the palace at night during select periods, known as night viewing. However, please note that due to the limited number of tickets available, advance reservations are required. Night viewing is immensely popular, making it challenging to secure a reservation. Nonetheless, there are special options available for foreigners, so it's certainly worth a try.

Gyeongbokgung Palace, the first of the Joseon Dynasty's palaces, was initially constructed but later destroyed during the Japanese invasion in the 16th century. It remained neglected until the 19th century when efforts were made to rebuild it. While the palace has not been fully restored to its original state, it still stands as a remarkable example of a Joseon palace. During select periods, Gyeongbokgung Palace is open for night viewing, and foreigners have relatively easy access to this experience.

When visiting Changdeokgung or Gyeongbokgung, a helpful tip is to rent a traditional Korean costume known as a "hanbok" from a rental shop near the palace. Wearing a hanbok allows you to immerse yourself in the historical atmosphere and capture unforgettable memories through countless photographs. These cherished moments will stay with you for years to come.

The Whanki Museum is a small yet impressive museum dedicated to the works of Kim Whanki, a pioneering figure in Korean abstract art and one of the most prominent Korean painters of the 20th century. While it may be a bit challenging to reach by subway, it is a must-see destination for art enthusiasts. After exploring the museum, I highly recommend taking a stroll around the neighborhood to visit Seokpajeong. Seokpajeong is a breathtaking Korean-style garden that once served as the villa of Heungseon Daewongun, the father and regent of King Gojong.

In the vicinity, you'll find a road where a scene from the movie "Parasite" was filmed. It's the scene where Song Kang-ho and his family hurriedly leave the host family upon their return from camping. If you happen to be British, I suggest visiting Scoff bakery, located just around the corner. It's a well-liked bakery in Korea that claims to be a "British bakery," and it could be interesting for you to see if they offer authentic British bread. Is there another restaurant that claims to be 'British' and performs well in Korea? Maybe there is, but I don't know. (How about in your country?) However, there is an intriguing establishment called the London Bagel Museum that enjoys immense popularity, with people often waiting in line for hours to gain entry. Despite the name, as you know, bagels are not originally British, so the origin of the bakery's name remains uncertain.

If you're curious about learning Korea's modern history, I highly recommend visiting the National Museum of Korean Contemporary History. This museum offers a well-documented look at the country's development from the late 19th century to the present day, covering colonization, war, and poverty. It's conveniently located near the stunning Gyeongbokgung Palace. For those interested in the Korean War and the turbulent recent past, the War Memorial of Korea is another must-visit site. Its exhibits focus on the Korean War in the 1950s.

Another meaningful site related to Korea's time as a Japanese colony is the Seodaemun Prison History Hall. Built in 1908, this prison was notorious for its torture, imprisonment, and execution of independence activists during the Japanese occupation. Even after Korea's liberation, it continued to be used as a prison until 1987, with many pro-democracy activists, including former presidents Kim Dae-jung and Kim Young-sam, incarcerated here. In 1998, it opened as a museum.

If contemporary art piques your concern, then the National Museum of Modern and Contemporary Art (MMCA) is a must-visit venue with four locations throughout Korea. The largest location, Gwacheon, sits just outside the city limits but remains easily accessible via subway line 4. The Seoul branch conveniently stands near Gyeongbokgung Palace. The Seoul Museum of Art (SeMA), situated near Seoul City Hall, offers a diverse array of intriguing temporary exhibitions. It's worth noting that RM, a member of the highly regarded Korean band BTS and an art enthusiast, even made an appearance at the David Hockney exhibit held at SeMA. (RM visited a lot of museums in Korea, so you might not be able to check out all of them.) SeMA also houses several offshoots, including the unique SeMA Bunker, an underground bunker discovered during site investigations for a transit center in 2005. Believed to have been constructed in the 1970s as a secret air defense bunker, its existence remained unknown for decades. It was transformed into an art museum in 2017. The entrance to the SeMA Bunker conveniently sits next to the IFC Mall. Another intriguing museum to explore is the Amore Pacific Museum of Art, run by a cosmetics company, which consistently hosts captivating temporary exhibitions despite having a limited permanent collection.

We've discussed the excitement of visiting big box stores like E-Mart, Lotte Mart, and Homeplus, but let's not overlook department stores as well. Shinsegae Department Store Gangnam in Korea had sales of nearly $2.5 billion in 2022, making it the highest-grossing department store not only in Korea but in the entire world. If you assume all department stores are the same, you're mistaken. On weekends and during sales, there are usually crowds of people, with lines sometimes forming even before the store opens. Finding a parking spot can take 30 minutes or more. Some department stores are so crowded that you'd think they were giving something away for free (although they do occasionally offer gifts to loyal customers called VIPs). It can be surprising to find people purchasing luxury items in such a bustling and vibrant atmosphere that may not immediately give off a customary sense of luxury.

It's even more surprising that some people wait in line overnight or in the early morning to enter ultra-expensive luxury brand stores. While wealthy individuals in other countries shop for high-end brands like Hermès, Louis Vuitton, and Chanel in department stores or flagship stores, enjoying their shopping experience with a sip of Evian or Perrier, why do Koreans engage in this practice? The truth is, those who spend the night in sleeping bags are not necessarily wealthy individuals themselves. They purchase high-end handbags with the intention of reselling them for a profit, without even opening the packaging. It's a lucrative business proposition – imagine buying a $10,000 handbag and selling it for $11,000, earning $1,000 for a night's work. Of course, not everyone is inclined to resell. Some people are willing to stay up all night to acquire something that is highly sought-after and unattainable even with ample financial resources. Now, how do the truly affluent manage to obtain these products? They either travel abroad to make their purchases or secure appointments or invitations to each brand's flagship store, a privilege reserved for those with a significant track record.

The Galleria Department Store in Apgujeong-dong, situated in one of Korea's most affluent neighborhoods, stands out from the typical department store experience. Despite its smaller size and annual sales of less than $1 billion, it boasts the highest sales per unit area in the world, primarily due to its emphasis on high-end products. (West wing is more luxurious among two buildings.) Consequently, the crowds at Galleria are not as overwhelming as those at other department stores. If you're interested in observing the fashion and style of Korea's wealthy elite, this is the perfect destination. Begin your visit by exploring the food section located in the basement level of east wing, where the prices of fruits, fish, beef, and other items reach unimaginable heights.

If you have a penchant for large and sophisticated shopping malls, COEX is a must-visit destination. Its vast size can be overwhelming, so it's recommended to familiarize yourself with the mall's maps, conveniently posted throughout the premises. The exterior of the building showcases impressive giant LED screens with exceptional resolution, adding to its allure. Inside, you'll discover a multitude of shops and restaurants, an enchanting library, a decent-sized aquarium, hotels, department stores, and much more.

Indeed, the IFC Mall and The Hyundai Seoul in Yeouido are both beloved shopping destinations that offer compelling experiences. Situated adjacent to each other, these malls provide a wide range of stores and amenities for visitors to explore. Another must-visit shopping spot is the Lotte World Mall in Jamsil. This iconic mall is home to the impressive Lotte World Tower, which stands as the tallest building in Korea. The Lotte World Mall also houses Lotte World, one of the city's premier theme parks. Additionally, the mall features a sizable aquarium, providing a fascinating aquatic experience.

Among the many markets in Seoul, Noryangjin Fisheries Wholesale Market is a must-visit for foreigners who love seafood. South Korea leads the world in seafood consumption per capita, surpassing countries like Norway, Japan, and even eating twice as much as the United States (which may be one of the reasons for Korea's low obesity rate). Naturally, the market attracts a large number of customers with its vast variety of seafood. While the construction of a new building has somewhat diminished its exotic atmosphere, the market still maintains its unique and captivating character. It caters to both wholesale and retail customers, with wholesale auctions mostly taking place in the middle of the night and early morning, while the rest of the day is focused on retail sales. Interestingly, customers can choose and purchase live fish on the first floor and enjoy it right away on the second floor. After buying the fish on the first floor, they can head to any of the restaurants on the second floor, where the fish is expertly prepared as "hoe" (a Korean style raw fish dish) and served with spicy soup, vegetables, and side dishes. While patrons are required to make an additional payment on the second floor, it remains reasonably priced compared to dining at a standard restaurant.

When it comes to exploring a big city, many people want to experience the panoramic views from the highest observation deck available. In Seoul, you have three solid options to choose from. The first is the Lotte World Tower deck, soaring at an impressive 500 meters above sea level. However, it's located on the city's outskirts and comes with a higher price tag. The second option is Building 63's deck, which has held the title of Korea's tallest building for decades and truly comes alive at night. Finally, there's N Tower, perched atop Namsan Mountain in the heart of the city.

While it stands at a height of around 240 meters, when combined with the elevation of the mountain, it offers equally breathtaking views as the Lotte World Tower. You can enjoy stunning vistas from every angle, whether it's day or night. To reach the top of Namsan Mountain, you can take a leisurely walk from various directions or opt for a more scenic ride on the cable car.

If you're not particularly obsessed with heights but still desire a remarkable vista, there's a fourth option. Head up to the 13th floor of the Seosomun Building, an annex of Seoul City Hall, where you'll find a cozy observation deck that won't cost you a penny. Additionally, it conveniently sits next to Deoksugung Palace, allowing you to witness both Seoul's past and present simultaneously. (The Seoul Museum of Art is right next door.)

For those who prefer exploring a city on foot, Seoul offers plenty of exciting places to visit. Start your journey in the famous tourist area of Insadong. From there, you can head east to Iksun-dong or venture north to Bukchon, an old neighborhood with a fascinating history. To the west of Bukchon, you will find Samcheong-dong. Just north of Gyeongbokgung Palace, adjacent to Samcheong-dong, lies the Blue House, which has served as the official residence of the

South Korean president for a long time. If you continue west from Gyeongbokgung Palace, you'll come across Seochon, an old neighborhood brimming with charm and character. And if you're up for an even greater adventure, journey further west to Inwangsan Mountain. One must-visit spot on the mountainside is The Forest Choso Chaekbang, a cozy cafe and bookstore situated in an old post that once served as a guardhouse for Seoul's soldiers. The view from the cafe is absolutely breathtaking!

If you're feeling energetic and the weather is favorable, consider taking a walking tour that starts from Gyeongbokgung Palace. This tour will allow you to explore Seochon, make a stop at the Hwanki Museum, and return to Gyeongbokgung Palace via the filming locations of Parasite and The Forest Choso Bookstore. The total walking time, excluding visits to the museum and cafe, is under two hours.

If you're looking to explore a vibrant neighborhood with a youthful atmosphere, Seoul offers plenty of options. Near Seongsu Station on Line 2, you'll find a variety of excellent cafes, restaurants, shops, and small museums, making it a great destination. Additionally, Hongik University Station on Line 2 and Sangsu Station on Line 6 are bustling with clubs, cafes, and diverse shops, attracting a young crowd. The Itaewon area has long been renowned for its international vibe and vibrant nightlife. You can discover wide-ranging hot spots located to the south and north of Noksapyeong, Itaewon, and Hangangjin stations on Line 6. While it's exciting to wander around without a set plan, keep in mind that the area is quite extensive, and the streets can be winding. It's advisable to have at least two or three destinations in mind to navigate more efficiently. (Our thoughts and condolences go out to those affected by the tragedy that occurred on October 29, 2022, in Itaewon.)

There are quite a few places on the outskirts of Seoul that might be of interest to foreigners. The most prominent one is the DMZ. While it may not be a top choice for locals, many foreigners are curious about it. Foreigners visiting the area are often surprised to find that the DMZ is so close to Seoul. It's only an hour's drive from the center of Seoul. The DMZ extends two kilometers north and south of the Military Demarcation Line. It has been untouched for 70 years since the 1953 armistice, creating a huge natural ecological park 248 kilometers long and 4 kilometers wide. It's difficult to visit on your own, but there are several DMZ tour programs for foreigners.

Here's a fascinating tidbit: the barbed wire often seen on

the news and during DMZ tours is not actually the Military Demarcation Line. It represents either the Southern Limit Line, which is two kilometers south, or the Civilian Control Line, which is even further south. Surprisingly, there is no barbed wire on the Military Demarcation Line itself. Instead, there are 1,292 small stakes spaced approximately 200 meters apart.

Everland, South Korea's premier amusement park, is also located near Seoul. Now, if you're from cities like Orlando, Los Angeles, Tokyo, Paris, or Shanghai, you may not find Everland particularly noteworthy. However, for tourists visiting from other parts of the world with more than four or five days in Korea, spending a day at Everland is a fantastic option—especially if you've been a roller coaster fan since childhood.

On scorching summer days, the adjacent water park, Caribbean Bay, offers a refreshing oasis. Don't let the whimsical name fool you—it's actually the "world's largest water park" and definitely worth a visit instead of Everland. (You'll probably have the most crowded water experience of your life.) And one important note: no matter how much you love amusement parks, you should never go to Everland on May 5th. That's Children's Day in Korea, and Everland becomes the most crowded place in the country. It's best to leave the weekend to the Koreans and go on a less crowded weekday instead. You can take the subway to Everland, but it's not a good option. It's much faster and more convenient to take a regular bus or shuttle bus.

To conclude this highly subjective list, I'd like to add a word of caution: a common mistake many travelers make is to get caught up in the guidebooks' lists of popular destinations. Just because it's famous, just because other people like it, doesn't mean you'll like it. Remember, you won't be able to see them all anyway. A good place is not necessarily a great place; a great place is a place you genuinely enjoy. While guidebooks can be helpful, it's essential not to rely solely on them. (In that sense, you're a great traveler for picking up this book and not just reading guidebooks. But don't solely rely on my book either!) Use multiple sources and multiple people's opinions, but only you can plan your own trip that you will enjoy the most. And don't feel like you have to do everything you planned. Life often takes us on unexpected paths, and sometimes the most remarkable experiences come from moments of spontaneous serendipity. It is my sincere hope that at least half of your travel plans will be fulfilled, and that the other half will be filled with unexpected delights.

19.
매우 주관적인 서울의 최고 맛집들

이 책에서 그렇게 많은 한국 음식 이야기를 했으니, 당신은 분명히 그중 몇 가지만이라도 맛보고 싶을 것이다. 무엇을 먹을지 선택하는 것도 괴롭겠지만, 그 음식을 어디에서 먹을 것인지도 큰 고민일 터. 같은 이름의 음식이라도 이왕이면 더 맛있는 곳에서, 이왕이면 더 유명한 곳에서 먹고 싶은 것은 인지상정이다. 『미슐랭가이드 서울편』을 비롯한 국제적인 맛집 목록은 여러 개 있지만, 그 목록을 작성하는 사람들은 한국인이 아닌 외국인인 경우가 많다(일부 한국인 심사위원들도 있을 수 있지만, 누가 심사하는지 공개된 바가 없다). 한국인이 진정으로 사랑하는 서울의 진짜 맛집들은 어디에 있을까?

여행자가 먹을 수 있는 끼니 수는 제한되어 있다. 체중을 신경

쓰지 않고 하루에 네 끼씩 먹기로 마음먹었다면(어쩌면 과감하게 다섯 끼를 시도할 거라면), 당신의 용기를 매우 칭찬한다. 하지만 당신이 한국 음식을 최대한 많이 맛보고 싶다고 해서 하루에 열일곱 끼를 먹는 것은 이룰 수 없는 꿈(어쩌면 악몽)에 불과하다. 그러니 친애하는 동료 미식가들이여, 전략적이고 현명한 식당 선택이 필요하다.

고백하건대, 한국에는 맛없는 식당도 많다. 도대체 이 집이 왜 망하지 않는 것인지 이해가 되지 않는, 그런 식당들도 있다(물론 그런 집은 조만간 문을 닫을 가능성이 높다). 음식 선택은 잘했더라도 식당 선택을 잘못하면 당신의 귀중한 한끼는 만족스럽지 않을 수도 있다. 그래서 여기, 스무 개의 맛집을 추천한다. 누구의 의견도 참조하지 않은, 온전히 나의 주관적인 목록이다(하지만 목록에 있는 음식점에서 먹은 음식이 당신을 만족시키지 못했다면, 그건 그 음식점의 책임이다).

선정 기준은 이렇다. 첫째, 내가 직접 방문한 적이 있는 곳 중에서 골랐다. 서울에 오래 살면서 정말 많은 음식점을 가보았지만, 모든 식당을 다 가보는 것은 당연히 불가능하다. 나름대로 유명한 맛집들 중에서 이런저런 이유로 가보지 못한 곳도 많다. 내가 직접 경험하지 않은 곳을 유명세만으로 추천하지는 않았다는 뜻이다. 단순히 내가 방문한 적이 없다는 이유로 목록에 오르지 못한 맛집 사장님들께 죄송하다는 말씀을 드린다.

둘째, 극단적으로 웨이팅이 길거나 극단적으로 예약이 어려운 가게들은 제외했다. 여기서 '극단적으로 웨이팅이 길다'는 것은 한 시간을 줄서서 기다려도 입장이 불가능한 정도를 말한다. '극단적으로 예약이 어렵다'는 것은 한 달 전에 전화해도 예약을 할 수 없는 정도를 말한다. 한국인들의 맛집 사랑은 유별나서, 예약을 받지 않고 반드시 줄을 서야만 먹을 수 있는 가게인 경우 문을 열기 몇 시간 전부터 사람들이 줄을 서기도 한다(궁금하겠지만, 안 알려준다. 그런 곳일수록 가보고 싶겠지만, 참으시라. 당신의 짧은 여행 기간 중 몇 시간을 그렇게 허비하는 건 바람직한 일이 아니다). 식당에 전화를 걸어서 가장 가까운 예약 가능 날짜를 물으면 두세 달 후를 알려주는 곳도 있는데, 그런 곳도 그냥 포기하시라(한국인들도 대체로 그냥 포기한다. 흥 칫 뿡).

셋째, 극단적으로 비싼 집은 제외했다. 여기서 '극단적으로 비싸다'는 것은 술이나 음료를 제외하고도 한 사람당 3백 달러 이상 지불해야 하는 곳을 말한다. 아래의 목록에 있는 식당들의 한 사람 식대는 대체로 15~50달러면 충분하다(몇 개의 예외가 있지만, 이들도 2백 달러를 넘지 않는다). 음식은 매우 훌륭하지만 그에 비해 너무 비싼 가격을 받는 특급 호텔 구내에 있는 식당들도 제외했다.

넷째, 한국 음식을 파는 식당들 중에서만 골랐다. 서울에서는 온갖 나라의 음식을 먹을 수 있고, 외국 음식을 파는 음식점 중에도 대단히 멋진 곳이 많다. 하지만 여기서 굳이 훌륭한 일식당, 중식당, 이태리 식당, 프랑스 식당, 스페인 식당 등을 소개할 필요는 없다고 생각해서다. 소위 '컨템퍼러리'로 분류되는 식당도 일부 포함시켰지만, 이들은 모두 한식을 기본으로 하여 현대적이고 창의적인 음식을 내는 곳들이다.

다섯째, 한국인들 중에서도 비교적 소수의 사람이 아주 좋아하는 음식은 제외했다. 이런 음식들은 '개성'이 강한 편이어서, 외국인들이 먹기엔 다소 어려울 수 있기 때문이다. 물론 그런 음식들도 한국의 음식 문화에서 중요한 위치를 차지하고 있지만, 다양한 배경을 가진 외국인들이 좀더 보편적으로 즐길 수 있는 음식들에 초점을 맞췄다는 뜻이다.

이런 원칙하에, 서울에 있는(딱 한 곳은 서울 밖에 있고, 서울이 아닌 지역에도 분점들이 존재하는 곳도 있지만) 많은 식당 중에서 내가 외국인들에게 추천하고 싶은 식당을 스무 곳 골랐다(단 하나의 매장만 존재하는 곳도 있고, 몇 개의 분점이 존재하는 곳도 있고, 아주 여러 개의 분점이 존재하는 곳도 있다. 그래서 당신이 방문할 수 있는 실제 음식점 수는 스무 개보다 훨씬 많다). 당신이 놀랄까봐 미리 말하는데, 이 책에서 아직 한 번도 언급되지 않은, 상대적으로 덜 유명한(물론 외국인들에게만 그러하고, 한국인들에게는 대단히 익숙한) 음식들도 등장한다. 한국 음식의 종류는 정말 많다. 심혈을 기울여 골랐으니, 이 목록에서 최소한 한 곳, 혹시 여러 가지 조건이 맞는다면 두 곳 이상 방문해보기를 권한다. (반드시 예약이 필요한 곳은 따로 표기해두었다. 휴무일과 영업시간은 각자 확인하시라.)

또한, 각 음식점을 방문했을 때 당신이 주문해야 하는 가장 대표적인 메뉴들을 (주로 성인 남자 2인 기준으로) 설명해놓았다(친절하기도 해라). 최대한 다양한 음식을 주문하여 일행들끼리 나눠 먹기를 권한다(같이 여행하는 사이면 꽤 가까운 관계이니, 평소엔 그렇게 하지 않더라도 여행지에선 그렇게 하자). 그리고, 당신이 아래 목록에 있는 식당을 실제로 방문할 경우, 반드시 이 책을 꺼내어 직원에게 보여주기 바란다. 그렇게 하면 특별한 혜택이 있느냐고? 그렇지는 않다. 다만, 다음에 내가 그 식당을 방문하여 외국인들 여러 명이 들고 왔던 그 책을 쓴 사람이 바로 나라고 말하면, 나에게 뭔가 좋은 일이 생길 수는 있으니까.

- 필동면옥(Pildong Myeonok): 시작은 내가 가장 사랑하는 식당부터. 이곳은 평양냉면 가게들 중에서 매우 유명한 곳 중의 하나로, 내가 외국에서 2년간 지내는 동안 가장 많이 그리워했던 곳이기도 하다. 평양냉면 전문점 중에서 맛이 유난히 밍밍한 편이다. 평양냉면 하나, 비빔냉면 하나, 만두 한 접시, 그리고 메뉴판에 나와 있지 않은 '반반'을 주문하여 나눠 먹으면 된다. 반반을 주문하면 소고기 수육과 돼지고기 수육을 절반씩 맛볼 수 있다. 소식가라면 비빔냉면은 생략해도 된다. 뭔가 건더기가 있는 디핑 소스가 나올 텐데, 모양은 없지만 맛은 끝내준다. 만두와 수육 모두 이 소스를 찍어먹으면 된다. 피크 시간엔 웨이팅이 있지만, 회전율이 높아서 기다릴 만하다. 1985년 개업.

- 우래옥(Woo Lae Oak): 한국에서 가장 유명한 평양냉면집이라고 해도 과언이 아니다. 필동면옥보다는 국물이 진한 편. 식당 이름의 의미가 '다시 방문하는 집'이니, 이곳에서 한끼를 먹

는다면 한국을 다시 방문할 가능성이 높아질지도 모른다. 서울식 불고기도 상당히 맛있는 집이니, 불고기 2인분과 평양냉면 두 그릇 혹은 평양냉면과 비빔냉면을 한 그릇씩 주문하기를 추천한다. 특이하게도 '고기를 포함해서 주문하면 후불, 면만 주문하면 선불'이라는 시스템을 갖고 있으니, 냉면만 주문할 경우엔 참고하시라. 주말은 매우 혼잡. 1946년 개업.

• 한일관(Hanilkwan): 1939년에 개업한 유서 깊은 식당. 상당히 많은 메뉴를 파는데, (내 생각으론) 육개장이 전 세계에서 가장 맛있는 집이다(우리 엄마가 만든 것보다 맛있다. 엄마한텐 비밀). 비빔밥도 아주 맛있는데, 이 집에서는 '골동반'이라는 다른 이름으로 메뉴에 올라 있다. 두 사람이 가서 골동반과 육개장을 하나씩 시켜서 나눠 먹으면 딱 좋다. 평양냉면도 매우 훌륭하니, 위의 두 냉면집에 갈 시간이 없는 사람은 여기서 맛보아도 된다. 채식주의자가 먹을 수 있는 황태구이, 탕평채, 낙지볶음과 소면 같은 메뉴도 있다. 서울에만 다섯 개의 매장이 있다.

• 벽제갈비(Byeokje Galbi): 한국 최고의 갈비 레스토랑이라고 할 수 있다. 하지만 가격도 놀라울 만큼 비싸다. 1986년에 개업한 이후, 언제나 '(가장 비싸더라도) 가장 훌륭한 갈비'를 지향해왔다. 고기의 품질은 당연히 최상급이고, 고기를 구워주는 직원의 기술도 최고. 여러 종류의 반찬들도 매우 맛있다. 여러 부위의 소고기를 파는데, 대표 메뉴이자 가장 비싼 메뉴인 한

우설화생갈비를 주문해서 먹자(경고. 1인분에 백 달러 이상). 여러 명이 방문했다면, 양념갈비와 육회까지 맛보면 더욱 좋다. 고기를 다 먹은 다음에는 평양냉면을 작은 사이즈로 주문해서 맛보면 된다. 냉면 역시 최고 수준이라서, 이 집을 방문할 거면 굳이 앞에서 언급한 다른 냉면집을 방문할 필요가 없다. 서울에 네 곳이 있지만, 2호선 신촌역과 연세대학교 사이에 있는 것이 처음 생긴 곳이다. 이 회사에서 운영하는 다른 브랜드 '봉피양'도 추천할 만하다. 벽제갈비 못지않은 훌륭한 고기를 훨씬 저렴한 가격에 판매하는데, 사실 봉피양에서 가장 추천하는 음식은 돼지갈비. 봉피양은 서울에만 열 개 이상의 지점이 있다.

• 버드나무집(Budnamujip): 혹시 외국에 있는 한국 식당에서 달착지근한 양념갈비를 맛있게 먹은 기억이 있다면, 이 집을 강력히 추천한다. 다른 메뉴들도 많지만, 그건 이 가게에 자주 가는 한국인들을 위한 것들이고, 관광객인 당신은 무조건 양념갈비를 주문해야 한다. 고기를 먹은 후에는 된장찌개 하나와 누룽지 둘을 주문하면 좋다. 누룽지는 밥을 지을 때 밥솥 바닥에 눌어붙은 밥을 말하는데, 한국인들은 스낵으로 그냥 먹기도 하고, 물을 부어 끓여서 밥 대신 먹기도 한다. 두 개의 매장이 있다. 1977년 개업.

• 하동관(Hadongkwan): 1939년부터 지금까지 사실상 같은

음식만 팔고 있는 곰탕 전문점이다. 당연히 곰탕을 먹으면 되는데, 보통과 특 중에서 '특'을 추천한다. 보통은 평범한 고기만 들어 있고, 특에는 거기에 더해 양이 추가되어 있다. 국물 맛은 똑같다. 주문할 때 돈을 내는 시스템이고, 자리에 앉으면 '늦어도' 3분 안에 음식이 나온다. 보통의 한국인들은 다 먹는 데 10~15분 정도 쓴다. 음식을 받자마자 테이블 위에 비치되어 있는 파를 적당히(이게 얼마큼인지 모르겠으면 옆 테이블을 훔쳐보라) 넣은 다음, 김치를 곁들여 먹으면 된다. 총 네 곳의 가게가 있는데, 코엑스몰에 있는 것을 제외하면, 아침 7시에 문을 여는 대신 오후 4시 반이면 문을 닫는다. 숙소 근처에 하동관이 있다면, 술 마신 다음날 아침 식사로 안성맞춤이다.

• 고려삼계탕(Koryeo Samgyetang): 삼계탕에 관심이 있다면, 이 식당이 일순위다. 서울에는 삼계탕을 파는 식당이 무척 많고, 그중에는 여기보다 더 유명한 집들도 있다. 하지만 이 식당에서 파는 삼계탕이 가장 전통적인 편이다(너무 많은 재료를 추가하여 맛이 복잡한 식당도 많은데, 이 식당의 삼계탕은 클래식하다). 1960년에 문을 열었고, 지금도 서울 도심에 딱 두 개의 식당만 운영한다. 메뉴는 여러 가지가 있는데, 굳이 고민하지 말고 메뉴판의 맨 위에 있는, 아무런 수식어가 붙지 않은 삼계탕을 주문하면 된다. Goryeo, Koryo 등으로도 표기된다.

• 봉추찜닭(Bongchu Jjimdak): 앞에서 '치킨' 이야기를 아주 많

564

이 했다. 교촌, BBQ, BHC 등의 가게를 찾아가면 된다는 조언도 이미 했다. 그런데 놀랍게도, 그렇게 많은 치킨집이 있음에도 불구하고, 한국에는 프라이드치킨과는 전혀 다른 종류의 또 다른 닭요리도 매우 인기가 있다. 그것은 간장을 베이스로 한 소스로 요리한 찜닭이다. 그중에서도 가장 성공적인 프랜차이즈 회사가 봉추찜닭이다. 2000년에 창업한 이 회사는 현재 전국에 150개 이상, 서울에만 50개 이상의 지점이 있다. 메뉴는 뼈가 포함된 것과 뼈 없이 살코기만 있는 것 두 종류인데, 첫번째 메뉴를 고르면 된다. 매운맛, 보통, 안 매운맛 중에서 선택이 가능한데, 당신은 '안 매운 맛'을 고르는 게 좋겠다. 크기는 대, 중, 소에서 고르면 되는데, 소는 2~3인용, 중은 3~4인용, 대는 4~5인용이다. 토핑을 추가할 수 있지만 굳이 하지 않아도 되고, 닭을 거의 다 먹은 다음에는 '누룽지'를 주문하여 마무리하면 좋다. 여기서의 누룽지는 그냥 누룽지가 아니라 누룽지를 사용한 볶음밥이다.

• 나리의 집(Narieui Jip or Nari Sikdang): 당신이 한국에서 단 한끼만 먹을 수 있다면 삼겹살을 먹어야 한다고 했다. 사실 삼겹살 맛집은 전국에 수백 곳이 있고, 식당마다 조금씩 특색이 있어서 '손님이 많은' 곳이면 어디를 가든 즐거운 식사가 가능하다. 이 식당은 생삼겹살이 아니라 냉동 삼겹살을 파는 식당 중에서는 가장 인기 있는 집이다. 피크 시간에는 한 시간쯤 기다려야 할 수도 있다. 삼겹살과 함께 주문해야 하는 대표 메뉴

는 청국장과 밥이다. 청국장은 된장의 일종으로, 오랜 숙성 기간을 필요로 하는 보통의 된장과 달리 2, 3일 동안만 숙성시켜서 만든다. 맛이나 향은 보통의 된장보다 오히려 강한 편이다. 한남동에 있는 본점은 나리의 집, 청담동과 잠실에 있는 두 개의 분점은 나리식당으로 이름이 다르지만, 음식은 거의 똑같다. 1986년에 개업했다. 근처에서 쉽게 찾을 수 있고 믿을 만한 삼겹살집으로는 전국에 백 개 이상의 매장이 있는 하남돼지집이 있다.

• 연타발(Yeontabal): 이 책에서 아직 한 번도 언급되지 않은 음식 중에 '곱창'이라는 게 있다. 동물의 창자를 포괄하는 말인데, 한국에서는 특히 소의 창자가 인기 있다. 부위에 따라 곱창도 여러 종류가 있는데, 그중에서도 가장 귀한 것은 '양'과 '대창'이다(두 가지 부위는 거의 늘 같이 판매되기 때문에 한국인들은 '양대창'이라고 붙여 말한다). 한 번도 소의 창자를 먹어보지 않은 사람은 약간의 거부감이 생길 수도 있겠지만, 양대창 숯불구이야말로 별미 중의 별미다(망설이다가 나를 믿고 맛을 본 모든 외국인들은 엄지를 치켜세웠다). 양대창을 주로 판매하는 식당도 꽤 많은데, 그중에서도 연타발이 최고다. 서울에 다섯 개의 매장이 있다. 두 사람이 가면 양 2인분과 대창 2인분을 (소주와 함께) 주문하면 적당하다. 너무 많아 보이겠지만, 한 사람이 1.5인분 정도 먹는 게 흔한 갈비나 삼겹살과 달리, 양대창은 한 사람이 2인분을 먹는 경우가 많다. 고기를 다 먹고도 배가

남으면 '양밥'이라는 이름의 볶음밥을 추가할 수 있다. 2000년에 개업했다.

• 진주회관(Jinju Hoegwan): 어느 한국 음식이든, 그 음식을 판매하는 음식점 중에서 최고가 어디인지에 대해서는 논쟁이 있을 수 있다. 하지만 콩국수에 관해서만은 그렇지 않다. 진주회관은 자타가 공인하는 콩국수 최고 맛집이다. 삼성을 세계적 기업으로 키운 고 이건희 회장과 이명박 전 대통령을 비롯한 수많은 유명인사가 이 집의 단골로 알려져 있다. 콩국수는 정말 많은 식당에서 판매하는 (적어도 한국인들에게는) 평범한 음식이지만, 진주회관의 콩국수는 아주 특별하다. 뭔가 특별한 노하우가 있음이 분명하다. 당신이 냉면을 비롯한 몇몇 한국 음식들을 이미 맛보았다면, 그리고 당신의 여행 시기가 여름이라면, 1962년에 개업한 이 식당을 한 번쯤 방문해볼 만하다. 콩국수 중에서는 아마도 한국에서 가장 비쌀 텐데, 그래봐야 10달러 정도다. 오피스가 즐비한 도심 한가운데 있어서, 평일 점심시간에는 상당히 붐빈다.

• 황생가칼국수(Hwangsaengga Kalguksu): 칼국수로 유명한 식당은 많지만, 가장 추천하고 싶은 곳은 여기다. 칼국수도 물론 상당히 맛있지만, 함께 판매하는 '전(Jeon)'도 정말 훌륭하기 때문이다. 역시 앞에서 한 번도 등장하지 않은 음식인데, 전은 여러 재료에 밀가루와 달걀물을 입힌 다음 기름을 두른 팬

에 구운 음식을 통칭하는 말이다. 고기, 생선, 채소 등 매우 다양한 재료로 만들 수 있어 종류가 아주 많다. 이 식당은 만두도 상당히 맛있다. 그럼 주문은 어떻게 할 것인가. 칼국수 하나, 만두 한 접시(큰 만두가 일곱 개 나온다), 그리고 모듬전 작은 사이즈를 주문하면 두 사람이 배불리 먹을 수 있다(이렇게 시키면 40달러 정도다). 모듬전은 'Assorted Pan-fried Delicacies'라고 메뉴에 적혀 있다. 중요한 것은, 칼국수는 '하나를 둘로 나눠달라'고 말해야 한다는 것이다. 이걸 한국어로 하기는 쉽지 않을 테고, 아마도 주문받는 분은 영어에 능통하지 않을 것이다. 손과 손가락으로 최선을 다해 표현해보시라. 이렇게 주문하는 사람이 워낙 많아서, 아마도 뜻이 통할 것이다. 몇 개의 지점이 있지만, 경복궁 근처에 있는 본점이 가장 맛있고, 손님도 가장 많다. 2001년 개업.

• 삼청동수제비(Samcheongdong Sujebi): 전국에서 가장 유명한 수제비 맛집이다. 수제비를 파는 수많은 가게 중에서 이 집만큼 웨이팅이 긴 집은 없다. 평일에도 피크 시간에는 30분 정도, 주말에는 그 이상 기다려야 한다. 예약도 불가능하고, 한국의 여러 맛집에서 사용하는 번호표 같은 것도 없다. 그냥 줄을 서서 차례로 입장한다. 하지만 워낙 금방 먹고 나오는 집이라, 줄의 길이에 비해 대기 시간이 극단적으로 길지는 않다. 둘이 가면 수제비 2인분과 감자전 하나를 시키면 적당하다. 2인분이든 3인분이든 한꺼번에 작은 항아리에 담겨서 나오니, 앞에

놓인 그릇에 덜어 먹으면 된다. 테이블 위에 있는 두 가지 김치를 곁들여 먹는데, 매운 고추가 들어간 양념장을 조금 첨가해서 먹어도 된다. 그런데 수제비는 숟가락으로 먹기도 약간 불편하고 젓가락으로 먹기도 약간 불편한 음식이다. 두 가지 도구를 번갈아 혹은 한꺼번에 활용해볼 것.

• 원조1호장충동할머니집(Wonjo Ilho Jangchungdong Halmeoni Jip): 이렇게 긴 이름을 어떻게 외우느냐고? 그럴 필요 없다. 지하철 3호선 동대입구역 3번 출구로 나가면 유명한 '족발' 음식점이 여러 개 있고, 대부분은 맛이 비슷하다(사실은 미세하게 달라서, 한국인들은 각자 가장 좋아하는 가게가 따로 있다. 저 긴 이름의 식당은 내가 가장 좋아하는 집일 뿐이다). 그런데 족발이란 무엇인가? 여러 가지 소스를 섞은 물에 돼지의 다리를 푹 삶은 음식이다. 말하자면 한국식 슈바인스학세(Schweinshaxe)라고 할 수 있다(맛과 식감은 전혀 다르다). 슈바인스학세와 달리 먹기 좋게 썰어서 나오며, 사우어크라우트(Sauerkraut) 대신 일종의 김치 및 채소들과 함께 먹는다(맥주가 아니라 소주와 잘 어울린다는 점도 다르다). 족발은 한국인이 사랑하는 음식들 중의 하나이며, 유명한 식당도 정말 많다. 반드시 장충동에 가야 하는 것은 아니고, 당신의 숙소 주변에도 제법 괜찮은 족발 전문점은 많이 있다. 대체로 대, 중, 소 세 가지인 사이즈만 고르면 되는데, 두 사람이면 가장 작은 걸 고르면 된다. 어떤 가게는 여러 종류의 족발을 팔고, 그중에는 아주 매

운 것도 있다. 당신은 무조건 메뉴판의 맨 위에 있는 것을 고르면 된다. 여러 족발집에서는 '보쌈'이라는 음식도 판매하는데, 보쌈은 삶은 돼지고기를 김치 및 다양한 채소들과 함께 먹는 것이다. 족발과 보쌈은 식사나 안주로도 많이 소비되지만, 치킨과 더불어 한국인이 무척 사랑하는 야식 중의 하나다.

• 할머니 현대 낙지아구감자탕(Halmeoni Hyundai Nakji Agu Gamjatang): 역시 황당하게 긴 이름의 식당인데, 한국인들도 정확한 이름을 잘 못 외운다. '할머니'는 Grandmother라는 뜻이며, '현대'는 당신이 아는 자동차 회사의 이름인 동시에 식당 근처에 있는 아파트 이름이기도 하다. '낙지'는 small octopus의 한국어인데, 이 가게에서는 영화 〈올드보이〉에 나오는 것과 같은 낙지가 아니라 낙지볶음을 판매한다. 매운 음식을 전혀 못 먹는 사람은 도전하지 말 것. 상당히 좋은 낙지를 사용하기 때문에 가격도 꽤 비싸다. 아구찜도 팔고 감자탕도 판매하는 이 식당의 모든 음식은 소주와 잘 어울린다. 이 식당은 구글에서 영어로는 잘 검색되지 않는데, 지하철 3호선 압구정역 5번 출구에서 걸어갈 수 있는 거리에 있으며, 신구초등학교 바로 옆에 있다.

• 화해당(Hwa Hae Dang): 간장게장이 정말 맛있는 식당이다. 간장게장 역시 이 책에서 처음 등장하는 음식인데, 여러 가지 향신료를 넣고 끓인 간장에 신선한 게를 적당한 시간 동안 두

어 숙성시킨 다음 먹는 것이다. 그냥 먹으면 당연히 짜기 때문에 밥과 함께 먹는다. 외국인에게는 맛이나 모양이나 먹는 방법이 모두 낯설겠지만, 한국인이 엄청나게 좋아하는 고급 음식이다. 간장게장의 별명은 밥도둑이다. 하도 맛있어서 밥이 빨리, 그것도 많이 없어지기 때문이다. 서울 여의도에 있는 식당은 분점이고, 본점은 서울에서 150킬로미터쯤 떨어진 바닷가에 있다. 다른 간장게장 맛집으로는 신사동의 프로간장게장이 있다.

• 정식당(Jungsik): 한국의 대표적인 파인 다이닝 레스토랑 중의 하나다. 한식에 흔히 쓰이는 재료들을 활용하지만, 한국인들에게도 새롭게 느껴지는 창의적인 음식을 낸다.『미슐랭가이드』에서 두 개의 별을 받았고, 뉴욕에도 같은 이름의 식당을 냈을 만큼 성공한 레스토랑이다. 반드시 한 달 전에 예약을 해야 한다. 식당 홈페이지에 영어로 자세히 설명되어 있다. 디너는 주류 제외 2백 달러 수준이고, 런치도 백 달러를 훌쩍 넘는다. 채식주의자 메뉴도 있는데, 가격은 똑같다.

• 온지음(Onjieum): 정식당이 한식을 새롭게 재해석한 창의적인 음식으로 유명하다면, 온지음은 훨씬 전통적인 한식을 낸다. 과거 왕실에서나 먹던 음식부터 현대의 한국인들이 자주 먹는 음식까지 모두 맛볼 수 있다. 전자는 원형에 가깝게 재현했고, 후자는 좋은 재료와 세련된 플레이팅으로 (한국인들이)

'아는 맛' 중에서 최고를 지향한다. 외국인인 당신도 한국이 음식 문화가 얼마나 발달한 나라인지 실감할 수 있을 것이다. 경복궁 바로 옆에 위치해 있으며, 반드시 예약을 해야 한다. 디너는 2백 달러가 조금 안 되고, 런치는 백 달러 정도다. 와인 페어링 대신 한국의 전통주 페어링이 가능하다. 『미슐랭가이드』에서 한 개의 별을 받았다.

• 에빗(Evett): 이 목록에 있는 식당 중에서 유일하게 한국인이 아닌 오너 셰프가 운영하는 식당이다. 음식도 사실 '한국 음식'이라고 부를 수는 없는 것을 낸다. 하지만 여기 포함시킨 것은 호주 출신의 조셉 리저우드(Joseph Lidgerwood)가 한국의 식재료와 음식 문화에서 영감을 받아서 창의적으로 재해석한 음식을 제공하고 있기 때문이다. 디너는 주류 제외 2백 달러 수준이고, 런치도 백 달러를 훌쩍 넘는다. 일반적인 와인 페어링 외에 한국 술 페어링도 가능하며, 한국의 식재료를 활용하여 셰프가 배합한 음료들을 제공하는 논알콜 페어링도 독특한 매력이 있다. 2019년에 개업했으며, 에빗은 셰프의 미들네임이다. 『미슐랭가이드』에서 한 개의 별을 받았는데, 내가 심사위원이면 두 개를 주고 싶은 곳이다.

• 마방집(Mabangjip): 이 목록에 있는 식당 중에서 유일하게 서울 바깥에 있는 식당이다. 지하철 5호선 하남시청역에서 1.5킬로미터 떨어져 있고, 서울의 동남쪽 지역에서는 택시를

타고 30분 정도면 갈 수 있다. 이 식당은 1920년경에 개업한 것으로 전해지는, 한국에서 손꼽히게 오래된 식당 중의 하나다. 15달러가 채 안 되는 세트 메뉴를 시키면 스무 가지가 넘는 반찬과 밥, 그리고 된장찌개가 나온다. 대부분의 반찬은 나물이라 부르는 채소들이다. 채식주의자라면 이것만 먹으면 되지만, 대부분의 손님들은 소불고기 혹은 돼지불고기를 추가한다. 두 사람이라면 둘 중 하나를, 네 사람이라면 둘 다 추가하면 된다. 이 집의 불고기는 수분이 매우 적은 스타일이다. 소불고기는 15달러 정도, 돼지불고기는 10달러 정도. 전통 한옥 구조로 되어 있는데, 여러 개의 방 중 하나로 처음 안내받으면 조금 당황할 수 있다. 방에 아무것도 없기 때문이다. 주문을 하고 나서 바닥에 어색하게(불편하게?) 앉아 있으면, 잠시 후에 직원들이 커다란 상을 들고 들어온다. 상 위에는 스무 가지 넘는 반찬이 놓여 있다. 안타까운 것은, 백년의 역사를 가진 이 식당이 도시 재개발로 2024년에 다른 곳으로 이전할 예정이라는 사실이다. 당신이 그전에 여기를 가볼 수 있으면 좋겠다.

19.

Curated Collection of Seoul's Yummiest Restaurants

With all the mouthwatering Korean food buzzing in this book, you'll undoubtedly want to indulge in a few culinary pleasures. However, the real challenge lies not only in deciding what to eat but also in choosing the perfect place to savor it. It's only natural to crave the same dish but in a more upscale or renowned setting. While we have these 'international' restaurant lists circulating, such as the esteemed Michelin Guide to Seoul. But, let's be honest, the individuals curating those lists are often foreigners rather than authentic Koreans. (They may include a few local judges, but that's a well-kept secret.) So, where in Seoul can you discover those authentic eateries that truly make Koreans' taste buds dance with joy?

Travelers often have their limits when it comes to indulging in the delectable offerings of Korea. Now, if you're willing to loosen your belt and relish four meals a day (or even five if you're feeling audacious), kudos to you! Forget about dieting. However, let's be realistic here: attempting to devour seventeen meals in a single day is a feat achieved only in dreams (or perhaps nightmares). So, my fellow gastronomical adventurer, it's essential to make strategic choices. It's all about selecting wisely.

I must confess, there are plenty of lackluster restaurants scattered across Korea. You know, the kind that leaves you scratching your head, questioning how they manage to stay in business. (Trust me, they might just shut down sooner or later.) Even if you make impeccable food choices, one wrong turn into a subpar eatery can shatter your dreams of a memorable meal. Fear not, for I present to you my personal top 20 recommendations—an entirely subjective list devoid of any reference to others' opinions. (But if you happen to dine at one of these establishments and walk away disappointed, well, that's on them, not on me, my friends.)

These are my selection criteria, folks. Firstly, I only included places that I've personally ventured into. Having resided in Seoul for quite a while, I've had the pleasure of exploring countless eateries. However, trying every single one of them is an impossible feat. There are a plethora of famous establishments out there, but due to a variety of reasons, I haven't had the chance to grace their premises. Hence, I excluded many well-known restaurants with high reputation simply because I have never been there. To the owners of those excluded eateries, please accept my sincerest apologies.

Secondly, I made sure to exclude restaurants with extremely long wait times or incredibly challenging reservation processes. When I say "extremely long wait," I mean enduring an hour-long wait and still not securing a table. And when I mention "incredibly challenging reservation," I'm referring to the frustration of calling a month in advance only to be met with a resounding "fully booked." Koreans have such a profound love for their cuisine that some establishments, which don't accept reservations and require you to stand in line, witness eager food enthusiasts queuing up hours before they even open their doors. (I know you're curious about their locations, but it's best to resist the temptation. Trust me, sacrificing precious hours of your limited travel time is not worth it.) If you happen to call a restaurant and they offer you a reservation two or three months down the line, it's best to throw in the towel. (Even Koreans themselves often utter a disgruntled "Humph!" and give up.)

Thirdly, I made a deliberate choice to exclude exorbitantly expensive establishments. When I say "exorbitantly expensive," I'm referring to places where you can expect to spend $300 or more per person, excluding alcoholic beverages. The majority of the restaurants on this list fall within the range of $15 to $50 per person. (Of course, there are a few exceptions, but they don't exceed $200.) Furthermore, I've decided to omit restaurants located within luxury hotels. While the food in these establishments may be exceptional, the prices are simply too steep considering the overall value they offer.

Fourthly, I intentionally focused on selecting restaurants that specialize in Korean cuisine. While Seoul offers a diverse array of international dining options, including outstanding Japanese, Chinese, Italian, French, Spanish, and more, I deemed it unnecessary to include them all in this list. However, I did include a few noteworthy "contemporary" restaurants that offer innovative and modern interpretations of Korean cuisine, combining traditional flavors with their unique creative flair.

Fifthly, I chose to exclude dishes that are favored by a relatively niche group of Koreans. These particular foods often have a distinct and robust flavor profile, which may pose a challenge for foreigners who are not accustomed to such tastes. While they hold significance within Korean culinary culture, I wanted to focus on more widely accessible dishes that offer a friendly introduction to Korean cuisine for visitors from various backgrounds.

With these principles firmly in place, I have painstakingly curated a list of twenty restaurants in Seoul (with one exception located just outside of Seoul) that I wholeheartedly recommend to foreign visitors. It's worth noting that, since some restaurants have multiple branches, even nationwide, the practical number exceeds twenty. I must confess, I've kept a few surprises up my sleeve, introducing you to some lesser-known (to foreigners, not to Koreans) culinary pleasures that haven't been mentioned in this book until now. The realm of Korean cuisine is incredibly diverse, and I've conducted thorough research to carefully select a variety of restaurants that I urge you to explore. I encourage you to try at least one restaurant from this list, and if you're feeling particularly adventurous, indulge in two or more. Please note that for those requiring reservations, I've indicated as such, but it's always prudent to double-check for any potential closures or changes in operating hours.

Additionally, I've provided descriptions of the quintessential dishes you should consider ordering at each restaurant, keeping in mind an average appetite of TWO adult men. (What a kind-hearted guy am I!) My suggestion? Embrace the rapture of culinary diversity by ordering a generous assortment of dishes and sharing them among your travel companions. Even if sharing meals isn't your usual practice, let this trip be the catalyst for breaking free from routine and savoring the joy of communal dining.

And here's a little insider tip for you: if you happen to dine at one of the restaurants mentioned in the list below, don't forget to proudly present this book to the staff. Will it earn you any immediate special perks? Well, not exactly. However, let me share a little secret with you. The next time I visit that same restaurant and mention that I'm the author of this very book that many foreigners have been carrying around, who knows? Something wonderful might just come my way.

- Pildong Myeonok: Let's kick off with my personal favorite eatery. Brace yourself for a rendezvous with one of the most renowned Pyeongyang Naengmyeon joints in town, and trust me, the longing for this place consumed me during my two-year sojourn abroad. The distinctive feature of these noodles is their unexpectedly mild flavor compared to other Pyeongyang Naengmyeon joints. Here's the game plan: order yourself a bowl of Pyeongyang Naengmyeon, complemented by a serving of Bibim Naengmyeon and a plate of delectable dumplings. Now, let me share a little secret not listed on the menu—a must-try specialty known as "banban" (half & half). Brace yourself for a tantalizing combination of "suyuk" (boiled beef slice) and "jeyuk" (boiled pork slice), perfectly harmonized for your pleasure. If you're not feeling too hungry, you can skip the Bibim Naengmyeon. Now, prepare your taste buds for a dip into an enigmatic sauce adorned with tantalizing chunks. The dipping sauce may not win any beauty contests, but trust me when I say it's an explosion of flavor. Take pleasure in dunking both the dumplings and the meat into this magical elixir. Keep in mind, my friends, that peak hours may bring about a wait, but fear not, as the high turnover rate ensures the wait is relatively short compared to the length of the line. This gem has been serving yummy dishes since its inception in 1985.

• Woo Lae Oak: Undoubtedly one of the most famous Pyeongyang Naengmyeon restaurants in Korea. The broth here has a thicker consistency compared to Pildong Myeonok. Translating to "house of revisiting," the restaurant's name holds a special meaning, suggesting that dining here may increase the possibility (and desire) to revisit Korea. Since their Seoul-style bulgogi is also exceptional, I highly recommend ordering two servings of bulgogi and two bowls of Pyeongyang Naengmyeon, or one bowl of Pyeongyang paired with one bowl of Bibim Naengmyeon. It's worth noting their unique payment system: post-payment if you order with meat, but prepayment if you opt for noodles alone. So keep that in mind when placing your order. Be prepared for weekend crowds as this place tends to get quite busy. Woo Lae Oak has been satisfying diners since its establishment in 1946.

• Hanilkwan: This historic restaurant holds an indispensable place in Seoul's culinary landscape since its establishment in 1939. Hanilkwan offers a diverse array of dishes. In my humble opinion, their Yukgaejang (spicy beef soup) surpasses all others in the world, even surpassing my mom's version (don't tell her!). Another highlight is their Bibimbap, which goes by the name "Goldongban" on the menu. It's highly recommended for two people to share a Goldongban and a bowl of Yukgaejang, creating a harmonious dining experience. If you're unable to visit the aforementioned two restaurants, Hanilkwan also serves excellent Pyeongyang Naengmyeon. Vegetarian options are available as well, including Pan-fried Dried Pollack, Mung Bean Jelly with Mixed Vegetables, and Spicy Stir-fried Baby Octopus with Noodles. With five locations in Seoul alone, Hanilkwan is easily accessible for a memorable dining experience.

• Byeokje Galbi: Known as one of the finest establishments for "galbi" in Korea, this restaurant lives up to its reputation. However, it's worth noting that dining here comes with a surprisingly high price tag. Since its inception in 1986, Byeokje Galbi has consistently aimed to offer the best (albeit priciest) galbi experience. The quality of the meat is unparalleled, the grilling staff's expertise is remarkable, and the selection of side dishes is equally exceptional. While they offer various cuts of beef, I highly recommend their signature and most extravagant dish, the Seng Galbi (fair warning: it comes with a price tag of over $100 per person). If you're dining with a group, consider trying the Yangnyum Galbi (marinated galbi) and the yukhoe (seasoned raw beef). Once you've relished the meaty bliss, you can savor a small bowl of Pyeongyang Naengmyeon, which is equally exceptional. With the excellence of their noodles, there's no need to visit any other noodle shops mentioned earlier if you choose to dine here. Byeokje Galbi has four locations in Seoul, with the first one conveniently situated between Sinchon Station on Line 2 and Yonsei University. Additionally, their sister brand, Bongpiyang, is also worth exploring. While offering meat of (almost) equal quality to Byeokje Galbi, Bongpiyang comes at a fraction of the price. My personal favorite dish at Bongpiyang is their pork ribs. With over a dozen branches in Seoul alone, you'll have no trouble finding a Bongpiyang near you.

• Budnamujip: If you've ever had the pleasure of enjoying the delectable sweetness and savoriness of marinated ribs at a Korean restaurant abroad, then Budnamujip is a must-visit. While there are plenty of options available tailored to the tastes of the local patrons, for tourists, I highly recommend indulging in their Seasoned Beef Ribs. Once you've relished in the meaty goodness, make sure to order one serving of doenjang-jjigae and one or two servings of "nurungji" (scorched rice). Nurungji is the delightful crispy rice that forms at the bottom of the rice cooker, and Koreans enjoy it as a snack or as a rice substitute by adding water and boiling it. Budnamujip features two locations, both of which have been serving satisfied customers since their opening in 1977.

• Hadongkwan: This esteemed establishment specializes in gomtang, a classic beef soup that has remained virtually unchanged since 1939. When visiting, indulging in their delectable beef soup is a must, and if you have to choose between the regular and original, we highly recommend the original. While the regular version features plain meat, the original adds an extra layer of rumen, enhancing the overall flavor. The broth itself remains consistent across both options. Payment is made at the time of ordering, and once seated, your food will arrive in no later than 3 minutes. It's interesting to note that the average Korean diner typically takes around 10-15 minutes to complete their meal at this restaurant. Once your food arrives, feel free to add an "appropriate" amount of scallions to your dish, conveniently provided on the table. If you're unsure about the quantity, a quick glance at neighboring tables can serve as a helpful reference. Don't forget to savor your meal alongside the well-matching accompaniment of kimchi. Hadongkwan has four locations, with the exception of the COEX Mall branch, which operates from 7 am to 4:30 pm. If there's a branch of Hadongkwan near your accommodation, it's perfect for breakfast the next day after a night of drinking.

• Koryeo Samgyetang: If you have a craving for samgyetang, look no further than this establishment. While there are countless samgyetang restaurants in Seoul, some more famous than this one, Koryeo Samgyetang stands out as the epitome of authenticity. Unlike many establishments that tend to overcomplicate the flavor with excessive ingredients, Koryeo Samgyetang stays true to the classic recipe. Since its inception in 1960, it has remained committed to its roots and continues to operate with only two restaurants in the heart of Seoul. The menu offers several options, but don't feel overwhelmed. Simply order the

Samgyetang listed at the top, without any additional labels. Keep in mind that the name may also be spelled as Goryeo or Koryo, among other variations.

• Bongchu Jjimdak: We've delved into the world of chicken quite extensively, discussing places like Kyochon, BBQ, and BHC. However, Korea has another immensely popular chicken dish that stands apart from the realm of fried chicken. Enter Bongchu Jjimdak, a franchise that has garnered significant success with its soy-based braised chicken. Established in 2000, the company operates over 150 branches nationwide, with more than 50 located in Seoul alone. The menu offers two types of chicken: bone-in and boneless, and we recommend opting for the former. You can choose from three spice levels: spicy, normal, and non-spicy, but it's advisable to go for the non-spicy option. Sizing options include large, medium, and small, with the small portion serving 2-3 people, the medium portion serving 3-4 people, and the large portion serving 4-5 people. While there are additional toppings available, they are entirely optional. Once you've relished the flavors of the chicken, consider ordering the "nurungji" to round off your meal. At Bongchu Jjimdak, their version of nurungji is not just scorched rice but an appetizing fried rice made with nurungji.

- Narieui Jip or Nari Sikdang: As I mentioned before, if you could only have one meal in Korea, it should be samgyeopsal. It's important to note that there are countless samgyeopsal restaurants across the country. The number of renowned "matzip" establishments is well over a few hundred, and each venue offers its own satisfying experience. In fact, you can always enjoy a satisfying meal wherever you find a lively crowd of customers. This particular restaurant holds a prominent reputation as one of the most favored establishments specializing in frozen pork belly rather than fresh. Be prepared for potential wait times during peak hours, which can stretch up to an hour. The must-try accompaniment to your pork belly is "cheonggukjang" served with rice. Unlike conventional doenjang that requires a lengthy aging process, cheonggukjang is aged for just two to three days, resulting in a bolder flavor and aroma. The original location in Hannam-dong is known as Narieui Jip, while the branches in Cheongdam-dong and Jamsil go by the name Nari Sikdang. Although the names may differ, the culinary offerings at these branches remain nearly identical. Narieui Jip opened its doors in 1986, standing as a testament to its enduring popularity. For a convenient and dependable pork belly experience in your neighborhood, you can also consider Hanam Doejijip, maintaining over 100 branches nationwide.

• Yeontabal: One food that hasn't been mentioned in this book yet is "gopchang". Gopchang is a broad term for animal intestines, and cow intestines are particularly well-loved in Korea. There are several types of gopchang, depending on the specific part of the animal, with the most prized cuts being "yang" (cow stomach, rumen) and "daechang" (cow tripe). These two cuts are commonly sold together, referred to as "yangdaechang" in Korean. If you've never tried cow intestines before, you might initially hesitate, but trust me when I say that charcoal-grilled yangdaechang is an exquisite delicacy. Every foreigner who hesitated, then took a leap of faith and tried it, ended up giving it a thumbs-up. While there are a lot of restaurants specializing in yangdaechang, Yeontabal stands out as the best. They have five locations in Seoul alone. If you're dining with a companion, I recommend ordering two servings of yang and two servings of daechang, accompanied by some soju. It may seem like a substantial amount, but unlike beef ribs or pork belly, where one person commonly consumes about 1.5 servings, in the case of yang or daechang, two servings per one person is standard. And if you still have room for more after indulging in the meat, you can add a side of "yangbap", a delicious fried rice dish. Yeontabal has been serving customers since 2000, offering an exceptional dining experience.

• Jinju Hoegwan: When it comes to Korean cuisine, there can often be debates about which restaurant serves the best dishes. However, when it comes to kongguksu (soy milk noodle soup), there is no contest. Jinju Hoegwan is widely recognized as the ultimate destination for enjoying this delicacy. It has even gained popularity among notable figures, including the late Samsung Chairman Lee Kun-hee and former President Lee Myung-bak. While soy milk noodle soup is a common dish found in many Korean restaurants, Jinju Hoegwan's version is truly exceptional. Their expertise and unique approach are evident in every bowl they serve. If you have already experienced various Korean dishes and are visiting during the summer, I highly recommend visiting this restaurant, which first opened its doors in 1962. It's worth noting that Jinju Hoegwan's soy milk noodle soup is considered one of the pricier kongguksu in Korea, but it costs only around $10 per bowl. Located in the heart of the city center, amidst numerous office buildings, it tends to get quite crowded during weekday lunch hours.

• Hwangsaengga Kalguksu: Here is my top recommendation among the many renowned kalguksu noodle soup restaurants. While their kalguksu are undeniably delicious, it's the "jeon" that truly steals the show. Jeon refers to a variety of ingredients coated in flour and egg wash, then pan-fried in oil. It can be made with diverse food materials such as meat, fish, and vegetables. The dumplings at this restaurant are also exceptionally tasty. Now, let me guide you on how to place your order. I suggest ordering a bowl of noodles, a plate of mandu (seven large dumplings), and a small plate of modum-jeon, which is a multifarious assortment of pan-fried delicacies. This order will satisfy two people and cost you approximately $40. It's important to note that when ordering kalguksu, you should request "one kalguksu, split into two bowls."

When the staff is not fluent in English, expressing this phrase in Korean might be a bit challenging. Try your best to convey the message using hand gestures and finger count. Since many people order in this manner, it's likely to be understood. Hwangsaengga Kalguksu has several branches, but the main branch near Gyeongbokgung Palace is the most acclaimed and crowded. It first opened its doors in 2001.

• Samcheongdong Sujebi: This is the most famous sujebi restaurant in the country, known for its long waiting times. Among the scores of sujebi restaurants, none compare to the length of the queue here. Even on weekdays, expect to wait around 30 minutes during peak hours, and even longer on weekends. Reservations are not accepted, and the restaurant does not use numbered tickets either. Instead, you join the line and enter the restaurant in order. However, the wait time is not excessively long considering the length of the line, as the food is served promptly. If you visit with a companion, I recommend ordering two servings of sujebi and one portion of "gamjajeon" (potato pancake). Regardless of whether you order two or three servings, they are served together in a small jar, allowing you to transfer them into your own bowl at the table. You can enjoy the sujebi with the two types of kimchi provided and add some spicy chili sauce for extra flavor. It's worth noting that eating sujebi can be a bit challenging with just a spoon or chopsticks. I suggest trying to alternate between both utensils or even using them simultaneously for a more enjoyable dining experience.

• Wonjo Ilho Jangchungdong Halmeoni Jip: Don't worry about memorizing such a long name. If you take Exit 3 of Dongguk Univ. Station on Subway Line 3, you'll come across several famous "jokbal" restaurants. While most of them offer similar flavors, each has its own subtle variations. (Koreans recognize the subtle differences, and have their own favorite restaurants. Wonjo Ilho Jangchungdong Halmeoni Jip is my personal favorite.) Now, what exactly is jokbal? It's pig's trotters simmered in water with a variety of sauces, often referred to as the Korean version of Schweinshaxe. (The taste and texture are completely different.) Unlike Schweinshaxe, jokbal is served in bite-sized pieces with kimchi and vegetables (instead of Sauerkraut), accompanied by soju (instead of beer). Jokbal is immensely popular in Korea, and you'll find numerous restaurants serving it. Keep in mind that you don't have to specifically visit Jangchung-dong, as there are plenty of excellent jokbal restaurants near your accommodation as well. In general, these restaurants offer jokbal in three sizes: large, medium, and small. If your party size is two, the smallest size should be sufficient. Some places may offer different types of jokbal, including spicy options. It's advisable to choose the one listed at the top of the menu. Additionally, many jokbal restaurants also serve a dish called "bossam", which consists of boiled pork served with kimchi and assorted vegetables. Jokbal and bossam are often enjoyed as meals or snacks, and alongside fried chicken, they are among Korea's favorite late-night indulgences.

• Halmuni Hyundai Nakji Agu Gamjatang: This restaurant indeed has an unusually long name, and even Koreans struggle to remember it precisely. "Halmuni" translates to "Grandmother," while "Hyundai" shares its name with a well-known car company and an apartment building located nearby. While "nakji" refers to small octopus in Korean, this restaurant specializes in Nakji Bokkeum, a spicy stir-fried small octopus dish, not the octopus featured in the movie Oldboy. If you have a low tolerance for spicy food, I advise against trying it. The dish is relatively expensive because they use high-quality small octopus. In addition to Nakji Bokkeum, they also serve Agujjim (spicy braised monkfish) and gamjatang (pork backbone stew), all of which pair excellently with soju. This restaurant is not widely listed on search engines, but it is conveniently located within walking distance of Exit 5 of Apgujeong Station on Subway Line 3, right next to Shingu Elementary School.

• Hwa Hae Dang: This restaurant is highly acclaimed for its "ganjang gejang," a dish of marinated crabs in soy sauce. Ganjang gejang is another culinary astonishment that hasn't been mentioned in this book yet. To prepare it, fresh crabs are immersed in a soy sauce mixture simmered with a variety of spices and then cooled. The crabs are left to marinate in the flavorful sauce for an appropriate duration, allowing the exquisite taste to permeate the crab meat. The dish boasts a naturally salty flavor and pairs exceptionally well with rice. While the flavor, appearance, and eating method may be unfamiliar to foreigners, ganjang gejang is a beloved luxury food among Koreans. In fact, it is often referred to as the "rice thief" because its delectable taste entices diners to devour copious amounts of rice in a twinkling. Hwa Hae Dang has a branch in Yeouido, Seoul, while the main restaurant is located approximately 150 kilometers away, near the beach. Another notable ganjang gejang restaurant is Pro Ganjang Gejang, also known as Prosoycrab, situated in Shinsa-dong.

• Jungsik: Jungsik is a prominent fine dining establishment in Korea, eminent for its innovative approach to Korean ingredients. While it incorporates common elements of Korean cuisine, it presents them in creative dishes that are novel even to local diners. The restaurant has been honored with two stars by the prestigious Michelin Guide and has achieved such success that it has opened a namesake location in New York as well. To secure a reservation at Jungsik, it's recommended to book one month in advance. For the convenience of international visitors, the restaurant's website provides a comprehensive description in English. The dinner experience at Jungsik costs around $200 per person, excluding alcoholic beverages, while lunch prices exceed $100. Additionally, Jungsik offers a dedicated vegetarian menu at the same price point as the regular menus.

• Onjieum: While Jungsik is prominent for its inventive take on Korean cuisine, Onjieum specializes in offering more authentic Korean dishes. The restaurant presents a diverse range of culinary experiences, ranging from dishes once exclusively enjoyed by the royal family to those commonly savored by modern Koreans. The former category seeks to recreate the original flavors and techniques, while the latter focuses on showcasing the best of the ordinary Korean cuisine with premium ingredients and refined presentation. Dining at Onjieum will provide you with a deep appreciation for the rich and well-established food culture of Korea. Situated in close proximity to Gyeongbokgung Palace, reservations are highly recommended to secure a table. The dinner experience at Onjieum costs just under $200, while lunch is priced around $100, excluding alcoholic beverages. Instead of a typical wine pairing, the restaurant offers an enjoyable option of a traditional Korean liquor pairing, further enhancing the authentic dining experience. Onjieum has been awarded one Michelin star.

• Evett: This is the only one on our list that features a non-Korean owner-chef. The cuisine, crafted by Australian Joseph Lidgerwood, doesn't strictly adhere to traditional Korean recipes. Instead, it is celebrated for its innovative interpretations that draw inspiration from Korean ingredients and culinary traditions. Dining here comes with a price tag of approximately $200 for dinner, excluding alcoholic beverages, with lunch offerings surpassing $100. Besides the expected wine pairings, there are options for Korean liquor pairings, and the non-alcoholic pairings are anything but ordinary, featuring chef-crafted drinks that incorporate Korean elements. Opened in 2019 and named after the chef's middle name, Evett has earned one Michelin star, though in my estimation, it merits two.

• Mabangjip: This unique restaurant stands out from the others on this list as it is located outside of Seoul. Situated approximately 1.5 kilometers from Hanam City Hall Station on Subway Line 5, or a 30-minute taxi ride from the southeastern part of Seoul, Mabangjip offers a dining experience that takes you away from the bustling city center. With its origins dating back to around 1920, it holds the distinction of being one of the oldest restaurants in Korea. For an affordable price of less than $15, you can enjoy a satisfying set menu at Mabangjip. The set menu includes a meticulous assortment of over 20 side dishes, rice, and doenjang-jjigae. The majority of the side dishes consist of flavorful and refreshing "namul", a variety of seasoned vegetables. Vegetarians will find this offering to be a satisfying meal on its own, while many guests choose to complement their dining experience by adding beef or pork bulgogi. If you are dining as a pair, you can opt for one type of bulgogi, and for a group of four, both options are available. Notably, the bulgogi here is prepared in a low-moisture style, ensuring a distinct and enjoyable taste. The beef bulgogi is priced at around $15, while the pork bulgogi is priced at around $10.

The restaurant is housed in a traditional "hanok" structure, which may initially feel disorienting as you are guided to one of the many minimalist rooms. These rooms are devoid of furnishings, creating a simple and authentic atmosphere. After settling down on the floor (which may be perceived as slightly inconvenient or clumsy for some) and placing your order, the staff will arrive with a large dining table in a few minutes. The table will be adorned with an impressive array of over twenty different side dishes, each offering an appetizing taste and texture. It is important to note that Mabangjip, with its century-old history, is scheduled to relocate in 2024 due to urban renewal. Therefore, it is highly recommended to seize the opportunity to visit and experience this distinguished restaurant before it moves to its new location.

20.

서울 밖으로 나간다면 어디를 갈까?

한국을 처음 방문하는 것이고 한국에서 머무는 날이 닷새 안 팎이라면, 모든 일정을 서울 안에서 보내도 좋다. 서울은 충분히 크고 충분히 다양해서, 일주일 혹은 그보다 좀더 길게 머물러도 갈 곳과 할일과 먹을 것이 끊이지 않을 것이다. 하지만 여정이 충분히 길다면, 혹은 이번 한국 방문이 처음이 아니라서 이미 서 울은 웬만큼 둘러보았다면, 이제는 서울 밖으로 눈을 돌려야 한 다. 그럼 어디를 가면 이 놀라운 나라의 숨은 보석들을 만날 수 있을까?

한국은 작은 나라이지만, 바티칸이나 모나코보다는 훨씬 크다. 싱가포르보다 열 배 이상 크고, 홍콩보다 열 배 가까이 크다. 덴 마크, 네덜란드, 스위스보다도 두 배 이상 크다. 아일랜드, 체코,

오스트리아, 포르투갈보다도 크다. 여행자가 단기간 내에 모두 돌아볼 수 있는 크기는 결코 아니라는 뜻이다. 하지만 고속도로 가 엄청나게 발달되어 있고, 시속 3백 킬로미터로 달리는 고속철 도도 전국 곳곳에 깔려 있어서, 당신이 마음만 먹는다면 못 갈 곳 은 없다. 당신이 무엇을 원하느냐에 따라 목적지가 달라질 뿐, 가 능성은 무궁무진하다.

가장 먼저 결정해야 하는 것은 렌터카를 빌려 직접 운전을 할 것인지 여부다. 물론 서울에서는 당신이 운전을 할 이유가 전혀 없다. 하지만 서울 밖으로 나가려 하면 운전 여부에 따라 여행 계 획은 크게 달라질 수밖에 없다. 나는 내가 방문한 거의 모든 나라 에서 렌터카로 다녔다. 심지어 주행 방향이 다른 나라에서도 그 렇게 했다. 하지만 누구나 자동차 여행을 좋아하는 것은 아니고, 낯선 나라에서 운전하는 것은 그리 만만한 일이 아니다. 특히 주 행 방향이 다른 나라에서 운전하는 것은 힘들고 위험하다(그러니 당신이 영국, 아일랜드, 호주, 뉴질랜드, 피지, 타이, 말레이시아, 인도, 인 도네시아, 일본, 싱가포르, 홍콩, 남아프리카공화국, 케냐, 나미비아, 탄 자니아 등의 국민이라면 한국에서는 운전을 하지 마라).

이유가 뭐든 운전을 하지 않기로 마음먹었다면, 가장 쉽게 갈 수 있는 장소는 KTX라고 부르는 고속철도가 정차하는 도시다. 그중에서도 관광객들에게 가장 추천할 만한 곳은 부산, 경주, 안 동, 전주, 강릉 등이다. 부산은 서울에서 세 시간 가까이 걸리지 만, 다른 곳들은 모두 두 시간 안팎이면 갈 수 있다.

먼저 부산은 한국에서 두번째로 큰 도시이며, 동남쪽 끝에 있는 항구도시다. 바다를 보기 힘든 곳에 살고 있어서 바다라면 무조건 관심이 간다면, 그리고 시골보다는 대도시를 선호하는 편이라면, 부산은 좋은 선택지다. 매우 비싼 곳부터 저렴한 곳까지, 바다가 보이는 숙박시설이 아주 많다. 다양한 생선 요리도 발달했고, 돼지국밥이라는 로컬 푸드도 유명하다. 돼지국밥은 돼지 뼈를 오래 끓여서 만든 육수에 밥과 여러 가지 양념을 넣어서 먹는 것으로, 한국식 바쿠테(Bak kut teh)라고 할 수 있다.

부산은 지형부터가 독특해서, 도시 면적의 대부분이 산이라고 해도 과언이 아니다. 산과 산 사이의 좁은 공간들에 도시가 만들어지다보니, 산중턱까지 각종 건물이 빼곡하게 지어져 있다(심지어 고층 아파트도 산중턱에 지어져 있다). 한국전쟁 시기에 피란민이 대거 몰려들어 갑자기 인구가 늘어났던 영향이 지금까지 남아 있는 것인데, 아이로니컬하게도 결핍에서 비롯된 그 모습이 특이하여 지금은 관광 명소가 되었다. 감천문화마을이라는 곳에 가면, 산과 바다와 밀집된 건물들이 묘하게 어우러지는 특이한 풍경을 볼 수 있다.

부산에는 전 세계에 딱 하나밖에 없는 유엔군 묘지가 있다. 한국전쟁에서 평화와 자유를 위해 싸우다가 목숨을 잃은 군인들이 여기에 잠들어 있다. 한국전쟁은 UN의 이름으로 연합군이 파병된 유일한 사례인데, 당시 전투 병력을 지원한 나라는 호주, 벨기에, 캐나다, 콜롬비아, 에티오피아, 프랑스, 그리스, 룩셈부르크, 네덜란드, 뉴질랜드, 필리핀, 남아프리카공화국, 태국, 튀르키예,

영국, 미국 등 16개국이며, 병원선과 의료진 등을 지원한 나라는 덴마크, 독일, 인도, 이탈리아, 노르웨이, 스웨덴 등 6개국이다. 대한민국 국민들은 이들 22개 나라의 국민들에 대해 특별히 감사하는 마음을 갖고 있다.

한국전쟁 기간 중 17개국(의료지원국 중 노르웨이 포함)에서 총 40,896명이 희생되었으며, 부산의 UN기념공원에는 그중 약 11,000명의 유해가 안장되었다(상당수가 그들의 조국으로 이장되어, 지금은 11개국 2,319명의 유해가 잠들어 있다). 지금은 공원으로 조성되어 있으며, 매년 한국 시각으로 11월 11일 오전 11시에는 세계 곳곳에서 부산 방향으로 서서 1분간 묵념을 올리는 행사가 열린다.

자갈치시장은 한국에서 가장 유명한 해산물 전문 시장으로, 이곳에서도 마음에 드는 (살아 있는) 물고기를 고른 다음 위층에 올라가 그것을 먹을 수 있다.

해운대 일대는 해수욕장, 호텔, 맛집 등이 밀집한 곳인데, 해운대블루라인파크가 추천할 만하다. 과거에 사용됐던 철길을 따라 해변을 오가는 관광 열차와 스카이캡슐이라 부르는 초소형 (2~4인승) 기차를 타고 해안의 절경을 감상할 수 있다. 중간 중간 자유롭게 타고 내리며 산책을 겸해도 좋은데, 주말에는 상당히 혼잡하다. 여기에 디해 매년 10월에는 아시아 최대의 영화 축제인 부산국제영화제도 열린다.

해운대에서 외곽으로 조금만 더 가면 나타나는 해동용궁사라는 절도 유명하다(아주 가까운 것은 아니고, 10킬로미터 정도 떨어져 있어서 자동차로 20분쯤 걸린다). 이 절은 1970년대에 지어진 '신생' 사찰로 역사적인 가치는 전혀 없으며, 특별한 문화재도 없다. 절 자체가 특별히 아름답지도 않고, 다른 사찰들처럼 경건한 분위기도 없다. 14세기에 이 자리에 처음 절이 건립되었다는 주장이 있으나, 근거는 주말 백화점의 주차 공간과 마찬가지로 매우 희박하다. 그럼에도 불구하고 유명한 이유는 절묘한 위치 때문이다. 한국의 사찰들은 대부분 산속에 있지만, 이 절은 바다에 면해 있어서 전망이 매우 좋다. 이름도 독특한데, '용궁'은 바다를 관장하는 신의 거처라는 뜻이다. 한마디로 '특이한' 절로 유명한 셈이다. 어디서 소문을 들었는지, 외국인 관광객도 꽤 많이 방문한다 (나는 방문을 추천하지는 않았다. 유명하다고 했을 뿐).

안동이라는 도시는 여러 명문가의 본산으로, 수많은 학자를 배출했을뿐더러 한국의 전통문화가 지금까지도 가장 진하게 남아 있는 곳이다. 영국의 엘리자베스 여왕이 1999년에 방한했을 때 안동을 방문했고, 마침 생일을 맞은 여왕을 위해 한국식 전통 생일상이 차려졌던 일화도 유명하다.

안동에서는 하회마을이라는 곳을 반드시 방문해야 한다. 한국의 전통가옥인 한옥이 밀집되어 있는 곳으로, 시대를 초월한 아름다움을 확인할 수 있다. '하회'는 아주 작은 지역의 지명인데, 목가적인 분위기의 이곳은 '하회탈'의 고향이기도 하다. 하회탈은 이 지역의 전통적인 역할극에 출연하는 배우들이 썼던 탈로, 다양한 형태가 있지만 주름이 많은 할아버지가 활짝 웃는 듯한 모습의 탈이 가장 유명하다. 한국의 수많은 기념품점에서 하회탈을 모티브로 만든 소품들이 판매되고 있다.

전통문화의 도시 안동은 전통적인 방식의 소주로도 상당히 유명하여, 시내 대부분의 음식점과 기념품 가게에서 '안동소주'라는 것을 판매하고 있다. 안동소주는 쌀로 만들어지며, 한국 어디에서나 싼값에 마실 수 있는 그 소주와는 다르다(이 책에서는 '프리미엄 소주'라고 표현했다. 안동소주는 서울에서도 구입 가능하고, 심지어 공항 면세점에도 있다).

안동에는 유명한 음식이 두 가지나 있는데, 하나는 '안동찜닭'이며, 다른 하나는 '간고등어'다. 안동찜닭을 전국 곳곳에서 판매하는 체인 식당이 앞에서 언급한 '봉추찜닭'인데, 안동 시내에는 개별적으로 운영되는 안동찜닭 전문 식당이 수백 개 있다(그중 수십 개가 '찜닭거리'에 모여 있다. 맛은 대부분 비슷하다). 그러니 당신이 안동을 방문할 예정이면 굳이 서울에서 봉추찜닭을 찾아갈 이유가 없다. 간고등어는 굵은 소금으로 염장한 고등어인데, 내륙 도시 안동이 고등어로 유명한 점이 특이하다. 오래전, 유난히 쉽게 상하는 고등어를 안동 사람들이 먹기 위해서는 바닷가에서 고등어를 소금에 절인 다음 수송하는 수밖에 없었던 데서 유래한다(발음은 'gan go deung eo' 네 음절로 하면 되는데, 대충 말해도 안동 시민들은 잘 알아들을 것이다).

안동까지 갔으면 최소한 하루는 그곳에서 숙박을 해야 할 텐데, 이왕이면 '구름에'라는 이름의 리조트를 이용하면 좋다. 한국에는 한옥에서 숙박할 수 있는 전통 호텔들이 곳곳에 있는데, 그중 가장 추천할 만한 곳이 여기다. 하루 숙박비는 2백 달러 수준으로, 한국의 다른 숙박시설들에 비해 특별히 비싸지도 않다. 이 호텔에서 머문다면, 걸어갈 수 있는 거리에 위치한 안동시립민속박물관을 들러도 좋겠다.

다음으로 경주가 있다. 경주는 '벽 없는 박물관'이라 불릴 정도로 고대 유물이 많은 도시. 10세기 중반까지 천 년 가까이 지속된 신라왕조의 수도였던 경주에는 한국에서 매우 중요한 문화유산이 많다. 신라는 특히 불교문화가 발달했는데, 특히 유명한 곳이 불국사와 석굴암이다. 불국사는 한국에서 가장 유명하고 가장 아름다운 사찰 중의 하나이며, 석굴암은 석굴 내부에 석불을 모셔놓은 곳으로 신라 과학기술 및 미술의 절정으로 손꼽는다(석굴암은 보존을 위해 워낙 엄격하게 관리되어, 실제로 관람할 수 있는 부분은 매우 적다).

경주 시내 곳곳에는 고대 왕족들의 거대한 무덤이 지금까지 남아 있다. 가장 대표적인 곳인 대릉원에는 23개의 봉분이 모여 있으며, 그중 천마총은 무덤 내부에까지 들어가 과거의 신비로운 유물들을 볼 수 있다.

경주 시내에서 자동차로 20분 정도 떨어진 곳에는 양동마을이 있다. 이곳은 한국 정부가 지정해놓은 7개의 전통 마을 중에서도 가장 가치가 높은 곳으로, 수백 년 전에 지어진 백여 채의 가옥이 있다. 안동 하회마을과 마찬가지로 지금도 주민들이 거주하고 있으며, 에어비앤비를 통하면 이곳의 한옥에서 숙박을 할 수도 있다. 하회마을과 양동마을 모두 2010년에 유네스코 세계문화유산으로 등재됐다.

경상도에 경주와 안동이 있다면, 전라도에는 전주가 있다. 전주도 한국의 전통문화가 매우 발달했던 도시이며, 예술과 음식 문화가 특히 유명하다. 전주한옥마을은 여러 채의 한옥으로 이뤄진 관광지로, 비교적 저렴한 한옥 호텔과 음식점, 공예품점 등이 밀집해 있다. 즐비한 상점들은 갖가지 종류의 길거리 음식들로 관광객들을 유혹한다. 한복을 대여해주는 가게도 많으니, 이왕이면 한국의 전통 복장을 갖추고 돌아다니면 더욱 좋겠다. 그곳에는 전통술박물관도 있다. 소주 외에도 한국의 전통 술은 종류가 아주 많다. 시음도 가능하고, 직접 술을 빚는 체험도 해볼 수 있다(역시 BTS가 방문했던 장소다. 예약과 체험은 한국어로만 가능하다).

인근에는 조선왕조를 세운 태조 이성계의 초상화를 모셔놓은 경기전이 있다. 경기전 내부에 있는 어진박물관에 가면, 사진이 없던 시절에 왕을 그린 그림이 얼마나 중요한 물건이었는지 실감할 수 있다. 전동성당은 한국 최초의 순교자가 순교했던 자리에 세워진 성당이다. 첫 순교는 1791년에 있었고, 이 성당이 건립된 것은 1931년이다.

전주에서는 웬만한 음식점 아무 곳이나 들어가도 다 맛있을 뿐더러, 서울보다 훨씬 많은 종류의 반찬이 제공된다(좀 너무하지 않나 싶을 만큼 다양한 종류를 주는 곳도 있다. 심지어 별로 비싸지도 않다).

서울에서 동쪽으로 2백 킬로미터쯤 떨어져 있는 동해안의 강릉도 외국인들의 방문이 늘어나는 도시다. 2018년 평창동계올림픽이 열린 도시들 중 하나이기도 하고, 아름다운 해변과 맛있는 커피와 순두부로 유명한 곳이다. 세계에서 유일하게 어머니와 아들이 모두 화폐에 등장하는 나라가 한국이라고 말했는데, 그 어머니와 아들이 모두 태어난 장소도 강릉에 있다. 오죽헌이라는 고택인데, 이는 약 6백 년 전에 지어진 건물로 한국에 남아 있는 주택 중에서는 가장 오래된 것들 중의 하나다. 강릉까지 왔으면, BTS 뮤직비디오에 나오는 유명한 버스 정류장이 있는 향호해변까지 방문할 수 있겠다(강릉 시내에서 20킬로미터 떨어져 있다).

기차로 가기는 좀 어려운, 그러니까 운전을 선택해야 편리하게 구경할 수 있는 멋진 곳도 많이 있다. 그런 곳들을 본격적으로 살펴보기 전에, 한국에서 운전을 하려는 외국인들에게 필요한 내용들을 먼저 알아보자. 우선 국제운전면허증, 여권, 본국의 운전면허증이 모두 있어야 하고, 만 21세 이상이며 운전면허 취득 후 최소 1년이 지나야 차를 빌릴 수 있다. 본인 명의의 신용카드도 있어야 한다(이건 세계의 거의 모든 나라에서 비슷하다). 보험은 의무적으로 가입해야 하는 것만 들어도 되지만, 아무래도 낯선 곳에서의 운전이니 조금은 더 보장 범위가 넓은 것을 택하면 좋겠다.

한국의 고속도로는 유료인데, 통행료가 있는 다른 선진국들과 비교하면 그리 비싸지 않다(하지만 휘발유 가격은 제법 비싸다). 통행료는 현금이나 신용카드로도 낼 수 있지만, 하이패스라고 부르는 전자 결제 시스템을 이용하는 것이 편리하다. 많은 렌터카에는 이를 위한 단말기가 부착되어 있어서, 나중에 차를 반납할 때 한꺼번에 결제하면 된다(단말기 부착 여부를 미리 확인해야 한다). 하이패스 이용자는 톨게이트를 지나칠 때 파란색 유도선이 그어져 있는 레인을 따라 지나가면 된다.

제한속도는 구간에 따라 다르지만 대부분은 시속 백 킬로미터이며, 일부 고속도로는 시속 110킬로미터다. 과속 차량을 단속하는 카메라가 곳곳에 설치되어 있는데, 두 가지 특징이 있다. 첫째, 거의 언제나 전방에 카메라가 있다는 사실을 알려주는 노란색 표지판이 설치되어 있다(뭐 바람직한 건 아니지만, 대부분의 운전자들은 카메라가 없는 구간에서는 어느 정도 과속을 하다가 카메라가 있는 곳에서만 속도를 줄인다). 둘째, 예고 표지판을 보고 속도를 줄이면 잠시 후 실제로 정면 혹은 측면에 카메라가 나타나긴 하는데, 실제로 작동하는 카메라보다 작동하지 않는 카메라가 더 많다. 심지어 카메라가 놓여 있어야 할 자리에 카메라가 없는 경우도 흔하다(실제 카메라의 위치는 가끔씩 바뀐다). 어디에 진짜 카메라가 있는지 알 수 없으니, 운전자는 예고 표지가 보일 때마다 속도를 줄일 수밖에 없다. 이걸 내가 왜 알려주고 있는지는 모르겠지만, 아무튼 그렇다.

그러니 한국의 고속도로에서는 웬만하면 과속을 하지 않는 게 좋겠다. 게다가 두 개의 지점을 통과하는 시간을 측정하여 과속 여부를 판별하는 방식도 병행하고 있다(이런 숱한 장치에도 불구하고, 한국의 교통사고율은 높은 편이다. 서유럽 국가들 중에서 가장 교통사고가 많이 일어난다는 이탈리아보다 조금 더 높다. 이탈리아와 한국은 모두 사람들이 성격 급하기로 유명하다). 그러니, 운전을 할 때는 안전을 최우선으로 생각하길.

고속도로의 일부 구간에 버스 전용 차로가 지정되어 있다는 사실도 알아야 한다. 서울 주변을 비롯하여 교통량이 특히 많은 구간의 1차로는 버스만 다닐 수 있다(엄밀히 말하면 9인승 이상의 차량에 7명 이상 탑승했을 때만 가능하다). 파란 실선으로 구분되어 있으니, 이 레인만 유독 차량이 없다고 기뻐하며 진입하는 일이 없도록 주의해야 한다(다른 운전자들도 바보가 아니다). 버스 전용 차로 운영 시간은 구간마다 다른데, 당신이 표지판만 보고 알아 차리기는 쉽지 않을 것이다. 그냥 다른 차들의 움직임을 보고 눈치껏 운전하면 된다.

한국에서 고속도로를 달릴 때 경험할 수 있는 최고의 즐거움은 휴게소다. 한국의 고속도로 휴게소는 매우 규모가 크고, 정말 다양한 상품들을 판매한다. 주유소, 식당, 편의점 등이 있는 것은 물론이고, 앞에서 소개한 수많은 길거리 음식을 휴게소에서 맛볼 수 있다(도심에서는 찾아보기가 쉽지 않은데 고속도로 휴게소에서만 유난히 흔한 음식들도 있다). 다양한 자동차용품, 생활용품, 의류, 해당 지역의 특산물 등도 판매한다. 주로 트로트 계열의 음악을 수록한 CD도 흔히 판매한다(길거리 음식 말고 당신이 사야 할 품목은 없다). 휴게소 사이의 간격은 대부분 30킬로미터 내외로 촘촘하게 있으며, 아무리 멀어도 50킬로미터 정도 떨어져 있을 뿐이다.

마지막으로, 당신이 한국에서 자동차 여행을 떠날 때 고려해야 할 가장 중요한 사실을 알려준다. 서울에서 출발하는 시점을 토요일 낮으로 잡지 말고, 서울로 돌아오는 시점을 일요일 오후나 저녁으로 잡지 마라. 무조건 최소 한 시간 이상 더 걸린다. 운이 나쁘면 두 시간 이상 더 소요될 수도 있다(다른 요일이라고 해서 뻥 뻥 뚫린다는 것은 아니다. 러시아워 때의 대도시 주변 고속도로는 늘 막힌다). 서울 밖으로 나갔다 돌아오는 건 평일에 하자.

이제 KTX를 타고 가는 것보다는 자동차를 몰고 가는 것이 더 좋은 명소들을 몇 군데 알아보자. 가장 먼저 소개하고 싶은 곳은 뮤지엄 산(SAN)이다. SAN은 Space, Art, Nature의 앞 글자를 딴 것이기도 하지만, mountain을 뜻하는 한국어 발음이기도 하다. 실제로 이 미술관은 깊은 산속에 있다. 일본의 건축가 안도 타다오(Tadao Ando)가 설계한 건물도 근사하고, 소장하고 있는 작품들도 훌륭하다. BTS의 RM을 비롯한 여러 K팝 스타들도 다녀간 곳이고, 드라마·영화·CF 등의 촬영지로도 여러 번 선택된 곳이다. 서울에서 두 시간이 채 안 걸린다.

당신이 서울과는 완전히 다른, 지극히 전통적인 분위기를 느껴보고 싶다면 '아원'도 추천한다. 여러 채의 한옥으로 구성된 이곳은, 다른 지역에 있던 오래된 한옥들을 옮겨와서 다시 지은 건물이다. 2백 년 이상 된 목조건물에서 하루를 지내는 근사한 체험을 하려면 객실에 따라 250~400달러를 지불해야 한다(최대 5명까지 묵을 수 있는 가장 큰 객실은 약 천 달러 수준이다). 여기서 숙박을 하지 않고 그냥 돌아보아도 좋다. BTS도 2019년에 이곳에서 화보 촬영을 했다. 아원 바로 옆에 있는 소양고택도 고급 한옥 호텔이며, 인근에는 조금 저렴한 한옥 호텔이 여러 개 있다(하지만 홈페이지들이 한국어로만 되어 있어서 아쉽다). 서울에서 차를 몰고 가면 세 시간 정도 걸리는데, 앞에서 소개한 전주 시내에서는 30분이 채 걸리지 않는다. KTX와 자동차를 모두 이용하여 전주와 이곳을 함께 돌아보는 것도 멋진 아이디어다.

속초라는 도시도 재미있다. 속초는 동해안 북쪽에 위치한 도시로, 오랫동안 서울에서 가장 가기 힘든 도시 중 하나였다. 기차로는 아예 갈 수 없고 자동차로는 다섯 시간 이상 걸리는 곳이었지만, 2017년에 서울양양고속도로가 개통된 이후 서울에서 두 시간 20분이면 갈 수 있게 됐다. 속초는 아름다운 해안과 맛있는 생선 요리로 유명하고, 인근에 있는 양양해변은 한국에서 서핑을 즐길 수 있는 몇 안 되는 장소 중의 하나다. '오징어순대'라는 음식도 맛보아야 한다. 이것은 돼지의 창자가 아니라 오징어를 이용해서 만든 순대다.

등산을 좋아한다면 설악산 국립공원을 방문해도 좋겠다. '한국의 요세미티'로도 불리는 설악산은 단풍이 물드는 가을철이 특히 아름답다. 당신이 미술 애호가라면, 속초로 가는 길에 박수근 미술관을 들러도 좋다(한 시간 정도 더 걸린다). 박수근은 한국인이 매우 사랑하는 20세기 화가 중 한 사람이다.

서해안 도시 중에는 보령이 유명하다. 서울에서 자동차로 두 시간이면 도착하는 이 도시는, 아름다운 해수욕장이 몇 개 있기는 해도, 한국인들이 즐겨 찾는 수많은 여름 휴양지 중의 하나에 불과했다. 하지만 1998년에 보령머드축제가 열리기 시작한 이후 국제적으로 유명한 곳이 되었다. 매년 7월 말경에 2~3주 정도 열리는 이 축제는 사람들이 온몸에 진흙을 바르며 노는 행사다. 진흙에 건강에 좋은 성분이 포함되어 있다고는 하는데, 하루나 이틀 동안 진흙을 바른다고 몸이 특별히 건강해질 리는 없으니, 그냥 '재미'를 위한 행사라고 보면 된다. 이 축제를 위해 보령을 방문하는 외국인만 매년 30만 명에 달한다. 당신이 한국에 오는 계절이 여름이라면, 반드시 고려해볼 만한 축제다. 운전을 하기 싫으면 고속버스를 타고 가도 된다.

마지막으로 소개하는, 하지만 가장 중요한 장소는 제주도다. 제주는 서울에서 비행기로 50분 거리에 있는 아름다운 섬이다. 동서로 73킬로미터, 남북으로 31킬로미터 크기이니, 제법 큰 섬이다. 당연히 한국에서는 가장 큰 섬이며, 하와이의 마우이섬보다 조금 작다. 화산활동에 의해 형성된 섬으로 중심에 한라산이 있으며, 섬 전역에 약 370개의 기생화산이 있다. 한반도에서 남쪽으로 멀리 떨어져 있는 섬이라, 기후·음식·문화·생태 등 모든 것이 독특하다. 제주도 사투리는 한국인들조차 잘 이해하지 못할 정도다(물론 제주도 사람들도 표준어를 구사할 줄 안다). 한국인이 가장 사랑하는 대표적인 휴양지로, 서울의 김포공항과 제주공항을 오가는 항공편은 연간 8만 편에 육박한다. 놀라지 마시라, 매일 2백 편이 넘는 것이다(웬만한 지하철보다 자주 다닌다). 이렇게 비행편이 많지만, 주말에는 표를 구하기 어렵다. 제주를 방문할 계획이 있으면 오래전에 예매를 해야 한다. 실제로 서울-제주 노선은 전 세계에서 가장 붐비는 노선으로 유명하다. 코로나 이후 조금 감소하긴 했지만, 한때는 서울-제주 노선에 탑승하는 여객의 숫자가 연간 1,500만 명을 넘기도 했다.

당연히 제주에는 유명한 관광지도 매우 많다. 사실 섬 전체가 관광지다(물론 70만 명 가까운 사람들에게는 생활의 터전이다). 일단 한라산국립공원이 있고, 여러 개의 폭포와 동굴, 크고 작은 공원이 많다. 해수욕장, 숲, 산책로, 미술관, 맛집 등도 아주 많다. 그리고 제주가 아닌 다른 곳에서는 찾아볼 수 없는 독특한 장소들도 있다.

대표적인 곳은 제주 4.3평화공원이다. 한국 현대사의 비극적인 사건 중 하나인 제주 4.3 사건의 희생자를 추모하는 공원이다. 한국이 일본의 식민 지배에서 벗어난 것이 1945년이고 남북이 각각 정부를 출범시킨 것은 1948년, 한국전쟁은 1950년부터 1953년까지다. 그 혼란의 시기에 본토와 멀리 떨어진 제주에서는 좌익과 우익의 대립 등 여러 가지 복잡한 요인으로 무려 7년여 동안(1947년부터 1954년까지) 군인, 경찰, 반란군, 주민 들이 서로를 죽이는 비극이 발생했다. 사망자는 약 3만 명으로 추정되는데, 이는 당시 제주 인구의 10분의 1을 넘는다.

제주는 또한 '해녀'로도 유명하다. 해녀는 산소공급 장치 없이 바닷속에 들어가 전복, 성게, 소라, 미역 등을 채취하는 것이 직업인 여성이다(당신이 제주에서 먹게 될 해산물 중의 일부는 해녀들이 채취한 것이다). 1970년대에는 제주 해녀가 만 4천여 명이 있었다고 하는데, 지금은 많이 줄어들어 3천여 명만 활동중이다. 2016년에는 유네스코 인류무형문화유산으로 등재됐다. 제주의 몇몇 지역에서는 관광객들이 직접 해녀 체험을 할 수도 있는데, 본격적인 관광 프로그램은 아니다. 직접 체험하지는 못하더라도 해녀박물관을 방문하면 해녀에 관한 흥미로운 사실들을 알게 된다.

제주는 걷기 좋은 곳이기도 하다. 올레길이라고 부르는 산책로가 해안을 따라 섬 전역에 조성되어 있는데, 총 연장은 400킬로미터가 넘는다. 또한 수백 개에 이르는 한라산의 기생화산을 '오름'이라고 부르는데, 이들 가운데 10여 개는 특히 아름답기로 유명하다. 대부분은 높이가 2백~3백 미터 정도라서, 그리 어렵지 않게 오를 수 있다. 당신이 매우 부지런한 편이고 전날 과음을 하지 않는다면, 새벽에 일어나서 성산일출봉에 올라도 좋겠다. 주차장에서 30분 정도 올라가면 정상에 도착하고, 그곳에서 바라보는 일출은 매우 근사하다(날씨가 화창하면 더욱 좋겠지만, 적당히 구름이 있는 날도 나쁘지 않다). 일출을 포기하고 그냥 낮에 방문해도 좋다.

축구 팬이라면, 제주 월드컵경기장을 방문할 수도 있겠다. 2002년 월드컵 때 활용된 이 아름다운 경기장에서는 한라산도 보이고 바다도 보인다. 제프 블래터(Sepp Blatter) 전 FIFA 회장이 이곳에 왔을 때 '세계에서 가장 아름다운 경기장'이라고 말하기도 했다(아마 다른 경기장에 가서도 비슷한 말을 했겠지만). 만약 당신이 제주에 있는 동안 K리그 경기가 이곳에서 열린다면, 축구를 보며 치맥을 즐기는 좋은 추억을 만들 수 있다. 매진되는 경우는 흔하지 않으니, 예매 없이 가도 된다. 입장료도 상당히 저렴하다(가장 비싼 좌석이 20달러가 안 되고, 50달러 정도 되는 패키지 티켓을 사면 테이블이 있는 좌석 두 자리에 치킨과 맥주 두 잔까지 준다).

제주도는 섬인 만큼 신선하고 다양한 해산물 요리가 발달했다. 거의 모든 종류의 해산물을 맛볼 수 있는데, 그중에서도 외국인을 깜짝 놀라게 할 메뉴로는 통갈치구이가 있다. 갈치는 한국인이 매우 좋아하는 생선으로 과거에는 서민들의 음식이었지만 지금은 가격이 매우 비싸다. 다른 지역에서는 이 긴 물고기를 적당한 크기로 잘라서 요리하는 것이 보통이지만, 제주에서는 한 마리를 통째로 구워서 그대로 테이블에 올리는 경우도 있다. 일행이 네 명 정도 된다면, 통갈치구이를 주문해보라. 놀라운 모양의 생선 요리가 나타날 것이다(물론 맛도 아주 좋다). 제주 음식을 판매하는 대형 식당에서 흔히 판매한다.

제주의 토종 돼지인 흑돼지도 아주 유명하다. 흑돼지는 보통의 돼지보다 훨씬 맛있고, 가격도 조금 더 비싸다. 서울에 있는 식당들 중에도 제주도 흑돼지를 판매하는 곳은 반드시 그 사실을 커다랗게 표시해놓을 만큼 한국인이 '믿고 먹는' 돼지고기다. 다양한 조리법이 존재하지만, 당연히 가장 인기 있는 것은 삼겹살 혹은 오겹살이다. 당신은 아마 서울에서도 삼겹살을 맛있게 먹었겠지만, 제주도를 방문했다면 한번 더 먹어도 좋다. 좀 과장하자면, 제주를 방문하는 한국인들은 거의 모두가 최소한 한끼는 흑돼지 삼겹살을 먹는다. 소금에 찍어 먹어도 좋지만, 제주도에서는 멸치젓(멜젓)에 찍어 먹는 방식이 더 흔하다. 따로 주문하지 않아도 당연히 제공된다(그러고 보니 삼겹살로 시작해서 삼겹살로 끝나는 책이다!).

스무 개의 챕터 중에서 가장 길어졌다. 매력적인 장소들 중에서 아주 일부만 소개했는데도 그렇게 됐다. 그만큼 한국에는 매력적인 곳이 많다는 뜻일 게다. 당신이 충분히 긴 시간 동안 한국에 머무르거나 여러 번 한국을 방문해서, 서울 이외의 지역에 있는 이 모든 멋진 장소들을 전부 방문할 수 있기를 기원한다. 당신의 한국 여행이 비할 곳 없이 놀라운 경험들과 잊지 못할 추억들로 가득하기를, 그래서 당신의 인생에서 잊지 못할 한 챕터로 영원히 간직되기를 간절히 바란다.

20.

Beyond Seoul: Exploring the Best of Korea's Regions

If you're visiting South Korea for the first time and have around five days, you can spend all of your time in Seoul. Seoul is big enough and diverse enough that you'll never run out of places to go, things to do, and things to eat, even if you stay for a week or longer. But hold your horses! If you've got some extra time on your hands or you're a seasoned South Korea traveler who's already soaked up the Seoul vibes, it's high time to venture beyond the city limits. Yup, we're talking about exploring what lies outside the bustling capital. Now, where should you head to uncover the best-kept secrets of this marvelous country?

South Korea may not be the largest country out there, but it sure dwarfs some of those pint-sized places like the Vatican or Monaco. We're talking more than ten times the size of Singapore and nearly ten times bigger than Hong Kong. It's over twice as big as Denmark, the Netherlands, and Switzerland. It even outshines Ireland, the Czech Republic, Austria, and Portugal in terms of landmass. This ain't your average 'blink and you'll miss it' kind of country. But let me tell you, with the jaw-dropping highway system and high-speed rail clocking in at a staggering 300 kilometers per hour, there's absolutely nowhere your wanderlust can't take you if you put your mind to it. The only thing left to decide is where your heart desires to wander off to. The possibilities are limitless, my friend!

The first decision you'll need to make is whether you're up for some adventure behind the wheel. Now, when you're exploring Seoul, trust me, driving is the last thing on your mind. But once you venture beyond the city limits, your entire travel experience will transform based on whether you take the driver's seat or not. Speaking from personal experience, I've embraced the thrill of renting cars in nearly every country I've set foot in. I've even dared to take on the challenge of driving in places with different driving directions. But let's face it, not everyone finds joy in hitting the road, and navigating unfamiliar territories can be both mentally demanding and potentially hazardous, especially when you're used to driving on the other side. (So, my friends from the United Kingdom, Ireland, Australia, New Zealand, Fiji, Thailand, Malaysia, India, Indonesia, Singapore, Hong Kong, South Africa, Kenya, Namibia, or Tanzania, it's best to steer clear of driving in South Korea).

If you happen to opt against driving, fear not, for there are convenient alternatives that will whisk you away to your desired destinations. The cities with KTX, Korea's high-speed rail system, are the go-to spots accessible with ease. For fellow travelers seeking memorable experiences, I highly recommend exploring cities such as Busan, Gyeongju, Andong, Jeonju, and Gangneung. While Busan may take nearly three hours to reach from Seoul, the other cities can be reached in approximately two hours.

Firstly, Busan is the second-largest city in Korea, situated on the vibrant southeastern coast of South Korea. If you reside in an area where glimpses of the ocean are rare and you're an avid ocean lover, and if your heart leans more towards the dynamic atmosphere of bustling cities over the tranquility of the countryside, then Busan is a must-visit destination. The city offers a myriad of accommodations providing breathtaking ocean views, catering to a range of budgets from luxurious to more affordable options. And, of course, let's not overlook the tempting seafood cuisine that awaits you. One local favorite is Dwaeji Gukbap, a mouth-watering Korean-style pork soup, akin to a Korean-style Bak Kut Teh. It's crafted with rice and various seasonings, simmering pork bones to perfection for a rich and flavorful broth.

Busan's unique geography is a sight to behold, as the city is predominantly nestled amidst mountains. The city's development has taken place in the narrow spaces between these mountains, leading to various buildings constructed right up against the mountainsides. In fact, even high-rise apartments can be seen perched on the hillsides, showcasing the impressive utilization of space. This distinctive characteristic stems from the rapid population growth during the Korean War when many evacuees flocked to the city. Ironically, what was once a result of necessity has now become a captivating tourist attraction. A notable spot that exemplifies this captivating landscape is Gamcheon Culture Village. Here, you'll encounter a truly beautiful vista where mountains, sea, and densely packed buildings coexist harmoniously.

In Busan, the world's only United Nations Military Cemetery stands as a poignant tribute. It is the final resting place for numerous soldiers who sacrificed their lives in the Korean War, fighting for peace and freedom. The Korean War marked the only instance when a coalition of nations deployed under the banner of the United Nations. Sixteen nations contributed combat troops, including Australia, Belgium, Canada, Colombia, Ethiopia, France, Greece, Luxembourg, the Netherlands, New Zealand, the Philippines, South Africa, Thailand, Turkmenistan, the United Kingdom, and the United States. Additionally, six nations provided hospital ships and medical personnel: Denmark, Germany, India, Italy, Norway, and Sweden. The people of South Korea hold deep gratitude for the citizens of these 22 nations.

Throughout the Korean War, a devastating toll of 40,896 lives from 17 countries (including Norway among the medical donors) was endured, with approximately 11,000 remains interred at the UN Memorial Park in Busan. While many have been repatriated to their homelands, the sacred grounds hold the eternal rest of 2,319 individuals from 11 nations. The UN Memorial Park in Busan stands as a solemn homage, and each year on November 11th at 11 a.m.

local time, people around the world face Busan and observe a poignant moment of silence.

The Jagalchi Fish Market stands as the epitome of seafood markets in Korea, celebrated for its lively ambiance and a wealth of enticing catches. Visitors here enjoy the enjoyable experience of handpicking their favorite live fish and then ascending to one of the many dining establishments upstairs to savor their choice.

In the Haeundae neighborhood, a treasure trove awaits with captivating beaches, luxurious hotels, and a variety of charming restaurants. To kick off your Haeundae adventure, the Haeundae Blue Line Park serves as an excellent starting point. Along the former railroad tracks, you can board a sightseeing train that shuttles you to and from the beach, offering a delightful journey. Additionally, seize the chance to ride the Sky Capsule—a charmingly compact train accommodating 2 to 4 passengers—for an extraordinary coastal perspective. From its lofty vantage point, you'll be treated to awe-inspiring vistas of the picturesque coastline. While you can freely hop on and off both the train and capsule with a single ticket, it's worth noting that weekends tend to draw sizable crowds. Adding to Busan's allure, every October, the city takes center stage as the highly esteemed host of the Busan International Film Festival (BIFF), the largest film festival in Asia.

Haedong Yonggungsa temple is conveniently located just north of Haeundae Beach. While it may not be a stone's throw away, a short car ride of approximately 20 minutes or a distance of around 10 kilometers will get you there. Now, this temple may not be a relic from ancient times or boast any fancy cultural artifacts. As a newbie temple built in the 1970s, it may not win any beauty pageants or have that serene temple vibe. There are rumors of an ancient temple on this spot way back in the 14th century, but the evidence is about as scarce as parking spaces during rush hour. But hey, it's got something going for it - a killer oceanfront location! While most temples in Korea are located in the mountains, this one faces the ocean and has a great view. Even the name is eccentric: "Yonggung" means "the Sea God's Palace," the abode of the god who oversees the sea. In short, it has a reputation as an 'unusual' temple, and, interestingly, many curious foreign tourists are drawn to it. (I'm not saying I recommended it, just pointing out its fame.)

Andong, a city steeped in rich heritage, maintains a distinguished lineage of esteemed families, nurtured countless scholars, and proudly upholds the traditions of Korean culture. Its significance was further elevated when the late Queen Elizabeth Ⅱ of England graced its grounds during her 1999 state visit, where a remarkable twist awaited her in the form of an authentic Korean birthday meal.

While in Andong, a visit to the Hahoe Folk Village is an absolute must. This charming enclave is adorned with an abundance of hanoks, traditional Korean houses that exude timeless beauty. Nestled within this idyllic village is the famed Hahoe mask, known as Hahoetal. These intricately crafted masks play an integral role in the region's vibrant cultural performances, adorning the faces of actors who bring the stories to life. With a diverse range of designs available, the most renowned Hahoetal is the one portraying a jovial, wrinkled old man with a wide, beaming smile. Such is its popularity that shops across Korea offer souvenirs and keepsakes inspired by the captivating hahoetal.

Andong has left an indelible mark on the world of spirits with its distinctive Andong soju. Unlike the ubiquitous and inexpensive soju found throughout Korea, Andong soju stands as a premium offering, crafted meticulously from rice. (In this book, we've referred to it as 'premium soju'.) This revered elixir graces the shelves of restaurants and souvenir shops across the city. (It is also available in Seoul and even in airport duty-free shops.)

There are two famous dishes in Andong: Andong Jjimdak (soy-based braised chicken) and Gangodeungeo (salted mackerel). The chain restaurant that sells Andong Jjimdak nationwide is the aforementioned Bongchu Jjimdak, but there are hundreds of independently owned Andong Jjimdak specialty restaurants in Andong. (Dozens of them are clustered in Jjimdak Street, and the flavors are mostly similar.) So if you're planning to go to Andong, there's no reason to visit Bongchu Jjimdak in Seoul. Gangodeungeo is coarsely salted mackerel, and it may be peculiar that the inland city of Andong is famous for its mackerel. The name comes from the fact that long ago, the only way for Andong residents to eat mackerel, which spoils very easily, was to salt it on the beach and then transport it. (You can pronounce it in four syllables: "gan go deung eo," but even if you say it roughly, the people of Andong will understand very well.)

If your travels lead you to the enchanting city of Andong, consider immersing yourself fully by spending at least one night at the esteemed Gurume Resort. Among the myriad traditional accommodations in Korea, Gurume stands as a pinnacle of excellence, offering a valuable opportunity to experience a hanok, a traditional Korean house. A night's stay at Gurume is a worthwhile investment, with prices averaging around $200. Rest assured, this expense is by no means exorbitant when compared to other accommodations throughout Korea. If you choose to stay at this hotel, you may also want to explore the Andong Folk Museum, conveniently located within walking distance.

Gyeongju, often referred to as 'the museum without walls,' is a treasure trove of ancient history. As the former capital of the Silla Dynasty, which reigned for almost a millennium until the mid-10th century, Gyeongju holds a special place in Korean heritage. Buddhist culture thrived in Silla, and two notable landmarks showcase its grandeur. Bulguksa Temple, celebrated as one of Korea's most famous temples, stands as a majestic testament to the Silla Dynasty's rich heritage. Another awe-inspiring site is Seokguram, a stone grotto temple housing a magnificent stone Buddha. Seokguram is considered the pinnacle of science, technology, and art of Silla. However, visitors can access only limited parts of it due to the need for preservation.

Within the city of Gyeongju, you'll discover the sprawling tombs of ancient royalty scattered across the landscape. The prominent Daereungwon, also known as the Tumuli complex, encompasses 23 majestic tombs. Among them, the Cheonmachong, also referred to as the Heavenly Horse Tomb, allows visitors to venture inside, unraveling the mysteries of the past.

For a glimpse into historic Korean village life, a brief 20-minute drive from downtown Gyeongju takes you to Yangdong Folk Village. Designated as one of the seven traditional villages by the Korean government, this remarkable village harbors over 100 well-preserved houses dating back centuries. Similar to Hahoe Village, Yangdong Village remains a vibrant community. Through platforms like Airbnb, you can even experience the authentic charm of staying in a hanok, a traditional Korean house. Both Hahoe Village in Andong and Yangdong Village in Gyeongju received the prestigious honor of being inscribed on the UNESCO World Heritage List in 2010.

If Gyeongsang Province has Gyeongju and Andong, Jeolla Province presents Jeonju. This cultural hub captivates visitors with its vibrant heritage Korean culture, flourishing art scene, and tantalizing culinary scenes. At the heart of the city is Jeonju Hanok Maeul (Jeonju Hanok Village), a picturesque tourist area showcasing a collection of hanoks. These classic Korean houses offer affordable accommodations, charming restaurants, and artisan craft shops, creating an idyllic setting for an immersive and authentic experience. The bustling streets are adorned with an abundance of street food stalls, tempting passersby with a wide array of mouthwatering treats. To truly embrace the cultural ambiance, don't miss the opportunity to rent a hanbok, ancestral attire that allows you to step back in time. Enhancing the cultural journey is the Traditional Wine Museum, where you can sample a variety of indigenous Korean alcoholic beverages and even try your hand at concocting your own unique blend. Please note that reservations and experiences at the museum are currently available only in Korean. It's worth mentioning that the celebrated Korean group BTS once visited this remarkable destination.

Within close proximity is Gyeonggijeon, a distinguished historical site that houses portraits of Taejo Lee Seonggye, the esteemed founder of the Joseon Dynasty. Immerse yourself in history by exploring the Royal Portrait Museum within Gyeonggijeon, offering a glimpse into the era when royal portraits played a vital role in capturing the essence of Korea's leaders in the absence of photography. Another notable landmark in Jeonju is the Jeondong Catholic Church, built on the sacred grounds of Korea's first martyrdom in 1791. This solemn place of worship, constructed in 1931, serves as a testament to the nation's religious history.

When it comes to culinary experiences, Jeonju leaves no stone unturned. Whether you choose humble local eateries or upscale establishments, almost any restaurant you step into will elate your taste buds with delicious fare. Jeonju takes pride in its generous servings of side dishes, often surpassing those found in Seoul. Be prepared to be spoiled for choice, as some dining establishments offer an extensive array of options that might leave you pleasantly overwhelmed, all at an affordable price.

Located approximately 200 kilometers east of Seoul on the picturesque east coast, Gangneung is an increasingly popular destination for foreign visitors. This coastal city gained international recognition as one of the hosts of the 2018 PyeongChang Winter Olympics and offers a blend of stunning beaches, delectable coffee, and renowned soft tofu. One fascinating aspect of Gangneung is its connection to South Korea's currency. As we've mentioned before, South Korea is the only country in the world where both mother and son are featured on its currency, and Gangneung is where both were born. The place is an old house called Ojukheon, which is about 600 years old and one of the oldest remaining houses in Korea. A visit to Gangneung would be incomplete without exploring Hyangho Beach, famous for its iconic bus stop featured in a music video by the BTS, situated approximately 20 kilometers from downtown Gangneung.

If you plan to explore the more remote and less accessible destinations in South Korea, driving becomes an ideal option. Before embarking on your road trip, it's essential to acquaint yourself with the requirements for foreigners driving in the country. To drive in Korea, you will need your International Driving Permit, passport, and driver's license from your home country. Additionally, you must be at least 21 years old and have held your driver's license for at least a year before being eligible to rent a car. Having a credit card under your name is also necessary (similar to requirements in many other countries around the world). While 'basic' insurance is mandatory, it's advisable to opt for coverage with higher limits, considering you'll be driving in an unfamiliar area.

South Korea's highways are tolled, but the fees are not as expensive as those in other developed countries with tolls. (Gasoline is relatively costly.) Payment can be made with cash or credit card, but the convenience of using an electronic payment system called hi-pass is notable. Many rental cars come equipped with a hi-pass terminal, allowing you to settle all toll fees at once upon returning the car. (Make sure to check in advance if the terminal is available.) As a hi-pass user, passing through a tollbooth is simplified by moving into the lane marked with blue guidelines.

The speed limit varies by section, with most roads allowing a maximum of 100 kilometers per hour, while certain highways stretch their limits to 110 kilometers per hour. Now, let's talk about those sneaky speed-catching cameras. They are everywhere, and can be identified by two things. First, there are almost always yellow signs warning you that there are cameras up ahead. (Not that it's desirable, but many drivers tend to put the pedal to the metal in camera-free zones, only to slam on the brakes when they see those signs.) Secondly, believe it or not, there are more non-functioning cameras than functioning ones. Actually, when you see the sign and slow down, a few moments later, you may find no camera in front of you or to the side. (But you can find an 'empty' camera box! And, the actual camera locations love to change their minds.) Since you never know where the real cameras are, drivers have no choice but to slow down every time they see a warning sign. (Anyway, I don't know why I'm telling you this. Hey, can you guess?)

So, it's highly advisable to avoid speeding on Korean highways whenever possible. Moreover, they even measure the time it takes for you to zip through two points just to catch those speedy drivers. Despite all these high-tech gadgets, South Korea has a bit of a reputation when it comes to traffic accidents, with a rate that's only slightly higher than Italy's, the reigning champ of traffic mishaps in Western Europe. It's no secret that both Italy and Korea are known for their passionate and short-tempered individuals. So, my friends, let's prioritize safety and enjoy the journey with a little extra caution!

It's crucial to note that specific sections of highways in Korea are designated as bus lanes, primarily around Seoul. These lanes are exclusively for buses, and regular vehicles are not allowed to travel in them. (Technically, you can only do this if you have at least seven passengers in a vehicle that seats nine or more.) Identifying these bus lanes is easy; look out for the solid blue lines marking them. Therefore, don't be deceived by the seemingly empty lane. Other drivers refrain from entering for a good reason. The operating hours of bus lanes can vary from section to section, and it can be challenging for foreigners to spot the signage. That's why it's essential to stay alert and closely monitor other vehicles while driving.

One of the highlights of driving on the highways in Korea is undoubtedly the rest stops. These Korean highway rest areas are acclaimed for their spaciousness and an impressive range of offerings. Alongside the usual amenities like gas stations, restaurants, and convenience stores, you'll also have the opportunity to indulge in the diverse array of street foods mentioned earlier. Moreover, these rest stops often feature enjoyable culinary delights that are uncommon in city areas. But that's not all! They also showcase a wide selection of car accessories, household goods, clothing, and local specialties, allowing you to shop to your heart's content. You might even stumble upon CDs of 'trot' music, a popular genre in Korea, adding a musical touch to your journey. (Though, there may be no items you need to buy other than street food.) Conveniently spaced about 30 kilometers apart, the rest stops on Korean highways ensure you won't have to wait long for the next one. (The farthest rest stop is usually within 50 kilometers.)

Lastly, as you prepare for a road trip in Korea, it's crucial to keep these important facts in mind. Avoid leaving Seoul on a Saturday afternoon and returning on a Sunday afternoon or evening, as it can add at least an extra hour to your travel time, and sometimes even more. Don't assume that roads will be clear just because it's a different day of the week—highways around major cities are often congested during rush hour. Whenever possible, plan your travel outside of Seoul on weekdays to minimize traffic delays.

Now, let's turn our attention to some destinations that are best explored by car rather than taking the KTX. Our first stop is Museum SAN. The name 'SAN' encapsulates Space, Art, and Nature, while also representing the Korean word for mountain. True to its name, the museum is nestled deep within the mountains. Renowned Japanese architect Tadao Ando has crafted a breathtaking structure, complemented by an extraordinary collection of artwork. Notably, it has drawn visits from popular K-pop stars such as RM(Kim Namjoon) of BTS and served as a backdrop for a lot of dramas, movies, and commercials. With a travel time of less than two hours from Seoul, it's an accessible gem waiting to be explored.

For those seeking a truly enchanting and culturally immersive experience, Awon Museum & Hotel stands out as a fantastic choice. This charming establishment comprises several hanoks, traditional Korean houses, painstakingly relocated from other neighborhoods to create an authentic setting. Immerse yourself in history by spending a night in a wooden building that is over 200 years old, with room rates ranging from $250 to $400, depending on your preferred accommodation. For larger groups, the spacious five-person room is available at around $1,000. If you prefer a daytime visit, you can freely explore the premises without staying overnight. Notably, even BTS chose this location for a photo shoot in 2019. Adjacent to Awon, you'll find Soyang Gotaek, another upscale hanok hotel, along with several more affordable hanok accommodations nearby. (Regrettably, the neighboring small hanok hotels in the area do not provide English-language services on their websites.) The drive from Seoul takes approximately three hours, but if you're visiting downtown Jeonju, it's less than a 30-minute drive away. Exploring both Jeonju and the region by both KTX and car is a great idea.

Sokcho, positioned as the northernmost city on the east coast, historically presented a challenge to reach from Seoul. Formerly inaccessible by train and requiring over five hours by car, the opening of the Seoul-Yangyang Expressway in 2017 significantly improved travel time to just two hours and 20 minutes from Seoul. Sokcho offers a stunning coastline renowned for its beauty and delectable seafood dishes. Nearby Yangyang Beach offers a rare opportunity for surfing in Korea. Don't miss the chance to savor the 'Ojingeo Sundae,' a squid-based sundae, not the classic pig intestines version.

For hiking enthusiasts, a visit to Seoraksan National Park is a must. Often dubbed the 'Yosemite of Korea,' Seoraksan unveils its true magnificence during the autumn season when the foliage paints the landscape with vibrant hues. Art aficionados can make a detour to the Park Soo Keun Museum, adding an extra hour to the journey. Park Soo Keun is revered as one of Korea's beloved 20th-century painters.

Boryeong, a city on the west coast, holds its own charm. Just a two-hour car ride away from Seoul, it offers not only picturesque beaches but also a history as a well-attended summer getaway for South Koreans. However, its international recognition soared in 1998 with the inception of the Boryeong Mud Festival. This annual extravaganza spans two to three weeks, usually towards the end of July, where participants gleefully engage in mud-based activities, covering themselves from head to toe. While the mud is believed to contain beneficial ingredients, don't expect an immediate health boost—it's all about the sheer enjoyment.

Remarkably, around 300,000 foreigners flock to Boryeong each year to partake in this festival. If you find yourself in Korea during the summer, this is an event you should definitely consider. And fear not if you prefer not to drive, as there are express buses available for convenient transportation to Boryeong.

And finally, we come to the captivating Jeju Island, a true gem of South Korea. Located a mere 50-minute flight away from Seoul, this beautiful island stretches across 73 kilometers from east to west and 31 kilometers from north to south, making it quite sizable. In fact, it proudly holds the title of being South Korea's largest island, falling just slightly short of the dimensions of Hawaii's Maui. Shaped by volcanic activity, Jeju Island boasts the majestic Hallasan Mountain at its center, surrounded by approximately 370 parasitic cones scattered across its landscape. Due to its southern location, Jeju Island exhibits a uniqueness that permeates every aspect, from its climate and culinary wonders to its rich culture and vibrant ecology. Even for Koreans, the island's dialect remains a fascinating mystery, as it differs from the mainland. (Rest assured, though, as Jeju Islanders also fluently speak standard Korean.) Serving as a classic vacation destination for many, the island enjoys an impressive frequency of nearly 80,000 flights per year shuttling between Seoul's Gimpo Airport and Jeju Airport. In fact, there are over 200 flights daily—surpassing the frequency of some subway lines. With such high demand, securing weekend tickets can be quite challenging, so it's advisable to book well in advance if you plan to visit Jeju. In fact, the Seoul-Jeju route ranks among the busiest air routes globally. At its peak, the annual number of passengers traveling between Seoul and Jeju surpassed a staggering 15 million, although this figure has slightly dipped due to the impact of the pandemic.

Indeed, Jeju Island is a treasure trove of tourist attractions that fascinate visitors from near and far. As an island that hosts nearly 700,000 residents, every corner of Jeju holds its own allure. To begin with Hallasan National Park stands as a crown jewel, and there is a mesmerizing array of waterfalls, caves, and parks of varying sizes. The island also features an abundance of pristine beaches, lush forests, picturesque trails, captivating museums, and splendid dining establishments. Moreover, Jeju Island is home to a myriad of unique sites and experiences that cannot be found elsewhere.

One notable site worth mentioning is the Jeju April 3

Peace Park, which serves as a poignant memorial to the victims of the Jeju April 3 incident, also known as the Jeju uprising. This tragic event holds a significant place in the modern history of South Korea. In the aftermath of Korea's liberation from Japanese colonial rule in 1945, the establishment of separate governments in the North and South in 1948, and the ensuing Korean War from 1950 to 1953, Jeju Island, situated apart from the mainland, became embroiled in a profound tragedy. Lasting for over seven years from 1947 to 1954, the conflict involved a complex interplay of soldiers, police, rebels, and residents, fueled by a range of factors including ideological divisions. The consequences were devastating, resulting in the loss of an estimated 30,000 lives, accounting for more than one-tenth of Jeju's population at that time. The Jeju April 3 Peace Park stands as a somber reminder of this painful chapter in Jeju's history.

Jeju Island is famous for its amazing "haenyeo", also known as sea women. These fearless women dive into the ocean without the use of oxygen tanks to gather a variety of seafood, including abalone, sea urchins, conch, and sea mustard. Some of the fresh seafood you'll enjoy on Jeju is harvested by these skilled haenyeo. While there were over

14,000 haenyeo in Jeju during the 1970s, their numbers have drastically declined, with only around 3,000 active haenyeo today. In recognition of their cultural significance, haenyeo were inscribed as a UNESCO Intangible Cultural Heritage of Humanity in 2016. In certain areas of Jeju, visitors can experience a glimpse of the haenyeo's world, although it is not a fully developed tourist program. For those seeking further knowledge, a visit to the Haenyeo Museum offers fascinating insights into the lives and traditions of the haenyeo.

In addition to its colorful attractions, Jeju Island offers a wonderful environment for walking enthusiasts. The Jeju Olle Trail, a scenic walking trail that stretches along the island's coastline, covers a remarkable distance of over 400 kilometers. Explorers can immerse themselves in the island's natural beauty while traversing this trail. Moreover, Hallasan is adorned with numerous parasitic volcanoes known as "oreum," with a dozen of them displaying exceptional beauty. These oreums, typically ranging from 200 to 300 meters in height, provide relatively accessible hiking opportunities. If you are a very diligent tourist and didn't drink too much the night before, you can get up at dawn to climb Seongsan Ilchulbong. It takes around 30 minutes to hike from the parking lot to the summit, where an awe-inspiring sunrise awaits. Even on moderately cloudy days, the experience remains rewarding. Alternatively, visitors can choose to explore Seongsan Ilchulbong during daylight hours, skipping the sunrise expedition.

For soccer enthusiasts, a visit to the Jeju World Cup Stadium is a must. This magnificent stadium, which hosted matches during the 2002 World Cup, offers breathtaking views of Hallasan Mountain and the ocean. It has received high praise, including being hailed as "the most beautiful stadium in the world" by former FIFA president Sepp Blatter during his visit. (I'm sure he's probably said similar things about other arenas.) If you happen to be in Jeju and a K-League game is taking place at the stadium, you're in for an exciting experience. Immerse yourself in the vibrant atmosphere of the matches while savoring some delicious "chimaek" (a combination of chikin and beer). It is common to find available tickets for matches at the Jeju World Cup Stadium even without purchasing them in advance. Fortunately, admission prices are reasonable, with the most expensive seats priced under $20. For a more enhanced experience, consider purchasing a package ticket that includes two seats with a table, along with chikin and two beers, all for around $50.

Jeju Island offers a superb array of fresh and diverse seafood cuisine due to its coastal location. While you can sample various seafood dishes, one that might surprise foreign visitors is the grilled "tong galchi gui". Galchi, also known as cutlassfish or hairtail, is a very favorite fish of Koreans, and while it used to be a commoner's food, it is now quite expensive. Unlike other regions where the fish is typically cut into smaller pieces, in Jeju, the whole fish is grilled and served at the table. If you're dining with a group of around four people, I recommend trying the grilled whole galchi, a visually stunning and delicious dish commonly found in larger restaurants specializing in Jeju cuisine.

Jeju Island is renowned for its native black pig, known as "heukdwaeji", which offers a distinct and flavorful pork experience compared to regular pork. While slightly pricier, it has become a go-to choice for Koreans, as indicated by the prominent signage in Seoul restaurants that proudly serve Jeju black pork. Among the several recipes, Samgyeopsal (grilled pork belly) and Ogyeopsal (grilled five-layered pork belly) are the most popular. While you may have already indulged in pork belly in Seoul, a visit to Jeju Island presents a special opportunity. It's almost a tradition for every Korean visitor to enjoy at least one meal of black pork samgyeopsal in Jeju. While some prefer to eat it with salt, in Jeju Island, it is more common to savor it by dipping it in "myeolchi-jeot" (a.k.a. "meljeot", salted anchovies), which is often served alongside the dish without your order. (Did you notice, my friend? Indeed, this book commences with a captivating tale centered around samgyeopsal, and ultimately concludes with another intriguing account featuring samgyeopsal!)

This final chapter is the longest among the twenty chapters, yet it only scratches the surface of the multitude of fascinating places that await you in Korea. Such is the abundance of wonders spread throughout the country. Hopefully, your time in Korea will allow for extensive exploration or you can visit Korea more than twice, enabling you to experience the enchantment of all these remarkable destinations beyond Seoul. May your journey in Korea be filled with unmatched experiences and unforgettable memories, creating a cherished chapter in the story of your life!

The end.

K를 팝니다

다 아는데 왜 재밌을까 싶은
대한민국 영어 설명서
ⓒ 박재영 2024

초판 1쇄 발행 2024년 6월 30일
초판 2쇄 발행 2024년 7월 31일

지은이 박재영
펴낸이 김민정
책임편집 유성원 편집 김동휘 권현승
디자인 퍼머넌트 잉크
저작권 박지영 형소진 최은진 서연주 오서영
마케팅 정민호 박치우 한민아 이민경 박진희 정유선 황승현
브랜딩 함유지 함근아 박민재 김희숙 이송이 박다솔 조다현 정승민 배진성
제작 강신은 김동욱 이순호
제작처 천광인쇄사

펴낸곳 (주)난다
출판등록 2016년 8월 25일 제406-2016-000108호
주소 10881 경기도 파주시 회동길 210
전자우편 nandatoogo@gmail.com
페이스북 @nandaisart | 인스타그램 @nandaisart
문의전화 031-955-8865(편집) 031-955-2689(마케팅) 031-955-8855(팩스)

ISBN 979-11-91859-99-7 03810